^{THE} **FOOD BLOCK**

THE FOOD BLOCK

by Alexei Ivanov

Translated from the Russian by Richard Coombes

First published in Russian as *Пищеблок* in 2019

© by Aleksei Ivanov

Agreement via Wiedling Literary Agency

Proofreading by Melanie Moore

Translation © Richard Coombes, 2024

© 2024, Glagoslav Publications

www.glagoslav.com

ISBN: 978-1-80484-128-0
ISBN: 978-1-80484-129-7

First published in English by Glagoslav Publications in September 2024

A catalogue record for this book is available from the British Library.

ALEXEI IVANOV

THE FOOD BLOCK

TRANSLATED FROM THE RUSSIAN BY RICHARD COOMBES

GLAGOSLAV PUBLICATIONS

CONTENTS

Part Three: The Vampire Chain

Part Four: A Vampire's Fear

Part 5: A Vampire's Death

A NOTE ON THE NAMES

Russian given names have both 'full' and 'short' (including 'diminutive') forms. Short forms tend to be used between relatives, classmates, friends, and colleagues.

A single name can have multiple short forms. Where an author uses several variants of a name, translators often choose one and stick with it, rather than replicate the original range. In *The Food Block*, however, the author consciously selects each variant with a particular purpose in mind, sometimes to convey affection and sometimes a hint of negativity, teasing, or outright insult. This translation reflects the author's intentions by retaining all the variant forms.

PROLOGUE

THE BUGLE'S SONG

Sunrise starts with the bugle's song
Of pioneer times, vibrant and young.
Mikhail Sadovsky, 'The Bugle's Song', 1972

'They were signallers. The boy beat his drum and the girl sounded her bugle. Together they welcomed every sunrise and escorted home every sunset. But people did not hear the song of the bugle or the thunder of the drum. They did not notice the wind setting the signallers' pioneer neckerchiefs aflutter, nor did they see the pioneers' eyes shining in the sun. Everyone believed that the girl with her bugle and the boy with his drum were made of plaster. But they were alive, and very much in love.'

The young group leader with the modish moustache looked around the boys in the dorm. The boys were not asleep; they were goggling, anticipating the very worst. Everyone knew who the leader meant. The plaster girl with the bugle stood on a low plinth at the gate of the pioneer camp. The plaster boy with the drum was missing altogether; a square of earth darkened on the spot once occupied by his vanished stone pedestal.

'One night,' the young leader continued in muted tones, 'a group of pioneers from our camp gave their young leaders the slip. They picked up stones and smashed the drummer to pieces. The morning sun lit up a pile of rubble. Workers came, gathered up the rubble, and took it to the dump. No one noticed the girl with the bugle crying. She was left alone, forever, without her beloved.'

The boys on their bunks stayed quiet, ashamed. The reason was no mystery: each of them had more than once tried to come up with a way of demolishing the bugler. Not from malice, of course; simply casual naughtiness.

'The girl did not forgive the boy's murder. She decided she would have her revenge. Each night she jumps down from her plinth and walks through the camp looking for whoever destroyed her drummer. And if she meets anyone in the camp after lights out, then without a hint of mercy she will strangle them with her stone hands.'

The lads lay there stupefied, pinned down by their own terror.

'Well, that's it. Good night,' said the moustachioed young leader.

He closed the dorm door behind him and went to his room, where his colleague was waiting for him, a tubby chap with curly hair.

'Scared them half to death,' chuckled the young man with the moustache. 'Made up a horror story for them, about the plaster bugler girl by the gate coming to life at night and prowling through the camp strangling everyone. Taking revenge for her poor shattered drummer.'

The curly-haired young leader did not approve of his moustachioed colleague's conceit. 'Nurturing them on fear is bad pedagogical practice,' he said.

'Effective, though. They won't go slipping out of their dorms at night.'

'Effective?' said Curly doubtfully. 'I rather think they'll batter the bugler to bits in the daytime, to break her psychological hold over them.'

Moustachio was genuinely puzzled. 'That's a twist that hadn't occurred to me,' he admitted.

Curly heaved a sorrowful sigh.

Meanwhile, the boys in the dorm were already asleep, sheets hauled up over their heads. Only the boy in the bed tucked away in the corner was awake. He was staring silently out of the window, as if waiting for something. He wriggled his hand free and reached towards the bedside cabinet for his glasses. Sat for a moment. Then he stood up and started dressing, trying not to make any noise. He made his way to the window, worked the catch loose, cautiously pushed the casement wide open, climbed up on to the window sill, and jumped out.

The boy walked through the night-time camp, finding cover behind thick acacia bushes. Street lamps brightly lit the long, deserted avenue. The leaves set up a faint whisper. A dog howled somewhere far off. It was warm, but chills coursed through the boy's body. He was very afraid, but he straightened his glasses and firmly resolved to find out whether or not the plaster bugler stayed on her plinth at night.

Out on the avenue, an indistinct figure appeared briefly, and the boy froze. The light of the mercury street lamps was blinding him, burning out all the shadows, and he could not make out who it was coming along the avenue. Coming slowly. Uncertainly, as if unused to walking. The way bedridden patients hobble when they are finally allowed to get up and take a few steps. Except that very sick patients always had someone to support them. The person on the avenue was alone. If it was a person at all.

Coming down the avenue was a girl of about the same age as the boy taking refuge behind the acacia. With every movement, the girl's whole body trembled strangely, as if something were breaking inside her. White blouse. White skirt. White pioneer neckerchief. White arms and legs, white eyeless face, white stone plaits. It was the plaster bugler. She looked like a robot, except that robots are activated by electricity and the bugler was animated by darkness. The bugler was looking for the person who had killed her drummer. Looking for them, to kill them too.

The boy behind the bushes backed off, turned, and raced away.

If the darkness is stronger than you, do not leave your house until you hear the bugle's song.

PART ONE

THE VAMPIRE'S TRAIL

Head all wrapped in bandages, sleeve with blood bright red,
Across the sodden grass the bloody trail will spread and spread.
Mikhail Golodny, 'Song about Shchors', 1935

CHAPTER 1

PASTA AND DRUMS

The Olympic rings were ensconced in the elastic circularity of the letters:

Olympics 80!

White streamers had been strung along the railings of the upper deck of the river bus to both starboard and port. True, the little craft was not chugging along the Moscow River against the backdrop of the magnificently modernised Luzhniki Stadium. This was the Volga, and the backdrop was the Zhiguli mountains, ancient, sloping, and covered with tangled forest. And the river bus was bringing not broad-shouldered Olympic athletes, but burlap sacks of buckwheat and sugar, cardboard boxes of pasta and dried fruit, and aluminium canisters of milk – in short, provisions for the food block of the Storm Petrel Pioneer Camp. None of that prevented the pennant on the little ship's mast from flying with Olympic vehemence.

Ivan Palych Kapustin, the captain, was sitting at a helm that was rather more like a car steering wheel. Ivan Palych had pulled a black tunic with blue stripes over his soiled and tatty sailor's vest and hoisted a cap sporting a crab and a gold rim onto his head. Steering the river bus was no more complicated than driving a car, but captains are captains wherever they are: to a man a tad overbearing, and that was making Igor Korzukhin self-conscious, like a schoolboy on an excursion, although he had grown up knowing Ivan Palych. Ivan Palych was friends with Igor's father, also a captain, except that Alexander Yegorych Korzukhin was not the commander of a 'galosh', that is, a Moskvich-type motorboat, but of a Volga-Don dry cargo ship, an enormous vessel, almost like an aircraft carrier. Igor was sitting in the wheelhouse in the engineer's seat, and Kapustin was throwing him sidelong glances, checking that he did not touch the lever that switched the engine from normal to reverse – that would properly foul up the works. Dials darkened on the panel in front of Igor: revs, oil pressure, cooling water temperature. Igor knew how to operate the ship and was certainly not about to yank the crank: was he a fool or what? But Ivan Palych did not trust the brat. There was too much of the peacock in the boy: those jeans, that badge he had knocked up himself with some guitarist on it; his lanky locks.

'Why didn't you get your hair cut before the shift?' grumbled Kapustin.

'I did,' said Igor.

Kapustin, naturally, did not understand that hair over the ears was the height of fashion. Igor had let his moustache grow as well. The result of that endeavour, it had to be said, was a young man's few sparse hairs. Well, so be it. The boy could be a hippy in summer while there was still time. Come autumn, the university military department would open its doors and a razor would be taken to every head, shaving them all to the universal boring butch.

Igor had finished his second year in the university's Philology Department the previous spring. Each year, after the end-of-year exams, the philology students would set off around the villages of the Volga region for a folklore practical. They questioned old women about forgotten rituals, and recorded folk songs, local tales, and dialect words. Most of the students in the faculty were girls, and these trips to the back of beyond were always filled with the yearnings of the lovelorn. The rickety fence of morality swayed under the pressure of susceptibility, and was held in place only by upbringing and natural timidity. Igor had no problem with timidity, and was hopeful of overcoming his upbringing, but in June, to his intense annoyance, he had caught a cold on the Volga and was not taken on the expedition. The Dean's office swapped out folklore for pedagogy: he was to see out one shift as a young group leader in a pioneer camp. Well, that was not bad, either. Students of the Pedagogical Institute worked as group leaders. More precisely, female students, because in the Pedagogical Institute, just as in the University Philological Faculty, girls were in the majority. Igor took the view that the girls from Pedagogy would be no worse than the girls from Philology. They might even prove better, if he had no desire to maintain relations once his practical was over.

The wide stretch of water ahead of the bow of the river bus glistened in the bright sunshine, and, in the distance, the brittle brilliance merged into a solid blinding blaze. The bus's engine gave out a dull rattle from somewhere in its guts beneath the wheelhouse. The wheelhouse windows looked out to all four points of the compass. Over by the low left bank, Igor saw a dredger, splayed out like an iron spider. Its pipe, resting on a lattice boom, spewed liquid slurry in a solid stream into the gaping hold of a moored self-driven barge.

'You won't miss the Olympics in camp?' asked Kapustin.

The Olympic Games began in a week. Everyone was waiting for the opening with an inexplicable feeling of holiday, the way people waited for New Year, hoping that all bad things would beat a retreat of their own accord and remain in the past. But what could the closed city of Kuibyshev, into which foreigners were not admitted, gain from the Olympics? Fanta and sausages in the grocery shops? Natty trainers in the sports shops? Dream on. For everywhere in the USSR except Moscow, the benefits of the Olympics were limited to Olympic jackets for the women and decorative Olympic roubles. Igor felt no reverence towards the global tournament, nor any sense of nervous excitement at the thought of impending blessings. Blessings that no one, in fact, had promised anyone.

Igor chose not to share his scepticism with Ivan Palych.

'I don't suppose there's a telly in camp,' he replied diplomatically.

'There's a telly in the main building, where the radio room is,' countered Kapustin.

'How do you know?' asked Igor in surprise.

'I just do,' replied Ivan Palych evasively.

The penny dropped. Igor fell silent. Dimon Malosolov, a sailor on board the bus, had already broadcast the story that Palych had formed a liaison in the Storm Petrel Pioneer Camp with the lady in charge of the food block. The bus went to the camp almost every other day, and often tied up overnight at the jetty, whereupon Palych would relocate from the captain's cabin to his lover's bunk. Igor envied the captain: an old guy – he had already hit the big five-oh – and still a player with the ladies. Meanwhile here he was, Igor, young and frisky and at the end of his second year and still without a girlfriend.

Dimon Malosolov had also managed to find himself a girl in camp, one of the young leaders. While Palych was bagging forty winks in the food supremo's bunk, Malosolov had been strolling out romantically along the bank of the Volga with his group leader. Not that he had managed anything beyond a quick grope. Dimon had wearied of her, and his mind was set on changing his girlfriend for one more accommodating. He was not the least embarrassed that the woman scorned would see and understand and be hurt. Igor envied Dimon's unwavering selfishness. With selfishness like that, life was a breeze.

There were three girls on the river bus, students on their way to the camp. They were sitting on the foredeck among the sacks, boxes, and canisters, their construction brigade[1] jackets slung over their shoulders. Igor was observing the deck through the large windows of the wheelhouse. The wily Dimon waited for one of the students to make her way to the rail, then steered his way over towards her as if he were planning a quick smoke. She was the plainest of the three young leaders – plump, with glasses and a light brown ponytail. A typical girl from philology. She was

....

[1]   In the USSR in the 1970s, a number of major construction projects were undertaken for which young people were encouraged to volunteer. Such 'construction brigades' worked, for instance, on the Baikal-Amur Mainline Railway ('BAM'), the 'Atommash' nuclear engineering plant in Volgodonsk, the Kama Automobile Plant ('KamAZ'), and the Sayano-Shushenskaya hydroelectric plant.

exactly what Dimon needed: with a girl like her he would find it easier to reach his goal.

From inside the cabin, Igor could not hear what Dimon was saying out on deck, but he had all Dimon's wiles by heart. Dimon would ask, as if offering his help: 'Young lady, does your mother need a son-in-law?' At which the girl would melt away. It always happened that way with girls, and Igor's ears would burn red at the banality of Dimon's chat-up lines. This was not something Igor could do. He needed a girl to show an interest in him first. Which was precisely why he had wormed his way into Ivan Palych's wheelhouse. The young leaders at the pioneer camp would be sure to wonder who was this guy who had come sailing down to meet them. Why, he had not left the captain's side the whole way.

Igor was fully aware of all the goings-on in Dimon's life. They had been friends at school since first year. At the end of year eight, Igor had stayed on into year nine, while Dimon had gone to technical college to train as a helmsman. Their friendship had been rekindled over the summer: both were mooching unenthusiastically around Kuibyshev. Igor, refused a place on the folklore expedition, hung around the apartment block, smoking in the yard to avoid the sharp edges of his mother's tongue, while Dimon passed his evenings drinking beer on the bench by the front door. Navigation bored Dimon: the river bus, unlike bigger craft, did not make long voyages to Moscow, Leningrad, or Astrakhan. Dimon complained to Igor about how he slaved for Kapustin: he lubricated the engine and scrubbed the decks, and when they berthed he wound the mooring ropes around the bollards and stood watch at the gangway. Kapustin kept Dimon away from the helm. And rightly so.

Ivan Pavlovich steered the little boat towards the left shore past the white buoy marking shallow water, and the river bus left the channel. Meanwhile a snow-white 'Meteor' was powering slowly along the fairway. The whole craft was pointing upwards, as if frozen in an unfinished leap: unearthly, fantastic, lifted above the waves by the might of antigravity. Even in the wheelhouse, Igor could hear the aeroplane roar of its turbines. That was the sound of real life, in which existed skyscrapers, transatlantic liners, powerful computers all but capable of intelligent thought, shuttles in orbit, and the search for extraterrestrial civilisations. Not the Storm Petrel Pioneer Camp with its pasta and drums.

A small village of a dozen or so houses roofed with iron or slate came into view. Thin-slatted painted fences, vegetable gardens, telegraph poles with crossbars. A light breeze from the Volga stirred the crowns of lindens and apple trees. The village was apparently considered so insignificant that no guard ship had been stationed there. There was not even a pontoon.

'Pervomaiskaya,' explained Igor Kapustin. 'Only oldies here. Those who are up to it work in the camp. Security guards, carpenters, scullery maids.'

'What about in winter?' asked Igor.

Pioneers did not go to camp in winter.

'In winter there's a clinic and a DOSAAF[2] ski camp.'

Beyond the village, a stream tumbled into the Volga, festooned with willows along its banks.

'The Bishop, they call it,' said Kapustin.

'Odd name.' Igor was surprised.

'Used to be the Archbishop. The camp's a lot of old Samaran dachas. All sorts of merchants and nobility had places here. Archbishop had a dacha there, too.'

At length, Igor made out the former dachas, now the pioneer camp. Under the tall carvel pines lining the Volga stood fairy-tale gingerbread houses, outlandish, like Christmas tree decorations, whimsically jolly, with convoluted carvings, ornamented stoops, attics and balconies, glass verandas, multicoloured facades, turrets, and roofs of various kinds: hipped, boat, tent. Not so much a dacha village as a brood of frisky wooden roosters with combs and colourful plumage. Here and there, though, among the throng of elegant houses, others not quite so elegant had squeezed in: panel barracks and white-brick boxes. A chain link fence separated the village from the Volga, clearly to stop the pioneers from scampering down for a dip.

....

[2]   DOSAAF (the Volunteer Society for Cooperation with the Army, Aviation, and Navy) was a Soviet Union sports organisation centred on weapons, vehicles, and flying.

'Isn't there an ordinary road that comes here?' asked Igor.

'There's a dirt track, but the backwater keeps flooding it.'

Ivan Palych was referring to the backwater of the Saratov Reservoir. In spring, and when the Balakovo hydroelectric station reduced its discharge, the water level in the reservoir rose, and the old lake bowls below Kuibyshev flooded, swamping the country roads on the low-lying left bank. In terms of reaching the camp, it was more reliable to bring in supplies by river transport.

'Already waiting for us up there,' said Kapustin, and the bus's klaxon let out a hoarse quack.

A pier had been built for the pioneer camp, a wooden jetty reaching a long way out into the water. It rested on iron pipes, driven into the river bed like piles. The sides of the jetty were hung with car tyres. An asphalt path led to the gates, near which stood a plaster pioneer girl on a pedestal, sounding a bugle. On the pier were a few men and a cart whose wheels had been taken from a car. They were ready, it seemed, to unload the supplies brought in on the river bus.

Igor squinted, checking over the people come to meet them. He could not see a single girl group leader on the bank. Bollocks. A crying shame. No one would know he had been in the wheelhouse with the captain.

CHAPTER 2

NEWBIE IN THE RANKS

The plump group leader stepped tentatively onto the gangway, and Dimon Malosolov, standing on the pier, gallantly supported her under the elbow, and then gently pulled her toward him, as if for an important and private conversation.

'Listen, Ira, a mate of mine's been sent to work in your camp but he's not one of your lot,' said Dimon with a friend's frankness and lowering his voice. 'Could you get him set up properly? Deal? Pretty please.'

Igor frowned, annoyed. He had spent the whole journey preening himself in the company of the captain, but when it came to patronage, he was reliant on a lowly sailor.

'And grab something tasty for me in the canteen,' added Dimon.

The crew of the river bus usually ate a meal in camp.

The plump group leader blushed with pleasure.

'Well, if there is anything,' she agreed, with feigned reluctance.

'Igoryokha, take Irishka's bag,' ordered Dimon in his friendly way. 'I got a ton of junk to chuck into the cart.'

Igor could not refuse. It would be impolite to refuse. Not good.

The young leaders greeted the men with the cart, evidently winos from the village moonlighting as handymen in the camp, then went up to the gates with the plaster bugler girl. Igor traipsed after them, checking out the handmade stencil drawings on the construction brigade jackets of the female students. Christmas trees, bonfires, tents, and arching over the top the name of the brigade: The Romantics. BAM, most like. Though KamAZ, Atommash, or the Sayano-Shushenskaya hydroelectric plant were also possibles, or even just work as conductors on long-distance trains. Igor's backpack was hanging off one shoulder, and in his hand he was clutching Irina's bag.

The camp surprised Igor. Or not the camp, to be exact, but the pre-revolutionary dacha village – a picturesque and unregimented scattering of small wooden palaces. Igor recalled excursions through the old part of Kuibyshev: among the merchants' passages with their displays and brick mansions with rows of arched windows you stumbled across decorative wooden houses of pseudo-Russian appearance. This was a kind of modernist swirl known as the Ropet style. Igor had not known that thirty kilometres from the city was a whole nesting site of puppet firebirds. An ensemble, one might say. Granted, its unity was godlessly violated by publicly funded replicas, and its harmony sliced in two by an asphalted avenue sporting pioneer stands and gas lamps. The carvel pines, however, preserved the spirit of the fretwork of former days.

The plump group leader stopped and pointed to one of the gingerbread houses.

'You're in that building. Volodya Kiselev has left, and you've been taken on in his place. Put your things in the group leader's room and come over to the canteen.'

'My name is Igor,' said Igor, handing over her bag.

'You can call me Irina Mikhailovna and nothing else.'

It was clear to Igor that this young lass wanted to enjoy all the pleasures in one go. One lad hitting on you, so you can afford to give another the brush-off: nice!

The building was bright and empty and smelled of fresh linseed oil and wooden boards. The indistinct noise of a radio floated down from upstairs. Igor climbed the creaking stairs to the first floor, where the leaders' room was located. A cubby hole with a sloping ceiling and boasting two beds, two bedside cabinets, a writing table, and a wardrobe. A curly-haired, stoutish lad was pointing a telescopic transistor antenna out of the window, searching for any suitable station.

'Hi,' said Igor, dumping his backpack on the floor. 'I'm the new group leader.'

'Take that bunk,' said the other, pointing with his antenna.

Igor shifted his backpack to the bunk and held out his hand to the curly-haired lad. 'Igor.'

'Alexander,' replied Curly, with gravitas.

'Philology?' asked Igor. 'Physics? History?'

'Foreign languages. Eengleesh.'

Igor was glad his neighbour was not from the Physical Education faculty. PE was mainly populated by athletes who had done their stint in the army. Even before the army, they had not been not overburdened with brains, and national service had merely cemented their blockheadedness beyond the capacity of the workers' schools to right them again. They turned out often enough to be not such bad people, but they dragged their hazing (handy at work) and conventional sergeants' wisdom to school, sports club, and pioneer camp: *I'm the boss and you're an idiot; the stronger guy's top dog; the colonel said the fly's a helicopter so it's a helicopter.*

'Can you translate the Beatles into Russian?' Igor asked Sasha.

'I have to say I don't approve of anything like that.' Sasha nodded at Igor's homemade badge with a picture of Paul McCartney on it. 'We're in a Soviet camp.'

'Understood,' said Igor dryly.

Even so, Sasha could not stop himself glancing at Igor's jeans.

'So ... what brand?'

Sasha's principles, it seemed, did not apply to all areas of life.

'Montana.'

Alas, alas, Igor's Montana jeans were fake, from a shop on Deribasovskaya Street; they were all he had the money for.

Still, he was hoping that no one would rumble the forgery.

The prestigious label was clearly a source of discouragement for Sasha. 'I'll say this straight away,' he said, turning off his radio. 'Don't plan on bringing any girls here. I'm not giving up this room.'

'I'll find somewhere we can hide away,' said Igor with a smirk.

He was far from being a Casanova, but he was not going to let this Sasha pull the commanding officer on him.

'Let's go to lunch. We're not hippies here; everything's timetabled.'

The faceless one-storey silicate brick building of the food block looked like a laundry, except that laundry windows tended to be fitted with thick panes of bottle-green glass, whereas the food block had ordinary windows with wooden frames. Grilles had been fitted over them on the outside. The bars made a pattern resembling a rising sun with rays, like on the emblem of the USSR. Above the kitchen roof protruded two black iron pipes. A ventilator howled in a fanlight and hurled out a stream of air scented with hot cutlets. Vegetable crates and crumpled scrap cans were piled up by the back door. The top of the wide main entrance was hospitably decorated with a faded banner reading 'Enjoy your meal.'

Rows of tables stretched across the spacious hall. On the strips of wall between the windows hung homiletic posters: a rosy-cheeked pioneer in a cap peeling potatoes with a knife; a pioneer girl with pigtails washing a dish with a sponge, and smiling; a boy and a girl with red neckerchiefs lugging a heavy bucket together, hands outstretched. This was how conscientious children were supposed to behave.

At this time, the only people in the canteen were the camp staff. They were used to going unnoticed during the shift. A few middle-aged men and women working variously as carpenters, security guards, and cleaners; a young doctor and an elderly nurse, both in white coats; a fat man who looked like an accountant; a chap in blue overalls who had to be a radio technician. Not just workers, though: some of the group leaders were there too. Dimon Malosolov had settled himself next to the plump Irina. Sitting on a bench beside Captain Kapustin was a woman whose curls had come straight out of a bottle. This was evidently his mistress, the food supremo. Igor heard her talking quietly to Kapustin, who was eating soup.

'You can keep the potatoes, but go through them – the ones here are already rotten. And dry them. Split the rice in half: three kilos for you and three for me. Don't touch the sugar. I'll take that for myself. I'm going to be making jam in August.'

At the serving hatch, Igor took borsch, pearl barley porridge, and a glass of compote, and then went back to sit next to Sasha. He would have felt awkward eating on his own.

'Kiselev worked in the fourth brigade, and that's where you'll be assigned,' said Sasha. 'I'm in the third. All day in number three, but I live in number four.'

'Why?' asked Igor, surprised.

'They don't put guys and girls together. That's depraved.'

We have a moralist among us, thought Igor.

'So who's my number two?'

'You're number two,' Sasha corrected him superciliously. 'Your number one is Irinka Kopylova.'

'Her?' Igor nodded towards Dimon's plump friend.

'Her. And I'm not giving you the room key yet.'

'Why not?' asked Igor, aggrieved.

'Start by taking your documents to Natalya Borisovna. And show the doctor your certificate. On the last shift we had head lice in the second brigade.'

'You think I've got lice?'

Sasha shrugged: *Any reason why not?*

Igor thought about it and decided not to argue. Why would he? His aim was to pay out his practical, not to remake the world for the better. In any walk of official life, the template was the medical examination at the military recruiting office: turn yourself into a cross-eyed, flat-footed idiot and you'll be declared unfit for the front line.

CHAPTER 3

JUST LIKE EVERYWHERE ELSE

In the afternoon, all the young leaders gathered in Company House. The meeting was taken by the selfsame Natalya Borisovna, to whom Igor was supposed to have handed over his referral for the practical. She was the Senior Pioneer Leader, and her last name was Svistunova.

Igor warily examined the Flag Room, ablaze in the sun with the glint of brass bugles and drums with metal rims. In doorless cupboards among rolls of wall newspapers and tattered magazines, nickel-plated sports cups shone, and the walls were aflame with draped silk pennants. The folded Company banner, placed on a special stand, possessed an inner royal grandeur that made it appear impossibly heavy, like the gun barrel of an artillery piece.

There were twelve young leaders, counting Igor and Sasha: four boys and eight girls. The other two boys were called Kirill and Maxim, and they were like two peas from the same pod, with the same Olympic tops and tracksuit bottoms. The girls, almost all of them, had put on their construction brigade jackets dappled with chevrons, shoulder stripes, and insignia; their badges were so tightly packed you could read their jackets like a newspaper. Construction brigade cockiness created the sense that these girls had been enjoying a vibrant personal life, although the romance of it all had most likely taken the form of cooking for a brigade of riggers working on the building of some hydroelectric station or other. That did not stop Igor feeling the stirrings of jealousy. Snipe all you like, the construction brigade was not one of your get-togethers with a bunch of old grannies in the philology department.

Also present at the meeting was the head of physical education, a tall young man with a disgruntled, bored expression. He was sitting in the corner, knees spread wide, twitching his thigh as if he was in a hurry to be somewhere else but forced to be here. Svistunova herself was a shapely lass with a stentorian voice who, in her pioneer neckerchief, looked for all the world like a little fighting girl.

'You're a feeble lot,' she told the young leaders feistily, tossing her dyed bangs out of her eyes. 'Come on, straighten up. I want to see those ponytails standing out like pistols.'

'We're always prepared,' answered the girl leaders; this seemed to be a standard joke among them. They broke into forced laughter.

'We have a new colleague. Igor Korzukhin. Where are you from, Igor?'

'The philology department at uni,' said Igor.

'Well, that's good. Meld with our collective, Igoryok.'

'Melding with immediate effect,' he said.

He did not like being called Igoryok, but the girls turned to him with friendly interest, and he did not get angry.

'Irishka, you can be a guiding light: be the newbie's patroness.'

'Be good if he could at least dress decently,' sighed Irina.

The young leaders looked at Paul McCartney on Igor's badge.

'Can you play the guitar?' asked one of the girls.

'I can, but you'd be better off not hearing it,' Igor warned them candidly.

The girls broke into laughter, this time less forced.

'One of us,' concluded Svistunova. 'Now to business.'

With a sweeping gesture, she spread out on the table a large sheet of paper on which were columns filled out in coloured felt-tip pen. Much as a commander spreads out in front of his generals a map of the appointed battle.

'Here's the grid with the plans, fighters,' she said. 'Same as before. Let's distribute the activities. We remember, don't we Lenchik, that you didn't want to hold an inspection parade with the senior brigades on the last shift. But you managed, didn't you?'

'I did,' nodded curly-haired, big-eyed Lenochka.

'There you are. You didn't need to be afraid,' said Svistunova, satisfied, marking the paper with a pen. 'As we say, just your skirt got a little rumpled. Verunya, you'll do the drawing on the asphalt competition and the handicrafts of found materials. Yes?'

'Yes. Only don't give chalk and plasticine out. There weren't enough last time.'

'What are you doing, eating them?' asked Svistunova in surprise. 'OK, I'll keep that in mind. So who wants to be in charge of birthdays?'

'Maybe we should do without that?' came the doubtful voice of an overweight girl with a pigtail. 'It's impossible to bake a normal semolina cake here. And the cooks in the kitchen are grumpy.'

'Yes but if you want to get the little girls out of there you'll need to hitch a tow-rope to their ears,' objected Svistunova. 'I'll put it to the food block boss. She can give her old girls the sharp edge of her tongue.'

'I'll take chess as well,' said Sasha, Igor's roommate. 'I've got a qualification. I'll organise a tournament at the end of the shift.'

'A tournament is good, just what the doctor ordered,' agreed the senior group leader. 'You're a *wunderkind*, Sasha.'

Sasha gave a condescending smirk. The girls looked at him obsequiously.

'And yours, Veronichka, will be the festival of pioneer songs.'

'Have they sent a recording?' asked Veronichka.

Igor thought that reducing her first name to a diminutive did not suit this young lady. She carried herself haughtily, and that made her seem more complicated than the others. She was not wearing a construction brigade uniform, and she had her hair done differently from the other young leaders: no ponytail or plaits, but short like a boy's; there was something sassy about it. Gold earrings sparkled in Veronika's ears, again not chiming in with pioneers and pioneering. Igor had met girls like her in the philology department. They smoked, shunned their classmates, did not eat lunch in the cafeteria, and read the Silver Age poets.

'They'll be sending a recording,' said Natalya Borisovna, speaking a little more harshly than before. 'Just bear in mind, my lovely, that if you choose a song about love, it should be about love for the motherland. Let's leave the lyric poetry at home, shall we?'

Veronika's only answer to this was a disdainful smile.

'I'll run a pioneer-ball championship,' said Maxim.

'Good,' said Svistunova approvingly. 'So who's going to do SIF?'

SIF stood for School of International Friendship. Put simply, it was a programme of writing letters to pioneers from socialist countries outside the USSR who were attending other camps, such as Artek and Orlyonok.

'Irinka and Galka, you'll do SIF. Only we need more boys.'

'Boys are too lazy to do writing,' objected Galya, a dark-haired, dark-skinned girl.

'What does that mean? They have to do it and that's that. If the older ones don't want to, take the younger ones. But bear in mind I'll be reading them. So let's not have them asking their foreign friends for chewing gum and stickers. We'll be having a regional competition for the best letter.'

'Understood, Natalya Borisovna.'

Svistunova was looking at the grid plan and nibbling on her pen.

Igor felt uncomfortable. His own school years were not so distant and he could remember them well enough. He had been secretly hoping that adult life would ease all the preening and bureaucracy to one side. Apparently not. Here, in the Storm Petrel Pioneer Camp, the crimson hand had him by the throat as firmly as before.

'Well?' Svistunova finished studying her cross-hatched plan and looked expectantly at the others. 'Any more ideas?' she asked. 'Why so gloomy, fighters? Anybody find themselves blessed with a sudden flash of intelligence?' The leaders were silent. 'No? Then that's all.'

'Hey, stop, Natalya!' This was the PE teacher, suddenly sounding upset. He closed his legs. 'I somehow missed the news that Wildfire's been crossed out.'

The PE teacher's familiar manner surprised Igor. It did not mesh with the style of a session with the Senior Pioneer Leader – and yet appeared not to jar on Svistunova at all.

'Crossed out, Ruslan, crossed out,' she replied agreeably.

'Why?' One of the girls was upset.

'Running through the woods is great.' One of the others joined in, on her side.

'No harm in dreaming,' grinned Svistunova.

'You get to go running and then I get to go looking for morons,' snorted the PE teacher contemptuously, giving the impression that he had to go round fixing everything, and without his superhuman efforts the work would fall apart, and he was already tired.

'We get fighting in Wildfire,' explained Svistunova. 'The older ones beat up the younger ones. So we'll do without Wildfire. And without the Neptune Festival.'

'Why without Neptune?'

Everyone had always liked the Neptune Festival in pioneer camp, adults and children alike. You got the chance to yell, push, and duck people forcibly in the water.

'Better to show aggression in sport.'

From the PE teacher's satisfaction, Igor understood that at the Neptune Festival too, he was obliged to manage the 'morons', and he, as was well-known, was already tired.

'Self-Governance Day is also crossed out,' Svistunova informed them. 'Take note. All that ever did was turn the camp into a bear garden.'

The PE teacher nodded authoritatively, and the girl group leaders raised no further objections.

Understanding dawned on Igor: the PE teacher was the Senior Pioneer Leader's man. That was why she was carrying out his wishes. Igor leaned over to his neighbour, Lenochka.

'Are they married, or what?'

'They're common-law partners,' whispered Lenochka reverently.

Or in terms that curly-haired Sasha might use, they were living together unlawfully.

Igor straightened up, relieved. At first he had felt like a stranger here. He knew no one, and was sitting there all trendy like a dummy while the girl group leaders, under the command of the decisive commissar Svistunova, were fighting for international friendship, world peace, and other right things. Poppycock. Here it was just like everywhere else. Flags were flags and sickles were hammers, but even in pioneer camp people wanted a simpler, easier, and better life.

CHAPTER 4

PIONEER AVENUE

Valerka chose not to suffocate in the crowd of boys huddled together at the exit onto the gangway. Where was there to rush off to? What for? All that would happen would be the handle of his suitcase would get ripped off. Above the deck and the wheelhouse of the river bus, now tight broadside to the pier, seagulls were swooping and screeching. A young sailor at the gangway was roughly shoving the boys away from the open doors, grabbing them by the shoulders, and letting them through one by one, like Sportloto balls. All the way, the same sailor had been chatting about something with one of the young leaders, the plump and bespectacled Irina Mikhailovna, flirting with her, and now he was showing her what a tough guy he could be.

'One at a time! One at a time!' he shouted at the boys. 'My fist's about to make a date with someone's head.'

The girls milled about behind the boys, chirping. 'Rin Khalovna!' they shouted. 'Galkin's kicking! Rin Khalovna, someone's left a top there. Rin Khalovna, Morozova's panama's blown off!'

Valerka stayed where he was, letting the girls go ahead as well.

'Lagunov!' Irina Mikhailovna had seen him. 'Get a move on.'

'Lagunov!' the girls immediately started shouting and looking around. 'What you doing sitting there? Get off that bench, you idiot. We've arrived. She's talking to you. Can't you hear?'

Valerka got up reluctantly and made his way forward, suitcase dangling from his hand. Teachers always noticed him because he was short, slim, and wore glasses. Teachers thought he needed looking after, so that he would not be squashed or lost. But Valerka Lagunov had never needed looking after.

He was sorry they had arrived so quickly. He had found it interesting on the boat.

Irina Mikhailovna led her brigade off the pier and gathered them in a group near the gates – two iron pillars over which had been fixed an iron-framed arch with iron letters: 'Storm Petrel Pioneer Camp'. Irina Mikhailovna began to run down her list, checking her brigade: fifteen boys and fifteen girls. All of them had just finished their fifth year, at different schools in the same district, and almost all of them were twelve years old. Valerka was looking at the now-empty river bus, graceful, like an enormous toy, but the other lads were staring at the monument by the gates – a plaster sculpture of a girl bugler. Even while they were on the bus, Valerka had marked and committed to memory the names of the most boisterous and loud-mouthed boys in his brigade; boys with the ability to become acquainted instantly and who were not remotely inhibited.

A boy by the name of Tityapkin looked up the plaster bugler's skirt and reported sorrowfully, 'Crap, it's all blocked up.'

'Ugh, Tityapkin, you creep!' wailed the girls.

Nobody knew Tityapkin's first name. With a last name like that, who needs a first name.

One of the other boys, Seryozhka Domrachev, said, 'We had this thing that if you got a pine cone in the horn without it bouncing back out it meant good luck.'

Seryozha Domrachev had spent the first shift at Storm Petrel and was back for the second. He knew everything about Storm Petrel.

'I'm going to find a cone right now!' A small sprightly lad who looked like a frog with ADHD started zipping about, hunting. His name was Zhenya Guryanov, nickname Gurka. 'I'll come here every night! I'll stuff her horn with cones!'

'Guryanov, get back in your place!' barked Irina Mikhailovna.

'Chuck what you like, not a cat in hell's chance it'll come true,' grunted a tall boy with thick lips and a sour face. His name was Venya Gelbich.

'That kind of thing always comes true!' objected Kolka Gorokhov. 'You what, you don't believe it? You'll see for yourself! You don't believe it, your bad luck.'

'The bugle bell's not that deep,' observed Lyova Khlopov reasonably. 'You won't get a cone to stick in there.' Lyova was a sturdy lad with fair hair.

'Chap on our shift got one stuck,' objected Seryozha Domrachev. 'Went home and his old folks bought him a bike.'

'Remember, boys!' announced Irina Mikhailovna loudly. 'We are the fourth brigade! We are now on our way to Building 4! Get into pairs!'

'Sod this for a lark,' said Slavik Mukhin, offended. 'We're not at nursery.'

Irina Mikhailovna parcelled the boys into pairs herself without any discussion. Valerka got Seryozha Domrachev.

The childish flurry under the plaster bugler gradually spent itself, and the young leaders led their groups to the buildings where they would be living. The younger ones – the sixth and fifth brigades – were taken first, after which Irina Mikhailovna led a procession of the fourth brigade. From the gates into the very depths of the camp ran Pioneer Avenue, planted with acacia bushes and decked with outsized glass-fronted stands. Street lamps lined the avenue, like in a city. The hot asphalt bristled with fallen pine cones.

'You stepping on the cones, boys?' asked Kolka Gorokhov of everyone. 'You mustn't! Anyone stepping on a fir cone means he's left something at home. Sure sign.'

Spirited pioneer music was playing all through the camp on invisible loudspeakers. The girls made to hurry straight after Irina Mikhailovna to ply her with questions on the way, but the boys hung back. They were confident they could think for themselves, and the leader would do nothing but hinder their exchanges of views.

'How's life here, Sery?' asked Lyova Khlopov.

'It sucks!' came in Gelbich with his opinion. 'I spent one shift here last year. Better off in jail. We had to march in line for a month!'

'It's all right here,' said Seryozha. 'Quiet Hour's a pain is all.'

'I'm not going to sleep a single wink!' declared Zhenka Guryanov.

'Everyone says that but they still sleep,' replied Seryozha acidly.

Paths branched off the avenue, leading to the living quarters and other camp buildings. Valerka gazed at the outlandish gingerbread houses with their elaborate carvings; there was something accepting about them, unlike one another as they were, as if none of them were insisting on anything: you do as you wish. It was as if instead of inspection drill and singing they were proposing a game of hide-and-seek; very off beat. The plank walls and painted metal roofs were dappled with patches of yellow-green light. The lofty, straight pine trees shot up as if they were taking off vertically. Gaps in the crowns of the pines scattered the sun into separate fires, as through wisps of pine smoke. Between red trunks like the strings of a musical instrument sparkled a long swath of the Volga.

'This is Building 2. The oldies live here,' explained Seryozha Domrachev. 'That's Company, Company House. All sorts of activity circles go on in there, and they show films. That's the canteen. That over there's the bathhouse. That's Building 5, got all the wimps.'

'Tell us something we can't see for ourselves,' grumbled Gelbich irritably. 'Blah blah blah.' He was jealous that they were asking Seryozha and not him.

'Are there any locals?' asked a scrawny little boy whose name Valerka did not yet know. He sounded fearful.

'There are no locals here,' Seryozha reassured him. 'There are Escaped Convicts.'

'Wicked,' whistled Gurka admiringly.

'There weren't any convicts last year,' declared Gelbich.

'Could have still been in the slammer last year,' said Seryozha. 'And now they're living in the forest, the other side of the fence.' His eyes darkened. 'They got hideouts there. Seen them myself. You're not allowed over the fence. They'll catch you.'

Hanging out with the other kids back home, Valerka had heard plenty of tales about Escaped Convicts. When they escaped from penal colonies, the cons turned into monsters, half-human, half-beast.

'If they catch you, what then?' asked Gurka, alarmed.

'If they catch you without a neckerchief, they might let you go.' Seryozha was referring to the pioneer neckerchief. 'You have a neckerchief on, they'll kill you. The oldies were saying that one year a boy went out and vanished. All they found was a skeleton.'

The boys were impressed.

'Not all cons are like that, Sery,' said Lyova Khlopov, reluctantly expressing doubt. 'Coach told us at club there was one footballer, an Olympic champion, he became a con too. They let him out and he went back to being a footballer.'

'He didn't escape,' objected Seryozha.

Lyova breathed a sigh. That was right. If the footballer con had escaped, he might have turned into a cannibal as well and be grazing near a pioneer camp somewhere.

Meanwhile, the girls could not have cared less about the threats of the world around them. They were pressing in on Irina Mikhailovna from all sides.

'Rin Khalovna, is there going to be a song contest? Rin Khalovna, I can do macramé! Rin Khalovna, are they going to put on a disco? Rin Khalovna, can I move to another brigade? My sister's there!'

'There's basically a ton of black magic around here,' Seryozha Domrachev told the boys darkly.

Valerka's heart sank. He did not like black magic. Grown-ups could try all they liked to say that black magic was a relic of the past or a pack of lies, but still it was frightening.

'You see that house over there?' Seryozha pointed to what was very probably the most beautiful of all the gingerbread houses: blue and white, two-storey, with a veranda, a balcony, and a little tower.

'Some old codger lives there. Pensioner. He has a Black Room. People go in there and no one ever comes out.'

Valerka looked at the nice blue house, and a shiver ran down his spine. Grown-ups had never told him anything like this about the world. Their world was dull and obvious, like a bus stop, geared towards their various common or garden needs. Black magic, obviously, was evil and wrong; it wreaked vengeance on everyone for no one knew what – but it made the world more colourful, mysterious, and alive. Meaning that black magic was real.

'Some old bum got lost in the woods last year and they found him,' said Gelbich, just to argue with Seryozha.

'If kids went missing in camp the cops'd come,' said Lyova Khlopov angrily. He liked football, and wanted nothing to do with black magic.

'The old buffer doesn't let kids in. But there's people been missing for ever.'

'What people?'

'These were bourgeois dachas before the revolution,' said Seryozha, his voice lowered. 'When the Reds came, all the bourgeoisie went into the Black Room and disappeared.'

'Get this,' said Gurka, sounding inspired. 'They must have left ghosts behind!'

'You have to put the Queen of Spades under your mattress against ghosts.' Kolka Gorokhov spun round and looked at the others. 'Men, who's got cards?'

'I'm going ghost hunting!' declared Gurka impulsively. 'Tonight!'

'You'll piss yourself!' warned Slava Mukhin authoritatively.

A woman who looked more like a girl, wearing a pioneer neckerchief, suddenly came skipping up to the fourth brigade, by now spread out comfortably along the avenue.

'Why the sour faces?' she cried out heartily. 'Missing your mums? Come on, let's hear a good old pioneer song!' And she started bellowing, '*Who walk together, undismayed?*'

A song that everyone knew.

'*Our Young Pioneer Brigade!*' The girls took up the chant, completely untogether.

'Boys, I can't hear you!' cried the lady, urging them on. '*Friendly!*'

'*Capable!*' replied the boys, feebly and out of tune.

'*Honest!*' bawled the lady, still driving them.

'*Indomitable!*' shouted the boys.

'*Our motto, by all declared!*'

'*Be prepared! Always prepared!*' the boys finished in unison.

'Now that's more like it!'

The woman patted the back of Tityapkin's head and moved on.

'Who's that cretin?' asked Tityapkin in a low voice.

'Svistunova. Everyone calls her Whistler. Chief Young Leader,' said Seryozha Domrachev.

CHAPTER 5

THE COMMANDER'S PLACE

They talked as they walked along the avenue towards their building, and that prompted the beginnings of friendship. They realised that they would be able to keep hanging together, at least in four pairs: Valerka and Seryozha Domrachev, Lyova Khlopov and Kolka Gorokhov, Tityapkin and Gurka, and Slava Mukhin and the eighth boy, a little scrap of a thing whose name they had not yet found out. The whole way he had hung back and simply gone along with everything. The tall, universally disliked Gelbich was left without a companion.

Building 4 turned out to be a two-storeyed slab of gingerbread that looked to all points of the compass at once. Irina Mikhailovna led the brigade onto the spacious, baking veranda. The second young leader was waiting there: a lad with a trendy haircut and dark moustache. He stood there smiling and looking lost, not knowing what to do, while Irina Mikhailovna handled the pioneers like an experienced drover.

'The building has four dormitories, so we'll have four squads,' she said, her glasses flashing sternly. 'Two squads of boys, two of girls, seven or eight in each. Split yourselves into squads and look lively about it. I'm giving you five minutes.'

Gurka immediately flung his arms wide and grabbed everyone he had been walking with – Lyova Khlopov, Tityapkin, Valerka, and all the others except Gelbich. He started to bundle them towards the window.

'This is our squad!' he bellowed at the rest of the boys. 'Don't mess with us, scumbags.'

'Guryanov, watch your mouth!' chided Irina Mikhailovna.

As any teacher should, she had quickly fixed her charges in her memory by sight and name.

The main question that had been tormenting all the boys from the moment they had seen the building was put to Irina Mikhailovna by a boy from the other squad, not Valerka's.

'Rin Khalovna, who'll get the top floor?'

The top floor was top in every way, the place to be; everyone knew that.

'You can bet it won't be us,' grouched Gelbich.

'The girls' dorms are on the top floor,' Irina Mikhailovna told them.

'Whaa?! Whaat's that about?! Sod that!' The boys showed their displeasure by all howling all at once.

'Because you're psychopaths!' Irina Mikhailovna cut them off. 'You have no idea how to walk quietly and you'll break your necks on the stairs.'

'Yeah we do. We can do whatever.'

'This conversation is over. Igor Alexandrovich, take the girls upstairs.'

The leader with the long hair and the moustache smiled again.

'Girls, follow me,' he said politely. 'Don't break the steps.'

The dorm into which Irina Mikhailovna ushered Valerka's squad was like the bunkroom of a wooden ship. A large window. Eight neatly-made bunks, four to a row, towels hanging at the foot, flannelette blankets drawn tight, pillows plumped up like pies. By each bunk stood a bedside cabinet. On the panels of the walls, on the floorboards, and on the flannelette blankets were bright squares of sunshine.

'Get settled in,' said Irina Mikhailovna. 'Fetch out what you need and your parade uniform. In half an hour I'm taking the luggage to the store-room.'

''Salright, this dorm,' said Lyova Khlopov, looking around and offering a summary.

His words came out like the command 'Forward!'

Gurka flung off his backpack and flew towards the window.

'Mine!' he yelled, dropping star-shaped on the bunk.

Valerka knew that the bunks under the window were always considered to be the best. Why, was unclear. His own preference was for the bunk in the corner, and he wordlessly placed his suitcase on it. No second neighbour, the door nearby, and it was easier to make a little house out of the sheet to take refuge from the mosquitoes.

Valerka had been to pioneer camps many times before, since third year. His dad considered that Valerka read too much and did not spend enough time with his peers. Valerka did not argue, though he found the camps somewhat boring. Valerka's father worked as an engineer in a secret design department, sketching the engines for military rockets. It was a state secret, though it was not clear from whom. As a man thinking of his Motherland, Valerka's dad wanted his son to be closer to the people. But the people bugged Valerka. To be alone, without comrades, without teachers, and without his stupid little sister: that was what he needed.

Tityapkin immediately occupied the other bunk under the window. He flopped down on his back and began to twist back and forth, as if screwing himself in for a more secure hold. Lyova Khlopov unhurriedly went up to him.

'Listen,' he said, his voice charged with feeling. 'I'm a footballer. I run, and I have these highly developed lungs' – at which Lyova indicated with his hands something resembling women's breasts. 'I need oxygen. Let me have the window, eh?'

Tityapkin stopped wriggling. Lyova was undoubtedly the strongest in the dorm, but that was not the point. Even in such a short time, it had become apparent that everyone in their newly-joined company listened to Lyova. Lyova was imperceptibly becoming their acknowledged commander. What was poor Tityapkin to do now? Quarrel with Lyova, when all the others had started to be his friend?

'Yes, sirree!' declared Tityapkin jauntily, as if giving in to Lyova was a positive source of joy, and he jumped deftly onto the bunk opposite.

'I've bagged this one!' shouted Slava Mukhin, peeved.

'I'm with Lyovka!' Tityapkin yelled at him. 'Lyovka's got no oxygen!'

'Piss off!' Slava pushed Tityapkin straight to the floor without debate.

'Whaddid you say?' flared Tityapkin. 'Let's step outside.'

'It's Slavik's bed,' Lyova observed censoriously.

Level-headed Lyova did not want to be next to the nincompoop Tityapkin. Meanwhile Tityapkin would have been a fool to quarrel with Lyova over Slavik's bunk if he was not prepared to quarrel over his own. Still, Tityapkin felt that he had been humiliated. He needed to retrieve his losses. His gaze swept across the dorm and came to rest on Valerka, small and wearing glasses. Glasses wearers were all wimps and assholes, of that there was no doubt in Tityapkin's mind. And the place in the corner looked pretty good.

Valerka was sitting on the floor, transferring a neatly rolled up jumper and his parade clothes (a white shirt and blue school trousers) from his open suitcase to the bedside cabinet. Tityapkin leaped over Seryozha Domrachev's bed and clambered on to Valerka's bed like a monkey on to a branch.

'I'm going to be here!' he announced. 'You shift yourself to that empty one.' He pointed to an empty bunk next to the eighth boy, the boy with no name.

Valerka realised that a fight was brewing, and stood up. His heart was pounding.

'You go!' he answered.

'What did you say to me, Four Eyes? You off your trolley?' Tityapkin was acting like a regular hoodlum.

'You weren't sitting down, Valerych!' Kolka Gorokhov took Tityapkin's side. '*Move your base, you'll lose your place*! Don't you know the rules?'

'You ain't fighting, we ain't watching!' shouted Gurka from across the room.

'Hop it, Titka!' said Valerka resolutely.

The boys guffawed, not attempting to hide it, and even Lyova smiled. Tityapkin's face was twitching with indignation. He rushed towards Valerka, clenching his fists.

At that moment the door swung open and Irina Mikhailovna stepped into the room. To look at she seemed a weak-willed old girl, plump, short-sighted, but inside – Valerka had already realised this – she had a core of steel.

'What's all this hullabaloo?' she asked fiercely.

The boys were silent. Irina Mikhailovna looked quickly round at everyone.

'Tityapkin, you're out of line!' she said grimly; she had sized up the situation at once. 'Get off Lagunov. Take an empty bunk. I'll be back to check!'

Never doubting that they would do as she said, Irina Mikhailovna went out.

Tityapkin very nearly burst into tears.

'It's not fair!' The animal had already all gone out of him, and he whined. 'You all got to choose your own bunks, and I'm left the last one like a spare part.'

'All right,' said Lyova, taking pity on him. 'Let's draw lots like in football: the one who gets the empty place goes there, and Tityapa takes his place.'

'Might be better to count?' suggested Kolka Gorokhov.

'Count,' agreed Lyova.

Kolka began to count, pointing his finger. He left Lyova out of the draw in acknowledgement of the commander's right to bunk where he wanted.

'*All the guests were ea-ting bread with a rusty nail stuck in their head,*' said Kolka, turning round on the spot with his arm outstretched and his finger pointing. '*I'm the one who bashed it there so ev-ry-one got stuck to their chair.* You!'

Kolka pointed at the nameless boy. A choice that suited everyone.

'What's your name?' asked Lyova.

'Yura Tonkikh,' mumbled the boy, barely audibly.

'Move over there, Yurik.'

'I've already parked my things in the drawers...'

'So move them!' shouted Gorokhov. 'Don't you respect the law?!'

'Tityapa, take that bunk,' ordered Lyova.

Tityapkin was satisfied, though he had ended up with basically the same place against which he had rebelled. Heading towards his new bunk, Tityapkin turned and threw a blistering look at Valerka.

'As for you, Four Eyes, get ready to rumble, you got that? Tonight.'

'Shut your mouth, your guts'll catch cold,' answered Valerka fearlessly, in the manner expected of tough boys, though he did not care for the threat one little bit.

The voice of Irina Mikhailovna rang down the corridor, summoning them. 'Brigade muster! Everyone to the muster!'

CHAPTER 6

ALL ABOUT YOURSELVES

Rise and shine, exercise, morning assembly. Breakfast, lunch, afternoon snack, dinner. Work details, quiet time, evening assembly, lights out. Activity circles, competitions, contests, shows. Parents' day, grand concert, farewell camp fire. Swimming, games, films… Irina Mikhailovna was explaining in detail the order of camp life, but Valerka was not listening. He already knew everything. He was screwing up his eyes to read the brigade roll pinned to the stand. More precisely, the list of girls: Boyarkina, Gulyayeva, Kasimova, Lebedeva, Sergushina, Styazhkina, Vishnyova, Zavyalova… No one he knew.

The brigade was sitting on the veranda on benches along the walls. Everyone was dressed for formal assembly: light top, dark bottom, pioneer neckerchiefs.

'So then, my young friends, we need to choose a commander,' said Irina Mikhailovna. 'Any suggestions?'

There were no suggestions. The young friends did not yet know one another well enough – though they knew from school that commanders were not people who were themselves in command; they made the others follow the commands of teachers or young leaders. Why the hell would anyone want that job?

'Who was a brigade commander at school?'

'I was!' one of the girls suddenly declared.

Her voice carried a note of pride and a desire to be admired.

'Come here, Sergushina,' ordered Irina Mikhailovna.

There was something of the ballet dancer in the way Sergushina came out in front of the brigade. She stepped lightly on her tiptoes, turned, displayed herself, and smiled as if she were a film star. She had a fringe and two ponytails with yellow plastic bows. She had coloured her lips with pomade and touched up her eyes and eyebrows with black pencil.

'What is your name?' asked Irina Mikhailovna.

'Anastasiika!' sang the girl.

Irina Mikhailovna looked at the painted coquette and sighed. It was no part of being brigade commander to be dolled up like this. Still, the teachers at her school had confirmed Sergushina in the responsible post of commander, meaning they had reason do so. She should trust the opinion of her colleagues and tolerate girlish silliness.

'The brigade agrees to choose Nastya?' asked Irina Mikhailovna.

'I'm not Nastya, I'm Anastasiika!'

The girls started whispering and the boys broke into laughter.

'Everyone agrees,' said Irina Mikhailovna, wrapping the matter up. 'Sit down, Sergushina.'

Anastasiya sashayed back to her place.

'And wash that off before assembly,' said Irina Mikhailovna, her glasses flashing.

Without looking round, Anastasiika let out a snort that signified *I knew it!*

'We also need a tall boy to carry the flag,' continued Irina Mikhailovna. 'Venya Gelbich, a job made for you.'

Gelbich was half a head taller than anyone else.

Gelbich declined the offer. 'No, I don't want to,' he said.

'Come on, don't be a nuisance,' scolded Irina Mikhailovna. 'Pick up the flag and a cap and shoulder sash from Igor Alexandrovich in his room.'

'Ba-a-lls to this,' said Gelbich, upset.

'We also need a brigade name, a motto, and a song.'

It struck Valerka that there was children's black magic: the Black Room, Escaped Convicts, Coffins on Castors, Meatgrinder Buses, Blue Nails. And then there was adult black magic: brigade commanders, flags, stars, mottos. Children's black magic was probably to instil fear: not to open doors to anyone who happened to knock, not to go off with strangers, not to eat unknown food. But what was adults' black magic for? To create the appearance that all children were pioneers, *always prepared, friendly, capable, honest,* and *indomitable?*

'Someone, give me some possible names,' said Irina Mikhailovna giving the brigade a jolt in the form of a stern look. 'Well now, where is your initiative?'

'There's totally no need to name it at all!' Gelbich twitched his shoulder irritably. 'Brigade Four and there you are! Nobody will remember a name anyway.'

'And if you hadn't been named at all, would you like it?' Anastasiika asked him, schoolma'am-like.

The pioneers broke into laughter. Gelbich pulled a scornful face; the idea seemed to suit him just fine.

'Do we have any more sensible suggestions?' asked Irina Mikhailovna.

'Let's call it "Rose Ecstasy",' said Anastasiika.

'"Rose Lavatory",' said one of the boys instantly.

'What's that?' asked Irina Mikhailovna in surprise.

'A very beautiful flower,' explained Anastasiika dreamily. 'Girls are given it on the eighth of March.'

'It is not the eighth of March,' said Irina Mikhailovna, rejecting the suggestion. 'Let's move on. The brigade will be called "Danko". And our motto will be *Burn as bright as Danko's heart.'*

'That was the name of the brigade last shift,' Seryozha Domrachev reminded her.

'Is there something wrong with that, Domrachev?'

'Call it what you like!' Seryozha took offence for some reason, and turned away.

'Here's our song. Memorise it. *Take hold of your heart and kindle its light, be loving and it will forever burn bright!* So, let's practice...'

They repeated this stupid song over and over all together as they walked from their own building to Company Court. Irina Mikhailovna monitored the girls, and Igor Alexandrovich supervised the boys. Anastasiika strutted ahead as if she were a bride and the brigade was carrying her long train. Venya Gelbich trailed miserably behind Anastasiika as if he were the bridegroom;

he wore a cap, and a scarlet sash over his shoulder, and he carried the flag like an oar.

Company Court was actually a volleyball court, with gravel running lanes around its perimeter. The six pioneer brigades fell in on the gravel in even rectangles. A small group of adults, led by the Senior Pioneer Leader, stationed themselves so as not to have their backs to anyone. A radio technician pulled up a microphone stand. Wires stretched across to disco towers.

'Greetings, my young friends!' Whistler's upbeat voice boomed over the loudspeakers. 'Welcome to the best shift of the year – the Olympic shift!'

A flutter of excitement rustled through the brigades.

'Tell me all about yourselves!' blared Whistler, by way of invitation.

The leader of the first brigade gave a silent command: 'Three … four!'

'RHYTHM!' barked out the first brigade.

'Motto!' ordered their leader.

'Romantics! Seekers! Creators! Dreamers!'

'Song. Three … four!'

'*Decide! Seek! Create! Dream! In the rhythm of reason be a human!*'

Frightened birds erupted from the acacia bushes around the court.

'*Comet!*' The second brigade bellowed just as the first had done. '*The comet's motto, hear us cry: never fall down from the sky! The comet's up there and we are down here! Happiness always both far and near!*'

'*Crimson sails!*' The third brigade took up the squawking. '*The sails billow, the wild wind thunders, children still believe in wonders! Sail forever the whole world through, you'll find the place where dreams come true!*'

'Three … four!' whispered Irina Mikhailovna.

'*Danko!*' roared Valerka's brigade. '*Burn as bright as Danko's heart! Take hold of your heart and kindle its light, be loving and it will forever burn bright!*'

Then the fifth and sixth brigades howled theirs. Details such as what the names, mottos, and songs meant were of no interest. The main thing was that it came out right. The brigade which out-yelled the others were the champs. Or rather, it was the other way about: the brigade that shouted the worst were the chumps.

'Excellent!' said the senior leader approvingly. 'Now it's our turn to identify ourselves. Get to know us, my young friends… The strictest person in our camp is senior tutor Marina Fyodorovna Rodionova! A round of applause!'

The brigades clapped the tutor, who raised her hand in return. They then applauded Nikolai Petrovich Kolybalov (camp director), Ruslan Maximych Zakhvatkin (physical education), and Valentin Sergeich Nosatov, the doctor. No one even tried to remember all these names and positions.

'And now for the most important person in our camp!' Whistler turned to a lean old gent in a pioneer neckerchief. 'This is Serp Ivanych Iyeronov!'

Their interest piqued, the brigades awaited further explanation.

'Serp Ivanych is a veteran of the Civil War! He is a pensioner of national standing!' Whistler swept the brigades with a rapturous look. 'Our company has taken this remarkable man under its patronage! Salute!'

Whistler snapped her hand to her forehead, and all the brigades followed suit.

'To Serp Ivanych we are granting the honour of raising the flag of the Olympic shift! Over to you, Comrade Iyeronov!'

Serp Ivanych was a tall man, and he leaned slightly towards the microphone.

'Hello, my young friends,' he said simply. His voice was rich and appealing. 'I hope I shall not get in your way here in camp. I expect you have seen the little blue house with the red roof? That is my dacha. Such is the domain of which I am the landlord. Come in and visit me. I'll treat you to tea and biscuits.'

The pioneers laughed uncertainly. Naturally, no one would even think of simply waltzing in to see the old chap, but thank you, as they say, for the invitation.

Valerka was standing in the front row and was able to have a good look at the old man. He appeared kind enough. Grey hair in a hedgehog cut, a short, white stubbly beard and moustache, deep, pronounced wrinkles. Bony, slightly slouched, but strong.

'Serp Ivanych took part in the revolution and liberated our city!' Whistler shouted into the microphone from the side.

'Ah, yes, I don't suppose you even remember those goings-on,' said Serp Ivanych, embarrassed, and absolving the pioneers in advance.

'We remember!' came a rumble from the brigades. It was a pleasure to show respect to such a friendly and modest man.

'And who liberated our city?' Whistler interrupted again.

'Chapayev!' went up an enthusiastic shout from all sides.

Chapayev was one man they would not forget: near the theatre in Kuibyshev was a hulking monument of Chapayev on horseback and a mass of soldiers with rifles.

'And who was driven out?' asked Serp Ivanych mischievously.

'The Whites!'

Of course the Whites, not the violets. The Whites were not all the same, though. For Valerka, the far-off Civil War was a beautiful, heroic fairy tale which made his heart ache. He had read a lot about that time.

'The interventionists were driven out,' he said in a low voice.

Iyeronov, of course, did not hear him, but Anastasiika Sergushina, Valerka's brigade commander, did. She was standing half a pace in front of the line, so that she was visible to all.

'Interventionists!' she shouted, her voice ringing.

'Whoa!' cried Serp Ivanych in surprise. 'Well now, my lass, wait there, I'm on my way.'

He rounded the microphone and, smiling, headed for Anastasiika across the empty space of Company Court. The brigades fell silent and watched apprehensively. No one knew why the old man was making his way over to Anastasiika.

'She's going to get it in the neck,' suggested Slava Mukhin.

'We should never have chosen that cretin!' muttered Kolka Gorokhov to his neighbours in the line. 'A girl commander's a shitty omen. They'll make us do the watch.'

Iyeronov drew closer, menacingly blotting out the whole world with his body.

'It wasn't me, it was him said it!' Anastasiika lost heart at the sight of the old man, and quickly turned the blame onto Valerka. 'Him, in the glasses!'

Valerka stiffened. Oi, oi, he should have kept quiet. No good can come from drawing attention to yourself with your opinion.

Serp Ivanych went up to Valerka and put a hand on his shoulder. 'Well done!' he said, praising him quietly and with feeling.

Valerka looked into the old man's dark eyes, and for some reason his heart missed a beat. Serp Ivanych's sorrowful eyes seemed to have seen everything in the world. They were bottomless, secret; it was as if Valerka were looking through a telescope and had fallen into the vast depths of the night sky, only these were depths with no twinkling stars, just black smoke. He thought: the smoke of the Civil War, most likely.

'We shall raise the flag together,' announced Iyeronov, turning to the brigades.

The brigades broke into an animated buzz of chatter. Four Eyes had lucked out! Serp Ivanych took Valerka by the hand, as if the boy were his grandson, and led him to a mast planted at the edge of the court. Valerka felt the eyes of the whole camp on him.

A rope was stretched along the mast and round a pulley, and a red flag was attached to the rope. The Senior Pioneer Leader gave a discreet signal to the radio technician, and the speakers were suddenly filled with the piercing blast of bugles and the rumble of drums.

'Pull the halyard,' said Serp Ivanych with a grin. 'Don't be afraid.'

Valerka started to pass the rope through his hands, and up went the red flag, up, up. At the top of the mast, it opened out and began to flutter against the bright sunny blue of the sky. All the boys and girls of Storm Petrel Pioneer Camp tilted their heads to look at the flag. All the five-pointed stars, oaths, and budyonovkas[3] had long ago turned into tiresome, pointless, obligatory nonsense – for children and adults alike – but the raised flag retained something honest, pure, and authentic. Like the city's pigeons, who could be rooting around in rubbish bins

....

[3]   A *budyonovka* was a distinctive type of hat and an essential part of the Red Army uniform during the Russian Civil War.

and pecking at sunflower seeds on pavements and then suddenly take off in flight.

'*Be prepared!*' shouted Whistler, snapping her hand in salute.

'*Always prepared!*' came an answering volley from the brigades.

Valerka was on his way back to the line, sensing that the whole camp was jealous of him. He took his place between Slava Mukhin and Yurik Tonkikh and tried to turn into a nobody so that they would stop staring at him.

'One cool dude, Valeryanych!' Tityapkin whispered hotly at him from behind.

Valerka understood that Tityapa had already changed his mind about wanting a fight with someone who was so suddenly attended by such fame. That would be too costly for him.

CHAPTER 7

THE DARK TIME

Life is a paradoxical thing. In order to retain at least relative independence, one has to be in the role of a slave, that is, of one who ideally would have no independence at all. Protecting something one does not have is absurd.

Igor was used to the absurd. The call goes out to protect the ideals of communism, and no one bugs out in surprise. Anyway, it was Irina who was in command of the brigade, and Igor, to preserve his independence, simply implemented her directions.

For Irina, everything was wonderfully simple. She had grown up on an ordinary collective farm, and was now managing her subordinates with the unthinking economy of a peasant. What to occupy the children with? Anything at all: the camp was bursting with activity circles, clubs, and preparations for sundry competitions. How to find the right thing for each child? Nothing complicated there. The tall ones to volleyball, the noisy ones to choir, the smart ones to chess, grandstanders could go to drama club, and anyone caught with matches or breaking the rules would be handed a rake and sent off to clear up the grounds. The main thing was to see that no one slacked.

Irina showed up in the building even before the bugle that started the radio programme 'Pioneer Dawn' had sounded reveille, and she did not leave the brigade until lights out. Before lights out she held a 'candle' ceremony on the veranda – a general meeting to discuss and sum up the day. The original idea had been that the pioneers would pass a lighted candle one to another, and each one, on receiving the candle, would express their impressions of the day just finished. However, for reasons of fire safety, Camp Director Kolybalov had banned the lighting of any fire in the wooden houses, and the 'candle' ceremony had been cancelled. That did not stop Irina. She broadcast a daily summary herself, without assistants. She believed that if she gave the floor to anyone who wanted to speak, the pioneers would not be asleep before it was time to get up, and fights might even break out.

Irina remembered all the details of the day with the accuracy of an intelligence officer.

'Krivoshein threw porridge in the canteen today. Tomorrow he'll be sweeping the dorm floor,' she said. 'Sergushina has the Company Council tomorrow at ten. Potapova, you are not going to assembly in torn tights. Tsybastov, I heard you use a swear word. Once more and I'll report you to the militia. Is that clear?'

'Guryanov said he was going to leave the camp at night,' complained the girls.

'Igor Alexandrovich, check on Guryanov during the night,' ordered Irina imperiously. 'If he's not in his bunk we'll expel him from camp for breaking the rules. That's it. Do the Oryol Circle, and then it will be time to go to your dormitories.'

The Oryol Circle was the name given to a pioneer ritual in which everyone stood in a circle, placed their arms round one another's shoulders, and all together in low voices made various promises or wishes. Or sang an uplifting song.

The fourth brigade, with some pushing and shoving, lined up along the walls and adopted the Oryol embrace. Igor had his arm on Tityapkin's shoulder on one side and Masha Styazhkina's on the other. Hugging the girls embarrassed the boys, so Igor and Irina put themselves in between them.

'The day has flown, and the camp is hurrying to bed,' they all mumbled.

'Good night to you, our boys,' said the girls, making it sound somehow intimate.

'Good night to you, our girls,' said the boys in strangled tones.

'Good night to you, our leaders,' they said, all together again. 'We have a hard journey tomorrow! Let's start operation "Shh-shh-shh!"'

Relieved, the pioneers released themselves and hissed in warning, pressing their forefingers to their lips.

This action seemed to Igor so phoney as to smart. The Oryol Circle was predicated on the assumption that pioneer life was an uncompromising and dangerous struggle that knit warriors together in brotherhood. A feeling of awkwardness scalded Igor, making him itch furiously. He scratched as he herded the boys into their dorm.

In the young leaders' cubbyhole, Sasha was also getting ready for bed. It was summer, ten o'clock in the evening! Sasha must have been a very obedient child, wholly subdued under the strict guardianship of his parents, and had not yet shaken the habit of doing everything by the rules. Igor wanted to read for a while in bed. But, as was well known, the 'lights out!' signal marked the onset of the dark time.

'Will you be able to drop off with the light on?' asked Igor.

'You need to respect house rules,' answered Sasha.

Clear enough: reading was ruined. Igor did not want to sit on the veranda with a book. Resigned, he went out on the stoop and fished out a cigarette. He had not made a girlfriend yet, so all he could do was take a walk on his own.

Beyond the pines, beyond the Volga, the sunset was burning itself out. In its dying was a concentration of yearning eroticism, a bashful, burning blush and a movement downwards, towards bed. Through the gently dazzling crimson, black pine trunks like mooring cables pulled the blue sky towards the mossy pier of the earth. It was hot, like the air in the engine room of a motor ship when the diesel has only just stopped running.

Igor paced the long Pioneer Avenue, himself not knowing where he was going. To the Volga, most likely; where else was there to walk here? The ornamented gingerbread camp buildings, their angles drowning in the uncertain twilight, suddenly identified themselves among the bushes in crimson reflections of the sunset in the window panes. In Building 3, a window was open and girls' voices reached Igor, singing: '*Not a sound from the gaa-rrden, not even a whisperr, all quiet and still here until the new morr-ning...*' A proper evening get-together, with no idiotic pioneer botherations.

In the acacia trees behind the 'Glory to the Victors' stand, someone was jiggling about and giggling. Igor stopped.

'Come out of there!' he ordered sternly.

Two girls emerged from the undergrowth. Both were from the second brigade; one of them Igor already knew. She was Ruslan the PE teacher's brightest star and Lenochka the young leader's biggest problem. Her name was Zhanka Shalayeva. She was cheeky, big-mouthed, and big-eyed and had all the older boys falling in love with her one after another. She was a streetwise girl who plainly understood more about life than she should at her age. Her friend was a dour hooligan whose name appeared to be Olya.

'Rule-breaking, are we?' inquired Igor, narrowing his eyes.

'Eek, oh please, don't tell Lenka, Igor Sanych!' replied Zhanka, flirting and not the least embarrassed.

So she was already calling her young leader Lenka and had learned the names of all the men on the staff. Yes, the wild child will always find her way.

'Go straight back inside!' said Igor severely. 'In ten minutes I'll come and check!'

The girls huffed grudgingly, turned, and made their way back into the bushes.

Igor walked on. The street lamps over the avenue flickered as they burned. The sky faded at once, and the crowns of the pines, lit from below, turned into a slowly billowing ceiling. The space behind the tree trunks disappeared, and acacia trees emerged from the darkness in dense clumps of paper-white foliage.

In the distance, by the food block, under a dim light over the service entrance, Nyura, the old scullery maid, was feeding scraps of food to a shaggy dog.

'Ea, don be afrai,' she murmured. 'Ea, Mukhtar, I won take it away...'

One half of Nyura's face was twisted in paralysis, and the pioneers mimicked her grimace, which made Nyura bad-tempered and shout at everyone. Igor was surprised at the quiet kindness with which Old Nyura was treating the hound.

Igor skirted Company House from the rear so that no one would see him. Young Leaders were not encouraged to leave the camp grounds. The Senior Pioneer Leader Natalya Borisovna and the PE teacher Ruslan Maximych were sitting on a bench in the back yard. Trying not to make any noise, Igor snuck up behind them.

'I want a dacha just like Yeronych's,' Natalya Borisovna was admitting in a low voice, laying her head on Ruslan's shoulder. 'I'll grow strawberries.'

'Live to be a hundred 'n' fifty like Yeronov and they'll give you one.'

'Perhaps I should have a baby, Ruslik? Then they'll give me a flat out the fund.'

'While you're stuck out there on maternity leave, you'll lose your seat on the City Committee.'

'What if I stay on it part time?'

'Go part time and you can forget about a flat,' sighed Ruslan.

Natalya Borisovna sighed, too. So many good opportunities: a job, a flat, a child, but one precluded another. You had to choose. And that was hard. Natalya Borisovna was a clockwork commissar only at work.

Igor reached the gates of the pioneer camp, unwound the rusty wire in the retaining loop, and pulled the leaf from between the iron pipes. The spectral bugler, of course, still rose up on her plinth. The slats of the pier, showing light, led away into the darkness of the Volga. The river breathed its freshness into his face.

Igor walked a little further along the beach away from the entrance to the camp. The sand hollowed beneath his feet. The narrow sickle of the nascent moon hung in the sky. Igor felt deep, deep within him the huge, flat emptiness of the endless water stretching out alongside, like the invisible high-voltage current along an overhead power line. That was how the Volga sounded. Its mystical attraction was enthralling, severing all of life's ties.

Between the camp and the Volga was a chain link fence. Access to the river was the most unshakeable prohibition at Storm Petrel. The camp bosses inspired far greater fear in the young leaders with stories of drowned children than the young leaders did in the children with stories about evil spirits killing pioneers at night. Igor grinned humourlessly. If it was interesting, it was not allowed. No swimming in the river. No walking in the forest. No seducing the girls. What were they supposed to do? Watch the Olympics on the common room television?

Igor sat down on a log thrown up by the water and half smothered in sand. Behind him, beyond the pines, the street lamps of Pioneer Avenue burned. In front of him, out on the river, buoys glowed faintly, giving out scarlet sparks. The dying blue of the sky magically outlined the distant slopes of the Zhiguli. A cruise liner was sailing down the channel, looking as if it were lit from within, like an aquarium. Music travelled indistinctly along the telepathic whisper of the current. People were sailing towards sights that would stun them; they were dancing on deck, drinking wine, joking and laughing, while he, Igor Korzukhin, was bolted with every available nut and lock nut to the pioneer camp, his summer practical, his higher education, the task of filling out his curriculum vitae.

And somewhere the moon was silvering the colossal jagged edges of ancient pyramids. The ocean wind was rattling the scraps of rigging on the masts of the Flying Dutchman. A mysterious force awaited aeroplanes in the trap of the Bermuda Triangle. Rows of mute stone *moai* gazed into the horizon from the shore of Rapanui Island. The dragon's jaw of Stonehenge grinned wide with shattered teeth. A Nepalese Yeti on all fours sniffed at the footprints of mountaineers. The shadow of a Jurassic plesiosaur slithered bodiless through the cold depths of Loch Ness. The cosmic navigation of the Nazca Desert was forever frozen in the intersections of mysterious arcs and bisectors. The roots of the jungle went on slowly demolishing abandoned Mayan cities. Shoals of colourful fish wove their way between the colonnades of sunken Atlantis. None of this he, Igor Korzukhin, would ever see. Why not? Yes, well. Ask me no questions.

The chain link jingled behind him. Igor looked round. Someone was climbing nimbly over the fence. Not a child. A grown-up, but shapely, and agile. A gymnast, suddenly materialising? Igor saw with astonishment that it was a girl, but with a boy's haircut. Veronika. One of the young leaders of the third brigade; the other was Sasha, Igor's roommate.

Veronika walked out onto the beach, giving the appearance of not having noticed Igor. Igor immediately understood that her disdain contained a challenge – not to him personally, of course, but to the whole world. To all noes, nots and nevers. Veronika kicked off her shoes, wriggled her jeans down, yanked her T-shirt over her head, and then, twisting her hands behind her back, fearlessly unhooked her bra. The faint moonlight faintly illuminated her pale breasts. Igor went rigid; he was unable to move, or even avert his eyes. Apprehensively stretching out her arms, Veronika cautiously stepped into the water in just her knickers, waded out until she was waist-deep, then eased herself forward and swam away from the shore.

Igor watched her describe a circle and come back. She left the water glistening all over, still not covering her breasts with her hands. Confusion reigned in Igor's head. This was the moment to drop some careless sarcastic remark, or perhaps not: perhaps to express understanding and approval, or at least offer her a cigarette. He did none of those; he just sat there, as silent as one of the *moai* on the island of Rapanui. Veronika's white breasts had bewitched him. He was bewitched by the strange and daring thing she had done – to bathe half-naked in the face of everything. So what if no one had seen it (a dunderhead in a state of shock did not count). Veronika briskly wiped herself off with her T-shirt and started to dress.

Then she walked back to the fence, climbed over the chain link, and disappeared behind the bushes. Igor was left with the crazy feeling that out of the blue he had suddenly lost everything in the world.

Or maybe he had gained everything.

CHAPTER 8

THE GRIN OF THE OLYMPIC BEAR

Company House was a two-storey panel barracks built about thirty years previously as a state farm dormitory. Back then the village of Pervomaiskaya was still thriving, more or less. Company House now housed the living quarters of the Senior Pioneer Leader, the PE teacher, and the senior tutor, as well as rooms for the activity circles, the radio centre, and the Flag Room – a near-sacred spot. On the ground floor was a cinema with darkened windows. Sixty or seventy people could be crammed in there; the films shown in camp were changed every three days so that the whole company could watch them. Tonight was the night of the third and fourth brigades. Igor, Irina, Sasha Plotkin, and Veronika were sitting in the back row. Ruslan the PE teacher and Svistunova came to join them.

The radio technician Sanya was showing a tedious documentary about the preparations for the Olympics, but the Senior Pioneer Leader had promised that there would be cartoons later, and the disgruntled spectators were sitting it out, talking to one another in anticipation of the show. The projector whirred; in the darkness above the room glowed a widening smoky beam, in which coloured shadows flickered, and the tops of the children's heads turned blue, then red, then yellow.

'Hey, guess this one, people,' said Lyoshka Tsybastov from the other squad, not Valerka's. He was fidgeting in his seat. 'An hour and a half of pleasure in a dark room on a white sheet! What is it?'

'Give us a break, we all know that one!' muttered Venka Gelbich.

'Hey! Button it back there!' snapped the PE teacher Ruslan, sternly scolding the chatterers. He leaned in to Sasha Plotkin's ear and whispered, with a note of respect, 'I have no idea how you teach these morons to play chess. Genius.'

Sasha gave a shrug of his shoulders, signifying: it's a gift from above; you're not going to understand it.

Valerka was looking attentively at the screen. Unlike the others, he was interested. So much preparation for the Olympics! Valerka was struck by the strange other-worldliness of the new sports facilities. The bowls of the stadiums resembled meteorite craters, and the Krylatsky Velodrome was like a fantastic settlement on the moon. The Friendship Stadium splayed out like a many-legged Martian crab, and the Dynamo Sports Palace came barging into it, out of control and looking like an old tank. The burning sun beat rhythmically on the honeycombed concave glass sail of the Cosmos Hotel. Caravans of transparent and elegant *Ikarus* buses glittered. Fountains flamboyantly gushed white foam. Flocks of colourful flags pulsated. But what impressed Valerka most of all were the athletes. They marched harmoniously in rows and columns, flashing white-toothed smiles at the cameraman. Valerka examined the faces of the athletes – straightforward, open, and doughty. The athletes were like soldiers on parade: ahead of them lay genuine combat, fierce battles at the limit of their capabilities.

Valerka was jealous of the athletes. Not of their strength, of course. He envied the fact that the athletes had teams on whom they could rely completely, teams that would not let them down. He had no team of his own. No one on whom to rely, no one for whom to give his all. What united him with Tityapa or Kolka Gorokhov? A dorm in their brigade building? Wanting to watch cartoons? That was not authentic. Valerka had never known real unity. Friendship was not what he had in mind. Friendship was when you shared an interest with your friend, when you were alike. A team was when everyone was different but all shared a single common undertaking which all needed and which could not be completed by any one member alone.

Lyova Khlopov was also glued to the screen. 'Rinat Dasayev!' he was muttering in admiration, as he recognised members of the Olympic football team. 'There goes Cherenkov! Bessonov! Gavrilov!'

The documentary finally ended, the room breathed a sigh of relief, and Sanya changed the reels: cartoons time. Admittedly, the cartoons were also about the Olympics. They were called 'Baba-Yaga Versus.' Baba-Yaga the gypsy, skinny Koshchei in his overcoat and a crown, and the tinpot Snake-Gorynych attempted to play any number of dirty tricks on Misha the plump Olympic Bear, but in their ineptitude all they did was get in a muddle and one another's way. Idiots! None of their plans came to anything. Hilarious. The brigades dispersed to their quarters satisfied.

Irina Mikhailovna quickly conducted a 'candle'.

'Guryanov and Tityapkin, who was going yackety yak in the film?' Irina Mikhailovna glared at the silence breakers. 'Do you want to be sitting here in this building next time while the civilised among us are watching the film?'

Then the fourth brigade clinched together in an Oryol Circle.

'The day has flown, and the camp is hurrying to bed,' mumbled Valerka along with everyone else. 'Good night to you, our girls … good night to you, our leaders … we have a hard journey tomorrow! Let's start operation "Shh-shh-shh!"'

Valerka could not bear it: it was all pretension. Why the hell were they saying such a heartfelt goodbye? No one was going to snuff it during the night. The people here were not even family. Valerka had never hugged even his mother and grandmother so ardently before leaving for camp, nor had he ever shown such tenderness to his little sister.

Back in the dorm, the boys sorted themselves out onto their own bunks, and Gor-Sanych switched off the light and closed the door. The boys immediately jumped up and grabbed their towels. Before going to bed they had to whack as many mosquitoes as they could, otherwise they would be eaten alive. They thrashed the walls, and each other while they were at it, then lay back down. Now was their chance to begin a discussion about the day, a real one, not like the 'candle'. The mosquitoes, having waited out the flurry of thrashing, gradually restarted their whining.

'The cartoons were rubbish,' declared Gurka. 'About as funny as a fart in a lift.'

'The film was interesting,' said Lyova. 'I'd like to go up to Moscow, have a gander at the Olympics. The football, anyway.'

'No one's allowed into Moscow,' objected Seryozha Domrachev. 'All the trains are going round.'

'So how are people supposed to get there?' asked Tityapkin, surprised.

'How now brown cow,' muttered Slavik Mukhin.

'So where are they getting spectators from? To watch the races, you know.'

'All the spectators are fuzz and soldiers in civvies,' Seryozha informed them authoritatively. 'In summer they put soldiers in all the schools in Moscow. And they built new stadiums so they could put invisible windows in the walls and the soldiers can shoot their rifles through them if anything goes down.'

The boys took a moment for grim reflection. It all had the ring of truth. The Olympics were the same as war, only hand to hand and not to the death.

'Foreigners have got a ton of sabotage ready,' shy Yura Tonkikh suddenly piped up. 'There's a whole book been written about it ages ago. Anyone who needs to read it's already read it.'

'How do you know?' Slavik Mukhin did not believe him.

'My dad told me.'

Normal boys never referred to anything their parents said. It was considered wimpish, like calling the teacher for help in a school fight. Still, the boys managed to make an exception in this case. Even Kolka Gorokhov sighed but said nothing.

'It says in the book that foreigners'll give T-shirts with Misha the Olympic Bear on them as presents,' continued Yurik. 'The bear will be, like, normal, but when they wash it the dye'll come out and Misha'll bare his teeth like a dog.'

'Wicke-e-ed!' gasped Gurka admiringly. 'I need that T-shirt.'

'It also says they'll hand out chewing gum and inside'll be razor blades. And the black people're going to use the glasses in the drinks machines to spread diseases. And they're going to sell jeans with germs sewn into the seams.'

Gurka thrashed about on his bunk; his feelings had gone into overload.

'And, like, no one's going to catch them?' objected Tityapkin, offended. 'I mean, they're sabotaging us!'

'Papa said that during the night in Moscow the fuzz'll shake the trees and beetles'll fall out and they'll collect them in jars. Then they'll give them to the medical institute and those guys'll make an injection. But not straight away.'

The cunning of the foreigners amazed the boys; Valerka too. The cartoons had been right to show Baba-Yaga being 'against'. Only Lyova Khlopov was displeased. He leaned on his elbow, looking at Yurik. Sabotage was sabotage, but there was no need to drag football into it.

'Anything in there about football, Yurik?' he asked.

'It says foreign football players are going to bring boxes with fleas. They'll let them out, set them on our guys, our guys'll get all twitchy and itchy and lose.'

Lyova calmed down somewhat and laid his cheek on his pillow.

'They're not going to lose because of fleas,' he said with conviction. 'Fleas are bollocks.'

The boys stared at the ceiling and pondered the hardships of life. The pine trees beyond the window were illuminated by the blue street lamps of Pioneer Avenue.

'We need to get a football team together,' resolved Lyova firmly.

CHAPTER 9

'LET SLIP THE DOGS OF WAR!'

The order of the day was reproduced on the large stands set up near the canteen, in front of Company House and on Pioneer Avenue. The time between the 'work details' and lunch was set aside for activity circles and clubs, training, and rehearsals. This period was equipped with an explanatory poem: *Happy hour has come to call, time to play for one and all.*

Igor Sanych took the boys of his brigade to the stadium to play football.

'The oldies said that last year there was a swimming pool instead of the stadium,' Seryozha Domrachev told them as they walked. 'But the girls went for a swim once after the boys had been in and one of them got pregnant from the water. They practically put the camp boss in jail. He ordered the pool to be filled in.'

The boys, to be honest, did not have much idea how girls got pregnant. To the boys, the dramatic story of the pool's transformation into a stadium seemed quite plausible. Life was hard.

'There wasn't a pool!' objected Gelbich without much conviction. No one took any notice.

Every shift in the camp there was a football championship. The team from one of the older brigades – the first or second – always won. The oldies' teams consisted of steamrollers that it was impossible for anyone to beat. But Lyova Khlopov, armed with football theory, was raring to have a shot at breaking this tradition.

'In football it's brains that matter, not muscles,' he told the boys from his dorm. 'When the players are smart and the team is cohesive, you can crush any opponent. The main things are skills and the will to win.'

Everyone had the will to win, and Lyova was promising to equip them with the skills.

'The tricks I know, you'll beat anyone,' he assured them.

Lyova entered into negotiations with Igor Alexandrovich. Igor liked Lyova's idea very much. Igor basically had no idea what to occupy the pioneers with when it fell to him as young leader to occupy them with something. And it was boring to watch children's games when he himself was no longer a child. Igor had brought a couple of science fiction books with him to camp. He could read them while the boys were absorbed in what they were doing and did not need supervision.

Igor tracked down Ruslan, the head of PE and the man in charge of the stadium.

'Look,' he said. 'Give me the pitch once a day for an hour.'

'What for?'

Igor explained. Ruslan easily agreed. If someone else was using the stadium, he would have less work himself. Still, he issued a warning.

'One of the goals is wobbly. Your morons knock it down, you'll be digging it back in yourself.'

Lyova planned daily matches between his squad and Venka Gelbich's. Lyova was counting on using these confrontations to assess the quality of all the players. He would then organise a brigade-wide eleven-man team. At the end-of-shift championship, this trained team would come out against the steamrollers. It would then become apparent which was more important: intellect or strength.

When she heard about Igor's initiative, Irina's temper flared.

'That's not doing things with the children,' she hissed. 'That's just you shirking your responsibilities!'

'We're on the Olympic shift,' replied Igor, sounding like a true demagogue.

All the boys unanimously supported the idea. At least football was more interesting than clearing up fir cones during work detail, rehearsing the play 'In Defence of a Peaceful Sky', or writing letters to foreigners in the School of International Friendship.

Gelbich's squad immediately started shouting and yelling. 'Not fair! There are seven of us and eight of you!'

'I don't have to play,' suggested Tonkikh timidly.

'All right, Yurik, you'll be a sub,' agreed Lyova readily. A bean pod like him would be no use anyway.

Valerka was not inspired by football either. The mosquitoes had been so rampant during the night that he had spent almost the whole time until dawn swatting and scratching, and had had nowhere near enough sleep. Walking to the stadium, he thought that he really must make a roof out of his sheet that evening, stretching it over the back of the bed. There was a reason why he had taken a place in the corner of the dorm, where it would be easier to make a little shelter against the bloodsuckers.

Long benches for spectators ringed the well-tramped stadium. There were no markings on the pitch. The goals consisted of two bare posts and a crossbar. Igor led the boys into the stadium.

'That's it.' He spread his hands in a gesture of helplessness. 'That's all the help I can give you.'

Gor-Sanych understood nothing about football and made no secret of it.

'I'll take it from here,' said Lyova gravely.

While Gelbich's dummies dashed about booting the ball, Lyova busied himself with theory.

'Gurka, you'll be in goal,' he said.

'No!' wailed Gurka. 'I want to score goals!'

'You're the most agile,' Lyova patiently explained. 'Without you we're screwed.'

Gurka's passion wrestled inwardly with his vanity, and vanity prevailed.

'All right,' he agreed condescendingly.

'Right then, listen to me,' continued Lyova. 'Sery and Kolyan, you'll be the backs. Defence. It's your job to protect our goal.'

'What about scoring goals?' Kolka Gorokhov was jealous.

'The strikers score the goals.'

'Make me a striker!'

'Everyone will take turns.'

'So let's count then. That's the rules!'

'The rules are to listen to me! I'm the captain!'

'Stuff your football!' Gorokhov burst into a fit of rage, stomped away, and started kicking the ground in frustration.

'Tityapkin and Mukhin, you're the strikers.'

'I'll mow 'em all down!' promised Tityapa. 'They'll be taking the whole lot of 'em straight to the morgue.'

'Me and Valerka will be the half backs. We'll be in the middle of the pitch.'

Valerka did not like the term 'half-back'. Being a back was boring enough, and this was only half the job. Meaning only Tityapa and Slavik would be playing football for real. But Valerka did not argue.

'Give us the ball, Gor-Sanych,' ordered Lyova. 'We're ready.'

Igor Alexandrovich walked out onto the pitch and placed the ball in the centre. The teams readied themselves for the struggle: on one side Lyova's, and on the other, Venka Gelbich's. Venka's whole team, exhibiting a shameless lack of art and craft, consisted of strikers, and that made Gelbich's massed mob look a great deal more dangerous than Lyova's technically positioned team. Igor Alexandrovich stuck a whistle borrowed from the PE teacher into his mouth and blew it.

The Gelbichi rushed at the ball. Vovka Makerov quickly sent it forward with an accurate kick, and the Gelbichi broke straight ahead, bundling Tityapa and Mukhin aside. Lyova courageously darted in to intercept, bringing down a couple of Gelbichi. Valerka also broke into a run, though he had no clear thoughts on where he was going, and his movements were random.

Kolka Gorokhov jumped like a frightened rabbit out of the Gelbichi's way, Seryozha Domrachev got hopelessly lost in the crowd of enemies, and Lyokha Tsybastov, running at full tilt, aimed a shot towards Lyova's goal. Gurka, arms outstretched, flew into one corner of the goal while the ball flew into the other. Gurka tumbled, then jumped up and raced after the ball as if he wanted revenge on it, and the sooner the revenge was carried out, the less significant the defeat would be.

'OK, OK, everything's fine,' Lyova consoled his warriors. 'You shouldn't start with a victory; it makes you complacent.' Lyova sighed heavily and cast a judgemental look at the Gelbichi. 'What are you doing, attacking in one great herd? There are different types of player: forwards, half-backs, goalkeepers, but you've got nothing but forwards. You can't do that. We're training up a joint team, and we're going to play against the steamrollers as one team where each player has his own job. We need to work on that.'

'Piss off!' replied the Gelbichi, triumphant and lippy.

None of his own lads said anything to Lyova, but the lesson had been learned: the rules just stopped you from winning.

Gurka brought the ball and placed it prominently in the middle of the pitch.

'Let slip the dogs of war!' he cried.

Igor Alexandrovich blew his whistle. The battle erupted again. Slavik Mukhin and Tityapkin left their area of responsibility by the goal and plunged into the general meleé. Lyova was forced to join in as well. The boys yelled, shoulder-barged one another, and kicked out desperately, trying to make contact with the ball. Valerka, afraid of breaking his glasses, ran around the bloodbath, but could find no way of pushing his way into it. Fury had possessed all the players. They cared nothing for the team or the goal – their own or the other; the main thing was to stick a boot in and send the ball flying somewhere, anywhere, who cared where. Suddenly the ball soared vertically into the air over the crowd, and came hurtling back down. Lyova gave a leap, and met the ball smack with his forehead.

The ball landed right in front of Valerka and went bouncing on down the pitch. Valerka rushed towards it at once, kicked it, and chased it in front of him, charging at the Gelbich goal. In goal, arms outstretched, a panic-stricken Borka Podkorytov darted this way and that, his face white. A crowd of other players rushed after Valerka like a pack of strays after a cat.

'Stop, Four Eyes! Stop, you shitbag!' came shouts from both sides, his own as well as the other.

Tityapa caught up with Valerka first and kicked him in the heel. Valerka tripped over his own feet and went sprawling face down. The roiling crowd of players swept over him, and someone stepped on his hand. The battle rolled this way and that in the Gelbich penalty area, slowly spilling into the goal and taking Borka Podkorytov down with it.

'Goal! It's a goal!' hollered Lyova's team. 'You're pissing yourselves now, slimeballs!'

'No goal! Dun't count!' hollered Venka's team. 'Cheats!'

Valerka got up and walked off the pitch. He was no longer interested.

Yura Tonkikh was sitting on a bench beside Igor Alexandrovich. The young leader was reading a tattered book with a garish cover.

'Get out there and take my place, Tonky,' ordered Valerka angrily.

'I don't want to...'

'Go or you'll get a thick ear.'

Yurik trudged off towards the pitch. Valerka sat down on the bench.

'You don't like football, Lagunov?' Gor-Sanych gave him a sideways glance.

'Love it!' growled Valerka, in a strop.

Valentin Sergeich Nosatov, the camp doctor, came up behind them. 'Can I cadge a fag, Igoryok?' he asked.

Valentin Sergeich was on his way back to the sick bay from seeing Serp Ivanych Iyeronov. Two or three times a week, Nosatov paid a visit to the all-Union pensioner to take his blood pressure. Iyeronov was an elderly man, eighty years old, the same age as the century; his health needed to be kept under control. Otherwise he would die in the pioneer camp, as Palmiro Togliatti had in Artek, and then the doctor would be shown the door.

Nosatov drew on his cigarette and watched the game for a few moments.

'Disgraceful,' he said with feeling.

'What riches we have...' shrugged Igor Alexandrovich.

'Bring them to me after the match. They're going to need bandages and disinfectant.'

On the pitch, the combat continued. The dishevelled and bellowing mob scurried from goal to goal. Valerka understood that the fundament of football was the pass, when one player sent the ball to another, nimbly skirting the anarchy, but right now no one was willing to cede the ball: each wanted to hang on to it and score a goal by himself. A fierce battle raged around the spinning ball. The boys seemed to be fencing with their feet, cracking the knees and shins of their own side and the other indiscriminately. Red Chinese sneakers and worn-out sandals flashed; sand flew out from beneath soles. The use of hands was strictly forbidden, but in the commotion the boys shoved and elbowed one another willy-nilly. Kolka Gorokhov lost his self-control and grabbed hold of Lyokha Tsybastov.

'What the hell, you mad Dagestan stallion!' Lyokha howled indignantly.

Tityapkin jinked out of the crowd with the ball and, wheezing, sprinted towards the Gelbich half, but he was overtaken, and vanished into a pileup.

Gurka, in goal, was beside himself with excitement. He was alternately running round in circles and jumping up and hanging off the crossbar like a gymnast. Whenever one of the Gelbichi broke through into an attacking position, Gurka hopped in front of him in a half-squat in the penalty area and shouted madly, like a hero in front of a firing squad, 'Come on, then! Let's do this, scumbag!'

Meanwhile Lyova Khlopov was investing all of himself in the struggle, leaving nothing behind, although he could have kept something back. Lyova played with skill and dexterity. He cut inside, circled, took the ball away with ease, jinked and turned, sold dummies. His undoing was his self-sacrifice. Lyova wanted to demonstrate class and involve everyone in his team. He spread generous passes, sending the ball to his team mates with low and high crosses. He flung himself courageously into the thick of the fray, not sparing himself, covering his lads from the blows of the Gelbichi. He fell regularly and was left writhing on the ground on his own as the crowd ran away, but like a true man he rose and, at a limping trot, hastened back to intercept the enemy horde once more. He was panting. His knees were bloodied with cuts, his T-shirt and tracksuit trousers were smeared with dirt, his hair was dishevelled, the tongues on his sneakers were lolling out. You could say that Lyova was playing nobly, not for dear life, but to the death. Out on the pitch he was 'one for all', but, alas, alas, the 'all' were not 'for one'. The boys were scrapping every man for himself, and Lyova's team shipped goal after goal. Valerka started to feel sore for Lyova.

Would it not be marvellous to invent a special machine where you pressed a button and everyone became unquestioningly obedient? It would make living simpler. Valerka had no need of such a machine personally: he had no wish to be in charge. He would give the machine to Lyova. Lyova was a good man, but the boys were not listening to him.

A lacerated Lyova gathered the boys of both teams in the middle of the pitch.

'Why are you such toddlers?' he asked them. 'We don't need to beat each other. We're learning to play together. I mean, Tsybastysh, why didn't you pass to Vovchik? He was right in front of goal. And Yurik, you went scarpering off. You're supposed to guard your own area. We all need to be coordinated.'

The ball was on the ground next to Lyova. The boys looked at one another nervously. Unable to restrain himself, Tityapkin rushed at the ball and kicked it. At that, the whole mob rushed howling after the ball, abandoning Lyova and his useless sermonising.

Igor Alexandrovich marked his place with his finger, looked at the boys, looked at Valerka, and gave a knowing grin.

'Disappointed in collectivism?' he asked.

'You can't talk like that!' snapped Valerka. 'You're a teacher.'

'A teacher, but not an idiot.'

Valerka looked angrily at the game and did not answer. What did this have to do with collectivism? Collectivism was wonderful. The collective was always right. A collective was always better than one individual. Smarter, more honest, braver. But out there in the stadium, could you call that a collective? A team? No. A pack of macaques fighting over bananas.

CHAPTER 10

OUTWARD APPEARANCE

Serp Ivanych simply did not have enough seating for everyone hoping to watch the opening of the Olympics, so viewers brought their own chairs. Igor took the activists from his brigade across to Iyeronov's dacha: Venka Gelbich, Anastasiika Sergushina, Lenochka Romanova and Lyova Khlopov. Irina let them go and stayed in their building; the Olympics did not interest her, even though she demanded a hundred times a day that the pioneers be proud of the fact that they had come to camp for a special shift – the Olympic shift.

Igor made Venka and Lyova carry chairs for Lena and Anastasiika.

'Chicks and the Olympics, eh,' grumbled Venka Gelbich. 'What the hell?'

'You have chicks in your class,' replied Anastasiika. 'We are young women.'

There were only two television sets in the camp. There was a black and white *Rassvet* in Company House, but a whole crowd had gathered there: Whistler and Ruslan, the senior tutor Marina Fyodorovna, the camp director Kolybalov, the doctor Nosatov, the radio technician Sanya, the facilities manager, the bookkeeper and the linen keeper, the canteen manager and the cooks. The pioneers from the older brigades, eager to see the spectacle, could not get in, and the young leaders had asked themselves over to Serp Ivanych's; after all, Serp himself had issued a general invitation. The guests felt a little awkward away from their own territory; at the same time, Serp's dacha boasted a coloured *Rubin*.

Serp Ivanych was flattered. He felt an old man's enthusiasm at the presence of so many young people, and did not know how to be useful. Kirill and Maxim, the two peas, lugged Iyeronov's television out onto the veranda, set it up on a table, and positioned the aerial. Serp Ivanych helped arrange the chairs.

'Do we have enough or not?' he asked. 'I've got one more chair upstairs, but it's back's broken. Will anyone be needing it, eh, lads?'

The pretty and cheeky Zhanka Shalayeva was flirting with Serp Ivanych.

'And this dacha is, like, totally yours?' Zhanka looked at Serp with the innocent eyes of an idiot. 'You must have done something totally heroic?'

'I'm just very old,' explained Serp Ivanych. 'I became bored in town a long time ago, and they sent me here to die and not get in the way.'

'You're not at all old yet,' Zhanka objected. 'You won't be dead anytime soon.'

The sunset's beams were gaining such speed and power over the Volga that they were blinding even through the palisade of pine trunks. The veranda was suffused with an amber glow. Through the window, Igor saw Veronika standing on the stoop smoking. Veronika, the young leader who a few days back had gone swimming in his presence without a bra. Igor already knew that Veronika worked in the third brigade with the nerd Sasha Plotkin, and shared a room with the rule-loving Irina. It seemed probable that Veronika was fed up of the morality champions. Smoking among the young leaders, particularly the young women, was not encouraged at camp, and Veronika was drawing on her cigarette with the look of someone already weary of idiotic reproaches.

Igor was drawn to her, as if he had already received a promise of something. He made quickly for the door.

'Hi,' he said, fishing out his cigarettes. 'You here for the Olympics?'

'They likely to show anything else here?' growled Veronika.

That did not deter Igor from continuing in the same teasing tone.

'What kind of sport are you interested in? Swimming?'

Veronika wanted to snap back, but was unable to stop herself snorting a laugh. She was not in the least embarrassed by her own recent brazenness, and this guy with the moustache appeared to have no intention of judging her. Meaning he was all right, then.

'Got to do something in the evenings,' acknowledged Veronika. 'And I don't want to read teaching manuals.'

'It's tough finding entertainment here,' agreed Igor. 'I wouldn't go to Svistunova's to watch telly. End up in her line of sight again for no good reason. Got to thank Serp for letting us in here. He's a good old boy.'

'Yeah, decent guy,' nodded Veronika.

The conversation stalled.

'Serp's seen it all,' said Igor, just to keep the conversation going. 'Hard to believe. Sword fights with the whites, mobile artillery...'

Igor found it hard to get his head round, it was true. Serp Ivanych looked every inch a modern old man, so to speak. He did not hector the youth, did not press his own opinion, did not complain about his health, made jokes, and watched a colour television. But the television simply did not fit with being in the Civil War cavalry.

'Well, actually, the artillery's not really what he did,' remarked Veronika. 'I ... er...' she faltered. 'Long story short, I know people who know him, you know, in town, on the Committee. Anyway, they say Serp made his career through the Party. And he only rode horses at the very start.'

Meaning that all Serp Ivanych had in his biography were rallies and party meetings. 'Urrhh,' said Igor slowly, disappointed. 'And I thought he was a hero.'

Veronika flew up instantly. 'So only the guy who goes into battle with a bayonet's a hero?' she demanded. 'What if someone's spent their whole life slaving like a donkey?'

To spend one's life slaving was certainly deserving of respect. But to live all your time as a donkey... No, Igor did not want that.

'Serp gave his whole self to his work. He didn't get married, didn't have children – he didn't have time! That's why he does such a lot with the pioneers now: he hasn't got any grandchildren of his own.'

'I don't know if that's the right thing to do,' said Igor doubtfully.

'It's obvious from your appearance you don't think so,' snapped Veronika, alluding to his jeans and trendy haircut. She shot him a scornful look.

'You don't quite fit that picture either,' said Igor cautiously, alluding to her night-time swimming.

'You're disgusting.' Veronika was offended.

She threw down her cigarette, ready to leave, but Igor grabbed her arm.

'Wait, wait,' he said in a conciliatory tone. 'I've got nothing bad to say about Serp Ivanych. I really like him.'

'They don't make them like him any more,' declared Veronika, still in a strop.

'They don't,' confirmed Igor earnestly.

'If you understood him, you wouldn't be loafing about here, you'd be laying rails at BAM!'

This argument had been forever hanging over Igor's conscience like the sword of Damocles. If you're a good person, why aren't you participating in good work?

'You're not at BAM either!' snapped Igor.

What the hell was this girl trying to teach him?

Veronika snatched her hand away and walked quickly towards Serp Ivanych's cottage.

Igor drew gloomily on his cigarette, pondering. He was a good person, but not interested in building a railway in the taiga. If he had been interested, he would have gone to railway institute instead of a university philology faculty. He was neither a lazybones nor an egoist. He was neither philistine nor petty bourgeois. But he did not want to go to BAM, KamAZ, or Atommash. He wanted to sail on the reed boat 'Tigris' with Thor Heyerdahl and explore the routes of the ancient Sumerians. He wanted to study coral reefs with Cousteau in his Diving Saucer. To climb Annapurna with Reinhold Messner. To excavate the ruins of Mohenjo-daro, look for Eldorado in the Orinoco jungle, or climb the inaccessible Roraima plateau, where, of course, it was hardly likely that dinosaurs had survived and were still living, but nevertheless there would be a Lost World. There was nothing wrong with such wishes. But for whatever reason it was better to keep quiet about them.

And Veronika… She did not want to live like everyone else, either; that was why she had gone swimming without a bra. And it was not Igor she was angry at, it was someone else or something else. All she was doing was taking her anger out on him. Alas, in order to do so, she had had to accuse him of something for which in fact she did not blame either him or herself. She had pressed into service whatever accusations came to hand.

'It's starting! It's starting!' Sudden shouts came from Serp Ivanych's gingerbread house.

As Igor walked in, the screen was showing a muscular athlete in a white uniform running down a Moscow street with the Olympic torch in his hand. The torch was leaving a long trail of smoke. Behind the athlete stretched two chains of sportsmen and women. Police cars, beacons flashing, moved slowly with them.

About twenty people had gathered on the veranda in front of the television. Lyova Khlopov was keeping a place for Igor. Iyeronov, making sure his guests had the best spots, was sitting in the back row. Igor squeezed through to him. He wanted to show the old man some courtesy; an attempt to make up for his own scepticism, even though his scepticism was something of which Serp Ivanych was unaware.

'Take my seat,' whispered Igor. 'It's closer to the telly.'

'I'm long-sighted, dear boy,' smiled Serp. 'Go on, go on.'

In the Olympic stadium, trumpeters blew a proud fanfare. A procession in antique attire and laurel wreaths made its way around the running lanes, the men holding bowls of smoking incense, the women garlands of roses. Triumphal Greek chariots rolled by, black and white horses strutted, young women showered flower petals. Then the white Olympic flag with its five rings was carried past, pinned to the waiting flagpole, and hoisted into the sky. The Olympic hymn was played, the flag unfurled in the wind. Birds took flight.

The bowl containing the Olympic flame towered over the stands, looking like a huge champagne flute. The athlete with the torch ran upwards towards the bowl, a wave of blue unrolling with him. The people in the stands clapped their hands, and the extras on the field waved handkerchiefs. Tall tongues of flame erupted from the bowl. Birds once again took flight and headed in various directions; the announcer said they were five thousand carrier pigeons. On the huge decorative panel below the bowl with the flame, a picture of the Olympic Bear appeared. A fanfare again rang out. In front of the telly, a reverential silence reigned.

At the Luzhniki Stadium, astronauts in spacesuits sent the Olympians a sporting hello from a giant screen and said that from their orbit they could see Moscow and even Greece. Ovations rocked the stands. The announcers recited majestic poetry. Athletic dancers in white spun around the green field of the stadium, and the spectators were amazed at the unaccustomed freedom of the men and the sensuality of the women. Next, artists in national costumes filled the field with a glitter of *sarafans* and *beshmets*, *papakhas* and skullcaps. Asian drums thundered, *zurnas* wailed. The rows of actors constantly rearranged themselves, stretching in arcs and winding and unwinding into the flowing rings of roundels. The colourful performance contained none of the formalism of jubilee concerts, and the variety of faces and costumes was breathtaking. The diversity concealed within itself the incredible might of the superpower that had marshalled people into such intricate figures.

Next, a host of Olympic bear cubs spilled onto the field, somersaulting and waving their legs in the air. Then came children: a crowd of boys and girls riding on hobby-horses. The boys began to jump and do back flips, the girls in their yellow frocks danced with dolls and spread themselves out on the green field in the shape of stars made of sunflowers. The young gymnasts, agile and nimble, reflected the essence of childhood to perfection; much more so than the pioneers with their pretentious rituals. Igor suddenly felt an aching tenderness towards the children, both the ideals on the screen and the boneheads in his brigade. And his heart was flooded with love for his country, so mighty and huge, often heavy-footed, but deep down still warm and kind.

None of the viewers on the veranda saw Serp Ivanych lean from his seat at the back towards the young leader sitting in front of him and apparently whisper something fondly in her ear. Her face twisted in an expression of fright, soon replaced by bewilderment, and finally by a soft smile, her eyes squeezed shut. It looked as if the gallant old aristocrat had bestowed a very pleasant but not quite proper compliment on the trembling mademoiselle.

CHAPTER 11

SINGING AND DANCING

Lyova did not give up on his plan. He chased his hapless footballers to practice the next day and the day after. Igor Alexandrovich read his book. Valerka did not want to sit gawping blankly at the football; boring.

'Gor-Sanych, can I just go for a walk?' he asked.

'Nope.'

'Look, you can trust me. I'm not going to smoke or break windows.'

'You'll get caught and I'll get a reprimand.'

'I won't grass you up. I'll say I just snuck out. Word of honour.'

Igor Alexandrovich held out for a while, then let Valerka go anyway. Valerka thought that Gor-Sanych was a good young leader. He understood things.

Valerka promised he would not go breezing down Pioneer Avenue or into Company Court. He drifted round the outskirts of the camp along the mesh fence. He started his route at Building 6, walked along the bank of the Volga, turned into the forest, and ended up in front of the sick bay. From there he set off back. Birds twittered, and the smell of resin hung on the air. In several places, Valerka discovered deep tunnels beneath the fence. Who had made them? Dogs? Pioneers? Escaped Convicts? Ah, to have a hideout on the camp grounds like the cons did in the woods, only invisible, so that he could slip into it and disappear. He could sit there and observe, but not be present…

Around the corner of the sick bay were potato beds belonging to the elderly nurse, Miss Pasha. Miss Pasha did not waste a minute of the working day, and was growing crops. Valerka thought the Escaped Convicts were probably stealing her shaggy potato plants a few at a time: they had to eat something. Miss Pasha must know all about the cons. Valerka hid behind a bush, hoping to catch a glimpse of Miss Pasha making some kind of sign from the sick bay window for whoever was sheltering in the woods. Which was where he was spotted by Whistler.

'The biter bit!' The Senior Pioneer Leader hoicked him out from the bush. 'What are you doing skulking about here?' she asked suspiciously. 'Are you ill?'

'Yes, I … by mistake…' floundered Valerka. Where had Whistler appeared from? Why had she felt the urge to come lumbering over to the sick bay? She was as healthy as a horse! 'I was… I wanted to go to Company House. Sign up to a circle.'

'OK, come with me,' said Whistler. 'I'm on my way there.'

Valerka submissively tagged along behind the Senior Pioneer Leader.

'What do you like?' she asked in a businesslike manner. 'Drawing? Singing? Draughts? Table tennis? Or do you want to do a wall newspaper?'

'I'll sing,' decided Valerka, as if pronouncing sentence on himself.

He really did like singing. In his view, he sang very beautifully, but the school choir would not take him because the choir mistress was a stupid cow.

'Right. Music Circle,' decreed Whistler. 'Everyone has to take part in something. Anyone who doesn't, we'll punish them.'

The music club was held in the hall where films were shown in the evenings. The members danced as well as sang, so they needed space. A dozen or so girls were scattered along the benches, along with two quiet, unremarkable boys.

Under the benches were the girls' colourful plastic bags.

'A new singer for you,' announced Whistler. 'What is your name?'

'Valera.'

'Where is Veronika Genrikhovna?'

'She's gone to the … you know … the radio room. For … you know … a recording of something.'

'All right, trill away,' said Whistler, and left the hall.

Anastasiika Sergushina was among the girls. Seeing Valerka, she wrinkled her nose sceptically. 'You can't sing, Lagunov. You don't have a voice.'

'You can't sing yourself!' burst out Valerka, angry. 'You're the one with no voice!'

'I have an alto,' replied Anastasiika haughtily.

Two other girls came giggling into the room, as relaxed as they would be entering their own flat. Valerka knew them: the sporty Zhanka Shalayeva from the second brigade, and her friend Olya, an acerbic and dangerous beanpole of a girl who enjoyed the nickname Lyolik. Both of them had been in the room earlier, but were out when Whistler brought Valerka in.

'Wo!' said Zhanka loudly, leaving her mouth open on the 'o'.

Valerka realized that Zhanka was showing the girls her glossed lips.

The girls looked on admiringly. Anastasiika alone broke ranks and sniggered.

'There's a bit smeared underneath,' said one of the girls.

'Dab it off,' Zhanka ordered her.

The girl licked her finger and wiped the lipstick from the corner of Zhanka's mouth.

'The mirror in the crapper sucks,' explained Zhanka. 'Can't see squat.'

Valerka realised that Zhanka had slipped off to the bathroom to make herself up.

'Give me a go too?' fawned the girl who had fixed Zhanka's errant lipstick.

'After Lyolik.'

'And me,' said another girl.

'When it's cold in hell,' said Zhanka.

She was used to being the centre of attention. A star on the street, smiling, sociable, and cheeky, Zhanka was liked by bad boys, and because of that she lived as free as the wind and basked in impunity.

'Sharing lipstick is unhygienic,' said Anastasiika.

'Nobody's giving you any, Sergushina.'

'I've got my own.'

'Swiped it from Mummy?' sneered Zhanka, grinning.

'I never take other people's things, Shalayeva,' replied Anastasiika with dignity. 'Everything I have is my own.'

'What, that chain's yours?' Zhanka pointed disbelievingly to the thin gold chain around Anastasiika's neck.

'There's a cross on it!' Lyolik let out a bray of laughter, as if a cross signified something shameful.

'My gran gave it to me,' said Anastasiika, reverently placing a palm on her chest. 'She had me baptised when I was a child. It's not forbidden to be baptised.'

Zhanka was not bothered about whether or not baptism was forbidden. She was offended that this lucky cow had such an expensive and curious thing.

'I'll tell Beklya. He'll take it off you,' promised Zhanka.

Beklya was a notorious bully. How he had got into camp was a mystery.

'He won't,' countered Anastasiika confidently.

'He will, he will, I know he will.'

'No, you don't.'

'I know everything!' Zhanka flopped down on the bench. 'You want me to tell you what you're going to say on your wedding night?'

'No,' replied Anastasiika.

'I do!' said the girl who had not been allowed the lipstick.

'Close your eyes and give me your hand,' said Zhanka. 'Prepare for some black magic.'

The girl closed her eyes and held out her open palm to Zhanka. Zhanka blew on it and began to make a series of passes over the palm, as if throwing pinches of invisible salt.

Come grandma, come grandpa, come from the air, do your black magic, you great big grey bear.

Zhanka slyly looked round, inviting them all to laugh: *What a cretin.* She tickled the girl's palm with her fingernail. Lyolik grinned spitefully.

'Knock it off!' pleaded the girl undergoing the trial, squirming from the tickling.

'Yep. That's what you'll say,' announced Zhanka triumphantly. The other girls giggled obsequiously.

Pleased with herself, Zhanka finally noticed Valerka.

'Well, what have we here? Newbie. What school are you from?'

Somehow everyone always knew people like Zhanka, and no one ever – alas – knew people like Valerka. And as far as Zhanka was concerned, he was not even to be credited with his own name. The number of his school was enough.

'Not yours,' barked Valerka.

'Getting cute are we, Four Eyes?' Olya-Lyolik readily tensed up.

'We don't have wimps like him at my school,' affirmed Zhanka.

The door to the hall creaked again. It was Veronika Genrikhovna returning. She was carrying a large square envelope of an official green colour. In the envelope, no doubt, was a gramophone record. The girls immediately switched their attention.

'Vnika Grekhovna, Vnika Grekhovna!' they babbled all at once. 'We've got a new boy!'

'Good.' Veronika briskly looked Valerka over. 'If he likes it, we'll sign him up to our collective.'

Valerka had seen Veronika Genrikhovna a few times. She was a young leader in the third brigade. For some reason, Valerka did not much like her. There was something of Zhanka Shalayeva about her, that was it.

'What songs do we have the music for?' asked Anastasiika.

Veronika Genrikhovna turned the envelope over and read aloud. 'Pioneer songs. "The Land We Call Home", "Bonfire", "The Cruiser Aurora", "The Eaglets Are Learning to Fly", "Let There Always Be Sunshine", "Where the Motherland Begins". Children's songs: "Potato", "The Blue Wagon", "Chunga-Changa", "When my Friends Are with Me", "The Musicians of Bremen", "Lullaby". You choose which song we're going to rehearse.'

Of one accord, the girls dived into the bags under the benches and pulled out their songbooks. The songbooks were made from standard exercise books and were works of art. The words were written in coloured pens, the titles in felt-tip pens, and photos and pictures pertinent to the theme were neatly stuck on every page. A song about love was illustrated with flowers, a song about the sea with ships, a song about friendship by a pair of youngsters holding hands. After each song was inscribed 'The End!'

'We have to do "Eaglets"!' said Anastasiika in a tone that brooked no appeal.

'Why?' asked Veronika Genrikhovna in surprise.

'I have an alto voice, and I'll be the soloist. Everyone else will be the chorus.'

Anastasiika allowed no doubt that all must serve to glorify her.

'You'll be the so-lo-lo-what?' Zhanka was bemused.

'The so-lo-ist,' repeated Anastasiika repeated. 'Meaning I'll be singing on my own.'

Anastasiika stood up, cleared her throat, and sang out in a clear voice:

'*They say life's a war and rightly so, and there'll be no retreat, oh no no no! The Eaglets are learning to fly!*'

It was such a whole-hearted sound that a shiver ran right through Valerka. Slender and slight, Anastasiika suddenly glittered with something silver, high, and penetrating.

'Well, you got some sass from somewhere, Sergushina!' Zhanka was furious.

Zhanka, naturally enough, would not be able to sing like that even if she exploded.

'I've been singing at music school and in the city choir for five years,' Anastasiika informed the room. 'I need to use my skills.'

'Stuff that!' Zhanka kicked furiously at the leg of a nearby bench. 'We should sing "Chunga-Changa"! We sang it last New Year, didn't we, Lyolik? Come here, let's show them!'

Zhanka and Lyolik stood in front of the girls and looked at each other.

'Three, four!' commanded Zhanka. '*Happy days in Copa Cabana, coconut and ripe banana, coconut and ripe banana, Chunga-Cha-anga!*'

Zhanka and Lyolik sang and danced, both in tune and uncommonly sweet: with open palms against their heads like ears they imitated monkeys, merrily twisting and squatting. Valerka could not believe that here in front of him were streetwise scoundrels who knew how to black an eye or call a name such that their opponents lost the power of speech. At the same time, there was something in Zhanka and Lyolik's movements – too childish for girls who had almost turned into young women – that was strangely improper. It was not something Zhanka and Lyolik had picked up at school, of course.

'We can make these round hats,' said Zhanka, looking at Veronika Genrikhovna. 'And paint our cheeks and make ourselves tails. We'll totally be monkeys.'

Zhanka was not bothered what the other girls thought, let alone the insignificant boys. Not that the girls objected. Not that Valerka objected either, though he liked the song about the cruiser better – it was about war, not monkeys. But Zhanka and Anastasiika had gone straight ahead and decided for everyone.

Veronika Genrikhovna very clearly caught the light, sexy undertones of the dance. Valerka guessed it by the sudden hardening of the leader's face. But she reacted differently from the way a teacher might react.

'We have enough pioneer songs,' Veronika told the girls coldly. 'So we'll be rehearsing "Chunga-Changa".'

'Any comment, Sergushina?' asked Zhanka triumphantly.

Anastasiika haughtily turned her back.

Valerka felt something else, too: that Grekhovna was in some way related to Gor-Sanych. Both broke the rules and gave in to the wishes of their charges. Gor-Sanych, though, gave way to Lyova because Lyova was bored by the rules, while Grekhovna gave way to Zhanka because Zhanka was cramped by them. Still, Valerka firmly decided that he was not going to attach himself to Grekhovna's circle. He had no wish to sing and dance with a bunch of monkeys. And he liked Anastasiika better than Zhanka.

CHAPTER 12

THE DEAD BODY IN THE PIANO

'Igor, do you know where Khlopov is?' asked Irina.

'Where?' repeated Igor stupidly.

They were standing on the empty veranda. Through her glasses, Irina drilled Igor with an angry look. 'Candle' was over, and the pioneers had gone to their dorms.

'The girls told me he didn't feel well this morning. And no one's seen him since afternoon snack. Was he at dinner?'

Igor did not know. He was already used both to his work as a young leader and to his brigade. He did not count heads, and did not check the boys off against the list.

'There was no food left over in the canteen,' remarked Igor cautiously.

'Gelbich ate it. And Khlopov has disappeared somewhere. This is an emergency!'

'I'll go and look for him,' said Igor at once.

'High time! I'll wait here until we know what's happened.'

Igor went out. The sun had already set, but the sunset beyond the Volga had not had time to fade, and it was still light. The street lamps on Pioneer Avenue were not yet lit. In the rich blue of the sky, the shaggy crowns of the pine trees shone with infrared warmth.

Strange. Where had Lyova gone? He was a good boy; boys like him did not run away from home, did not fall in with bad company, and did not have a criminal record. Perhaps he had fallen seriously ill and had to go to the sick bay. In which case Doctor Nosatov would have reported it. Or was Lyova over at

Serp Ivanych's with the young leaders, watching 'Olympic Diary' on TV? Igor glanced across at Iyeronov's dacha, looming in the distance beyond the bushes. Reflections from the television screen were flickering in the ground floor windows. No, the other young leaders would have chased Lyova away.

Igor stomped along the avenue, trying to make up his mind where to go, and noticed movement in the acacia tree behind the big stand with the slogan 'Create! Invent! Try!'

'Khlopov!' called Igor at once, without really thinking.

Lyova came reluctantly out from behind the stand and started to brush himself down.

'Where have you been?' asked Igor sternly.

'There…' replied Lyova evasively. 'They were showing the Olympics…'

He was clearly lying, and was hiding his eyes. A real teacher would doubtless have grabbed hold of Lyova and shaken the truth out of him, but Igor felt sorry for the lad. Who knows what boyish need had made him disappear? Perhaps he was building himself a headquarters, the way children did – a hideout somewhere in the woods beyond the fence. Or perhaps he had been dared to try and get to the ruined chapel beside the Bishop. Inhabitants of Storm Petrel considered these ruins to be very sinister and dangerous, and the boys tested their bravery there. Or perhaps it was just that someone had upset Lyova and he had run away to cry, so that no one would witness his weakness.

'Everyone's been searching high and low for you,' said Igor disapprovingly. 'Let's go back in.'

On the stoop, Irina pitched into Lyova. 'Do you want to be kicked out of camp, Khlopov?' she hissed. 'You're taking liberties here. Where have you been?'

'All right, Irina Mikhailovna, don't beat him up,' said Igor, trying to quiet his fellow young leader. 'He overstayed at Serp Ivanych's.'

'You can't go soft on the children, Igor Alexandrovich!' said Irina, cutting him off. 'And I'm going over to your Iyeronov to let him know what time he needs to turn the telly off.'

Igor winced slightly. 'I'll do it,' he said.

He gave Lyova a nudge forward and was mildly surprised to feel how cold and stiff Lyova's shoulder was. And the boy's back was littered with pine needles and duff, as if he had been rolling around on the ground in the woods.

Igor was relieved to get Lyova settled back in the dorm.

The boys, it hardly needs saying, were not yet asleep. Valerka had built himself a kind of little house to protect himself from the mosquitoes: he had filched a handful of drawing pins from one of the young leaders and tacked the edge of his sheet to the wall, stretching it out over both bedposts to make a roof. The sheet was tied to the bedposts with strips of bandage. Half the sheet acted as a canopy covering the side of the little house. Inside the little house it was as cosy as on the top shelf in a railway carriage. The boys were green with envy, and began to fashion little dens for themselves, though none was as deftly done as Valerka's.

'Four Eyes has smashed it. Look at that comfy bunk he's made himself,' said Tityapkin.

Valerka threw back the canopy.

'You want my fist in your ugly mug, just keep calling me "Four Eyes", Titka,' he warned Tityapkin.

'Don't you name call either!' responded Tityapkin, offended.

Lyova made his way to his bunk, quiet and withdrawn.

'Where did you vanish off to? Gurka asked him. 'You wanted to break out of camp? Why didn't you take me?'

Lyova cleared his throat strangely, as if he had lost the habit of speaking.

'I was watching the Olympics,' he said hoarsely.

Not many of them in the dorm were interested in the Olympics, but everyone was interested in horror stories.

It was horror story time.

'Gorokh, count!' ordered Slavik Mukhin.

'*Fly-ing from the se-cond floor,*' began Kolka, '*one sharp knife and then one more. Red, sea blue, sky blue too, who to pick it's up to you! Domrya, take your pick!*'

'Red,' chose Seryozha Domrachev.

Gorokhov went through the counting rhyme again, starting with Seryozha, and it fell to Gurka to tell the story. The boys became very still. Gurka settled cross-legged on his bunk.

'So basically an old woman bought a black shawl and put it in the kitchen. The mother came home from work, went into the kitchen, and the shawl, like, flew up to her and shouted, "Give me blood!" and strangled her. Then the father came home from work, went into the kitchen, and the shawl flew up to him and shouted, "Give me blood!" and strangled him. Then the older brother came in and saw them, like, all sprawled about the kitchen and ran to them, but the black shawl yelled, "Give me blood!" and strangled him, too. Then the youngest brother came in and saw them all dead and the shawl flying about the kitchen. The brother took fright and ran into the main room to the old woman and said, 'What do we do?' The old woman, like, said, "Cut off your hand and burn it!" The younger brother cut off his hand, burned it, and the shawl caught fire and burned to ashes!'

The boys lay there, bit by bit settling in to the horror.

'Gorokh, count!'

Kolka counted again, and it fell to Yurik Tonkikh.

'There was a family with a dad, a mum, and a daughter,' he began. 'The mum and dad wanted their daughter to play the piano. They went to the shop, but they only had black pianos. The saleswoman said, "Don't buy one," but they bought one anyway. The next day the daughter started playing. She went on playing and playing and her mum said, "Stop playing that black piano!" but she couldn't stop. Then she did stop, and her mum was lying dead on the floor. The ambulance came and they said, "She's got no blood in her!" The next day the daughter sat down to play again. She went on playing and playing and her dad said, "Stop playing that black piano!" but once again she couldn't stop. Then she did stop, and her dad was lying dead on the floor. The ambulance came and they said, "He's got no blood in him either!" The daughter ran to the shop and said to the saleswoman, "Take the piano away!" But the saleswoman said, "Buy an axe!" The daughter bought an axe, went back home, and started chopping up the piano, and a stream of blood poured out of it! The daughter chopped the piano right up to kindling, and there was a dead man lying in there! He was the one who'd drunk all the blood!'

Yurik fell silent, brooding. The boys were silent too. In the quiet, the mosquitoes buzzed their nasal whine.

Valerka was scared out of his mind. Stop playing that black piano!

'Guys, we don't need to do any more,' he said.

'Scared, huh?' asked Gurka spitefully.

'And you're not?'

'Fine, we'll do more stories tomorrow,' said Gorokhov, deciding for everyone. 'I know the one about the Meatgrinder Bus. Lights out, guys.'

Valerka dropped the canopy of his little house, stretched out, and squeezed his eyes shut so as to fall asleep quickly and stop being afraid. To calm himself, he thought about the reasons why people were terrified. Terror came from the primeval monkey. The monkey had been afraid of everything, so he had taken himself a stick, sharpened a stone, and lit a fire: in short, he had become human so as not to be afraid. The human world contained no fear. This world may be boring or stupid at times, but it was not scary. Of course, even in this world, scary things happened: people were run over by cars, fell ill with incurable diseases, or were sent to prison. But that was from bad behaviour. Idiots ran red lights, drank, smoked, stole. In short, they bought the black piano. Live right and you would not be afraid.

He, Valerka, lived right – but there was fear, and plenty of it. Whose fault was that? The monkey's? The people who lived wrong? No, not them; the dead man had climbed into the piano by himself. No one could explain where fear came from.

The boys all appeared to be asleep, but Valerka suddenly heard the soft rattle of a mesh bed frame, the rustling of sheets, and the light slap of bare feet on the floorboards. Perhaps someone was trudging off to the toilet...? But no creak of the door followed. Instead, there came a strange slobbering sound, at which Valerka's hands crawled with cold. In this midnight slobbering Valerka sensed both insane pleasure and something unbearably creepy.

Valerka eased his canopy back an inch and peeked through the crack. Half the dormitory was swallowed up in shadow. Through the large window he could see the pine trees, illuminated by a blue street lamp, now somehow mysterious in their very essence, like the pillars of a wooden bridge when you look at them as you sail down a river. Strips of white light lay on the far wall. Slavik Mukhin was sleeping on his back, his left arm thrust out of the covers as if he were in hospital on a drip. Lyova was kneeling in front of Slavik's bunk. Kneeling, bent over, his lips touched to the crook of Slavik's elbow. Lyova shifted slightly, straightened, and Valerka's heart almost stopped. Lyova's wet lips shone black. Or rather, not black, of course, but red. Lyova was drinking blood.

Valerka could not tear himself away from the spectacle. Lyova stayed blissfully still, as if tuning in to his own sensations, then leaned over once more and pressed his mouth to Slavik's arm. Valerka heard the slobbering again.

'I'm asleep!' said Valerka to himself. 'I've been listening to scary stories and now I'm having nightmares.' Lyova straightened up again, as if to catch his breath. His face was all but indistinguishable in the shadows, but inside the dark sockets of his eyes shivered an almost imperceptible crimson glimmer. Valerka hastily tweaked his canopy back into place.

He lay there huddled up, trying to convince himself that Lyova had not noticed him, and that he was in fact imagining the whole thing. The room was quiet. No one was sniffing or muttering; they were as quiet as they might be at a formal assembly complete with carrying the flag. Then the light slap of bare feet sounded next to Valerka's bed, and etched on his canopy, now glowing blue in the light of the street lamp, Valerka saw Lyova's silhouette. Lyova squatted beside the bed. A whisper blew softly through the canopy.

'Lagunov, let me into your little house.'

Valerka was separated from Lyova by no more than the thin fabric of an over-washed institution sheet. Thin fabric, and the significance of the words 'little house'. His home.

'Lagunov, invite me in,' said Lyova. 'I'm your friend.'

Valerka stayed silent. On the blue fabric, black hands appeared. Lyova was touching the sheet, barely making contact, stroking the canopy as if hoping through his caress to be given permission to enter another's home. 'It'll be better for you,

Lagunov,' he whispered. 'It's what everyone wants, only they don't know it.'

Still Valerka stayed silent. Somewhere in the distance out on the Volga, a motor ship sounded its klaxon.

Lyova squatted beside Valerka a while longer, then got up. The slapping of his bare feet moved away towards the window, where Lyova had his bed. The frame rattled.

Valerka lay staring into his canopy with bulging eyes. No, it was a dream. It was a dream.

In the morning the bugler would play and the delusion would dissipate, leaving no trace.

PART TWO

LAUGHTER OF THE VAMPIRE

But in the fever of our blood we climbed,
But opened eyes that were as good as blind.
Eduard Bagritzky, 'We Were Driven by Youth', 1932

CHAPTER 1

THE MORNING AFTER THE NIGHTMARE

Morning came so untroubled that it was impossible to believe in the nightmare. Valerka did not immediately remember it. Yawning, he sat on his bunk and looked out of the window. A blue dawn mist threaded the air, and through it the scattered rays of the rising sun slanted among the verticals of the pine trunks. The dormitory was bustling with lads in shorts and T-shirts. They clattered things on the bedside cabinets, swore, made their beds, hauled up their trousers. From the corridor came Irina Mikhailovna's tedious invocation.

'Wash your faces, brush your teeth. Wash your faces, brush your teeth.'

Slowly, the nightmare pieced itself back together in Valerka's memory, and even though he did not want it to, it unfolded itself in every detail. Shivers ran down Valerka's spine. Had he really seen Lyova drinking blood in the night? No, it was a dream, it was not real...

Slavik Mukhin, as always fed up about something, was fiercely worrying away at his arm, the very place where in Valerka's nightmare Lyova had sunk his teeth and drunk. Slavik's arm was red with mosquito bites. Lyova was sitting on his bunk, too. He was dishevelled and morose. For some reason, he had put on his pioneer neckerchief, though in camp, unlike at school, a neckerchief was only required on ceremonial occasions.

'Bollocks to this,' said Gurka in surprise. 'What's with the goody-goody pioneer shit?'

Lyova sighed heavily.

'Boys,' he said. 'You're bad at football because you don't do what I say. Ruslan Maximych watched us yesterday and told Igor Sanych the captain needs changing. Gelbich should get the job, he said. He's the brigade standard bearer.'

The boys howled in unison, indignant not so much at Lyova's dethronement as at the besmirching of their dorm's dignity.

'We'll ram Gelbasty's flag up his backside,' promised Gurka.

This assurance brought Lyova no joy. He sat there, hands hanging tiredly down; his pose was a picture of resignation. Venka Gelbich was a high-ranking young man, and Lyova Khlopov, who was he? A simple labourer on the football field.

'I won't give up,' promised Lyova severely. 'Gelbich doesn't want to be the standard bearer. He doesn't appreciate the honour. But I'm going to be like a real pioneer. Perhaps that'll make Igor Sanych change his mind about Gelbich. Listen, guys, who's got a pioneer badge? I left mine at home. Give it here so I can wear it, please.'

'Tityapa's got one,' said Gurka immediately.

'I do not!' said Tityapkin, at once in a tizzy.

'You do. You wanted to swap it for Beklya's razor!'

To be honest, a pioneer badge, even at camp, had no special value. Needles, sewing elastic, matches, shells, pen stems, coils of coloured wire, magnets from electric motors – these were riches, not to mention such treasures as a knife, a magnifying glass, or an Olympic rouble. Exchanging a badge for a razor blade was a good deal, and it was easy to understand Tityapa.

'He said please!' Kolka Gorokhov yelled at Tityapkin. 'The magic word! You have to comply.'

'I'm your friend.' Lyova looked into Tityapkin's shifty eyes.

'What's with the friend thing all of a sudden?' Tityapkin, nearing capitulation, was upset.

'I've got a badge,' said Yurik Tonkikh quietly to Lyova. 'I'll give it you.'

Yurik reached into his bedside cabinet.

In the schedule for the day this time came equipped with a verse: *Make your bed and wash your face, it's exercise time, so find your place!* The communal washroom was outside: two rows of metal sinks and two pipes with taps – one for the boys and one for the girls. There was only cold water. Under Igor Sanych's stern gaze, the boys brushed their teeth, rubbed their faces, and drilled their fingers in their ears.

'Guys, here's one,' offered Lyokha Tsybastov, spitting out toothpaste. 'A hairy head whizzes smartly behind a cheek. What is it?'

'Shove off,' came the angry answer. 'Everyone knows that.'

Washing cheered them all up, of course, but exercise cheered them up even more. The camp loudspeakers were playing energetic gymnastic music, and the announcer was saying in a mellifluous voice, 'Hands on your waist, feet shoulder width apart. And-a-one, and-a-two! And-a-one, and-a-two.' Irina Mikhailovna did not appear for exercise. Everyone knew that she was embarrassed at the way her bulky tits bounced about during the exercises. The exercises were led by Igor Sanych. He had a feather from a pillow stuck in his fashionable but now slightly wild hair. The pioneers did their exercises under the pine trees by their building. Whistler came bustling along the avenue, a folded flag sticking out from under her arm, to be hoisted, as required, at morning assembly.

'Why so sleepy?' cried Whistler ardently.

The brigade lined up in pairs – girls in front, boys behind – and Irina Mikhailovna led the procession to assembly.

'Brigade chant, be-e-e-gin!' she commanded.

'*Marching on towards the goal!*' everyone bawled, in time to their steps; it was already a habit. '*Happy heroes one and all! 'Cos our brigade's the very best, victorious over all the rest!*'

Gurka and Tityapkin, meanwhile, bawled their own version in synch with the official song:

'*Piles of poop went out for a walk, saw a foot inside a sock, dashed to the bog at quite a caper, found a bum but out of paper!*'

The boys grinned. It was amusing that Gurka and Tityapa were howling their subversive words at the tops of their voices, but the blockheaded young leaders did not hear a thing.

At assembly, Valerka watched the red flag rise into the sky, and for some reason he once again remembered his nightmare about Lyova sucking blood. Probably because the red flag was the colour of blood. But this blood, the blood of fighters, had been shed for the happiness of people. Nothing bad could happen under a flag like that.

After morning assembly, the brigade went to breakfast.

'Guys, let's get Gelbich,' suggested the irrepressible Gurka, marching in the ranks. 'Bollocks to them making him football captain.'

Lyova had taken on the dejected look of a man punished undeservedly.

'Let's do it!' agreed Gorokhov joyfully, and immediately called out, 'Hey! Gelbich!'

'What?' Venka turned round.

'Nothing!' announced Kolka cheerfully. 'Hearing test!'

'Gelbich, how tall are you?' asked Tityapkin.

'One sixty,' answered Gelbich proudly.

'Good stick for stirring shit!'

'Suck a banana!' answered Gelbich angrily.

The lads snorted, even Valerka and Yurik Tonkikh. The only boys not to laugh were Slavik Mukhin, who had been in a dark mood since reveille, and Lyova.

'You don't need to do this, boys,' said Lyova, straightening his neckerchief. 'It's not good.'

'Venka, say "pot".' Gurka refused to quieten down.

'What for?' asked Gelbich, suspecting a trick.

'Ah come on, say it, you wuss.'

'OK, "pot".'

'Drink a can of snot!' said Gurka, and burst into gales of laughter.

'Yeah, yeah, sucker me in and slap me with slippers,' flared Gelbich.

'Gelbich, Gelbich!' called Kolka Gorokhov.

Venka, tight-lipped, took no notice.

'Ah, come on, Gelbich, say something. I won't take the whatever.'

'What?' said Venka reluctantly.

'Nothing!' crowed Kolka. ''Nother hearing test!'

'Chattering in the ranks!' Hearing the questionable laughter, Irina Mikhailovna put a stop to the fun. 'Brigade chant, be-e-e-gin! One, two...'

'*One-two, we want our food!*' The brigade enthusiastically took up the chant. '*Three-four, we're nearly dead! Open up, we're in the mood! Or we'll eat the cook instead!*'

Irina Mikhailovna stopped the detachment near the food block and issued an order.

'Sergushina, check the boys' hands are clean.'

At the entrance to the canteen they were greeted by a flurry of dogs, who had scampered into camp from the village of Pervomaiskaya. All the boys and girls knew the dogs by sight and by name: Chernysh, Dolka, Mukhtar, Bambook, Vaflya, Zhusya, and Fidel. In camp, the dogs dropped their feral village manners and became enthusiastic pioneers.

The canteen smelled of bread, chlorine, and something cooked. The sun shone brightly through the barred windows, and the glasses glittered. Clean and well-mannered pioneers smiled at the visitors from the posters. The brigades entered the main hall one by one and took their seats at the long rows of tables set together, the boys on one side and the girls on the other. Chairs clattered, aluminium spoons clinked against plates, and from the kitchen came the clanking of cisterns and the sound of water.

For breakfast there was semolina and kissel. The boys immediately snatched the bread from the trays: they could eat it during the day, or feed it to the dogs.

'Same old rubbish,' grumbled Gelbich, looking at his plate. 'Should drown kittens in it, put them out of their misery.'

'I don't like semolina either,' admitted Yurik Tonkikh guiltily.

'Well I do!' declared Tityapkin, and pulled Yurik's plate towards himself.

'You can still eat the semolina here,' said Seryozha Domrachev, pulling a face. 'But the soup's dangerous. Got dog meat in it. Old Granny Nyurka puts it in.'

'She nick the proper stuff?'

'She takes the proper stuff to the Escaped Convicts in the woods at night. Oldies told me last shift.'

'They always steal in canteens,' said Kolka Gorokhov authoritatively.

'You know why Granny Nyurka's so crooked?' Seryozha looked round at everyone, eyes dark with unease.

It was true that Old Nyura was a strange one. She dragged one leg, her left arm stuck out a little to one side, and the left side of her face was twisted by paralysis and did not move. She had a slight stammer, too. But for all that, she was a sturdy peasant woman and by no means a feeble old thing.

'Oldies said that one day she went out to the cons, and the cons were cooking their own meat. Invited her to eat with them. She tucked in. Then found out they were cannibals. Twisted her all up just like that.'

The boys shivered.

'That'd twist me up too.' Gurka scratched fiercely.

'She can't live without cannibalism now,' added Seryozha morosely. 'If she hears that someone's gone missing, she takes a dog, scoots out to the cons and swaps the dog meat for human.'

'She should be sent to prison!' Yurik was indignant.

'What for?' sighed Seryozha hopelessly. 'She doesn't kill people herself. She looks us all over, and anyone with a bit of fat on, she tells the cons. They do the killing.'

The boys turned towards the kitchen window. Nyura was standing behind a big table taking in the dirty dishes. She raked the leftovers deftly into a waste bin, stacked the plates, and threw the spoons into a tin trough.

'Let's take revenge on her!' suggested Gurka hotly.

'That's a yes!' agreed Tityapkin and Gorokhov.

'That's a no,' protested Lyova in a low voice.

Slavik Mukhin shivered timidly as he scratched the bite mark on his arm, while the boys paid no attention to Lyova's order.

Tityapych wolfed down his second helping, and the boys all stood up in concert, to take their plates to Old Nyura. The pioneers on the posters hanging on the walls between the windows seemed to frown. The girl with the sponge and dish looked reprovingly, while the boy peeling potatoes clutched his knife threateningly.

'Throw your spoons into the bin with the leftovers,' whispered Gurka conspiratorially. 'Then she'll have to stick her hands in there.'

He went up to Old Nyura's table ahead of the others, put down his plate and glass, and, as if by mistake, threw his spoon into the enamelled bin swilling with its mush of brown semolina and kissel. Bread crusts were floating in the slurry. Old Nyura cast a ferocious look at Gurka. Coming up next, Seryozha Domrachev threw his spoon into the bin. Unable to resist the urge, he looked at Old Nyura.

'W … w…' clucked Nyura indignantly, stammering.

'Don't do that!' Lyova told the boys firmly.

Valerka had no plans to play any dirty tricks. And Yurik most likely would not dare. Slavik Mukhin silently set his plate among the dirty dishes on the table and went away. But Kolka Gorokhov still threw his spoon into the waste bin.

'Wh-whaa?' screeched Old Nyura.

Tityapkin was holding his plate and glass in one hand and spoon in the other. Old Nyura shot him a searing look and at once understood everything. Tityapkin shoved his plate into the pile of dishes, but Old Nyura, without waiting for the crime, suddenly whipped a wet, dirty, heavy towel out of nowhere.

'Run, Tityara!' wailed Gurka despairingly from afar.

Clutching his aluminium spoon in his fist, Tityapkin froze in terror. Old Nyura took a full swing across the table and fetched him a delicious slap round the head. Dirty water splattered in all directions, as if Tityapkin's bonce had exploded. Tityapkin let out a gasp and staggered, dazed. Then he clattered at full tilt away from Old Nyura's table.

CHAPTER 2

'ALBERT THE WEASEL ONE IN THE EASEL'

Valerka wanted to have a comrade with him for moral support, but there was no point asking Tityapkin or Gorokhov – they were both brainless.

'Yurik, come with me to a circle, eh?' suggested Valerka.

Yurik jumped at the chance. 'Which one?' He, too, was bored at Lyova Khlopov's football. He was not appreciated there.

'I don't know. There's lots of different stuff. Let's choose one.'

After work detail, Valerka and Yurik asked the young leaders if they could be excused, and set off for Company House. Valerka tried to remember the list of circles.

'There's singing, drawing, chess, stuffed animals... There's one where you write letters to foreigners. Something else, probably, only I've forgotten.'

'I went to a model aeroplane club at home,' admitted Yurik.

Valerka looked at him approvingly. Good news that it was not dress-making.

At the door of Company House, Valerka and Yurik met Anastasiika.

'What brings you here?' asked Anastasiika snootily. 'Have you been kicked out of football for being too stupid?'

'You calling us stupid? Push off and sing your so-lo,' retorted Valerka.

Standing at the blackboard with the schedule were Natalya Borisovna, the Senior Pioneer Leader, and Alexander Nikolaich, the young leader who shared a room with Igor Sanych.

'Success to report?' Natalya Borisovna was asking in a low voice.

'We are making progress,' replied Alexander with dignity.

'Well, I don't expect anything else from you. You are at the forefront of our pedagogical labour.'

Valerka and Yurik hovered at the schedule, and decided to make for the creative arts. Perhaps something worthwhile would come of it.

'I'm better at drawing than painting,' warned Yurik.

'You draw and I'll paint,' said Valerka. 'We won't flop.'

His artistic capabilities were in the same league as his vocal prowess, namely, in his opinion he was pretty good.

There were seventeen or eighteen children doing art, about equal numbers of boys and girls. Valerka immediately sized up the boys: at school they would be considered wimps, mummy's boys and granny's favourites, all top performers or delicate little flowers like Yurik. At pioneer camp they felt like pet rabbits among street dogs. The circle was led by a dinky young leader called Ninochka Sergeyevna.

'Oh, boys,' she said to Valerka and Yurik, 'you're a tad late. The whole circle is painting pictures for peace. On Parents' Day there's going to be a big exhibition on the Avenue. Will you be joining us, then?'

Valerka looked around the big room cluttered with easels. 'So, what do we paint for peace?' he asked.

Truth be told, he liked painting knights in battle.

'We've decided that everyone should paint something they like. But feel free to look in a magazine for a cartoon about warmongers.'

Ninochka placed a pile of colourful and tattered *Crocodile* magazines on the table in front of Valerka and Yurik. Valerka leafed curiously through the top magazine. The caricatures there were amusing: skinny bellowing generals in caps with extremely high crowns; impudent soldiers in helmets and dark glasses; fat bankers in tail coats, with bowler hats on their heads and cigars between their teeth; predatory policemen with truncheons. All of them capered stupidly around huge bombs with tails.

The *Crocodile* artists made fun of their characters, but Valerka wanted something serious, something inspiring admiration.

'I can draw a nuclear explosion. I know how to do that,' said Yurik timidly.

'I'll make something up myself as well,' promised Valerka confidently.

'Wonderful!' smiled Ninochka. 'Self-reliance is very important for artistic thinking. Choose your own places, boys. I'll fetch drawing paper. Pencils and brushes are over there in the jar, paints are in the cupboard. Albert Stakhovsky from the first brigade is our creative director. Alik studies at the Pioneer House art studio.'

Albert was a tall, slender, and spiritual young man, his lush hair split by a neat parting. Intelligent faces like Alik's were usually referred to by the boys as 'faces begging for bricks'.

Yurik fell quiet in front of a blank sheet of paper, absorbed in his own ideas. Valerka furtively looked around to see what the other children were painting. They were drawing absolutely whatever they wanted, with no connection with any struggle for peace: children planting a tree; a striped cat on a fence; a village hut on a river bank; a giraffe in a zoo; a pine forest; a girl with balloons; a butterfly on a flower; an aquarium with fish; a bunch of ugly people on skis. Bollocks.

Valerka already knew what he would draw. He would draw a powerful bulldozer, on caterpillar tracks. The bulldozer would be pushing a pile of all kinds of weapons in front of it, like big toys: a tank, a plane, a battleship, a rocket. Pushing them into a hole in the ground at a landfill site. The driver's head would be sticking out of the bulldozer's window, in the shape of a globe. Meaning something like the Earth does not need war. Great! Valerka had no desire to draw cats and fish; he wanted beautiful, fierce machines that embodied the courage of battle, strength, vigour. War, of course, was very bad. It was pain and blood, fear and death. No one seriously, truly wanted war. But so many people worked in factories making planes and machine guns; so many people drove armoured vehicles and launched rockets. Valerka's own dad designed something secret, too, and his dad was a very kind man. And they showed parades on the telly.

Better, then, if all weapons could be for show, like in films, for example, or just for drills.

Valerka became absorbed in his work and stopped noticing what was going on around him. Pencils rustled on paper, brushes tinkled in glasses of water. Ninochka Sergeyevna was sitting at the table, leafing through old issues of *Crocodile*. Artistic Alik was walking between the easels, looking at the paintings and making remarks in a quiet cultured voice.

'Lena, the red and orange colours will run into each other. Better to separate them in chiaroscuro, maybe lilac. Vitya, your outline of the horse's legs is wrong. Seryozha, this corner is empty, you need to paint something else here.'

Alik stood behind Yurik for a long time. Yurik was still at the pencil sketch stage and was drawing a huge atomic mushroom in the middle of a city. Houses and trees were burning, and little figures were running away, waving their arms.

'Yura, I don't approve of your composition,' said Alik at last.

'Why?' Yurik was on the brink of taking offence.

Alik grasped his chin with his hand, not taking his eyes off the paper.

'You see, you've depicted the explosion in the centre. And it's flinging everything away from itself, as it were, pushing everything else beyond the boundaries of the paper. It's a mistake. I would advise you to place the explosion in the upper left. Then the force of the explosion would be directed horizontally, vertically and diagonally in all other directions, and the composition would obtain consummation and balance.'

Alik showed how the force of the explosion would be distributed. Yurik thought about it.

'All right, I'll redo it,' he agreed with a sigh.

Alik gave a slight nod, and moved over to Valerka. *He comes on to me with advice, I'll tell him to stick it where the sun don't shine,* thought Valerka jealously and coarsely. *I'll give Albert the weasel one in the easel.*

Alik noticed that Valerka was frowning, and maintained a tactful silence.

'Alik, tell him not to have a tank in his painting,' a flaxen-haired boy suddenly asked from across the room.

Valerka made a move as if to jump to his feet. His tank had come out marvellously. It had tipped over like a dead beetle under the impact from the bulldozer; one of its tracks had torn away, coming loose from its toothed wheel, and the turret had fallen off.

'What the hell?' shouted Valerka, offended.

Alik plainly felt awkward.

'You see,' he began to explain, embarrassed, 'you and Yura signed up later than the others, and we had an agreement that everyone would paint something different. We want the exhibition to show the world's diversity, and to do that we mustn't have any repetition in the paintings. And Pavlik already has a tank.'

Valerka strode resolutely towards Pavlik. The flaxen-haired Pavlik's heart failed. Valerka's glasses did not mislead Pavlik into the traditional misconception about Valerka's fighting ability. It turned out, though, that Pavlik could draw really well. He had already executed his chunky tank in paint. A soldier was standing in front of the tank. He had picked up a little girl in a red dress, and the girl was sticking a flower into the tank's gun muzzle. Valerka gloomily admired Pavlik's work. There was no point in objecting. It was wickedly well painted.

Valerka went back to his place.

'We are a collective,' said Alik guiltily. 'Comrade must yield to comrade.'

'All right, don't whine,' growled Valerka, and he took a rubber and started erasing from his drawing the overturned tank and its toppled turret.

'And he should get rid of the rocket, too,' said a curly-haired girl smartly.

'How does my rocket come into it?' said Valerka, starting up again.

The rocket was cracking in half, and all sorts of rubbish was spewing out of its insides.

'I'm drawing a cosmodrome,' answered the curly-haired girl. 'I have a rocket, too.'

'Please don't be upset, Valery,' said Alik sympathetically. 'You must understand.'

'And the plane!' Shouted demands started raining in on Valerka.

Valerka was uncommonly pleased with the plane. The plane's nose was sticking into the ground, and on its tail a parachutist was dangling from a parachute.

'Think of something else,' whispered Alik, prudently stepping back.

Valerka furiously erased the plane and the rocket, and stared, discouraged, at his paper. A huge bulldozer was pushing a toy ship into a hole. The globe-headed bulldozer driver was jutting out of his cab, smiling like a moron, to use the PE teacher's word. Seriously, this was a drawing for peace?

Beside him, Yurik let out a sob.

Valerka glanced round. He thought that Yurik was empathising with his drama, but Tonky was looking at his own creation, paying no attention to Valerka's at all.

'What's up? You taken the hump at this ragworm?'

'I started thinking about war,' acknowledged Yurik. 'If there's an atomic explosion, then everyone will die, including Mum...'

With broad movements of his rubber, Valerka fell to destroying whatever remained – the ship and the bulldozer. Then he unclipped the smudged paper from the easel and moved towards Ninochka Sergeyevna.

'I give in.' He put his drawing paper on the young leader's table.

'Has something happened?' worried Ninochka Sergeyevna.

Valerka cut her off. 'I'm signing out of your circle of dickwads,' he told her.

The children looked at him warily, hiding behind their easels.

Valerka stormed out into the corridor, angrily slamming the door. Company House shuddered. The painters could get stuffed, them and their exhibitions! Valerka turned to march off, and crashed face first into Whistler's firm tits.

CHAPTER 3

THE PSYCHO'S CHOICE

Igor drove the begrimed footballers to the washhouse, which, with its long pipes, tubs, and butterfly valves resembled the milking apparatus on a collective farm. Taps shuddered, jets of water smacked against the tin of the basins, and the footballers rubbed their dirty faces with slabs of laundry soap. Someone tugged at Igor's sleeve. Igor looked round. Behind him stood Yurik Tonkikh, shifting guiltily from foot to foot.

'Igor Sanych, Natalya Borisovna wants to see you.'

'Why?' asked Igor, surprised.

'She's arrested Valerik.'

'Bugger,' said Igor in a burst of annoyance.

Turning the boys over to Irina, Igor followed Yurik, listening to the story of the revolution organised by the pioneer Lagunov in the creative arts circle. Igor, truth to tell, did not see anything particularly terrible in Valerka's behaviour. Meaning they should be able to get out of it without bloodshed.

'And what were you drawing?' Igor asked Yurik, just in case.

'I was drawing an atomic explosion and he was drawing tanks and rockets for peace.'

'*A star fell from the sky straight into my sweetheart's drawers,*' muttered Igor. '*Eh, burn em low, burn em high, burn em ay-yi-yi-yi-yi, only thank you, no more wars.*'[4]

'What?' said Yurik blankly.

'Nothing, nothing.'

....

[4]   A reference to a song by the Russian group Balagan Limited.

The arrested Valerka was being held in the Flag Room. He was sitting behind a cabinet stuffed with rolls of wall newspapers, scowling and looking out of the open window. Whistler was in her place at the table and staring at Valerka as if he were some kind of rare overseas cactus.

'You seem to be normal, Lagunov. How do you get on at school? A lot of mediocre grades?'

'Nope.'

'Not MR, then. But your behaviour is.'

She was using 'MR' to signify 'mentally retarded'. Valerka did not know what to say. He did not consider his behaviour to be that of someone mentally retarded.

'Are you registered?'

'Where?' asked Valerka.

There were many places where a person could be registered. At a mental hospital, for example, or with the militia, in the juvenile detention centre.

'In Karaganda!' answered Whistler irritably.

Entering the Flag Room, Gor-Sanych, with his moustache and wavy locks, immediately defused the tension. Valerka assumed that Gor-Sanych would be on his side.

'Look on him and admire: I'm keeping him here like a mad dog on a chain,' Whistler said to Gor-Sanych. 'He's adopted a certain personal style: hurling himself at people.'

If the bespectacled and rumpled Valerka resembled a mad dog, it was a very small one, practically harmless to humans.

'Let him go, Natalya Borisovna,' said Igor Sanych. 'I'll sort it all out with him, I promise. He's a boy you can get through to.'

The Senior Pioneer Leader pulled a sceptical face.

'Yes, of course I'll let him go,' she agreed, her tone threatening, 'but he is never to set one foot outside the brigade again. And let him think over his behaviour. Off you go, Lagunov.'

Valerka walked sullenly to the door past Whistler and Gor-Sanych, like a man suspected of wrongdoing and acquitted on a technicality, but still considered guilty.

Whistler followed Valerka with her eyes, then turned to Igor. 'Your work with this young boy is a complete shambles.'

'Look, he had a bit of a wild moment,' said Igor in a conciliatory tone, taking a seat. 'It's no big deal. He's a kid. Something about the paintings rubbed him up the wrong way.'

'The paintings don't enter into it,' said Whistler. 'What do the boys in your brigade actually do with themselves?'

Igor inwardly gave thanks to Lyova Khlopov.

'Football!' he declared with conviction. 'They're preparing a squad. They're training in two teams for now, so that come the camp championship they'll have successfully sorted out a combined team.'

'And why isn't Lagunov with them? All boys like football.'

'Not all,' objected Igor. 'And Lagunov wears glasses. He's afraid of breaking them.'

The reason Valerka had given up on football was not his glasses, of course, but for Whistler this was a good enough explanation.

'You have no kind of a grip on your charge, Igoryok,' said Whistler with a certain disdain. 'I caught your Lagunov on the grounds the other day, bobbing about the camp like a you know what in a you know where. Lied to me about wanting to sign up for singing. Fine. I hoicked him over here, he signed up, and then what? He walked straight out. Today he signed up for painting, and again he's walked out.'

Igor twigged that the safest course would be for him to take refuge in banalities.

'The fellow's searching for himself,' he said.

'He's not searching for anything!' came in Whistler sharply. 'This Lagunov of yours is about as worthwhile as a knitted condom, pardon my French. I've seen youngsters like him. He's just an anti-social type. And you indulge him. You think just because he wears glasses, he's a decent boy? You haven't got a clue about life.'

Igor sighed heavily. He was going to have to speak seriously.

'It's true he's not an easy boy, Natalya Borisovna. But he likes to do things right. What he's looking for is not a hobby circle, obviously. He's an idealist. He's looking for the ideal collective.'

'And what is that exactly?' Whistler looked pained.

'A collective in which the common interest takes precedence over the personal. That's why I let him off football. The team isn't coming together there yet.'

'Don't you try and pulp my brains!' flared Whistler. 'It's you. You can't get your house in order. That's why everything's discombobulated! Your football, this kid. Lagunov is a pain in the arse, simple as that. Don't come here concocting excuses for him or yourself. In short, Korzukhin, you need to rein in your boys. Starting with Lagunov. That's all. Off you go. Get to work.'

Igor snorted. Same old story. No sausage in the shops – slackers on the collective farm. The bus doesn't turn up – the driver's taken his foot off the gas. Valerka Lagunov's read too many books – the librarian's to blame. Igor got up and left the Flag Room. Eat up what they give you, Pioneer Valerka!

The spat with the Senior Pioneer Leader, strangely enough, did not spoil Igor's mood. Perhaps because underneath Whistler the Pioneer, bright-eyed and ballsy, there was an ordinary Whistler waiting to be found: a grumpy old girl. An old girl who resembled the model pioneer leader no more than did Igor himself.

He decided to have a smoke, but smoking was only allowed in the back yard of Company House. Igor went down the steps and walked round the building. There was a little garden, in the middle of which was a bench, and on the bench sat Veronika, smoking.

'Hi,' said Igor, sitting down next to her on the plank, hot from the sun.

'I was pretty sure you'd get yourself out here,' said Veronika. She gave him a wry grin.

'What do you mean?'

Veronika nodded over her shoulder at the open window of the Flag Room.

'Heard you getting bawled out.'

'Ah-hah...'

In the delicate breeze coming off the Volga, the acacias in the garden trembled softly. The heat shamelessly hinted that clothes were superfluous. Igor liked the feeling of being alone with Veronika, as if they were both balancing on a dangerous lip, and a slight shift on the part of the shadows would rupture the equilibrium and ease them imperceptibly over it. Without doubt, Veronika also felt something similar, even though in his relations with her Igor had not yet indicated any of his wishes. But understanding passed between them; the sun saw to that.

'I know your Lagunov,' said Veronika. 'He signed up for my circle, too. Sat there quietly, didn't kick up any kind of rumpus. He's not a hooligan. He's a psycho.'

Igor felt offended on Valerka's behalf. Why was everyone piling in on the kid?

'He's self-contained. That's why he seems like a psycho.'

Veronika cut in. 'We don't have anyone like that,' she said, in a tone that brooked no argument.

'Yes, we do,' replied Igor assertively. 'Me, for instance. I'm self-contained.' He said it to Veronika even though he would never say it to himself. 'Even if the high-ups get on my back,' he added.

Veronika screwed her eyes up a little, and her dark pupils became even darker, dazzlingly dark on this dazzling afternoon.

'My parents love bard songs.' Veronika flicked the ash off her cigarette. 'They go to Grusha[5] every year. At home, they get together with friends and all sing along: *a rubber hedgehog walked and whistled with a hole in his right side.*[6] These are what – grown-ups who make their own decisions?' Veronika grimaced disparagingly. 'We're all children. We all live in one big pioneer camp and follow a common timetable.'

Igor had already realised that Veronika's main mode of communication was the challenge. It did not matter what or to whom. What should he do? If he took issue with her, they would quarrel, as had already happened once.

If he agreed, he would be a fool.

'No choice,' concluded Veronika.

....

[5]   The Grushinsky festival is an annual Russian bard song festival established in 1968. It takes place near the city of Samara, on the Mastryukovo lakes. The festival takes its name from Valery Grushin, a singer-songwriter who died in the river Ude trying to save children who had got into difficulties.

[6]   From a poem by Yunna Petrovna Moritz, born 2 June 1937 in Kyiv.

She was talking about her own thoughts, but she voiced Igor's at the same time. There was no choice. Like in the food block canteen. Eat up what they give you. Or eat nothing at all, like that ridiculous Valerka Lagunov. The boy had found within himself the strength to do that.

Igor did not eat up either – he did not argue. He simply leaned along the hot bench towards Veronika and pulled the delicate hand with the cigarette away from her face. Then he moved closer and kissed Veronika on the lips. Her lips did not respond.

Igor backed away a little – just a little, just enough for one word to find room between their lips.

'Answer,' he demanded quietly.

And Veronika answered.

CHAPTER 4

'SPACE FOOD'

After Quiet Hour and afternoon snack, the young leaders usually occupied their charges with 'brigade games', but Valerka had plans of his own. He was thinking of making his own 'space food'. The *Pomorin* brand toothpaste his mother had given him was not suitable for this purpose; *Pomorin* should not even be used for make-up; it burned. And if you ate half a tube of it, you could snuff it. Valerka had noticed that Vovka Makerov from the second squad had a tube of 'Orange' toothpaste, which was just the job. A couple of days previously, Valerka had started a rumour in the second squad that 'Orange' was only used by girls, for kissing, and now he was reaping the fruits: Makerych eagerly exchanged his 'Orange' for *Pomorin*, and threw in half a box of matches to boot.

Valerka wrapped the matches in a scrap of newspaper and buried them in a secret place; they would serve their purpose yet. He took the box and went to Company House, supposedly to write a letter home. In fact, once he was there he covered the box with white paper. On the front side of the box Valerka drew ten tiny squares with the numbers from zero to nine. It was a micro-calculator. Not like Dad's *Elektronika*, of course, but almost the same. In any event, it worked just as well.

Then Valerka went to the washroom, took the lid off the 'Orange', cut the tube with scissors, and washed out all the paste with water. A trace would be left, he realised that, but a touch of orange would be fine; it was not the chemical causticity of *Pomorin*. He was now in a position to head off into the forest for berries. Crushed strawberries in his tube would be 'space food'. He would consume it in bed after lights out.

Valerka left the camp grounds through a hole he had already found in the chain link fence. The pine grove floated in the sun, as if in honey. A woodpecker knocked. The air smelled of resin and the distant freshness of the Volga. A squirrel made scuttling progress, hopping from tree to tree. In the forest, life went on as it should. The thought struck Valerka that the pine trees were growing for the universal good: for the squirrels and woodpeckers, for the river and the sky. Huge as towers, the pines did not block the sunlight even for the insignificant strawberries.

Valerka did not dare go deeper into the forest, and stayed close to the fence. After all, the Escaped Convicts did not live by the law. If they caught him, they would make 'space food' out of him, out of Valerka. At the same time, you could understand the cons. Who would want to languish in prison when they could live in this beautiful forest? Valerka crawled in the grass, picking strawberries and thinking about life.

Why had Whistler called him mentally retarded? He wanted to find a circle where everyone genuinely worked on something shared; did that really make him mentally retarded? Of course the lads in his brigade were all right, they were normal boys, but somehow always out for themselves; there was something not honest about them. They peeked in blind man's bluff and wouldn't stay dead in war games. Just yesterday, they had hidden Tityapa's trainers, and nobody would say where until Irina Mikhailovna had bawled all of them out when Tityapa showed up at exercise in just his socks. And they had all whinnied with laughter, except Lyova Khlopov. Lyova was a good guy, but there was something not quite right about him, too. Well, yes: he was hung up on his stupid football, but that was not it. It was as if Lyova turned only one side of himself towards the boys, and no one knew what was on the other. There was a reason why he, Valerka, had dreamed that Lyova was drinking Slavik Mukhin's blood. Before Quiet Hour, Valerka had asked Slavik how he was feeling. A vampire's bite should have had Slavik pegging out like an invalid. But Slavik had said that Valerka should piss off over to sick bay and have them pump him an enema, if he was so interested in medicine.

Valerka filled the tube with strawberries, pinched and folded over the end, and put the 'space food' in his pocket. He decided to go back into camp through another hole in the fence, by the back yard of the food block. The hole was covered by thick bird cherry shrubs. Under the bird cherry, Valerka caught sight of two boys sitting in the grass playing cards. Valerka stopped, hiding behind a pine tree.

He knew the card players. Everybody knew them. One was Sanya Beklemishev from the second brigade, nicknamed Beklya, chief hoodlum in camp. The other was his sidekick, Vasilyok, called Siphilyok behind his back. Beklya usually had a third type with him, Lyoshka Rulet. Rulet ran for Beklya and Siphilyok ran for Rulet. The juvenile detention centre wept for all three of them.

'Strickle,' said Beklya, throwing down a card. 'Boniface to you!'

Beklya liked strange words. He probably thought they made him seem clever.

Valerka was about to retreat and disappear without attracting attention, but suddenly the cherry shivered, and Valerka stopped dead as Anastasiika Sergushina came tumbling out into the clearing. If there was one person who did not fit with Beklya's cabal, it was her. Then Valerka realised that Anastasiika was being pushed forward by Lyoshka Rulet. Valerka froze.

'Where are the puppies?' asked Anastasiika. She had not yet worked it out.

Valerka straightaway guessed what stunt had been pulled. News had flown round camp the last few days that someone had finally tracked down the little house where Vaflya, one of the food block dogs, had hidden her puppies. Apparently Anastasiika wanted to have a look at Vaflya's brood, except that behind the cherry was Beklya's brood, and that was much worse. Rulet had played a mean trick on Anastasiika. Lured her into a trap. Beklya and Siphilyok jumped up, and Anastasiika was surrounded.

'Who are you calling puppies, sweety-pie?' asked Beklya, screwing up his eyes.

'Who are you mouthing off at?' bristled Siphilyok menacingly.

Beklya was big-nosed and thick-lipped, tall and skinny, as if smoking had burned him out from within.

Siphilyok was small and frail, like Losharik.[7]

'You're going to eat your words,' Rulet told Anastasiika.

To look at, Rulet seemed a normal boy. Only to look at.

'Get lost!' shouted Anastasiika angrily.

Beklya stretched out a long arm towards her. Before she could back away out of reach, he deftly hooked his finger in the gold chain round her neck, as a thief might, and hoicked the gold cross out from under her T-shirt. In one movement, he wrapped his fist around it.

'Give it to me,' he asked her, sneering. 'I believe in Goddy-wod too.'

'It was Grandma's!' Anastasiika did not dare pull away or she would break the delicate chain. 'Don't touch it!'

'You're going to eat your words,' repeated Rulet stupidly.

'Eat what words, you idiots?'

'You lammed into Zhanka back there, right?' Beklya reminded her.

'Have you been mouthing off at Zhanka?' Siphilyok flew up. 'Lyolik?'

Valerka recalled the spat between Zhanka and Anastasiika in the singing circle, and immediately guessed that the spiteful Zhanka had set Beklya on to her, and Beklya was happy enough to play the bully.

'I did not quarrel with your Shalayeva! Let go of my cross!'

'You'll pay for it, my little slice of potassium permanganate,' promised Beklya.

'If you take it off me I'll go to the militia!' Anastasiika refused to give up.

'And they'll give you a black eye! You're the one who'll end up sorry!'

'Let's do an umbrella on her,' suggested Rulet.

'Umbrella her!' yelled Siphilyok enthusiastically.

....

[7]   A character in a 1971 Soviet animated film. Losharik was a circus animal made of brightly-coloured juggling balls.

'Doing an umbrella' meant pulling a girl's skirt up and flipping it inside out, so that everyone could see her knickers. Valerka flared with anger at Beklya and his sidekicks. He would not have abandoned his hiding place for the sake of saving a gold cross; gold was a relic of the past, and not worth risking his bones for. But hoisting Anastasiika's skirt into an 'umbrella' was something else entirely.

Valerka moved out from behind his pine tree and stepped towards Beklya's group. His stomach tensed horribly. Preparing for a fight, he clenched his fists.

'Look out!' Seeing Valerka, Siphilyok was suddenly alert.

If you attack a group on your own, you need to act quickly and decisively, and the first thing to do is to take out the least imposing of the enemy. Valerka broke into a run. The least imposing was Siphilyok, a weed's weed. Valerka came at full tilt and jabbed him in the solar plexus. Siphilyok doubled over, mouth wide open and tongue out as if he was being sick. Glasses glinting threateningly, Valerka turned on Rulet.

'Who are you?' panicked Rulet, skipping back. 'What you after? A taste of my fist?'

'Whack him!' shouted Beklya imperiously.

He was still holding Anastasiika by her chain, as if on a leash.

Rulet did not heed his gang leader. He was jiffling about, wondering in which direction to make a dash, looking from Valerka to the bushes and back. Siphilyok was coughing violently, sending out thick strings of spittle. Beklya, annoyed, let go of Anastasiika's cross and rushed at Valerka. Valerka himself was already sizing up an attack on Rulet and was nimbly manoeuvring in front of him in a boxer's shuffle: a step forward, a step back, as the other lads had taught him in the yard. Suddenly a terrible explosion in his ear knocked Rulet and the whole clearing around the bird cherry out of his sight line. Valerka went staggering, and sprawled on his back in the grass. His micro-calculator matchbox and tube of space food flew out of his pockets. It was Beklya who had swept Valerka from his stance with a blow fit to pierce a tank, as if he had been knocking a cat off a fence with a brick.

Rulet, meanwhile, shot off as if propelled by an inner catapult.

'Nobody move!' barked Beklya at both Rulet and Anastasiika.

Anastasiika could have run away, but she was making no effort to do so. She was no longer alone, albeit that her saviour was lying on the grass, about as useful as an overcoat in summer.

'Jerk!' she cried fearlessly at Beklya, tucking her gold cross inside the neck of her T-shirt. 'Turd in the toilet!'

Beklya paid her no attention. He was curious to find out about Valerka.

'Where did you come from, penis ocularis?' he asked.

Through the ringing in his head, Valerka experienced surprise at this sudden show of education from Beklya. Maybe Beklya was not a complete idiot after all? Valerka sat up slowly, then struggled to his feet. The battle was over, the confrontation not yet.

'Let Anastasiika go,' Valerka stubbornly demanded of Beklya.

'Beat the crap out of him, Beklya!' sobbed Siphilyok at high volume from somewhere far off.

Rulet was warily making his way back to the battlefield.

'So, Four Eyes. Peeping, eh?' Beklya nodded towards Anastasiika.

'I was out for a walk,' answered Valerka angrily.

All boys tried to peep at girls in the buff, but getting caught doing so was considered a disgrace.

'Walking in the forest?' echoed Beklya doubtfully. 'There are cons there.'

On his way back, Rulet picked up Valerka's treasures: the tube and the box. 'Check this out,' he said. 'Had them on him.' He held out the box.

Bekla turned the homemade micro-calculator over in his fingers.

'What's this klaipeda?'

'A micro-calculator,' explained Valerka reluctantly. 'It calculates.'

Anastasiika was also showing an interest in Valerka's invention.

'And how does it work?' Beklya looked at Valerka without malice.

'Count,' suggested Valerka. 'What's eight sevens?'

Beklya and Rulet thought deeply.

'A hundred,' said Rulet, on the off chance.

'Fifty-six,' replied Anastasiika.

'Press the buttons,' said Valerka to Beklya.

Beklya carefully pressed the '5' and '6' buttons drawn on the box. Valerka took the box from Beklya's hand, and pulled out the drawer with a smooth movement.

'Zh-zh-zh-zh-zh,' he said, mimicking the sound of a small motor.

On the bottom of the box was written: 'Correct.'

'Rail grease!' offered Beklya in a tone of sincere admiration. He took the box back and shoved it in his pocket. 'What's with the toothpaste?'

'It's space food,' said Rulet. 'I seen the kiddies with it.'

Valerka was suddenly struck by an idea of pure genius.

'I take it out to the Escaped Convicts,' he said, his voice grim. 'I know the place. You leave food, the cons'll put a knife in return.'

'A real knife?' Beklya's eyes flashed.

'Finnish.'

Beklya bought it. 'Show me the place!' he said. 'We'll lie in wait for the cons!'

'Swap?' asked Valerka boldly.

'Swap what?'

Valerka jabbed his finger at Anastasiika.

'You get off her back, I'll show you the place.'

Beklya looked appraisingly at the prisoner. Any girl could be umbrellaed, not just this one. Zhanka Shalayeva could get by without her cross, especially as rob this little cow and she'd sure as shit complain to the cops. Cons, though… Cons! Real ones! Escaped! That was mystery, fear, power, and majesty!

'He'll screw you over.' Rulet did not trust Valerka.

'He does that he'll answer for it,' declared Beklya confidently. 'Done! Sinus!'

Beklya held a friendly hand out to Valerka, and Valerka squeezed it.

'Chop!' Beklya ordered Rulet.

Rulet slapped the handshake apart with his palm. The deal was done.

'Let's go,' said Valerka to Anastasiika, as if she were his own property.

This time, Beklya's gang made no effort to prevent them from retreating.

Valerka climbed through the bird cherry to the hole in the fence, and Anastasiika followed him. Valerka wriggled out into back yard of the food block and waited for Anastasiika. Vaflya the dog appeared from somewhere and started poking at Valerka with her wet nose. Anastasiika bent down and stroked Vaflya, who broke into a little jig of happiness.

'Well done, doggie, a true friend,' she said approvingly.

'It was actually me who rescued you,' clarified Valerka with a scowl.

'Yeah, right,' snorted Anastasiika dismissively.

Old Nyura came out of the canteen carrying a tub of slops. 'D-d-don't you t-t-ease the d-dog, you hooligans!' she shouted.

CHAPTER 5

HOW THINGS ARE

It was the first overcast morning of the shift. Clouds obscured the sky, but the weather did not venture as far as rain. The clouds were bloated with white light rather than water, and only their sinuous folds darkened with damp.

During work detail, Irina Mikhailovna made an announcement to Igor's boys. 'Lads, football practice is cancelled today.'

The boys did not object. They were sick and tired of running around the pitch and thumping the ball.

'Why is it cancelled?' Lyova Khlopov was alone in being put out.

'We're having a brigade meeting.'

Irina had considered sharing her plans with Igor unworthy of her office, so Igor seized an opportune moment to take her aside.

'What's this news?' he asked. 'What kind of meeting?'

'We've got work to do with your Lagunov.'

Igor did not like this at all. Was this not a little too much punishment for the hapless Valerka? He had done nothing: he had broken no rules, not fought with anyone in the brigade, not broken any windows, not cheeked the young leaders.

'How much are we going to knock him about? Svistunova's already given him a slap round the head.'

'She has, but I haven't. And the brigade hasn't.'

'Brigade? What brigade?' Igor grimaced. 'Why the hell would we set children against one another? They'll just say what you tell them to say!'

'It's a collective we have here.' Irina was completely free from any doubt.

'Have pity on the boy,' said Igor sincerely, not wanting to argue. 'Nothing will happen to him.'

'You're doing it so Svistunova doesn't accuse you of anything.'

That riled Irina. 'First of all, Igoryok,' she said, 'Svistunova is not accusing me of anything. I'm not to blame for Lagunov, you are. You're the one who's let him go to rack and ruin. And secondly, the collective's going to have to re-educate him, if his young leader isn't up to it.'

Irina's determination was impossible to shake, and Igor's mood slumped. He felt a kindred spirit in Valerka, and did not share Irina and Whistler's desire to squash his independence like a bulldozer.

After work detail, the fourth brigade gathered on the veranda. The boys and girls, shoving and bickering, sat along the walls on benches and chairs, as they were used to doing at 'candle'.

'That's my place, you cow!' Gurka clashed with Lenochka Romanova.

'Your place is in a zoo!' replied Lenochka.

'Quiet, quiet, children,' said Irina, calming the brigade down. 'We need to have an important conversation. Valerik Lagunov, come here, stand right here.'

Valerka left the ranks and stood, bewildered, next to Irina. Igor was pleased to be behind Valerka; he would not see the boy's shame.

'So, children, we have an issue. Here is your comrade, Valery.'

Irina pointed at him as at an exhibit. The brigade hushed, interested now.

'What about me?' muttered Valerka, not loudly, but still a challenge.

There was a burst of laughter from the pioneers.

'Let's discuss his behaviour,' suggested Irina.

'So what's he done?' asked silly Zhenka Tsvetkova from the corner.

Irina stayed silent and looked searchingly at the brigade: she wanted the pioneers themselves to uncover what Valerka had done wrong. The pioneers whispered among themselves, muttering in muted voices. Igor made out a rumour flying around the boys and girls: 'Lagunov killed Vaflya! Vaflya and Bambook!

Poisoned them with toothpaste!' Bambook, one of the food block dogs, had indeed been looking woebegone since morning.

'So he killed 'em,' said Gelbich. 'It's a dog, not the PE teacher.'

'I haven't touched anyone!' snarled Valerka.

'Lagunov does not want to be part of the collective,' Irina finally informed them. 'He can't find a place for himself anywhere. He joined the singing circle then threw it in. He joined the art circle: same story there, and he was even rude to Nina Sergeyevna. To say nothing of our football team. It's a long time since he went to that.'

There was another outbreak of chatter. The brigade was puzzled, not knowing what to make of Valerka's coming and going.

'What do you have to say for yourself, Lagunov?'

'I'm not saying anything!' snarled Valerka.

He found it unpleasant to be put in front of everyone and unscrewed into his constituent parts. The silvery light of the overcast day seemed surgical.

'Well, boys and girls, what do you say?' Irina addressed the collective. 'You're his comrades. Lyova, you're the football captain. Explain to Lagunov.'

Lyova reluctantly stood up and fingered the end of his red neckerchief, embarrassed. He had taken to wearing his neckerchief in training and during Quiet Hour. Valerka looked distrustfully at Lyova. Perhaps Lyova would behave like a friend and not condemn him?

'You, Valerik, want to hog the ball the whole time.' Lyova gave a laboured sniff. 'But football's a team game. You have to pass the ball to others. You don't like that. It's not right. You should put the interests of the team above your own.'

Valerka seethed with instant indignation. Had he really been the one playing like an egomaniac, with no regard for anyone else? The reason he had given up playing stupid football was that there was no team: the boys were even kicking the ball away from their own teammates.

'You what?!' shouted Valerka. 'I was playing fine! Tityapa's the one keeping the ball! Gorokh didn't make a single pass! Slavik came prancing out of his own zone!'

'Liar, liar!' yelled Tityapkin and Gorokhov. 'You're a bum, Lagunov!'

Igor knew that Valerka was right – he had seen the game.

'Gorokhov and Tityapkin, no name calling here!' barked Igor.

Irina dismissively cut off Valerka's self-defence. 'It's no good shifting your own guilt onto others, Lagunov! If you mess up, fess up!' Irina looked around for someone else to summon to Valerka's demolition. 'What about you, Sergushina? You're brigade commander.'

Anastasiika stood up and gave a weary sigh and rolled her eyes, as if Valerka had already so exhausted her that she had no strength left.

'He goes outside the fence without permission, Rin Khalovna.'

Irina straightened up as if she had been given a reward. So she was right to suspect that Valerka Lagunov's antisocial tendencies ran deep. Wandering about beyond the fence was a serious crime. Well done, Sergushina! For his part, Valerka could not believe what he had just heard. Anastasiika had given him away? Anastasiika? After he had defended her from Beklya? How mean was that?

'Snitch!' shouted Valerka angrily.

Anastasiika grimaced: Ugh, insulting a girl. How low can you get?

Irina sat on her chair as if in the turret of an invisible tank whose invisible gun was pushing invisibly right into Valerka's forehead.

'And you don't like criticism, Lagunov!' remarked Irina sternly.

Who does? thought Igor.

'Still, explain to us, Lagunov, how our collective does not suit you.'

Valerka did not know what to say. Everything had somehow got into a muddle. He looked at the boys and girls and realised that none of them would say a word to support him.

He had done nothing bad. Everyone went outside the camp grounds. Everyone quarrelled with someone from time to time, slacked off on some job, stayed awake after lights out. A human being was not a robot. He, Valerka, was being condemned for not being a robot. And it was dishonest of them to condemn him, because they were not robots either. They were just making themselves out to be robots. And why did they have to do that?

Of course, the collective was always right. But was the fourth brigade really a collective? Two weeks ago they did not even know one another. They had been gathered here, a random group, united by no common cause. Were they doing battle with an enemy? Were they building something useful? Were they proving something important to anyone? Were they deciding anything for themselves? They could not agree on anything with one another; the only thing they knew how to do together was break the rules – rules they had not even invented themselves.

A feeling of severe disappointment seized Valerka. Disappointment with the boys and girls, all ready to walk away from him without a word, if circumstances were such. Disappointment with people in general, because people had, for some reason, created a giant heap of rules and laws in life, according to which you were always guilty. Where was truth, where was friendship, where were common goals and a common cause? At the Olympics, on television?

'In short, we need to take action,' said Irina Mikhailovna. 'You're not a bad person, Lagunov, but you're completely all over the place. The whole brigade will stand bail for you. Right, boys and girls? Shall we help Valerik?'

The brigade maintained a wary silence, unsure of what was meant by bail. Maybe Lagunov would stab someone? What then – everyone would go to prison because of him?

'What can we do to help him?' muttered Gelbich, as though Valerka were terminally ill and on his death bed. 'Nothing!'

'From now on you'll spend all your time with us, where we can see you,' explained Irina. 'No circles, no doing your own thing. You'll be doing what everyone's doing.'

Relieved chatter broke out in the brigade. The retribution, it turned out, was not burdensome. A clear conscience, and no effort required of anyone. This was how life in camp began and this was what it came back to. Lagunov's punishment was that this was how things were.

'Meeting over.' Irina rose from her chair. 'Dismissed.'

CHAPTER 6

A BRIGADE OF YOUR OWN

For lap after lap the athletes ran in a compact group, giving the appearance of all being friends and supporting one another in the race. A subdued hubbub came from the grandstands; they were anticipating a furious final spurt. The television could not convey either the rhythm or the calculated belligerence of the running. The viewers were sitting on Serp Ivanych Iyeronov's veranda in a tight crowd just like the runners. The curtains on the windows were drawn so that the setting sun did not glare off the colour screen. As usual, Serp Ivanych was occupying a seat in the back row. Valerka had found himself a place to one side. He was not interested in the Olympics, but he simply had to get out away from his brigade somehow, and so had asked Gor-Sanych's leave to go over to Iyeronov's.

The clanging of the bell announced the final lap. Accelerating, the runners stretched out into a chain. Out of nowhere, a strange dark man took the lead, unremarkable, diminutive, and with an expansive bald patch shining evenly with sweat and with comical curls at his temples and the nape of his neck. His place was in a youth theatre, not a stadium. But the absurd black man set his elbows working and his legs pumping like pistons and, leaning forward, dashed like the very devil to the finish line, outstripping all the others.

'And the winner of the ten thousand metres is Miruts Yifter, an athlete from the Federal Democratic Republic of Ethiopia!' announced the commentator.

'He's a bit old even for cross-country but he floored it like a youngster,' said one of the young leaders on the veranda admiringly.

The Olympic newsreel came to an end when the sun had almost disappeared behind the Zhiguli mountains. The crimson light of sunset poured off the Volga in a broad wave. The painted gingerbread houses of the pioneer camp glowed every colour, like a promise of fairy-tale dreams. The viewers went away excited. There, on the telly, was the energy, the uprush, the battles of the Olympics, and here – what? Tea with biscuits, the singing of mosquitoes, a blast from a distant motor ship. A drifting, drowsing dullness, not life.

Valerka turned unnoticed round the corner of Iyeronov's dacha. He did not want to make his way back to the brigade. He would let them all fall asleep and then go in. He did not have the strength to face the others. Valerka sat down on a bench in shadow. He recalled the face of Miruts Yifter, caught by the television camera in his finishing burst. Scary bulging eyes, sharp cheekbones, sunken cheeks, mouth gaping and white-toothed. It was not the face of a victor, flying towards triumph on the wings of inspiration. It was the face of a man racing away from mortal danger. It was as if the Ethiopian had looked on the other runners as his fellow athletes the whole way round, and then just before the finish line had suddenly realised that they were his enemies. They were ready to barge him, trample him, disgrace him. And in the hope of salvation, he had desperately spurred himself forward. Pure terror had driven him on. Miruts Yifter was running away from the other athletes in a ferocious desire not to have them near him.

Inside Valerka was a growing sense that Miruts Yifter was – himself.

'Will I be interrupting?' came from close by.

Serp Ivanych was standing by the corner of the house.

'I'm sorry.' Valerka jumped up. 'I was just leaving.'

'Sit down, sit down,' replied Serp Ivanych. 'There's room enough.'

He lowered himself heavily onto the other end of the bench. He said nothing, but Valerka felt inhibited, and even bitter: there was nowhere he could take refuge, be alone. The camp was big, but he could not find a secluded spot.

'Something happened?' asked Serp Ivanych suddenly.

'No,' answered Valerka.

'I can see,' said Serp Ivanych, looking at Valerka. 'You feel bad.'

'I'm OK,' persisted Valerka.

'What have they done? Offended you? Given you a telling off? Banned you from something?'

Valerka did not know what to say.

'You can tell me a pack of lies about being homesick,' suggested Serp Ivanych. 'I'll pretend I believe you.'

'And if I really am homesick?' asked Valerka truculently.

'You'd do being homesick under the bedclothes,' grinned Iyeronov. 'Hiding out among strangers is about disappointment in your own.'

Valerka shot the old man a surprised look: how did he know?

'People not what you thought? You expected something good from them, believed in them, but they let you down, deceived you, turned out small-minded, indifferent?'

Something twitched in Valerka's stomach, and tears began to well up in his eyes. What Serp Ivanych was saying was the honest truth; it was all exactly what Valerka himself felt. Valerka turned away and sniffed. You can keep a stiff upper lip when you are on your own, but when someone understands you, holding back is too hard.

'Tell me,' asked Serp Ivanych. 'I really am interested.'

Iyeronov's face was strangely pale in the gloom. His dark eyes seemed to be calling Valerka somewhere. Valerka wanted to find a way to join up with the old man, to be near him, to love and obey him as a wise teacher. It would be really good to have a grandfather like Serp. Or a neighbour in the block. If Serp Ivanych had been a commander, Valerka would probably have dreamed of serving in his army.

Valerka began to talk. About Lyova Khlopov's football, about the singing circle, about his drawing with its tanks and rockets, about Anastasiika and Beklya, and about the pioneer meeting, where he had been punched in the face just for not being like everyone else. And he really wanted to be like everyone else, but he needed everyone else to be good. Serp Ivanych did not interrupt; he nodded thoughtfully.

'Eh, brother,' he sighed, and put a hand on Valerka's shoulder.

The hand was large, heavy, and strong like a young man's. Valerka felt that it was ready to clench and grasp tenaciously; but it did not clench.

'Do you know what the secret is?' asked Serp Ivanych, looking into Valerka's eyes.

And in the old man's gaze, an abyss once again split open for Valerka, but now something with authority was drawing him into it. There, in the abyss, he too would be made wise, fearless and all-powerful, like Serp Ivanych.

'The secret is that people can only give themselves up for a great cause. Not for the sake of singing a song or playing football. And a great cause only arises when people think about great things. If they think about themselves, about good things that might come their way, about relatives or friends, sooner or later they will betray the great cause. They will give it up. And they won't be what you want to see in them. Alas, my boy, this is how it is. I have experience.'

'Have you ever had a trustworthy brigade like that yourself?' asked Valerka. 'All for one and no one for himself?'

'I have,' nodded Serp Ivanych. 'I have, but it was many, many years ago. Some were killed, some lived to old age but are dead now. I'm the last one left.'

'So tell me about it now,' asked Valerka shyly.

Serp Ivanych looked away, over to where the sunset had gone out.

'It happened in '18. The Civil War had already broken out. Samara – Kuibyshev in today's speak – had been seized by the Whites. The Reds were putting up resistance in Tsaritsyn – Volgograd in today's speak. Me and the lads lived in the village by these dachas. We worked for hire for the gentlemen who used to holiday here in the summer. The dachas were called Shikhobalovsky's – they belonged to one of the bourgeoisie, owned steam mills. We were still boys – younger than your young leaders. But we wanted to join the Bolsheviks. And a rumour went round that battle steamships with Red Guards would be moving from Tsaritsyn to Samara. The Whites immediately brought a battery here, to the dachas, so they could shell the Tsaritsyn landing force from the cannons on the shore. Me and the lads had a bit of a chat and decided to destroy the battery. We had no weapons, just scythes and pitchforks, and my brother had a rusty revolver from somewhere. But we had to save our own at whatever cost. As I remember it now, on the evening of August 3rd we got together at the edge of the village and swore we wouldn't chicken out, wouldn't betray one another. And at night we attacked the Whites...'

Serp Ivanych fell silent, and kneaded his throat as if he were losing his voice.

'The fighting was pitiless. We were chopping and stabbing among the dachas left and right. They were firing rifles and revolvers at us. But none of the lads ran away, no one hid. Everything was drenched with blood, bodies were lying all around. We ripped the bolts off the White Guards' rifles, then commandeered a steamship tied up at the wharf and sailed off to Tsaritsyn. Less than half of us made it out of there. We spent three days in Tsaritsyn and then were taken into Budyonny's[8]... Those boys were my brigade. We dreamed of a great cause together. Not even about the Soviet regime – about a new world, a new man. We wanted all people to become something else. And what would happen to us was not important.'

Valerka stared about him, looking at the ancient dachas. He could not imagine the fighting that had broken out here. How selflessly the village lads had died to make sure the landing ships reached the captured city.

This was exactly how it was – the far-off Civil War. Fires blazing beyond the horizon. Scarlet flares lighting the sky. Budyonny's squadrons charging with bare sabres in the steppe dust. Light mobile artillery swivelling and mowing down the

....

[8]   Semyon Mikhailovich Budyonny was a Russian military commander during the Russian Civil War, Polish-Soviet War, and World War II, and a politician who was a close political ally of Soviet leader Joseph Stalin.

                                          ALEXEI IVANOV

ranks of White officers with their machine guns. Double-decker aeroplanes roaring overhead, their pilots in motorbike goggles dropping bombs on enemy headquarters with their own hands. Ironclad armoured trains battering their way into stations, guns chattering. Rebel cruisers with towers and smoking chimneys slicing through storm waves on the open seas. Sailors criss-crossed with ribbons of ammunition and lowered bayonets climbing into the attack. A mounted trumpeter with a fluttering red banner in one hand, a horn to his lips in the other. The weather back then was the same as at today's Olympics: constant sunshine, blue sky, white clouds. Back then, people were talking of revolution all over the world, and of a free mankind, and no one wanted anything for themselves alone.

'It's properly dark now,' said Serp Ivanych, patting Valerka's shoulder again. 'I'm afraid you'll be in for another telling off. Time for you to go back to your boys.'

'Yes, of course.' Valerka came to.

Lights in the windows of the old dachas. The smell of pine trees. The yapping of dogs by the food block…

'And don't upset yourself needlessly,' added Serp Ivanovich. 'Your time will come. You'll get a brigade of your own. Not all at once, my friend.'

CHAPTER 7

THE POROROCA

'I need to go out,' Igor said to Sasha. 'Will you keep an eye on the pioneers?'

The request was not burdensome. What was there to keep an eye on? Irina was already taking the evening 'candle' downstairs, after which the children would sort themselves into their dorms, and all the young leader had to do was go through and check that they were in bed. That did not stop Sasha darkening.

'Where are you off to? To watch the Olympics?'

'I have a date,' explained Igor.

Sasha's rounded, soft face became even harder and more severe.

'We came here to work, not to slope off on dates.'

'Don't be a drag, Plotkin.'

Igor knew that at this moment, Veronika was holding her 'candle' in the next building. When Irina returned, Veronika would be free. She had agreed to meet Igor by the monument to the girl bugler at the entrance to the camp.

Igor closed the door of the young leader's room, slid the bolt, and retrieved his backpack from under his bed. Seeing that Igor intended to change his clothes, Sasha, displaying good manners, turned away. Igor pulled down his jeans and replaced his sateen boxers with stylish swimming trunks embroidered with an anchor. What if the date got as far as the main event? A man had to look his best.

'I do not approve of this vulgarity,' declared Sasha, frowning.

'As they say in the telephone exchanges, one is providing a connection unimpeded by ceremony,' replied Igor cynically.[9]

'If you respect the girl, you won't do it.'

'And if the girl herself wants to?'

'A respectable girl wouldn't want to!' snapped Sasha.

'You just don't know girls,' returned Igor condescendingly.

Truth be told, Igor did not know them especially well himself. At least, he had never encountered a situation in which a girl herself 'wanted to'. But he was hardly going to pass up an opportunity to nettle his oh-so moral neighbour.

Sasha sniffed indignantly. 'As it happens, I have a fiancée,' he announced.

'Who?' Igor was immediately interested. His imagination instantly painted him a picture of Sasha Plotkin's fiancée: a simple, chubby woman with glasses, like Irina.

'I don't go blabbing about my fiancée on every corner.'

Igor swallowed Sasha's acidity without blinking an eye. He was curious.

'Do you live with her?' he asked straight out.

'I respect her. Premarital relations are unacceptable to me.'

'So when's the wedding?'

Sasha hesitated, mulling over whether or not to open up, but he was clearly jealous of Igor's liberties and wanted the upper hand.

'I don't know, in a year, maybe,' he said. 'My parents have joined a cooperative. By January, the house will be finished and they'll be given a flat. Snagging, decorating, exams – by the time all that's done it'll be summer again. The wedding'll be then.'

'You've hit lucky with your parents,' said Igor, sincerely envious.

....

9   The Russian telephonists' tag 'даёшь связь без брака!', which appeared also as a toast in the form 'за связь без брака!', relied on a play on the words 'связь' ('connection', 'relationship') and 'брак' (which means both 'marriage' and 'defect') to create an ambiguous slogan suggesting that a better connection might be achieved between a couple if they did not marry. Literally both 'a connection without a fault' and 'a relationship without marriage'.

A flat was the ultimate dream. Many people only got their own place when they retired. And a flat – especially a flat in a cooperative – was something it was not worth Igor even thinking about. His mother's salary was small; saving for a one-bedroom flat was beyond her. The best Igor could hope for when he got a job was a room in a communal flat, if he got married. Not that he was in any hurry to get married.

'Parents shouldn't get the credit for everything,' said Sasha importantly, as if he had earned the down payment on the flat himself.

'Will your fiancée wait?' said Igor, lobbing a spanner in the direction of the works.

'She has to!' said Sasha, surprised.

Igor realised that Sasha considered himself a remarkable match, and that he found the idea of being turned down surpassing strange. He had decided to get married, and that was it, the question was settled, no objections would be accepted. And indeed, who would refuse such a groom, with a flat and higher education?

Igor walked down Pioneer Avenue towards the camp gates, and thought about Sasha Plotkin. For people like him, life put out the welcome mat. Sasha could afford to have such high morals. He would be provided for come what may; he had no need to take chances.

While there was no one on the river bank, Igor peered under the bugler girl's hem. It just had to be done, so that he could stop tormenting himself.

Veronika arrived in jeans and a check shirt with the sleeves rolled up. Clothes were important. As they said in the philology faculty, they were a non-verbal message. The more complicated the clothes were to take off, the less in the mood for intimacy was the girl. Igor, though, found himself unable to evaluate Veronika's mood. He kissed her, testing her intentions, and Veronika accepted the kiss as a gesture of politeness – without resistance and without reciprocal movement towards him.

'Where shall we go?' asked Igor.

They headed in the direction of the Bishop and the village of Pervomaiskaya. The path stretched along the bank beside the edge of the pine forest and then rounded the rim of a vast open space called Concert Clearing, where a huge farewell camp fire was built at the end of each shift. The quiet, occasional plash of water sounded like the pent-up breathing of a lover. The fiery sunset behind the Zhiguli was burning out, as if awareness of the day was fading, and the expanse was drowning in a lilac half-light, immersing itself, it seemed, in a fragile and weightless folly. The freshness of the Volga lapped gently up against the stuffiness of the sun-baked forest.

'Don't be silent,' said Veronika, demanding conversation.

'Are you and Plotkin in the same class?' asked Igor.

'Same year, different streams,' said Veronika dryly. 'How does he come into this?'

'He's just been giving me his entire life story. He's getting a flat in winter and married next summer. I suspect his life is marked out right up to retirement. In two years, a child; three years, post-grad; five years, a car; seven years, a good position. Look on him and weep.'

'Wonderful!' sneered Veronika. 'If his ambition was to end up in prison, yes, that would be bad. But he's aspiring to decent things: family, work, prosperity. We should be following his example. And here you are pulling a face.'

Igor heaved a long-suffering sigh, and glanced sideways at Veronika.

'I'm not your enemy. Why are you picking a fight with me?'

'Well, what's your problem?' retorted Veronika, refusing to calm down.

'I don't give a monkey's about Plotkin,' said Igor, expressing himself clearly. 'I just find it surprising when people think their whole life being predetermined is a blessing.'

Veronika reluctantly yielded.

'How is it not a blessing, if everything mapped out is good? Plotkin's father works for the Regional Committee and his mother's high up in the Local Education Authority. Sashka will have everything: flat, car, good position, wife. He's right to plan it all out.'

'Fools' luck,' said Igor obscurely.

'Let's talk about something else.'

The copse came to an end, and the twilight cleared a little. Ahead, a small gulf took shape, the mouth of the Bishop. An enigmatic whisper reached them from somewhere beyond a group of low hazels: the swish of water around branches lowered into it. A round moon hung over the Volga, one edge slightly melted, and the flat surface of the reach gave back a pale gleam. In the distance glimmered the long faceted crystal of a tourist motor ship. Illuminated from within, the ship seemed to be a piece of glass trickery in which invisible lines taking fixes from the constellations crossed and flared.

Igor and Veronika perched nearby on a grassy knoll. Tiny sparks crackled faintly in the dark feline warmth of the night.

'There are reservoirs one after another from here to the Caspian Sea,' said Igor thoughtfully. 'It's all calm on the river, like a pond. I want to see the Pororoca. Do you know what that is?'

'What?'

'A gigantic wave on the Amazon. Twice a year, at the equinox, the waters of the Atlantic rush into the mouth of the Amazon and drive up the river for hundreds of kilometres. The Pororoca. You can hear its roar before it's even come over the horizon.'

'Class,' agreed Veronika.

Except that the Pororoca was not here; it was on the other side of the globe. Even astronomy worked differently there: the constellations did not revolve, like enormous hieroglyphs on an enormous disc; they rose and set like the moon and the sun. And along with Aquarius and Orion there shone Ophiuchus and Monoceros.

Igor moved closer to Veronika and put his arm around her. He placed a cautious hand on her breast. If Veronika objected, he would stop. His hand felt the stiff fabric of Veronika's swimming costume under her shirt. Veronika had put on her swimming costume for the same reason as he had pulled on his trunks. Meaning he was doing the right thing. He had guessed the direction of the current.

Veronika tilted her face to say something, and parted her lips, but Igor smothered her words with a kiss. And Veronika offered no further objection. But there was in her consent a sort of defiance, as if an echo from the Pororoca.

CHAPTER 8

WHEN NO ONE BELIEVES YOU

Stirred by his conversation with Iyeronov, Valerka did not go back to his own building. He had already skipped 'candle' and broken the rules by wandering abroad after lights out. Might as well be hung for a sheep as a lamb. In the thickening twilight, Valerka made his way to the food block and sat down on a crate by the service entrance. The scruffy red figure of Bambook at once materialised next to him; the dog spun a couple of times and then lay down, slumped against Valerka's leg. Valerka stroked him. Dogs latch on to people because they want friendship; they are capable of being loyal and reliable, whereas people do not need real friendship.

Valerka thought of the days when the young Serp Ivanych had been fighting in his brigade. Wonderful times. Disturbing, expansive, fierce. A pity they were over. Where was one to find comrades now?

No, all is not yet lost, Valerka consoled himself. When he grew up, he could become a geologist. He and his friends would pile into a squat green amphibian and force their way through the impenetrable taiga, or navigate wild marshes. Rucksacks with useful minerals would be piled in the back, but the geologists would value friendship above gold and diamonds. And when the amphibian stalled, and wolves surrounded them on all sides, he and his comrades would take cover behind their cargo, firing back at their predators, and together they would fight to the last bullet while they waited for a military helicopter...

Or he could become a polar explorer. A giant rime-coated nuclear-powered icebreaker would thunder its way through the ice massives, and the Arctic blizzard would whistle, but if he, Valerka, fell overboard into the black water, his friends would jump in after him with lifebelts… Or an astronaut. That would be good. If a meteorite were to hit his oxygen cylinder while he was in orbit, in a vacuum, and hurl him away from the space station into the abyss, a comrade would rush after him, after Valerka as he whirled in the void, and grab him and give him his own air… Bambook sighed, as if he were sorry that no one would ever take him, a mongrel, to the taiga or the Arctic Ocean or outer space, with his capacity for waiting faithfully.

Over the Volga, over the Zhiguli and the Storm Petrel pioneer camp, stars burned, piercing the ragged black pine crowns with sharp, pale blue electric pulses. There was nothing for it: it was time to return to his own building. Valerka patted Bambook on the scruff of his neck and rose to his feet.

He headed for Pioneer Avenue the most direct way – past Building 2, through the uncultivated land where the stadium was, and across the grounds of the fifth brigade. The avenue was fenced by a dense row of acacias, but Valerka knew a narrow gap in the bushes. Bambook had taken it into his head to follow Valerka, and slipped through the bushes behind him.

The smooth asphalted avenue was brightly lit by its mercury lamps. The large stands cast impenetrable rectangular shadows onto the road and the bushes. There was a bench hiding in one of the shadows, like in a black box, and Valerka froze where he was, still in the acacia, because on the bench were a boy and a girl. It looked as if they were kissing. Disturbing them would not be good; on the other hand, Valerka was curious to peep. Bambook, however, suddenly whimpered softly and backed away, out of the bushes.

It was difficult at first to see anything in the gloom. Then the faint glimmer of the stars showed the girl's upturned face and the line of the boy's shoulders. The two were not kissing at all. The girl was sprawling limply on the bench with all her weight on her back and her legs outstretched. The boy was hunched over; his posture was that of a predator. He was pressing the girl's arm to his lips. Valerka heard a hideous slobbering – the same as in his dream of Lyova drinking Slavik Mukhin's blood. Only this was not a dream. There was a vampire on Pioneer Avenue genuinely sucking the blood of his victim. Valerka was paralysed with horror. Behind him, Bambook barked, calling him back.

The vampire boy jerked and looked around. Valerka saw the dead-white gleam of his eyes. Was that Lyova…? Lyova…? Had he gone out hunting for people…? In an instant, the vampire was on his feet. He leaped over the bench, inhumanly agile, and with barely a sound disappeared into the bushes on the other side of the avenue.

Valerka stood stupidly like a tree stump, trying to comprehend what he had witnessed. If this was not a dream, then the last time was not a dream either. He had convinced himself that he had dreamed about Lyova drinking blood, because it was impossible to believe that such a thing was real. Lyova Khlopov a vampire? The stubborn and sensible footballer Lyova with his dirty T-shirt and crumpled red neckerchief was a creepy vampire from ancient tales? Impossible. But here was a victim – a girl on a bench.

That craven Bambook, the coward, had sensed it all and scarpered, leaving his comrade. Woozy from horror, Valerka took a step out of the bushes onto the asphalt. No one. The gas lamps hummed quietly over the avenue. The pointlessly cheerful pioneers in their pioneer caps stared from the stands, hands raised in salute. The girl lay on the bench, arms dropped. Valerka approached her. He thought he knew her. The curly-haired cretin from the art circle who had demanded that he should remove the rocket from his drawing. She was from the first brigade. The girls in the older brigades were irrepressible when it came to going out and kissing boys.

Valerka looked at the girl's face and could not tell whether or not she was alive. At length, the girl shuddered and sighed, as if she had woken up. Valerka did not wait; he hurtled away, unable to stay. Staying with a vampire's victim was more frightening than staying with the vampire itself. A vampire was nonsense, a nasty fairy tale, a granny's superstition, but a person whose blood had been drunk … this was truth. This was proof of something real.

Igor Alexandrovich was sitting on the steps of the stoop of Building 4, smoking. He had a strange look, simultaneously happy and dazed. He seemed to be somewhere else in his thoughts, with the result that the sudden night-time appearance of the vanished pioneer made no impression on him.

'Valera?' he wondered, vaguely surprised. 'Why aren't you in the dorm?'

'I was at Serp Ivanych's,' said Valerka, not quite lying.

'Well, good. Off to bed now.'

Valerka, rumpled and dishevelled, did not move. 'Gor-Sanych, there's a girl in the avenue in a bad way. She's lying down.'

'Lying down?' echoed Igor stupidly.

'Gor-Sanych, she's in a bad way!' repeated Valerka insistently.

Igor shook himself, brushing off his sweet confusion. Damn it! A child in a bad way. Something had gone wrong and here he was, dozing at the wheel like a moron.

'Take me to her,' ordered Igor, tossing aside his cigarette.

The avenue, washed in the chemical light of the street lamps, stretched away empty in both directions.

The stands looked like television sets turned off.

'Where's your girl?' Igor looked at Valerka suspiciously.

Valerka stared around, frowning. There was the bench vacated by the startled Lyova. The shadow of the escaped vampire was still lurking in the bushes. Perhaps there were drops of blood left on the bench. Valerka hurried forward, allowing the darkness to swallow him, and examined the planks of the bench and even sniffed the air, trying to pick out something with his nose. But the only scent he could find was the acacia.

'She was here,' muttered Valerka. 'She was lying here.'

'Perhaps she was just resting. Having a doze.'

Valerka breathed out hard through his nose. 'A vampire bit her,' he said dully. 'She fainted.'

Igor Alexandrovich stayed guiltily quiet for a moment.

'A vampire?' he clarified warily.

'Yes,' confirmed Valerka, totally defeated. 'Lyova Khlopov.'

Igor understood everything. This boy had spent the day being humiliated, insulted, offended. He felt that everyone had betrayed him, that he was alone and needed by no one. So he had made up a ridiculous story to bring attention back to himself.

'Let's go, Valer.' Igor took him by the arm.

Valerka complied. 'You think I'm lying?' he asked.

The lamps were humming quietly; a grasshopper was chirping somewhere; the barely audible call of a night cuckoo reached them from the forest. Valerka felt very bitter: once again he was not being understood. His disappointment in Igor Sanych was suffocating. Valerka had almost come to believe that Igor Sanych was one of his own, but he had turned out to be just as alien as the others.

'I'm not a psycho,' said Valerka angrily. 'Lyova's a vampire. He's one person during the day and another at night. He gets up and drinks blood. He drank Slavik Mukhin's. Now he's sunk his teeth into a girl from my old circle.'

'I've been hanging about on the stoop for nearly an hour. No one's come out of the building.'

'He got out the window,' persisted Valerka.

'Your dorm window is visible from the stoop.'

'He got out another window.'

Igor decided not to argue with the boy. This was not the time.

The ornate carved gingerbread housing their brigade appeared ghostly in the fragile luminescence of the half moon, as if it were made of blue smoke.

'Take you to the dorm?' asked Igor when they were at the stoop. 'We can both make sure everything's all right with Lyova.'

Valerka wanted to offer Gor-Sanych a proud refusal, to make him feel ashamed, but inside the dorm, terror was lying in wait for him, and even the young leader's superciliousness would help Valerka sneak into his little house.

Igor entered the dorm with exaggerated caution, to convince Valerka that he was taking it seriously. In the dorm, everyone was asleep. Not pretending, as at inspection, but for real. The slanting light from the lamps outside the window illuminated the white figures of the boys wrapped in dark folds on their bunks. The boys had crawled right under their sheets, heads and all, to escape the mosquitoes. One of them was letting out an occasional snore.

'All quiet,' whispered Igor, glancing around.

Valerka realised that Gor-Sanych was play-acting, but still his fear subsided.

'Lyova's asleep,' Igor added, leaning over the swaddled hulk.

'That's Tityapkin, not Lyova.'

Igor lifted a corner of the sheet above the boy's face.

'Suck a banana, you bum!' muttered Tityapa in his sleep.

Valerka quickly and dextrously built his little house, and ducked under the canopy.

'OK. Sleep,' whispered Igor guiltily. He hesitated for a moment, then tiptoed out of the dorm, noiselessly closing the door behind him.

Valerka lay there, resignedly giving his attention to the living silence, filled with shadowy rustling, the breathing of the boys and the creaking of the old wooden house. The window showed as an illuminated blue square on his sheet. The mosquitoes started up their singing. The summer night was warm and serene, but somewhere in it, evil was lurking. How could Lyova be a vampire? He was just a regular schoolboy, a pioneer, an athlete. He had a dad and a mum. A football coach. A class teacher. Vampirism, so monstrous in its abnormality, simply did not have a place in normal life. There was no war raging around; these were not the times of knights and witches. And there was no God. Where had this devil come from?

On the other side of the canopy, over by the window, bunk springs creaked and bare feet slap-slapped. Someone had got out of bed. *It's not Lyova!* Chilled to numbness, Valerka tried to convince himself.

A dark silhouette the other side of the sheet obscured the blue square of the window.

'Lagunov!' Valerka heard Lyova's voice. 'Lagunov!'

Valerka clamped his mouth shut. *Now he's going to tell me it'll be better for me.*

'It'll be better for you,' whispered Lyova's voice insinuatingly. 'It makes it better for everyone. Really, Lagunov. Invite me in.'

Valerka could feel the answer bursting out of him. *Come in!* Just one moment of terror and he would never be afraid again, never be tormented. It would be like diving into cold water:

splash! and then it was all right. But no, he must not. There were things to which you must not agree.

'You'll come to want it yourself, Lagunov,' promised Lyova, his voice sepulchral.

The dark silhouette moved away, and it was as if warm air rushed under the canopy into the little house. The bare feet slapped across the room, then bare knees knocked against the floor, there was a rustle of cloth being turned back, and a revolting slobbering.

CHAPTER 9

FOOTBALL WITH VAMPIRES

The boys waited for the start of the game as if waiting for the bell for class – with morose reluctance. Tsybastysh was chasing around with the ball. Lyova was using a stick to mark out the lines of the playing area on the churned-up dirt of the pitch. Tityapkin was plainly sick and tired of football.

'Why are you wearing a pioneer neckerchief like a dipstick?' Tityapa started niggling at Lyova.

'You should be the one running with the flag,' came in Gelbich, supporting Tityapa.

'Nah, 'scool,' said Gurka, boredom enlivening him. 'You can poke the flag like a spear. Guys, let's get the flags!'

'I'm the captain. I must catch the eye,' said Lyova patiently.

'Catch my bollocks,' retorted Tityapa, not letting up. 'Who doesn't know you're the captain?'

'Yes but in war does a commander take off his stripes?' asked Lyova rhetorically. 'Guryanych, do your laces properly. You're in goal.'

Gurka hunkered down to sort out his trainer lace and immediately got such a kick from Gorokhov that he almost fell over.

'You what, you freak?' he howled indignantly, jumping up.

'Law of the mountains,' whooped Gorokhov in reply. 'Bend over, you get booted!'

'I was squatting down, not bending over. Give me your arse, I'll boot you back!'

'Guryanov, as you were!' commanded Lyova in a military manner, and Gurka, always irrepressible, for some reason did as he was told.

Valerka recalled that the previous night Lyova's bare knees had knocked against the floor somewhere in the part of the dorm where Guryanov had his bunk.

Valerka thought that what Lyova had said about war was completely right. At night, in order to get to sleep in the same room as a vampire, Valerka tried to convince himself that he was, as it were, at the front, in a dugout into which at any moment a bomb or shell might fall or the enemy burst in with guns or grenades. But he still had to sleep, even if with one eye open.

'We're training without warming up, and that's not right,' said Lyova, sounding concerned and looking up at the sky like a farmer in a sown field. 'At least it's not hot or cold today.'

Gor-Sanych was smoking, away from the pitch. Valerka loitered resignedly on the bench, not knowing what to do with himself. He had been condemned to the collective by the court of his comrades.

Staring gloomily at Lyova, Valerka thought that no one would believe Lyova was a vampire. Valerka's own doubts had been dispelled during the night. Perhaps vampirism was an illness of some kind? Psychos and lunatics of all kinds abounded. Or perhaps it was a secret, black side of the ordinary world? The side where Escaped Convicts and cannibals and zombies and witches and wizards lived. Normal people were safeguarded from the black side by doctors and militiamen.

Meanwhile, Lyova set about preparing the players with a pep talk.

'I'm giving everyone a task. Goals are not important. Learn how to go round your opponent and make long passes. Pay special attention to corners. Your legs need to work. Technique, I mean; no physics.'

Igor was casting sidelong glances at Valerka. Valerka did not seem to notice him, and this was making Igor feel awkward. If Valerka had been telling a pack of made-up stories the previous night, then today shame would prompt him to avoid the young leader. Valerka was not avoiding Igor. He was simply holding himself aloof, as if bitterly disappointed. Igor did not like it. The tension was unpleasant and needed to be defused. Igor tossed aside his cigarette butt, walked over to Valerka, and lowered himself down next to him on the bench.

'How did you sleep?'

'Fine,' answered Valerka, not looking at Igor.

'I want to talk about yesterday. Do you mind?'

Valerka looked at the field and the players, and said nothing.

The boys were running back and forth, now bunching into a yelling mob, now scattering. The ball zigzagged across the ground or flew straight up in the air. To begin with, no one was particularly keen to immerse themselves in the football, but very gradually, all were drawn in and got properly worked up. Even Yurik Tonkikh, sports hater par excellence, was chasing the boys like a puppy after a pack of big dogs, and passionately shouting something.

'Mukhin, don't lose your position! Makerov, speed up, switch flanks!' Lyova was dashing down the pitch issuing orders to his own team and the other. 'Domrachev, bundle him off the ball! Gorokhov, make yourself available! Gelbich, take the corner! Carry it forward, don't lob it, Podkorytov! Tityapa, send him the wrong way!'

Surprisingly, Lyova succeeded in running a real game. The ball did not fly off into the bushes, the boys did not grapple with one another, and battle raged royally on one side of the pitch and then the other, like in real football on the telly.

'Don't toe-poke! Use your ankle!' panted Lyova, advising Slavik Mukhin.

'I totally did the splits!' replied Slavik ecstatically. 'Practically ripped myself open to the belly button.'

Igor Alexandrovich distracted Valerka from watching. Awkwardly, he tried to explain himself.

'You understand why can't I believe...' he began. 'A vampire doesn't just drink blood... It exists according to certain rules. And Lyova doesn't obey them. I mean, for example, a vampire is a dead person. But Lyova looks ... you know ... alive.'

Indeed, Lyova looked nothing like a dead man. He was dashing around the football field, his red neckerchief dangling from his neck, its tails flapping. A fresh abrasion on his knee was darkening. Valerka wondered whose blood was flowing out of him: his own, or the blood he had drunk? If only a doctor could take it for analysis.

Valerka did not argue, and that encouraged Igor.

'Another thing. Vampires can't tolerate sunlight,' Igor continued. 'The theory is they sleep in their coffins during the day, and wake up after sunset. Haul them out into the light and they'll burn up or crumble to ash.'

Glowing white clouds hung in the sky, haphazard, like the surviving pieces at the end of a chess game. The sun alternated, coming out and going in, and Lyova paid it not the slightest attention.

After the next goal, Lyova gathered the boys in the middle of the pitch.

'I'll tell you what,' he said thoughtfully, wiping the straggling blond hair from his wet forehead. 'Tsybastysh is king of the feints.'

Lyokha Tsybastov immediately assumed a look of contemptuous arrogance.

'We need to use him to practice how to get round a player. He'll try and confuse you, and you'll be like a mirror. You have to move towards his weak leg.'

The boys looked appraisingly at Tsybastysh's dirty tracksuit trousers, comparing his legs.

'How do you do that? The best way is to kick the ball to one side of the opponent and go round him on the other. But there has to be space there that you can operate in.'

'Bollocks to you lot getting round me,' promised Tsybastysh self-confidently.

'This is all rubbish,' said Gelbich, irritatedly rejecting Lyova's theory.

He had his arm cocked and was trying to lick a fresh bruise on his elbow. He resembled a vampire so hungry it was drinking its own blood.

'If you're going to go round a player, you need to work on your dribbling,' continued Lyova, ignoring Gelbich's scepticism. 'Learn three rules: change of direction, change of rhythm, strike in three phases. Our biggest problem on the pitch is tit … tot …'

Tityapkin immediately clenched his fists. From 'tit' to 'Titka' was a very short journey. And it was true: Tityapkin really was getting in everyone's way. He ran forward, pushing, kicking his opponents and his own teammates.

Lyova finally finished his word. 'Total lack of system,' he said.

But Tityapa had started up and was incapable of putting his foot on the brake.

'You're the biggest problem on the pitch!' he shouted. 'You and your cock and balls system!'

Tityapkin pushed Tsybastysh away and marched off resentfully.

Gelbich followed him with a glance, then turned back to Lyova.

'The only thing you know is how to torture people, Khlopov! You've already lost one. Jerk off and dribble on yourself. I'm out of here as well.'

Valerka watched as Gelbich followed after Tityapych.

'When it comes down to it,' said Igor from beside him, 'vampirism is transmitted like an infection. A vampire drinks blood from its victim, the victim dies and then rises from the dead, also as a vampire. The number of vampires has to go up. A vampire arrives and everyone else turns into a vampire as well. One today, two tomorrow, four the day after that, then eight, and so on. Geometric progression. But the other boys in your dorm aren't vampires, are they? It's not like they get up at night with Lyova.'

Consideration of geometric progression had always been Igor's main argument against vampires. If even one vampire actually existed, vampires would pretty quickly take over the world, and then die out from lack of victims. Elementary logic. Of course, counterarguments were available. Take the plague. In the Middle Ages there was no known cure for it. Plague victims died within a few days. The plague wiped out whole cities at enormous speed. There was no escape. Even so, contrary to obvious logic, humanity did not disappear, destroyed by the plague. And the plague virus somehow survived, even though it killed its host. The devil could rationalise how epidemics worked. For the pioneer Lagunov, Igor had enough arguments.

Igor did not want to destroy Valerka's picture of the world. Nor did he want to make excuses for his own disbelief. He hoped that Valerka would come to a common sense view himself, and then all his wrong-headed ideas about life would dissolve of their own accord. Notions of vampires and notions of friends who were traitors.

'Have I convinced you?' asked Igor cautiously.

'No,' answered Valerka calmly and firmly.

CHAPTER 10

MAKE-BELIEVE

Valerka came across Anastasiika on Pioneer Avenue. The pavement was marked out in chalk for hopscotch, and Anastasiika was jumping around the squares backwards on one leg, holding the other leg with her hand. From time to time she would freeze in bizarre poses. She was alone, and doing it entirely to amuse herself.

'Lagunov, stop!' she called out. 'Where are you going?'

'Nowhere,' retorted Valerka, scowling.

'You'll be my witness that I got all the way. Swear on a dead cat.'

He really did not need to get involved with a traitor like her, but Valerka still liked Anastasiika, even after she had betrayed him.

'*The cat's a goner, its tail's come off. Cheat and the tail you'll have to scoff,*' said Valerka.

Anastasiika began to jump again, providing a running commentary on the hopscotch squares.

'*One – butter a bun. Three – mop up pee. Five – add spit and chive. Eight – chuck it over the gate. Ten – make a little house!*'

Valerka was enjoying looking at Anastasiika, so nimble and beautiful.

'Your jumping is odd,' he remarked.

'We're having a competition,' explained Anastasiika, turning round. 'I've already jumped 'nursery', 'school', and 'hospital', and now I'm doing 'canteen'. If anyone asks you, you have to do this' – Anastasiika showed him crossed fingers – 'and tell the truth about me. And if you don't tell the truth, you'll die in your sleep.'

'Because of hopscotch?' Valerka was doubtful.

'There was a girl in our yard who always lied to everyone and then she broke her leg. Anyone'll tell you it's true. Her imp punished her.'

'What imp?' asked Valerka, surprised.

'Don't you have a single girlfriend, Lagunov?' asked Anastasiika, surprised in her turn.

Valerka snorted. Stupid question. How could he be friends with a girl?

'Every young lady has her own imp,' Anastasiika informed him importantly. 'You can check. Do you have a sister, any girl relatives, even a third cousin?'

'I got a normal sister.'

'Get her to write on a piece of paper: "I'm the lady of the house!" and put it under the door mat at the entrance to the block. In the morning there'll be another piece of paper and it'll say, "No, I'm the master of the house!" It's the imp'll write that.'

Valerka thought. His little sister Lyuska had finished her first year at school. She had not got as far as being a young lady yet, far less the lady of the house, and she wrote in squiggly letters and made mistakes. But having a go at teasing her imp was a must.

'What about you, though … aren't you afraid your imp'll punish you?' asked Valerka, hinting at Anastasiika's treachery of the day before. 'You'll die in your sleep and that'll be that.'

'I'm immortal,' said Anastasiika confidently. 'My name comes from the word "anaesthetic". They give anaesthetic to everyone in hospital so they don't die.'

She pulled a colourful bag out of the bushes and handed it to Valerka.

'Carry this. We're going to the same place.'

'Where?' asked Valerka, taking the bag. For some reason he found it very easy to submit to Anastasiika.

'Where we have to. How do you do at school at maths and Russian?'

Mathematics and the Russian language were his hardest subjects.

'Four.'

'I had you down as a two. I'm straight fives. I'll get a gold medal.'[10]

'You don't how the fifth year'll go yet,' objected Valerka.

'Who needs to know, knows. Why don't you come to circle any more?'

'I don't want to sing stupid songs like "Chunga-Changa".'

'Nor do I, but I do.' Anastasiika shrugged. 'You have to do silly things with someone, then they stop seeming silly.'

Valerka inwardly agreed. Left to himself, he would have considered going for a walk with Anastasiika a pointless exercise, but now he was enjoying it.

'Are you inviting me to the circle?' he asked cautiously.

Anastasiika neatly changed the subject. 'Who do you like more – Irina or Veronika?'

She was referring to the young leaders.

'No one,' admitted Valerka. 'Veronika's mean and Irina's like at school.'

'Well, I like Igor Alexandrovich the best. He has a moustache like this' – Anastasiika put her palms to her mouth, fingers curled – 'like a toothbrush. He's in love with Veronika. If they get married, their children will look like Frenchmen. French people are beautiful, Germans are frightful, and Chinese are identical.'

Valerka could not keep up with Anastasiika's rapid changes of tack.

'Guess this riddle,' she suggested. 'How many Chinese people does it take to change a light bulb?'

'Er … er … I give up,' conceded Valerka, lost. He had not heard that one before.

'Five,' said Anastasiika firmly and fell silent.

'Why five?' asked Valerka timidly.

'One to hold the lamp and four to turn the table it's standing on. Now you give me one.'

Valerka recalled another riddle about the Chinese.

'How many Chinese people does it take to put in a window frame?'

....

[10]   The reference is to the marking system in Soviet and Russian schools, in which 1 is the lowest and 5 the highest.

'How many? Get on and tell me, you idiot.'

'Loads. A million. All of them. One to hold the frame and the rest to move the house.'

The sun was burning over Pioneer Avenue, and the acacia bushes, full of chirping birds, resembled solar batteries. Invisible sparks crackled in the air.

Where the territory of the fifth and sixth brigades met there was an old plank gazebo under the pines, with a hipped board roof and benches. The young leaders usually sat in it to watch the pioneers tidying up their plots. Now the gazebo was empty. Anastasiika led Valerka to it.

'This is an enchanted place,' she said, her voice charged with significance.

'Wishes come true here?' guessed Valerka.

'Well, not wishes… If you stay here, everything will come out just right. But first you have to give the gnome a present. There's a gnome living under the floor.'

Anastasiika took her bag from Valerka and fished out of it a fat exercise book with a decorated cover. From inside the book's flap, she pulled a rolled up sweet wrapper.

'Yes, but I don't have a present,' said Valerka sorrowfully.

Anastasiika hesitated.

'OK,' she agreed, handing over the wrapper. 'It can be a present from you. I gave the gnome something gold just yesterday. Push it into the floor.'

They climbed the two steps into the gazebo, which the toddler brigades had left smelling of apples and caramel. Valerka looked around and then bent down and dropped the wrapper into a crack between the boards.

'Now we have to wait,' said Anastasiika. She sat down on one of the benches.

Valerka sat down too, and Anastasiika plunked the exercise book into his lap.

'Fill it out,' she commanded carelessly, and reached into her bag for a pen.

Valerka opened the exercise book – and his stomach caught fire and his cheeks flooded red. It was Anastasiika's secret diary – a book cherished by any girl. Girls let only their best girlfriends and the most exceptional boys anywhere near it. Since Valerka could not be considered exceptional, Anastasiika's action signified deep affection.

The first page boasted an advisory notice: *Please help this book stay clean, leave all the pages in, and, friends, don't write here anything mean!* Then came a section with wishes for Anastasiika. All of them were extravagantly done in thick, brightly-coloured felt-tip pens: flowers, cats, butterflies, princesses, birds, and various patterns. Valerka, worried, read: *Kitty put her paw in the blue ink and wrote Nastya be happy in everyfink!*; *I'm not an artist, I'm not a poet, I'm twelve years old and don't I know it*; *Love is happiness and happiness glass, it's ever so easy to break a glass vase!*; *Remember my words, remember my rhyme: don't fall in love with two at one time!*; *A girl can smile, you might not love her, but know this!!! If laughing at her is your style, she'll have revenge, so you take cover!*; *Don't fall in love with a fair-haired boy, a fair-haired boy won't give you joy, his heart is cold, his blood is cold, he'll break your heart before you're old!* Valerka felt that he was looking into some part of Anastasiika that was very private, into her soul, although, of course, the wishes had been written by other girls.

One page was folded diagonally in half, and on the flap it said: *Secret! Do not open!* Valerka glanced sideways at Anastasiika. Anastasiika was looking somewhere else, pretending not to be interested. Valerka unfolded the page. On it was a picture of a pig, underneath which was a message: *Well you're a total pig, that's clear! I told you not to peek in here!!!*

Then there were pages and pages with lipstick kisses to the book's owner from her girlfriends. Then began the questionnaire that Valerka was supposed to fill out. 'What's your name?' 'What's your favourite season, flower, holiday, girl's name, game, film, animal, artist?' 'Why do people kiss?' 'What is true love?' 'What will you be when you grow up?' 'Write something in French!' Valerka ran his eye over the previous answers. To the very personal questions, the respondents had all replied identically: *I'm not telling!* Who the girls and boys in the secret diary were, Valerka did not know. There was no one from his brigade in Anastasiika's album.

Valerka realised that Anastasiika had included him in the circle of her closest friends. He recalled her betrayal of the day before, and became bitter.

'Why did you snitch on me yesterday?' he asked darkly.

'Are you an idiot?' Anastasiika was genuinely surprised. 'That's what you're supposed to do. You what, you're offended? You a little boy, huh? It's all like make-believe. All those pioneer meetings, flags, stars, neckerchiefs – they're all make-believe!'

'Make-believe?' Valerka was borderline angry. 'And the gnomes and imps and secret diaries are for real, right?'

'Of course they're for real,' said Anastasiika with conviction.

CHAPTER 11

THE WORKER AND COLLECTIVE FARM GIRL

'We can't sit on the upper deck, we'll be spotted,' said Igor. 'We'll have to sit in the saloon. But it's how to get in there.'

Getting in would be difficult. The captain of a small motorboat such as a Moskvich river bus would lock it up like a car when he left.

'I've already thought that one out.' Dimon Malosolov chuckled, delighted at his own cunning. 'I dropped a word in Palych's ear that the pioneers had in mind to get onto the boat at night, like, you know, need to keep an eye. He's given me the key.'

Dimon jingled a weighty bunch of keys on his finger.

'Meaning I'll be with Irishka, you'll be on your own if your old girl can't make it, and the doctor and Lenka – that makes five of us.'

The enterprising Dimon had devised a brilliant plan to seduce Irina: a banquet on board ship. While the doughty captain Kapustin was ashore in the camp accommodation, resting exhausted in the arms of the food block supremo, Dimon would gather together a happy band on the river bus. Everyone would have a drink and unwind. Then the superfluous among them would depart, leaving Dimon alone with Irina, and the seafarer would possess the islander.

Igor readily agreed to help Dimon. Since Irina and Veronika shared a room, Veronika would have to keep an eye on her brigade whether she wanted to or not while Irina feasted on the boat, and these days, Igor was bored without Veronika. Veronika already occupied all his thoughts.

'Dimon, what the hell do you need the doctor for?' asked Igor.

It turned out that Dimon had foreseen a possible variation.

'I only had enough loot for a couple of bottles of wine and vodka. If Irishka's a no-go, I'll head off to the doctor's for a refill. He's got booze.'

'What if the doctor and Lenka want to be on their own?'

The doctor was a difficult old devil, and Dimon had invited Lenka as a lure.

'I'll send that cretin packing,' promised Dimon confidently.

Plotkin seethed quietly when he found out that Igor was going out again.

'Your dates are messing with the normal regime,' he said, teeth gritted. 'It's time you stopped. You're at work, not in a rest home.'

'I can't say no today,' replied Igor, concerned. 'Sorry. Tonight we're on the razzle, booze and all, and that's sacred.'

The fading glow of sunset had washed the river bus flesh pink. The windows of the little boat were aflame, burning fiercely, mute and blind as if in the heat of passion. The water lapped quietly, smacking gently against the hull. Seagulls wheeled over the Volga.

Igor stepped off the slatted pier on to the metal deck of the boat, flipping closed the little gate in the railing behind him. Dimon had set up the get-together in the fore saloon, which was one third the size of the aft saloon and therefore cosier. The way down was inside a dark metal grotto formed by the wings of the superstructure and the rounded bulge of the wheelhouse, which overhung the stairs. From the outside, this bulge, decorated with a five-pointed star, reminded Igor of a human nose. Above it, the eyes gleamed sternly – the windows of the captain's wheelhouse.

Dimon had opened the door to the cabin wide and considerately fixed it to the wall with a piece of wire. Dimon had, truth to tell, pulled out all the stops. He had brought slatted crates over from the food block and constructed a table between two rows of sofas. Adding a touch of culture, he had spread the table with newspapers. In the canteen he had dug up glasses and aluminium forks. Enamelled plates of squash paste and homemade lecsó awaited the guests.

A paraffin candle in a mackerel tin stood ready for darkness.

Dimon had already uncorked one bottle and was pouring port. The doctor, Valentin Sergeyevich, was fiddling with the foil cap on the vodka. Irina and Lena were waiting. The low saloon looked like a suburban train carriage, except that there was no jolting and no rattling of the wheels. The tightly sealed double-glazed windows let in no noise from outside.

Dimon was holding forth. 'Here's one,' he said cheerfully. 'A girl says to her bloke: "I'm leaving you! You're always wittering on about how I'm fat." The bloke's, like, "Come on, what about our kids?" The girl doesn't get it. "What kids?" The bloke's like, "Well, you're pregnant."'

The willowy Lena giggled, while the plump Irina pursed her lips.

Dimon was feeling irresistible.

'Here's another one,' he said, carrying on without a pause. 'A frog's swimming by the bank, thrashing its legs. A hare comes up and says, "Frog, is the water warm?" The frog's like, "For information, I'm here as a woman, not a thermometer."'

'Dimon was the sharpest wit in our class,' said Igor, taking a seat. 'He once put dog poo in a flask for our chemistry mistress.'

Dimon burst into happy laughter.

'Let's have a toast,' said Irina, interrupting Dimon and giving Igor a flash of her glasses.

'To the girls!' announced Dimon generously, raising his glass.

Lenochka's eyes darted round; she was trying to decide who to set a course for. Igor or the doctor? Igor was cheerful, the doctor somewhat gloomy. On the other hand, Igor was a mere student of philology, no more, while the doctor was older and already had a profession. There was a lot more advantage in having a doctor as a husband than a philologist – although it was a little early to be thinking about marriage. But considering how things might pan out was always useful.

'This is the second shift we've worked together, and we're still very formal.' Lenochka smiled at Valentin Sergeyevich. 'Let's try to relax. I'm Lena.'

'Valya,' said Dr Nosatov sourly.

He clearly had no interest in being with the others. *Why did he come?* wondered Igor.

'Here's another one,' said Dimon. 'A bloke and a girl lying in bed. Midnight. The guy says: "Irishka, can I?"'

'Choose your names carefully,' warned Irina, a note of studied threat in her voice.

'Ah, come on, no harm in it.' Dimon waved dismissively and moved closer to Irina. 'Anyway. Two in the morning. The guy's like, "Irishka, can I?" She doesn't say a word. Five in the morning. He's like, "Irishka, can I?" She says, "Yeah, OK, you can take a break now."'

Dimon secretly pinched Irina.

'You looking for a slap?'

'What's up with you?' Dimon shot her a grin. 'You're sounding like my wife.'

'You're married?!' Irina was astonished.

'On the way to,' Dimon assured her fervently.

Irina blushed with annoyance and pleasure.

'Grooms like you are ten a penny around here.'

Igor realised that the worker's spirit of Dimon Malosolov was irresistibly drawn to the collective farm flesh of Irina Kopylova. And however strange it might seem, there was indeed something very sensual about Irina. A natural excess of ripeness. Igor preferred a mysterious refinement, of the kind he found in Veronika. Igor recalled Veronika suddenly turning him over so that she was on top but then leaning nimbly over him and kissing his lips, as if apologising for taking over the higher place in love. Igor ran his eyes round the little boat's saloon. He wanted to put his head straight through the soldered-up window and rush off to Veronika.

'Have you really cut up corpses?' Lenochka naively asked the doctor.

Valentin Sergeyevich grimaced. 'We won't talk about that.'

'I don't suppose I'm of any interest to you,' said Lenochka, taking offence. 'You must have a lot of young ladies coming to your clinic. You've already seen everything.'

Valentin Sergeyevich sighed wistfully and reached for the vodka.

Beyond the Zhiguli, the sunset burned itself out, darkness fell over the Volga, and the candle was lit in the saloon. Every shining black window showed a reflection of the little flame. Gleams of light splashed across the low ceiling as the river bus swayed slightly on a wave from a distant motor ship, the wave's force already spent.

A tipsy Dimon put his arm round Irina and murmured in her ear. 'Palych retires in two years, he doesn't need a thing, and I know the ship like God, they'll make me captain, no sweat.'

A tipsy Lena, unaware of the futility of her efforts, went on flirting with the doctor, who was drinking himself deeper and deeper into melancholy. It appeared that the onrushing darkness was scaring him like the very devil, making him hang around in a group where he had nothing to do and nothing to say.

'I've had this kind of cough for two days,' complained Lena affectedly. 'In the sick bay do you have aspirin? Shall we go to your place there?'

'We do... No... You can't go there...' blathered Valentin Sergeyevich. 'I have a sick child on the ward... We'd be better off having a smoke.'

'I'm with you!' said Lena, seizing the moment.

Valentin Sergeyevich and Lena squeezed between the tables and couches, and headed for the stairs to the deck. Irina watched them go.

'Why'd you fluff your chance with Lena?' she asked Igor with a sneer. 'The girl's been snatched from under the booby's nose.'

'Igoryokha's not a booby,' guffawed Dimon. 'What's he want Lenka for? He's already splashing himself doing the pokey-pokey with Veronichka!'

Igor nearly exploded in annoyance. He had asked Dimon not to say anything. Shit, this was his own fault. Why the hell had he told this idiot about Veronika?

Irina pulled away from Dimon, looking at Igor with the kind of predatory interest she might reserve for someone she had just found out had a criminal record.

'With Nesvetova?' she repeated, as if she could not believe the enormity of this moral collapse. 'You and Nesvetova?'

'We're not talking about it,' replied Igor, setting up a boundary.

Irina sniggered knowingly.

'OK. Time to go.' She wriggled, freeing herself from Dimon's clutches. Igor's relations with Veronika had served as an instructive reproof to her.

'Where?' wailed Dimon in desperation.

'It's high time,' said Irina firmly. 'Let me go!'

'I'm off too,' said Igor at once.

If Irina was returning to her building, Veronika would be free.

On the upper deck, Dr Nosatov and Lenochka were standing by the railing looking out over the Volga. It was clear from Lenochka that nothing had happened – no cuddling, no kissing. The doctor and the young leader both looked as if they were wondering whether or not to throw themselves overboard. They clearly had completely different reasons for drowning themselves in the Volga, and they would each have drowned individually, without the other's help.

Valentin Sergeyevich was embarrassed to feel a surge of joy when Irina took Lena away.

Nosatov can get drunk with Dimon, thought Igor. *Sour Puss and Chatterbox: two boots of a single pair, both of them left.*

Irina marched resolutely beneath the lights of Pioneer Avenue, supporting a drooping Lenochka under the arm. Night birds chirped in the acacia bushes. Igor followed on behind. Irina led Lenochka to the place where the path branched off towards Building 1, and directed her home. Lenochka forgot to say goodnight to Igor.

Irina turned to Igor. Her glasses glinted under the street lamps.

'Tell Dima not to be offended at me,' demanded Irina. 'He's a nice guy, normal, not like you. But don't let him dream about anything like that. I'm a decent young woman, and there'll be none of that before my husband.'

Igor felt an urge to take off his hat, if he had had one.

'I'll tell him,' he agreed, 'if you tell Veronika to come out.'

'It's already late!' snapped Irina. 'Time to sleep. She won't come out to you.'

'Yes, she will,' countered Igor calmly.

CHAPTER 12

LOTS OF THEM

'Moustachio won't be here tonight, lads,' said Gurka authoritatively. 'He's on the ship boozing with his sailor. The doctor 'n' Fatty are with them too.'

Fatty was Irina Mikhailovna, of course.

'How do you know?' asked Slavik Mukhin, disbelieving.

'I'm a peeping top gun.'

'If the young leaders have done a bunk, we have to toothpaste the girls,' said Gorokhov, becoming agitated. 'You always have to do that at camp. It's the law.'

The boys were on their bunks in their dorm, but no one was sleeping. Beyond the window, the pine trunks were still glowing pink in the lilac twilight, like the cooling incandescent filaments of a light bulb that had just been switched off.

'Better not now. Wait till it's completely dark,' said Tityapa. 'The girls'll have conked out and you can do what you like to them, they won't feel sod all.'

Valerka was silent, thinking: the more commotion, the less fear.

'You don't need to go pasting the girls,' said Lyova suddenly, objecting firmly.

'Why not?' The boys flew up as one.

'It's a breach of discipline.'

'Like bollocks it's a breach of discipline!' Tityapkin sat up and looked at Gurka and Gorokh, demanding support from them. 'No Moustachio and Fatty, no discipline, right? Curly's not our leader.'

Curly was Sasha Plotkin. Plotkin was a young leader of the third brigade, and so was not considered a real commander in the fourth. Nor was that the nub of it. The boys sensed a weak spot in Curly. He was chicken. He was afraid that the pioneers of another brigade would not obey his orders, so he did not try to assume command. If the pioneers violated the regime, the pioneers were to blame, but if the pioneers did not heed a young leader, the leader was to blame. Why should Curly be blamed for other people's pioneers?

'If you don't like it, don't go, Lyovych,' said Gorokhov, summing up. 'But you've got no right to forbid us. Yes?'

Having stood up for their freedom, the boys calmed down.

'The oldies on the last shift said they pasted the girls,' recalled Seryozha Domrachev. 'Only one of them ran out of toothpaste. He like went somewhere and found some like cream from somewhere. They all got into the girls' dorm at night, and this guy daubed his stuff on one of the girls. Her whole face came off in the night, and she didn't even notice. She got up in the morning and was a skull.'

'Holy bollocks!' The boys were horrified.

'Crapola, I wish I could put some of that cream on!' Gurka's excitement was such that he sat down on his bunk, grabbed his pillow, and shoved it on his head as if it were a compress to cool his hot fantasies. 'I'd run round with a skull at night and frighten everybody!'

Gurka pulled his bottom eyelids down with his fingers, stuck out his tongue, and started wheezing.

There's someone here to run about scaring people without you, thought Valerka grimly.

'There's no such thing as that cream,' objected Yurik Tonkikh quietly.

'What do you mean, no such thing?' cavilled Gurka, returning normality of appearance to his mobile face. 'How do you know, you millipede? The smartest brain can pull the chain!'

Slavik Mukhin also decided to share a story from life.

'Guys, we had a girl who was told not to take photos of herself with the oldies from year nine because they had red film, but she said red film doesn't exist. Yeah, right, what a nut job. They were all laughing at her afterwards.'

Gurka and Seryozha Domrachev laughed knowingly.

'Red film exists, it's true,' agreed Yurik sadly.

'What kind of film?' Tityapkin wanted to know.

'You take pictures on it as normal, and then…' Slavik lowered his voice, embarrassed, 'and then in the pictures everyone's naked!'

'Wicked!' The boys were delighted.

'Foreigners invented it,' explained Yurik. 'At the Olympics they wanted to take photos like that of our whole team and then spread them about everywhere. But the police took the films out of their cameras.'

Valerka even forgot his fears for a moment, amazed at the perfidy of his enemies and the opportunity to penetrate into the secrets of girls. OK, it was bad, but shit was it cool! If he had film like that, he would have lifted his father's camera without asking and taken a picture of Anastasiika. Of course, he would not have shown it to anyone, but he would have seen everything for himself. Lucky devils, anyone getting hold of that film!

The frantic Gurka was wearing himself out waiting for the fun to begin.

'That's it, it's dark!' he announced and jumped up, hurling aside his blanket.

Exactly the way a hungry person announces 'It's boiling!' and scoops a ladle of uncooked porridge from the pot.

Lyova, lying in his bed, lifted himself up on his elbow.

'Don't go!' he repeated, looking round the dorm.

His quiet, confident voice held such a note of oppressive authority that Valerka felt as if the people and things around him had become twice as heavy. Still, it was no surprise that Tityapa and Gorokh followed Gurka in leaping up. It had long been clear that they were their own mob: a mob of wild-eyed psychos. Overcoming resistance, Valerka also sat down and lowered his bare feet to the floor.

'Are you coming?' he asked Yurik Tonkikh.

'I'm afraid,' admitted Yurik guiltily. 'If they catch us, we'll be punished.'

For Valerka, however, the society of Lyova was scarier than the reprisals of the young leaders.

'Give me your toothpaste, then.'

Valerka did not currently have any toothpaste of his own.

One by one Valerka, Tityapa, Gurka, and Gorokh slipped out of the dorm into the corridor. In the glow of the street lamps outside the window, the painted timbers and metal knobs on the stands gleamed, and the steps of the wooden staircase leading up to the upper floor, where the girls' dormitories were located, showed a dull white.

'*Darkness is the friend of youth!*' whispered Gorokhov in satisfaction.

'*It's dark – I'm on my way!*' came in Gurka. '*There's a blob of something – hey! Sniff, sniff – smells like shit! Yum, yum, this is it!*'

'Shut up you freaks!' hissed Tityapkin. 'They'll kill us!'

The treads creaked treacherously. The boys froze at every step.

Valerka had rarely visited the top floor. Only when he went up to the storeroom, where the suitcases were kept, or to Gor-Sanych's room. On the first floor everything seemed mysterious, and the boys stole along like partisans in the woods.

'Here's their dorm.' Tityapkin let out a barely audible breath and pointed to the nearest door. 'I'll go in first. Gurepooper next, then Gorokh.'

'I'll get you for Gurepooper!' promised Gurka.

Valerka knew that the dorm Tityapych was heading for was not where Anastasiika was staying; she was in the next, further on.

'I'm going to the next dorm,' Valerka advised the others.

'Shove off then. Be good not to have you with us,' agreed Tityapa readily. 'If the girls wake up, you'll give us all away. They'll recognise you by your glasses.'

'Yeah, right, like no one would ever recognise you,' snapped Valerka.

Tityapkin opened the door a crack, made himself small, and slipped noiselessly into the emptiness of the dorm. Gurka and Gorokhov disappeared after him.

Valerka tiptoed on. Reaching the entrance to Anastasiika's dorm, he stopped, and looked around. The ceiling with its beams, the walls with electric wires strung on isolators, the smooth floor. Deep shadows. The responsive silence of an old wooden house. It was an alien space, one he understood, but unusual, as if he had crawled under a friend's covers. The smells were even different on the girls' floor: milk, toffee, sweet watercolour paint.

Valerka ghosted the door open into the depths beyond it. And over him blew air so sudden and cold it was if a window in the dorm had been thrown wide open onto December. The mercury street lamps illuminated the room in a manner to which Valerka was not accustomed, as a reflection from the wall, like from the white screen in a cinema. Eight beds in two rows stretched out like graves in a snow-covered cemetery. The girls were asleep. Or rather, almost all the girls were asleep – but not all of them.

Masha Styazhkina was sitting in her bed, her head drooping and one arm held out in strange submission. Marinka Lebedeva was standing beside Masha's bed in her panties and T-shirt; standing, slightly bowed, and supporting Masha's suspended arm the way she might support a ladle of water in front of her lips. Marinka was sucking blood. Masha let out a sad sigh, and Marinka gave a dissatisfied shrug and returned her victim's arm to a comfortable position. Valerka saw the glint of two fangs dug into the girl's thin wrist.

Valerka did not even have time to be frightened. He stepped back and pulled the door to, removing the spectacle of the vampire from his sight. For some reason he had only one thought in his head: Gor-Sanych had not been lying! The night Valerka had spotted the vampire on the bench on Pioneer Avenue, Gor-Sanych, smoking on the stoop of their building, had not lied when he said that Lyova had not gone out. Lyova had not gone out. It had been another vampire on the avenue, not Lyova at all. Because at the Storm Petrel Pioneer Camp there were, in truth, a lot of vampires.

PART THREE

THE VAMPIRE CHAIN

*Drops of blood thick and red from the young fighter's breast
ran down to the green, green grass.*
Nikolai Kool, 'Far Away, o'er the River', 1924

CHAPTER I

THE FOURTH IMBECILE

'You blind?'

Venka Gelbich pushed Valerka aside, leaned over, and pulled out a crumpled sweet wrapper from the pile of rubbish. Cheap sweet bars were sometimes given out for afternoon snacks. The wrappers were considered trash in normal life, but in the camp they went up in value. There was a way of folding a wrapper tightly into a triangle to make it into a *butska*.[11] *Butska* fights were held on the steps of the stoop and on the windowsills. Legend had it that on the first day of the shift, Tsybastysh, with nothing more than an unassuming wrapper from a cheap bar, had out-butskaed one fashioned by Vovka Makerov from the luxurious gold of a very much more upmarket sweet. Not that Valerka cared about sweet wrappers just at the moment. Sweet wrappers? They were surrounded by vampires!

In the morning, as usual, the brigade was toiling away at work detail, tidying up their grounds. The boys were using rakes to scrape the ground beneath the pine trees; the girls had taken brooms and were shuffling along the paths around the building. No one knew where so much rubbish had come from in one day. Each squad had its own pile,

---

[11]   'Butska' was the name given by children to a sweet wrapper tightly rolled into a rectangle or triangle. The word is derived from the verb 'butskat', meaning to rap your fingernail loudly on something or to make the sound you get from kicking a tightly-inflated ball.

which was then transferred in buckets to a general pile near Pioneer Avenue. During Quiet Hour, a man on a cart would ride down the alley and take all the piles outside the camp fence.

Whistler and the camp director Kolybalov passed by the fourth brigade. 'Why the long faces?' Whistler shouted cheerfully to the pioneers. 'Come on, buck up! Let's have a competition: the first to collect a hundred cones gets a specially-cooked apple pie! Forward, fighters!'

The pioneers put on a show of smiling at the Senior Pioneer Leader, but no one sped up. Even Rin Khalovna tried to get lost accidentally-on-purpose among the pine trees. Everyone had long ago grown tired of the daily hoo-hah with the rubbish.

Valerka turned his rake this way and that, unwilling, moody. Gelbich approached him.

'Sick to death of combing an elephant,' he said irritably. 'Sick to death of everything here, especially football. I'd like to boot that ball straight at Khlopov's hooter. Look, Lagunov, what clubs did they kick you out of at Company House?'

'Drawing and singing,' answered Valerka, without warmth.

'No, can't draw.' Gelbich sighed heavily. 'Even a swastika comes out wonky. What do they do in singing?'

'Sing.'

'Ah-hah.' Gelbich dithered, glancing this way and that. 'Come with me to Company House, Lagunov, eh? Don't feel like it on my own, and you know what's what there.'

It turned out that the strapping loud mouth Gelbich was capable of being shy.

'I'm not allowed,' Valerka reminded him morosely.

'Bollocks to their blather. We'll ask them. I'll be your security. I'm the flag carrier.'

Valerka thought how easy it was for Gelbich. He was getting out of football. What circle should he sign up for to save himself from vampires?

A cone flew in from somewhere and whacked Gelbich on the back of the head.

'Which of you hooligans did that?' yelled Gelbich at once, whirling round.

Throwing cones was forbidden. Officially, because they could hit you in the eye; in reality, so that you were not distracted from your duties.

'Whoa, whoa!' shouted Igor Sanych threateningly, from somewhere far off.

Valerka took a look at the girls. Marinka Lebedeva was shuffling about with her broom by the steps of the stoop. Marinka was a squad leader and so had put on her red neckerchief. Masha Styazhkina was clumsily trying to shovel rubbish from her squad's heap into a battered bucket. The rubbish would not all go in, and was spilling to one side. Both Masha and Marinka looked perfectly normal: T-shirts, faded tracksuit trousers, scuffed sandals. Masha had pigtails, Marinka a ponytail with a hairpin.

Valerka put his rake down, walked over to Masha, took the shovel from her, filled the bucket himself, and tromped it down with his foot.

'Did you see me last night?' he asked, as if a propos of nothing. 'I came to your dorm to toothpaste you. And I saw you.'

Masha screwed up her eyes dubiously. Or perhaps she was squinting in the sun.

'Don't lie, Lagunov. The toothpasting was the first dorm, not ours. And not you. Those three imbeciles.' Masha nodded at Gurka, Tityapa, and Gorokh.

Gurka, Tityapa, and Gorokh had forgotten about work detail and were fighting one another with their rakes.

An irate Irina Mikhailovna was hurrying over to them.

Valerka looked Masha straight in the eyes.

'I saw Marinka Lebedeva drinking your blood.'

Masha was quiet for a moment, appraising Valerka.

'The fourth imbecile,' she said calmly.

Masha picked up the bucket and headed for the avenue.

Valerka suddenly remembered how he had tried to find out the truth from Slavik Mukhin in much the same way, and Slavik had also thought that Valerka was simply taking the mickey. Valerka silently watched Masha go. He was beginning to think that people bitten by a vampire did not even know about it. As if the vampire were casting a spell on them. Or putting them to sleep, the way doctors put a patient to sleep in order to remove their appendix.

Valerka felt like a spy watching everyone around him. Or a locator searching for an invisible enemy plane in a clear sky. Or a microscope, scrutinising every speck of dust. Valerka tried to identify anything that would somehow give away the vampires and their victims. It was not possible that during the day no evidence remained of the night's terror. The vampires must somehow show themselves in the sunlight. There must be some sign, of some sort, of the nightmare, whereby it would be possible to identify those who drank blood and those whose blood had been drunk. An everyday mosquito bite would make an itchy place itch.

'Mashka!' Marinka Lebedeva suddenly called out angrily from the stoop.

Valerka started. What did Marinka the vampire want?

'You mislaid some rubbish.' Marinka indicated a pine branch with her broom.

Masha returned, and without objecting picked up the dirty dry branch from the path, shoved it into her bucket, and headed back towards the avenue.

It was a trifle, a piece of nonsense… Except that now Valerka was observing his surroundings with the greed and haste with which a thief searches a flat, fearing that the owners will be back any minute. Masha had come back for a twig… Valerka would never have come back. He would have picked up the piece of rubbish on his second pass. But Masha had come back. *I need to go to the mental hospital*, thought Valerka. Perhaps Masha was just an obedient and good girl, and he, Valerka, was contrary, as his mother said, and basically a nut job, and that was the whole reason.

Valerka wandered back towards the boys. Gelbich was waiting for him, still thinking about a circle in which he could hide from football.

'Hey, Lagunov, how do they sing at the circle? All together or does just one person do the singing? What kind of songs? Your own favourites, eh? I like songs about prison.'

'You sing what they say,' grunted Valerka. 'It's not like you're at home, sitting in the kitchen and opening your gob. You can't sing about prison.'

'Pity,' said Gelbich sadly. 'Songs about prison are the truth of life. Not a picnic in the park. Fine. Let's go and tweak Moustachio's moustache.'

Igor was walking aimlessly between the boys with a rake and frowning, making out that he was meticulously controlling the work and its results.

'Gor-Sanych, say we can go to the singing circle instead of football,' said Gelbich, eschewing all niceties. 'I like singing, and I'll keep an eye on him.' Gelbich jabbed a finger at the silent Valerka. 'Pioneer's honour.'

Valerka hid his eyes. He was embarrassed that he had not believed Gor-Sanych's honest answer about Lyova that night. Igor, too, looked away. He felt guilty for having offended Valerka with his disbelief in vampires.

Igor hesitated, then made up his mind. 'Well, all right.'

Gelbich clapped Valerka on the back, like a patron with his charge.

Pioneer's honour. Valerka repeated Gelbich's words to himself. What kind of pioneer was Gelbich? He carried the brigade flag at assembly, but thought prison songs were the truth of life. Gelbich might not be a bad person, but he was a lousy pioneer. What if vampires were as phony as the pioneers? They took a bite and that was that, you walked away; nothing special had happened to you. It was not scary that there were vampires. It was not scary that they bit you. And a vampire was not a dead person who was afraid of the sun. And if you were bitten by a vampire, you did not turn into a vampire yourself; you simply carried on as before: *stick, stick, cucumberene, and look, you've got a human bean.*[12] Everything just as always. No more mobile artillery or Budyonnyites, though there were red flags and bugles. No vampires either, though there were strange people who drank blood by moonlight. Five-pointed red stars no longer meant anything at all, and the night-time blood drinkers these days made no one either warm or cold.

....

[12]   Lines about drawing a human being, from a song in a children's cartoon.

CHAPTER 2

A PIONEER'S DISTANCE

'Salute the Company flag!' commanded Whistler.

Every pioneer in every brigade lined up in Company Court threw up their hands in the pioneer salutation, as if shielding their eyes from the sun.

It was morning, they were still half asleep, and the everyday had not yet had time to capture their attention. So when the flag was hoisted, they all looked only at the flag and were silent, without fidgeting or whispering. The red cloth made its way jerkily up the mast, at the top catching the wind and spreading open like a wing. Igor, meanwhile, was examining the children's faces – simple, good, guileless. The girls, for now, were not ashamed of the freckles the sun had brought out, and the boys had grown shaggy like forest bandits: there was no hairdresser in camp.

Igor thought that an impartial observer might find the ways of the camp strange. This was not a military unit, and the adults and children were not soldiers, yet for some reason they all got up at the crack of dawn, went to Company Court, lined up, raised the flag, and saluted it. What for? Why? No one was forcing them to do it, but it was accepted. 'This is the way we live,' said Igor to himself with a kind of illogical satisfaction at the incomprehensibility of communal life. The incomprehensibility unified them, turning everyone involved into one of their own.

Of course, the reason for Igor's satisfaction was not the rituals of pioneering. The reason was his night-time assignation with

Veronika, when the two of them had gone to the Bishop and bathed in the warm creek, Veronika's supple body glowing green in the water like a mermaid's. And then lying in the soft grass on a standard-issue flannelette bedspread which Veronika had brought from her building, while above them an airliner sailed silently through the constellation of Cassiopeia, its red and blue lights winking. Yes, Igor had fallen in love. He had fallen in love, and Veronika had reciprocated, and now there were no barriers left between them, and for this reason Igor felt somehow firmly rooted, prosperous, furnished with everything he needed for a full existence. A victor's advantage made it possible to see the familiar world as if from outside and to appreciate the strangeness of the way it was ordered. Although this very strangeness was the foundation of prosperity.

At assembly, Whistler had told him to report to her after work detail, and now he was striding along Pioneer Avenue, squinting in the sun. Everything was wonderful. Stirring music was playing through the speakers. The camp was preparing for Parents' Day. Boys from the senior brigades were swishing brooms extravagantly across the asphalt and scraping the rubbish out of the bins. The girls were wiping down the benches, scrubbing off the graffiti and bird droppings. A handsome young man was unscrewing the plexiglass from a stand and pinning up children's drawings. The linen keeper was hauling a pile of clean bedclothes to the sick bay. Cleaning women were going somewhere with mops and buckets. From the food block came the clinking of crockery and the stuttering scolding of Old Nyura. A security guard was leading a horse harnessed to a cart with car wheels. Even Serp Ivanych Iyeronov was pruning the acacia bushes in his little square of garden with large rusty shears. The plank walls and canted roofs of the gingerbread houses were dappled with light and shadow.

In Company House, bustle and commotion reigned supreme. Little girls with silk ribbons in their hands were running back and forth, boys were shifting tables and cupboards with a clatter, someone was straining ineptly to sound a bugle. Igor stopped in the corridor, because in the Flag Room Whistler was arguing with Kolybalov, the camp director. For some reason, Kolybalov had lugged in a hefty chain saw and set it up on Whistler's table.

'You're like a child, Nikolai Petrovich!' raged Whistler. 'What logs for the stove? Do it this evening. To your heart's content!'

'Lights out,' said Kolybalov stubbornly. 'Can't make any noise.'

'You can! Tonight I'm allowing it. I need workers to clean up Concert Clearing. The parents will troop over there and what will they see? Weeds up to their arses. And there's a woman from the city council coming, she's got a daughter in the second brigade.'

'Natalya, I'm in charge here.'

'You, Petrovich, are in charge of reception procedures here, but Parents' Day is my responsibility. Who gets a reprimand if it's a shambles?'

'Me.'

'You my foot. You're about to retire. I'll be checking the situations vacant page. Get out, you're spoiling the view.'

Kolybalov picked up his chainsaw and stumbled out into the corridor, sighing.

Whistler was in jeans and a shirt, and she had wound a kerchief round her head, like a worker in a weaving factory workshop during *subbotnik*.[13]

'Pull the door to,' she said to Igor, coming out from behind her table. 'I need a little talk with you, sweetheart, and I don't want anyone's ears to start burning.'

She perched her mighty backside on the window sill and folded her arms.

'I'm ready,' nodded Igor.

The Senior Pioneer Leader was looking at him searchingly as she might at an artist who had stepped out onto an empty stage to perform. Her look carried a kind of threat.

'Intelligence has informed me that you and Nesvetova have started an affair,' she said at last, coming straight out with it. 'Is it true?'

....

[13]   *Subbotnik* was the name given to unpaid volunteer work carried out in the USSR on Saturdays. The work consisted mostly of cleaning the streets and other community services.

Igor's face flushed. He saw nothing wrong in his relationship with Veronika, but Veronika had wanted to keep it a
secret. Which was understandable. Premarital affairs attract
condemnation. Why would Veronika want that? Igor, though,
had let her down. He had shot his mouth off about Veronika to
Malosolov, Dimon had blabbed to Irina on the river bus, and Irina
had been more than happy to give away someone else's secret to
Whistler. Dimon was an idiot, but Irina was a little bitch.

'It's true,' Igor confirmed with a wry grin.

'What's the smile for?' snapped Whistler, suddenly angry.
'Laughing for no reason means your brain's in silly season.'

'There is a reason,' objected Igor reasonably.

Whistler fixed him with a fierce look.

'Don't try to be smart. Are you even aware that she has a
fiancé?'

Igor felt as if he had been slapped in the face a second time. A
fiancé? Of course Igor realised that Veronika had had someone
before him, but a fiancé? Now? So that was why she was so
keen to keep it secret. Did she really want to hang on to her
fiancé while simply having a summer of fun with Igor? Igor felt
cheated; insulted, even. Whistler observed him silently. Igor ran
his palm across his forehead as if wiping away a clinging cobweb.
No, Veronika was not like that.

'She hasn't told you, then?' Whistler sarcastically sought
clarification.

'I don't care if she has five fiancés,' answered Igor sullenly.

'And do you know who he is?' Mocking him, looking down
on him, Whistler went on with the job of finishing Igor off.
'Sashka Plotkin. Your roommate.'

Igor stared stupidly into the corner at the red company flag.
Shit in a bowl with custard. His self-satisfaction of a moment ago
melted away, leaving no trace. He suddenly felt like someone up
before the dean at university or standing in front of the army
recruiting officer or at a Komsomol meeting – an ordinary little
student, of no significance, a zero with no authority, a little grey
man obliged to carry out orders.

Now he understood why Veronika and Sasha Plotkin were
working in the same brigade. Igor recalled Sasha's jealous boasts

of his secure future: a flat, a wedding, a job. Igor could not promise Veronika anything to compare. But … happiness in life was not a matter of material possessions… Who was he trying to convince? Himself? Veronika had kept quiet about Plotkin, and that was a fact. She did not want to lose her curly-haired Sashenka? More like she did not want to lose her wedding, her job, her flat…? In bed, Plotkin could be replaced by someone else. By him, for example: Igor Korzukhin.

'I can guess what part of herself Nesvetova is thinking with,' said Whistler. 'But you must have a brain; you're a man. Who have you trained your sights on, big boy?'

'Who?' asked Igor, uncomprehending.

'Plotkin's father is on the Regional Committee. Head of capital construction. His mother's a deputy head in the Local Education Authority. You offend their son and they'll turn you into mincemeat. You'll be thrown out of college and land with a wallop in the army.'

Igor looked sullenly at Whistler. A grim defiance was building up inside him. Why was the Senior Pioneer Leader trying to scare him, as if he were a child? What did she think he was – a simpleton? Even if he was being used and taken for a ride, he did not need Whistler's concern. He would not march to the pioneer drum.

'What's it to you?' he growled.

Whistler jumped down from the window sill. 'I don't want people calling my camp a brothel, like I'm sponsoring sleeping around here,' she said. 'Who'll be punished if Plotkin's sent into a dizzy spin? Not Plotkin. And not you – you'll be pulling on your boots by autumn. Me. I'll be punished. I'm the one who works for the local authority, not you. And I don't need a dressing down from my boss.'

Of course, Whistler was trying to save her own skin. She did not care about Sasha Plotkin's feelings, or Veronika's wiles, or what happened to Igor.

'I'll decide what I do,' said Igor sullenly.

Whistler pulled a contemptuous face.

'Don't jerk around, Korzukhin,' she warned. 'I can fail your whole practical myself and I'll write a report to the dean about your dilly-dallying and you'll be out of that school before you can say boo, forget the City Executive Committee!'

This was becoming intolerable. Conflict with Sasha Plotkin's family was one thing: at least the Plotkins had a right to complain. Whistler's servile meanness was something else altogether. The Plotkins, if they were decent people, might not seek retribution, but Whistler would not die wondering – she would be off shitting all over him in a pre-emptive strike.

'Don't try and scare me, Natalya Borisovna. There are ways to deal with you, too,' said Igor, restraining his anger. 'I'm not your serf.'

Whistler snorted, turned away, and went to her chair at the table.

'Well, the man says he's not a serf,' she said carelessly. 'Your immoral behaviour is still your misconduct. I do not intend to tolerate it. I'll give you one last chance to put things right quietly: wrap it up with Nesvetova before Plotkin gets wind of it. Kopylova will keep her mouth shut, I'll take care of that. And you keep a pioneer's distance from Nesvetova. Put it away and look out for yourself. You've had the moon but you still want the stars. Dismissed, Young Leader.'

CHAPTER 3

'CROCODILE MUG'

Valerka and Gelbich arrived at Company – Company House. Music was playing. From the open windows came the clatter of furniture and irritated voices: Company House was being rocked by a big clean-up. The circle members, predominantly girls, crowded in front of the stoop and in the little garden, waiting out the disaster.

'Balls. This always happens,' grumbled Gelbich. 'You start doing something good and instant bollocks breaks out.'

Valerka went over to Albert, the handsome, cultured artist from the art circle. Albert was all dressed up in a white shirt and scarlet neckerchief, and was talking politely to a lad in a cap with a star on it. Valerka remembered the boy: Pavlik, who had drawn the wickedly good tank.

'Will there be classes today?' asked Valerka.

'Yes, but a little later,' replied Albert. 'You've decided to come back?'

'Not to you,' snapped Valerka.

He swivelled his head, looking for Anastasiika. Anastasiika was sitting on a bench; she had put her coloured bag down beside her and was leafing through a songbook. Valerka would have sat down next to her, but Gelbich was in the way, demanding empathy.

'My mother once sent me to the shop for milk but it was closed for lunch,' he was saying. 'I was thinking, like, I'll drop in on one of the lads for a bit, he promised me tyre valves for my bike, so I went, and got hit by a car!'

Inevitably, the scamp Zhanka Shalayeva spotted Valerka and Gelbich. She was fed up of chatting with her stupid and inseparable Lyolik.

'A-a-a, Vasya,' she cried, smiling happily at Valerka as she might at an old friend. She held out her hand. 'Give me five.'

'I'm not Vasya!' hissed Valerka through gritted teeth, and refused the handshake.

'Zhanka said Vasya, so you'll be Vasya,' said Lyolik threateningly.

'Push off, Marusya,' growled Valerka.

'You getting cute, Four Eyes?' said Lyolik, tensing up.

'He's not Vasya,' Gelbich interjected, honouring the debt of friendship, and Valerka felt a rush of warmth towards him. 'You need your ears cleaned out?'

Lyolik was stunned, unaccustomed to such impertinence, but the tall, unsteady Gelbich was obviously not a pussy cat from music school.

'And who are you?' asked Zhanka, interested.

Gelbich grinned widely and scrutinised Zhanka with pleasure. 'I've come to sign up for singing.'

'You what, you can sing?' Zhanka was surprised. 'Sing.'

'Sing what?' Gelbich readily yielded.

'"Chunga-Changa".'

Gelbich cleared his throat, sucked air into his chest, and suddenly broke out in an unusual, deep, strong voice:

'*Chunga-Changa, blue skies above the ground, Chunga-Changa, summer all year round!*'

Valerka looked at Gelbich's mouth in disbelief, mystified as to how such abilities could find a place there. Zhanka, however, hummed and hawed, not ready to relent.

'OK, but no one signs up without a password.'

'What's the password?'

Zhanka hesitated, weighing her decision. Finally, she said severely, 'Canada.'

Valerka was surprised: Gelbich and Zhanka Shalayeva clearly liked each other. Zhanka was backing off, and he could stop worrying about Gelbich now. Valerka moved casually towards Anastasiika and lowered himself next to her on the bench. Anastasiika paid no attention to him.

'Hi,' said Valerka. 'What song are you learning?'

'I know them all by heart.'

'So what are you preparing for the show?' said Valerka, not letting up. '"Eaglets"?'

He was remembering that Anastasiika had wanted to sing a solo in 'Eaglets', but Zhanka wanted to sing 'Chunga-Changa', which you could dance to.

'Obviously "Chunga-Changa",' Anastasiika informed him wearily.

Valerka nodded sympathetically. Teachers such as Veronika Genrikhovna for some reason always supported bad kids like Zhanka: defended them in front of other teachers, appointed them as commanders at children's sports days or scrap metal collection, awarded them certificates for achievements in their labour – the only thing there was to give them an award for. It would seem that if a teacher – or a young leader; it was not important – felt like an outsider in her collective, she singled out children who were likewise outsiders, most often, alas, hoodlums. And Grekhovna was different from the other female young leaders: she wore earrings, she did not dish out punishments for everything under the sun, she did not torment them with discipline. Gor-Sanych was also different from San-Kolaich, his roommate, or the PE teacher Ruslan. That, Valerka thought, was why Gor-Sanych had fallen in love with Grekhovna.

'Veronika does not understand the art of music,' said Anastasiika haughtily. 'She shouldn't be running more than a village club.'

Meanwhile, Gelbich was getting to know Zhanka. Zhanka was questioning him closely.

'Where do you live?' she asked.

'Hunker,' answered Gelbich proudly.

'Hunker' was what people called the village of One Hundred And Sixteenth Kilometre. No one knew where the one hundred and sixteenth kilometre was counted from. The hooligans from underprivileged 'Hunker' were renowned for their bravery and valour.

'Who do you know?'

'I know Sika. Box. Ballon.'

'You know Beklya?'

'My mate.'

Zhanka smiled. Gelbich's answers satisfied her completely, and Gelbich himself was all right – tall, normal. Test passed.

'Give me your neckerchief,' conceded Zhanka. 'I'll sign it for you.'

If a girl wrote something on a boy's pioneer neckerchief, it signified a deep liking. Gelbich's problem was that he did not have his neckerchief with him. He spun frantically on the spot, saw Albert, and rushed towards him.

'Look, give me your neckerchief!' he begged, grabbing Albert's hand. 'I've got one, only it's back in the building. I'll bring you mine this evening.'

A discomposed Albert attempted to detach Gelbich's hand.

'Uh … uh … no, no! I … uh … uh … I can't!'

'Word of honour I'll bring it!' Gelbich fervently tried to persuade him. 'The situation's desperate, man.'

'A neckerchief is a symbol!' Albert helplessly tried to resist, shaking his rich and well-kept hair.

'I'll iron it and bring it!' Gelbich insisted.

Albert grew angry. 'Stop it!' he said. 'Leave me alone!'

Gelbich looked around. Zhanka was smirking cattily, and so was Lyolik.

At which point Gelbich roughly twisted Albert's arm the way a policeman might grab a criminal. Albert let out a gasp and bent over double, his fringe falling over his face in a wave like a bird's wing. Gelbich, keeping his prisoner hunched over, thrust his finger into the knot of Albert's pioneer neckerchief and in one movement pulled the neckerchief out by the corner, the way a conjurer pulls a handkerchief out of his magic hat.

'It was your own fault!' Gelbich shoved Albert away from him, sending him spinning to freedom. 'You don't want to be mingy when the lads ask you for something.'

'Give me your pen,' demanded Zhanka of Lyolik.

Gelbich made his way back, victorious. Proudly squaring his shoulders, he stretched his neckerchief out by the ends and laid it across his chest like a shirt. Zhanka tried the pen on her own wrist – did it work? – and began to compose the words of a message on the neckerchief. Gelbich looked down at Zhanka fondly.

Valerka squinted and read two slanting lines: *There's a jug on the table and a lily in the jug, what you looking at me like that for crocodile mug.* Gelbich read them too, though it was inconvenient for him, and whispered with the effort to understand. The message delighted him. He grinned from ear to ear.

'Freaks,' Anastasiika summed up contemptuously.

Valerka shifted his gaze to Albert. Something strange was happening to him. He had turned an unnatural ashen colour, dark shadows had appeared beneath his eyes, his cheeks had become awfully sunken, and his lips had gone black. And he was sweating all over; his white shirt was plastered to his back. His body had gone into spasm and was jerking, twisting, shaking. Of a sudden, Albert rushed over to Pavlik, snatched off the boy's cap with the star on it, and clamped it on his own head. The blond-haired Pavlik froze in amazement. With trembling hands, Albert grabbed the pioneer badge from Pavlik's shirt and slapped it on, seemingly sticking the pin straight into his own body. Then he charged off towards Company House.

Everyone followed him with their eyes.

'He's pissed off to rat on me, the tedious little worm,' declared Gelbich with conviction.

A moment later he had no time to worry about Albert. Irina Mikhailovna and Lyova were striding resolutely along the path from Pioneer Avenue to Company House.

'There he is!' said Lyova, pointing Gelbich out to Irina.

Gelbich winced. He had not expected such a treacherous blow.

'Why did you skedaddle out of training?' Irina Mikhailovna attacked him head on. 'Why did you abandon the team?'

'I'm fed up with football!' yelled Gelbich, immediately indignant. 'I'm going to do singing. If Khlopov's so hung up on chasing a ball, he can do it.'

'Are you a pioneer or not?' Irina was bearing down on Gelbich, and he was backing away. 'Do you remember what responsibility is?'

'What responsibility?!'

'We've got a match against the third brigade on Parents' Day,' said Lyova peaceably. 'And you're our main striker. How can we play without you?'

'I don't want to!' howled Gelbich.

'Oh, diddums!' Irina Mikhailovna came charging in. 'I want – I don't want. Do you know what the word "must" means? Don't prance about! Don't be an embarrassment to your comrades!'

'That's enough, let's go,' Lyova commanded. 'Show some conscience.'

Gelbich was ready to burst into tears of hopelessness.

'Don't make me tell your parents how you've been behaving.' Irina Mikhailovna finished Gelbich off and, glancing round, dropped down on Valerka. 'And you, Lagunov, get yourself back. You are categorically forbidden to leave the brigade.'

Valerka glanced at Anastasiika. Anastasiika was leafing through her songbook.

CHAPTER 4

SPURT

The television camera lens could not accommodate the humungous interior of the Krylatsky Velodrome in its entirety, and the cameraman was showing only separate fragments of the racing surface. The wide track was inclined, and laid out to form an elliptical arena. The incline was gentle on the long sides of the ellipse and steep at the bends. In the sprint, the cyclists competed in pairs. Two riders, one blue and one red, raced down the track one after the other. Their bicycles were thin and delicate, as if made from steel spiders' webs, and at speed, their wheels appeared transparent. Reflections of the spotlights gleamed on the riders' white helmets.

On the big turn, the blue rider soared up to the canted edge of the track, and the red rider, flying after him wheel-to-wheel, suddenly slipped downwards at pace and smartly overtook his rival. Red stepped on it, racing as hard as he could, and Blue chased after him, hoping to regain the lead. He stood up on his pedals, his backside pointing skywards, his whole body suspended over the sharp horns of his handlebars.

'Heading into the third and final lap, Sergey Kopylov puts on a dramatic turn of speed and overtakes Anton Tkach,' said the commentator calmly, in a well-trained voice, and the impression created was that the clash in the velodrome had long been in rehearsal and there was nothing to worry about.

The thought struck Igor that he himself had suddenly overtaken Plotkin in their fight for the girl. But would the finish be a victory? Unlike the cyclists, Igor had not known beforehand that he was in a competition. If he had known, he would not have competed.

About fifteen young leaders and older pioneers were sitting in front of the television on Iyeronov's veranda. The evening Olympics watching sessions had become customary, and Serp Ivanych had even hung thick curtains over the windows to darken the room against the setting sun. The viewers were talking quietly, exchanging impressions, while Serp Ivanych invisibly appeared now this side and now that, carefully straightening the blackout, and then settled into his place in the back row. He was enjoying having young people come to his house.

Veronika was sitting beside Igor, their shoulders touching, but today Igor did not reach out and put his arm around her waist, although he very much wanted to. Igor was tormented by the doubts Whistler had sown. He did not know what to do.

'Why are you so gloomy?' asked Veronika without turning her head.

It would be best, of course, not to start this conversation, not to bring up the subject. They had had a little fun on their summer practical and gone their separate ways when the practical was over. Rather like a holiday romance. But Igor did not want them to go their separate ways; he did not want to lose Veronika. But if their relationship were to continue, he needed to understand the lie of the land. And that was difficult.

'Why didn't you tell me about Plotkin?' Igor could barely get out the words.

Veronika was quiet for a moment.

'A-a-a-a-ahhhh, I get it,' she drawled, mockery in her voice. It was not in her nature to justify herself.

'Why?' repeated Igor insistently.

Two racers were flying round the velodrome again, once more blue and red. The camera was following them. Across the screen flashed spotlights banked in fours, the faces of the fans, the yellow figures of the judges. The blue cyclist was holding the lead, but the positions of leader and outsider meant nothing yet. Everything would be decided by a frantic spurt on the final lap.

Jealousy was twisting Igor inside. Of course, Igor had not forgotten Sasha enunciating in his lordly way that there was nothing going on between him and his bride: sex before marriage was immoral. Well done, Sashok! But this declaration did not cool Igor's jealousy. It was not important who Veronika slept with; what was important was who was best for her. Mind you, if Veronika had been intimate with Sasha, Igor would have broken off the relationship immediately. He would not steal a bride from her fiancé; he was not a scoundrel.

'I didn't tell you, because I don't give a monkey's about Sasha Plotkin,' said Veronika almost soundlessly.

She did not turn towards Igor. Igor stared at her stiff profile. Blue and red reflections from the television ran across Veronika's face. At the quiet, ruthless words of his girlfriend, Igor felt no sense of relief whatever.

'What do you mean, you don't give a monkey's? I mean, he is a living human being!'

'And?' Veronika smiled wryly. 'And I'm what? Not a living human being? Are you suggesting Plotkin's actually asked me if I want to be his wife?'

'How has he not asked you?' Igor was astonished.

'Sashenka Plotkin is a *wunderkind*. People have been kissing his arse since he was a child. The thought simply wouldn't fit in his head that a girl could refuse to marry him. Point is, he's the one, not me, who decided we're getting married. And everyone believed it. I mean – it's Sashenka Plotkin! Such a wonderful match! But I haven't promised him anything. If he doesn't get it, he's the idiot around here.'

The two peas, the young leaders Maxim and Kirill, were sitting in front of Veronika. Maxim turned round and gave an irritated whisper.

'Stop muttering back there. We're trying to watch.'

Igor had already opened his mouth to reproach Veronika; he was going to tell her she needed to explain everything to Sasha. But he stayed silent. The situation was clear. Yes, Veronika should have dumped Plotkin – but then what? Then nothing good. Golden Boy would likely take offence and complain to parents, and one stroppy female student would go flying out of the institute like a bird, to stop her twanging the traumatised young man's nerves. It was simpler for Veronika to soft pedal, undermining Sashenka's plans bit by bit, waiting for him to give them up himself.

A surge of sympathy for Veronika warmed Igor's breast.

'The Leningrad gymnast Alexander Dityatin, a member of the Leningrad Dynamo sports society, has achieved outstanding results at the Twenty-Second Summer Olympics!' the television presenter told them.

Igor looked at the screen. A muscular athlete with a heroic face was performing miracles: in a single supple spring he soared into the air from the blue floor with no apparent effort, turning right over; he twirled fantastically above the horse, spreading his legs like scissors; he spun on the horizontal bars and flew from beam to beam, the way a juggler's rotating rings dart from hand to hand. It was as if gravity had been switched off just for him and he was floating in weightlessness like an astronaut, pushing off from invisible supports, bending beautifully and flinging his arms wide in aerobatics.

Igor felt totally worthless, and was ashamed of his own egotism. He had suspected Veronika of selfishness while having no idea that things had been so unpleasant for her, and for such a long time at that. He felt a burning need to justify himself to her with something good, something real.

'Svistunova called me in today,' he whispered. 'Told me about you and Plotkin. Gave me an ultimatum: either I finish with you or she'll write a report about me to the university and get me expelled.'

'Caught in the crossfire,' sniggered Veronika. 'What does Whistler want with us?'

'She's afraid Plotkin's parents will roast her for letting the young leaders at camp run wild. Meaning me and you. And she's got all sorts of career plans.'

'Bitch cow.'

'Bitch cow,' agreed Igor.

In front of them, Maxim wriggled again. 'Look, I asked you to shut up!' he hissed, suffering.

'Shut up yourself,' replied Igor.

'I don't give a monkey's about Plotkin,' said Veronika, as if she had not noticed Maxim's agonies. 'I don't give a monkey's about Whistler. I don't give a monkey's about anyone. I hate living the way they tell me to. I'm not a doggie, sitting and lying on command.'

Igor realised that their love was safe. No one could make Veronika give him up. They would be together as long as they wanted to be.

'Let's get out of here,' suggested Veronika. 'Let's not wait for night. They can all snuff it from anger and envy.'

Igor looked at the television, and smiled. There, at the Olympics in Moscow, people were fighting to become the best in the world, fighting with all their strength in a furious struggle with gravity or in a frantic spurt at the bend. And they managed to prevail. But he did not even have to fight; there's good fortune for you. To prevail it was enough simply to scamper off into the woods with Veronika.

CHAPTER 5

BRAIN CHECK

Bambook, the food block mutt, knew that the little people would sometimes gather in secluded areas of the pioneer camp and scoff a variety of delicacies; being unobtrusively close by guaranteed a treat. Bambook was lying in the grass, smiling, wagging his tail in a friendly way among the yellow flowers of the goldenrod, and observing. Valerka, Gelbich, Gurka, Tityapkin and Gorokhov were kneeling near the far corner of their building, rubbing strips of pine bark against bricks.

'By law whoever wins takes the sweets,' said Gorokhov.

Everyone would be given presents on Parents' Day, and the division had begun in advance.

'How many can we take?' asked Gurka.

'As many as you want, just not more than two.'

Valerka had only been allowed into the redistribution out of charity. He had warned them at once that his parents would not come to see him, meaning he would not have any sweets. But Lagunov was as blind as a bat, and the likelihood of his triumphing was equal to zero, so the boys let Valerka take part in their scheme just for company, so that they had more boats and the sea battle was more interesting.

The little ships were made of pine bark. When they had first arrived, Rin Khalna had gone through the boys' belongings and taken away their knives, meaning they now had to make their ships by the laborious method of whittling. It would have been more convenient to rub their pieces of bark against the asphalt of Pioneer Avenue, but that would have left brown marks, and the young leaders had forbidden them to dirty the asphalt because there was to be a chalk drawing contest on the avenue on Parents' Day. The lads were forced to use the brickwork at the foot of their building. Not that these obstacles stopped anyone.

'You've done well to have glasses,' Gelbich said to Valerka. 'They don't make you play football.'

'Balls. I wish I had glasses too,' agreed Gurka. 'I'm fed up to the back teeth of football. How'd you lose your eyesight, Valerych?'

'Complications after tonsillitis,' announced Valerka proudly.

'Bollocks,' said Gurka, upset. 'Luck of the devil. Guys, what pills do I have to take to get tonsillitis? I'll swipe them from the doctor.'

'You have to catch a really bad cold,' explained Valerka. 'When you're practically dead, you'll get tonsillitis. Except doctors haven't invented a pill for it yet.'

'Doctors. Can't do a thing,' growled Tityapkin.

He was another who would not have minded wearing glasses and getting out of football.

Gelbich was deep in thought, and pressed his piece of bark with such force that it broke in two. Gelbich stared stupidly at the twisted fragment in his hand, and then in a sudden burst of anger launched it into the distant bushes. Bambook, misleading himself, immediately darted off after it.

'Cutting straight to it, guys, we need to start a revolution. End of story,' said Gelbich, despair in his voice. 'We have to bring Khlopov down. Otherwise we're done for.'

'How do we bring him down?' asked Gorokhov, surprised. 'There's no law to help us.'

'I've worked it out,' said Gelbich. 'Listen.' He lowered his voice, and the boys crept a little closer. 'Tsybastysh's got jeans. In his suitcase. We'll take them and switch them into Khlopov's suitcase. Everyone'll think Lyovik stole the trousers. You get kicked out of camp for stealing. So on Parents' Day they'll hand Khlopov over to his folks to take home.'

The boys were silent, pondering. Gelbich looked anxiously at the frowning faces of the conspirators. Valerka did not like the revolution plan.

'It's bad, Venka,' he said reluctantly.

Although why was it bad? Was drinking your comrades' blood good?

'You can keep quiet, Lagunov!' snapped Gelbich, turning on Valerka. 'You're not part of this. You haven't suffered like we have.'

'A scam is the Chekist's friend,'[14] chimed in Tityapkin.

'Who'll switch the jeans?' asked Gurka.

'You.'

'Me? How'd you work that one out?'

'You're the most agile. I mean, Khlopov said you're the goalie.'

Gurka was pleased at being praised, and calmed down.

Music began to come through the Pioneer Avenue speakers, signalling that they should get ready for lunch and nap time. This was the time when the young leaders unlocked the luggage store so that anyone could go in and rummage through their things. Perfect conditions for starting a revolution.

'Here's the deal, lads,' said Gelbich, hurrying up. 'Guberaka goes to the storeroom. Tityapa and Gorokh keep guard. I'll detain Tsybastysh in the dorm.'

'I'm with you,' Valerka told Gelbich.

He did not want to split from the collective, however shitty it might be.

Everyone in the brigade knew that Lyoshka Tsybastov would be staying in the dorm until lunchtime. He was being punished for throwing a beetle into Zhenya Tsvetkova's compote at breakfast. Gelbich and Valerka bumped into Tsybastysh at the door of the dorm.

'Where are you going? You're not allowed!' shouted Gelbich angrily, standing so that his chest blocked Tsybastysh's way to freedom.

'The music's playing!' hollered Tsybastysh. 'I've done my time! Let me go!'

Tsybastysh pushed Gelbich away with both hands.

'Not yet!' persisted Gelbich. He did not back off, but apart from fighting, did not know what else to do to keep Tsybastysh in the dorm.

....

[14] The Cheka was the first post-1917 iteration of the secret police. To this day in Russia, the name 'chekist' is routinely given to someone who works for the security forces.

'Shove off! I need socks!'

The socks were doubtless in Tsybastysh's suitcase.

'Wait a minute!' cut in Valerka. 'Lyokha, we've got business with you.'

'What the hell business?'

'Brain check for the boys,' said Valerka, making it up as he went along.

Tsybastysh hesitated, stepped back, and sat down on his bunk.

'Well?' he asked distrustfully.

Valerka assumed an important expression.

'Answer these test questions. First: what is superspeed?'

'I don't know,' replied Tsybastysh, irritated.

'What's this about speed?' Gelbich wondered from the doorway.

'Superspeed is running around the house and kicking yourself up the backside,' said Valerka. 'What's superneck?'

'What?' asked Tsybastysh and Gelbich simultaneously.

'Taking an enormous dump in a world champion boxer's entranceway then calling his flat and asking him for bog paper.'

Tsybastysh and Gelbich brayed with laughter.

'What's supersweat?'

'Just tell us!'

'Lying on the ceiling and covering yourself with a blanket.'

The storage room with the suitcases was on the first floor. The revolutionaries Gurka, Tityapa, and Gorokh were skittering down the stairs, out of breath. Valerka caught sight of them behind Gelbich, who was still blocking the exit.

'Medical examination over,' said Valerka with relief. 'Lyokha, your brain is not working. That's all. Go.'

Tsybastysh made no effort to argue. He jumped up, shoved Gelbich away, and ran towards the stairs. Gelbich watched him go, smirking.

'Clock what's about to happen, boys,' said Gelbich, smugly offering advance notice.

A minute later there came a desperate cry from Tsybastysh on the first floor.

'Follow me!' ordered Gelbich enthusiastically.

The storeroom was a small windowless room. A dim light bulb burned up by the ceiling. Shelving units ran along the walls. Partitions divided the room into sections. Each section was allocated to one individual. Irina Mikhailovna had allocated the sections when the children had first moved into the building.

Tsybastysh had opened his suitcase wide right there in his cubicle and shaken out the contents. From one side of the suitcase, a pair of tricot legs dangled like strings of drool.

'My jeans are gone!' repeated Tsybastysh in shock. 'They were here!'

Around Tsybastysh, excited girls were crowding. 'Look harder!' they babbled. 'Perhaps you left them in your bedside cabinet? You sure you don't remember giving them to anyone? What were they like?'

'Stolen! Shitbags.' Tsybastysh was almost crying.

Turning up like a bad penny, Lyova Khlopov himself hove into view.

'It's not good to accuse your comrades,' he said, lecturing Tsybastysh.

'Fifty-five roubles! Fifty-five...'

Gelbich's revolutionaries came jetting in to stoke up the drama.

'We need to search all the other trunks and check!' Faking sympathy, Gelbich set about planting ideas, popping up now on Tsybastysh's right, now on his left. 'If anyone's filched them he'll have bunged them in with his own clobber.'

Tsybastysh's and Lyova's cubicles were, as it happened, next door to each other. Lyova, standing practically side by side with Tsybastysh, calmly clicked the locks on his suitcase, lifted the lid – and froze. There, in the suitcase, on top of all his things, folded into a neat square and flaunting themselves with no shame, were Tsybastysh's jeans.

'There they are!' Tsybastysh gasped in amazement.

The girls around sighed.

'Khlopov filched Tsybastov's trousers!' bellowed Gelbich without hesitation, aiming to fix in the public mind the fact of Lyova's wrongdoing.

At that moment, Igor Sanych entered the storeroom, attracted by the noise.

'What's going on?' he asked sternly.

The girls started calling out all at once. 'Khlopov stole Tsybastov's jeans! Tsybastov went to his trunk but his jeans weren't there! And Khlopov opened his suitcase, and we saw them! He took them and hid them for himself! Tsybastov started crying! Fifty-five roubles!'

Lyova was still standing in his cubicle, stunned and silent, hands hanging down. He did not reach into his case and touch Tsybastysh's jeans, as if they were filthy and he was too squeamish to touch them – or he was afraid of leaving fingerprints. Igor Sanych looked intently at Lyova and Lyokha in turn.

Gelbich, a coarse but simple soul, could not restrain himself.

'Khlopov's a thief!' he shouted, ablaze with hope. 'He needs to be thrown out of camp! His parents can pick him up tomorrow!'

Lyova swivelled slowly, like a beacon, and fixed Gelbich with a stare, his eyes sending out beams that pierced the boy right through. And Gor-Sanych, too, turned a searching gaze on Venka. The hapless Gelbich, invisibly squirming, very nearly went up in smoke. He seemed about to start crackling quietly, like a red-hot frying pan.

Valerka watched events from afar. And for some reason he was suddenly ashamed, even though the vampire Lyova did deserve severe punishment. It was immediatcly obvious to Valerka that both Lyova and Gor-Sanych had guessed about Gelbich's underhand ploy to set up Lyova. Gelbich's revolution had turned into a disgrace.

'What's all this pandemonium?' rang out from the corridor.

It was Irina Mikhailovna, hurrying after Gor-Sanych into the conflict. She pushed Tityapkin out of the way and entered the storeroom, ready to fight.

'What's going on?' she asked.

Igor Sanych moved through the crowd to the shelves, and took the folded jeans from Lyova's open suitcase, using both hands as if handling an anti-personnel mine. Carefully, he transferred them to Tsybastysh's open suitcase.

'No problem, Irina Mikhailovna,' reported Igor Alexandrovich with ostentatious nonchalance. 'Just a silly children's joke. Ha, ha, ha.'

CHAPTER 6

THE COLLECTIVE FARM AND THE TSAR

No one was remotely interested in the stupid wall newspapers. No one had ever read them in their lives, and absolutely no one wanted to put one together. On Parents' Day, however, the parents would be dragged round the various buildings, and it was essential to demonstrate that pioneer life in the brigades was blooming sumptuously. Of course, they could present the old wall newspaper from the previous shift, passing it off as a new one, but the old one, the dog, had already yellowed in the sun and the switch would have been obvious. Irina summoned three girls to the veranda – Anastasiika Sergushina, the brigade commander, and the squad leaders Marinka Lebedeva and Lenochka Romanova – and ordered them to make a fresh brigade publication.

There was no table on the veranda, so Igor arranged four benches together. Irina unpinned the old wall newspaper and spread it out upside down, clean side up. The girls got paints, a bunch of pencils, and a couple of tattered *Bonfire* magazines, to cut out the pictures.

'Visual activism should be a work of art,' said Anastasiika importantly. 'For the theme of our newspaper, I propose: "What children dream of".'

'Do it properly,' answered Irina, annoyed. 'Brigade name at the top. Under that the motto. At the bottom the columns.

Put "The Nature of our Native Land" here. "The Cleanliness Board"[15] here. "Our Achievements" here. "The Barb"[16] here.'

'What are our achievements?' asked Lenochka Romanova in surprise.

'Oh, ask the boys. Who jumps higher, who runs faster, who outplayed who at chess. You'll scrape together enough for one column.'

'Katya Shilova won the bouquet competition,' recalled Lenochka.

'That'll do. Write her up.'

'She's a cretin.'

'So what?'

The other girls had taken one look at the veranda and immediately disappeared, to avoid being set to do boring work. The warning swept quietly through the brigade: don't cross the young leaders' sightline just now or they'll press you into writing the wall newspaper. So Igor was surprised when he suddenly saw Lyova Khlopov on the veranda. Unlike the other bonehead boys, Lyova was perfectly suitable for a serious assignment. For example, he could put up the marks (awarded on an inspection of beds and bedside cabinets) on the Cleanliness Board. Lyova, though, had appeared looking ready to line up for inspection and start singing: he had put on trousers and a white shirt, ironed his neckerchief, and even combed his hair.

'Irina Mikhailovna, I need to talk with you,' he said sternly, seeming not to notice Igor Alexandrovich.

'God, what now?' asked Irina, instantly annoyed.

'I consider that I have been discr … credited,' said Lyova, barely getting out the word.

'How so?'

'Venya Gelbich planted Lyosha Tsybastov's things on me and everyone thought I'd stolen them. But I hadn't.'

....

[15]   In camp, the brigades were awarded marks each day for cleanliness and tidiness, and these marks were displayed on the 'Cleanliness Board'.

[16]   'The Barb' was a part of the wall newspaper reserved at this time for criticism of bad behaviour ('naming and shaming').

Irina threw a withering look at Igor. 'So that in the storeroom wasn't a joke?' she asked angrily.

'It was a joke,' repeated Igor firmly.

'I get it.' Lyova spoke again, ignoring Igor. 'Gelbich wants to leave the football team and I won't let him. So he decided to make sure I get sent home tomorrow. He has done a mean thing.'

Igor looked closely at Lyova, as if for the first time. He was a good-looking boy. A true little Aryan. Yes, he was honest, responsible, and fair, as a pioneer should be. But when he spoke, his words came with a waft of a strange, sepulchral cold. Something dead and dreadful. Igor immediately recalled Valerka Lagunov saying that Lyova was a vampire. And vampires were dead souls. Lagunov, of course, was making it up … although Lyova had not been so correct and merciless at the start. Well, he had not seemed so. But perhaps he had been.

'And what do you suggest?' asked Irina.

'That today at 'candle' the brigade discusses what Gelbich did.'

'You want him kicked out and not you?' asked Igor.

Lyova lowered his eyes.

'I don't want anyone kicked out. But he should be punished.'

'Irina Mikhailovna and I will think about it,' said Igor, speaking quickly to get in ahead of Irina. 'Run along now, Lyova. We'll think about it.'

Lyova turned and walked away.

'Rin Khalna, which should I cut out, bear or tiger?' Lenochka Romanova, who was cutting up a *Bonfire* magazine, immediately yanked at Irina.

'So what do we have roaming about our forest?' barked Irina.

'I don't know!' said Lenochka, scared. 'We're not allowed over the fence!'

'Cut out the tiger,' Anastasiika advised her authoritatively. 'He's beautiful and noble. The bear's full of fleas.'

These considered arguments wholly satisfied Lenochka.

'Borisovna was right when she said you'd let all the boys run wild,' said Irina, whispering so that the girls did not hear. 'And you're still lying to me!'

'I am not lying!' Igor was on the brink of taking offence. 'I said it was a joke to make things easier. Because we're all to blame, not just Gelbich.'

'What are we all to blame for?' snapped Irina, completely losing her temper.

'Khlopov has choked the life out of everyone with his football. And we gave Khlopov our support, and didn't want to understand that the boys had had it up to here with running around after a ball. They had no other way of changing how things were.'

'You're the one who pandered to Khlopov because you were too lazy to do anything with the children yourself.'

Irina was right, of course. Not that Igor even tried to deny it.

'We don't need to stick Gelbich in a kangaroo court,' he said, begging her, and trying to retain his composure.

'And why is that? Do tell.'

Igor thought for a moment. He remembered Valerka Lagunov being tried for breaking away from the collective. Valerka had been forcibly compelled to attach himself to the brigade, but that had only increased his aversion to common activities: Lyova Khlopov, captain of the football team, was now, as far as Valerka was concerned, a vampire.

'Because our kangaroo courts ruin the defendants' faith in the other children,' said Igor, picking his words deliberately. 'Ira, you and I are the young leaders here. Let's punish Gelbich ourselves. I'll give him a reprimand, and you put him under arrest.'

'You're an idiot, Korzukhin,' replied Irina. 'You know nothing about pedagogy. We have a pioneer camp here, and we're bringing them up the pioneer way, and that means collectively. The collective is always right. Let them decide about Gelbich.'

Irina was shorter than Igor, but just at that moment she seemed taller.

Igor hit out, unable to restrain himself. 'So why did you go snitching to Whistler about me and Veronika instead of bringing it to a general discussion? We could have told Plotkin and the collective plenty about what we were up to.'

Irina flushed bright red, pulled off her glasses, and fixed Igor with a myopic stare. In the naked simplicity of her plump, rustic face burned a confidence in her convictions that would keep her safe without optical reinforcements.

'Because Borisovna is the collective!' Irina's voice was a whip.

What was to be done with her? Kill her, perhaps? To every argument Irina instantly found a counterargument, because she revered both the collective farm and the Tsar. This unconscious doublethink tended towards one single end: forcing everyone to live as everyone else did, subjecting everyone to a set of common rules – those rules which had already become the norm. Everybody plays football: so do you. Everybody licks Plotkin's arse: so do you.

'Irina Mikhailovna!' Anastasiika Sergushina called the young leader from the wall newspaper. 'Who should we write about in "The Barb"?'

'The Barb' was a section for critical comment by the pioneers.

With some difficulty, Irina switched over to everyday life and put her glasses back on.

'Who's misbehaved recently?'

'Makerov overslept and missed exercise. Domrachev splashed water around.'

'So write about them.'

Igor himself did not know why he was so doggedly defending Gelbich. Gelbich deserved a good thrashing for his stupid dirty trick. The fact was that the invisible and meaningless boundaries so vigilantly guarded by Irina and Whistler were bugging Igor. He simply wanted revenge. The beauty of a debt was in its repayment. He offered Irina a warning.

'If Gelbich is kicked out of camp,' he said, 'I'll write a report that you, Irina, gave the storeroom key to the pioneers, and exercised no control over what they did there, and that's how Gelbich managed to take someone else's things.'

Irina sparkled her eyes through her glasses. 'Well, you are a bad apple,' she said with feeling.

'Just we won't get ourselves in a stew over this, OK? Let's punish Gelbich by banning him from tonight's film, and draw a line under the episode at that.'

CHAPTER 7

PARENTS' DAY

The parents were brought in on two river buses. The toy boats tied up elegantly one each side of the camp pier. The whiteness of the ships' superstructures in the bright sunlight was blinding. Their scarlet stars glowed as triumphantly as if the buses had broken through a blockade and delivered reinforcements to a battle-weary garrison. Shoreside, from the camp gates, the plaster bugler girl trumpeted a greeting to the guests. In reply, Captain Kapustin blasted the entire Volga with the rousing, not to say piercing, melody 'A Slavic Girl's Farewell', although it would have been more logical to switch on something on the theme of meeting. The chattering crowd of parents, mostly mothers with shopping bags, stretched along the plank pier to the gate.

The social being more important than the personal, the programme opened with a solemn assembly at which the flag was raised. Only then were the children released to their parents. The young leaders herded the guests from the entrance to Company Court. The guests waited. Finally, a squad of drummers lined up on the parade ground. To a resounding beat, all six brigades came out one after another, marched one complete, well-orchestrated circuit, and took their places. The grown-ups were silent, looking at the pioneers with their neckerchiefs; a few grandmothers shed a tear or two.

Valerka enjoyed working his elbows and stomping his feet. Many of the boys and girls marched in step only to please their parents, but Valerka was marching for himself alone. No one was due to come and see him. His mum and dad had warned him in advance that they had been given a permit for Baikal, and his aunt was babysitting Lyuska, his little sister, so she was not able to come either. Still, no matter. He was no longer a child; he would survive. And marching in formation was great. In the ranks Valerka felt part of a collective, as if he was doing something important together with everyone else, or as if they were all one people.

'Company, sa-lu-u-ute flag!' commanded Svistunova.

The flag was hoisted, of course, by Serp Ivanych. The visitors watched, smiling, as this young-looking scraggy old man deftly paid out the halyard. The pioneers snapped their hands up in a salute to the flag, but the guests did not know what to do, until someone suddenly had the idea of clapping, like in a theatre, and the other adults joined in, clapping their hands in relief.

'At ease!' Svistunova commanded. 'Fall out!'

The even rectangles of the brigades broke apart in an instant: children rushed to find their parents, and parents made for their children. But the older and more worthy among the men headed first towards Comrade Iyeronov and respectfully shook his hand. Serp Ivanych, a man with a personal pension and a veteran of the Civil War, was known and loved in the city of Kuibyshev.

'How is your health?' a stern woman in glasses asked Iyeronov.

'It was better in the Civil War,' joked Serp Ivanych.

'Can I get you any help from the City Council?'

'This is Alevtina Petrovna Plotkina,' Whistler butted in to explain.

'I remember Alevtina Petrovna,' said Serp Ivanych. 'I do not need help. You have a son working here as a young leader, am I right?'

'Yes.' The woman nodded and blushed slightly. 'Alexander.'

'A good young man!' said Whistler, squeezing in once more. 'He sets the standard for us.'

'Rest, Serp Ivanovich. Get your strength back,' said Alevtina Petrovna, and she moved away from Iyeronov and turned to Whistler. 'Natalya Borisovna, I appreciate the consideration you give my son, but I want to remind you: Sasha is an ordinary student. No indulgences for him, no favouritism. Undeserved praise will only spoil him.'

'I judge him by the results of his work,' shrugged Whistler.

Meanwhile Valerka set off on a wander round the camp. The young leaders were supposed to assemble parentless children like him in Company House to spend the day under the supervision of the PE teacher, but Valerka did not want to go and be with Ruslan Maximych. He had persuaded Yurik Tonkikh to lie that Yurik's mother would supervise him along with her son, and Rin Khalna had let him go. Valerka had obtained his freedom. He was curious to have a look at the camp in the role of an intelligence gatherer.

The camp was living a life that was overly noisy, over-populated, and laboured in its variety. Music played through the speakers. Voices and laughter were carried in from all quarters. Grown-ups were walking around, many staring at the gingerbread houses in amazement, not having expected such beauty. Someone's overweight mum was swinging on a swing, letting out peals of embarrassed laughter. The simpler dads had taken off their jackets and were playing volleyball with lads from the older brigades. The dads with slightly more upstairs were playing chess with the cleverer boys. Girls were drawing on the asphalt of Pioneer Avenue with coloured chalks. Someone's pesky granny, holding up her glasses, was reading the menu pinned to the wall by the entrance to the food block. Valerka wanted to see the concert Veronika Genrikhovna's group had got ready; he wanted to see Anastasiika sing, but Company House was so crowded that Valerka could not push his way into the hall. He managed no more than to hear the middle of 'Chunga-Changa' and a ripple of applause.

Valerka drifted in the direction of the stadium. Parents were sitting on the benches waiting for the football match to start, while the players were gormlessly charging about the field. Lyova Khlopov was holding a meeting with a muscled dad, clearly an athlete. Over by the goal, Gelbich was nimbly working the ball, knocking it up now with his knees, now with the toes of his trainers. Valerka made for Gelbich.

'What's this, Venka, they made you do it after all?' he began sympathetically.

'No, I agreed,' replied Gelbich carelessly.

'They re-educated you?' Valerka was taken aback.

Gelbich went after the ball, keeping his eyes on it. 'Lyovych explained everything, made it sound OK. We slug it out with the third brigade, then Lyovych'll pick the best players to be in the team against the steamrollers.'

Valerka already knew all this. What had Lyova found to say to Gelbich that was so different? How had he managed to bring him round? Valerka looked sceptically at Gelbich.

'You were yelling about how you'd rather drown than go to football...' he tried.

'Lyova said this comes first. I mean, he's got the biggest bollocks around here.'

A wave of something cold suddenly washed over Valerka. The fiery revolutionary Venka Gelbich no longer existed. Lyova had done something to him. What could he have done? Bitten him? Was Gelbich afraid of being bitten? But Gelbich did not have the look of someone who had been intimidated. Valerka backed away, one step, then another. Gelbich took no notice. He was preparing for the key match.

Lyova was ardently expounding something to his players, waving his arms. He looked exactly as he always did: tracksuit bottoms, T-shirt, neckerchief, tousled blond hair. Valerka was no longer afraid of him; fear had found its own place. By day, the vampire posed no danger, and at night Valerka simply hid in his 'little house' and covered his head with his pillow. Yes, his flimsy house was made of hemp, sheets, and pins, but it reliably protected him from Lyova. Lyova could get up to whatever he wanted as long as he did not touch Valerka. And Lyova did not touch Valerka.

For Valerka, Lyova had become something like a dentist. A dentist dragged people off to his place and tortured them there, but he did then let them go. It was horrible to imagine the dentist in his lair, wielding his drill and forceps, and even more horrible to imagine being held captive by him. But you could still live if you knew how to keep your head down and not think. Valerka could keep his head down, but not thinking was, alas, beyond him. He left the stadium bitterly disappointed.

He made his way to the canteen: on Parents' Day, compote was served to anyone who wanted it. On Pioneer Avenue, Valerka's gaze was snagged by the stands with drawings for peace. He recalled the artists in the circle puffing over their paper, depicting all sorts of flim-flam: cats and dogs, flowers, various grandmothers' villages, walks through green forests. Now, though, there were very different pictures hanging on the stand: foreign generals and soldiers, rich men, policemen, and black bombs. Valerka was surprised, and his surprise was joined by an unpleasant disquiet: what was going on here? Of course, a giraffe in a zoo and a New Year tree were girls' fluff, but at least the members of the circle had wanted to draw their own fluff, not caricatures from *Crocodile* magazine. What had prompted the artists to change their plans?

'Do you like them?' Valerka heard from behind him.

He looked round. Sitting on a bench in front of the stands was Albert. He was observing the impression the exhibition was making on the viewers.

'Why are the pictures different?' asked Valerka with a frown.

'They are more in line with our theme. We are criticising warmongers.'

Parents passed by the stands, but showed no inclination to linger.

'There's nothing there that's, like, ours,' grunted Valerka.

For some reason he had started to feel sorry for the earlier cats and dogs; they may have been ridiculous, but they were vibrant, sincere, genuine.

'Come back to the circle and draw what you want,' suggested Albert, straightening the red neckerchief on his chest. 'It really would be better for you to be with us.'

Valerka felt as if he had received an ice cold electric shock. *It will be better for you.* That was what Lyova had said, begging to be let into Valerka's little house. And the bench on which Albert was now sitting was the same one on which Valerka had seen a vampire drinking the blood of one of the girls that night.

Valerka recognised the outline of Albert's head and shoulders, recognised his hair… Albert had been that vampire.

Legs trembling, Valerka walked quickly away from Pioneer Avenue. Albert Stakhovsky, Marinka Lebedeva, Lyova Khlopov… Who else in the Storm Petrel Pioneer Camp sucked blood from people at night? And who could he tell about this horror? Gelbich? Gelbich had submitted to Lyova. Yurik Tonky? Tonky would piss himself and peg out on the spot. Natalya Borisovna or Irina Mikhailovna? They would consign him straight to the mental hospital. The only one capable of believing in vampires was Gor-Sanych, and he had already not believed on one occasion. Mind you, that was when Valerka had pointed the finger at Lyova, who had not left the building, and that was why Gor-Sanych had doubted him.

Valerka sat in the empty canteen, thinking and drinking his compote. The canteen was flooded with sunlight, but everywhere – on the floor, on the long tables, on the walls – lay shadows from the window bars. Of course, the bars had not been installed for the same reason as bars were put over prison windows. They were simply there to keep the glass from being hit by stray balls: children in camp were rascals. Nevertheless, they were still bars.

In the kitchen, Old Nyura, the scullery maid, was clinking glasses. From time to time she looked out into the hall, but no more visitors had come in. A little dark boy with glasses was sitting quietly miserable over his compote, like an abandoned puppy.

'Eh, eh there,' Old Nyura called out to him. 'H-h-hasn't M-m-mama c-come?'

The boy did not answer.

Old Nyura sighed heavily, wiped her wet hands on the apron over her stomach, opened a cardboard box of sweets on the grocery shelf, and scooped out a handful of the cheapest. She clumsily made her way out into the hall, walked over to the miserable boy, and tipped the sweets on to the table in front of him.

'T-t-treat yourself,' she stuttered, stroking the boy's head. 'D-d-don't b-be sad. Mama s-s-still l-loves you.'

CHAPTER 8

'WOZ ERE'

From the camp to Concert Clearing was no distance: half a kilometre through the pine grove. The clearing was on the gently sloping bank of the Volga. It was called Concert Clearing because it was the place where camp-wide activities were held, such as children's sports competitions, amateur performances, and the Last Camp Fire at the end of every shift. At the competitions and shows, the pioneers could lounge on the grass, which was better than on the stadium sand, and at the Last Camp Fire, of course, a huge bonfire as tall as two people was lit on the field. It would be impossible to build the fire in Company Court with its lawn and running track, and where in any event everything was clean and orderly.

On Parents' Day, motorboats docked alongside Concert Clearing, bringing the parents who did not want to use public transport, namely the river buses, from the town. Piloting the boats were fathers who were diehard fishermen: for them, this way of visiting their offspring was a compromise between a cherished passion and family duty. The fathers hauled their *Kazankas*[17] out onto the sand and immediately cast their rods into the water, thereafter periodically dashing down to check their catch.

Valerka stood at the fringe of the grove, looking at the small, scattered groupings dotted round Concert Clearing, and his eye alighted on Seryozha Domrachev.

....

[17]   A type of motor boat.

'Wait here,' Valerka ordered Beklya and his henchmen.

Seryozha's mother, father and older brother had come to see him. His mum mad spread an oilcloth on the grass and laid out their fare: cooked chicken, tomatoes, bread, gingerbread, and lemonade. The brother was already devouring a watermelon, hoping to gobble up at least half of it. The father sat with a guilty smile, listing unnaturally in the direction of the river as he kept one ear cocked for the ringing of the bell on his fishing rod.

'Sery, five seconds,' requested Valerka.

Seryozha stood up.

'Sery, where's the abandoned church?'

Valerka was taking Beklya to the place where goods were exchanged with the Escaped Convicts. There was in fact no such place; Valerka had lied about it to save Anastasiika, and he now needed urgently to invent it. The idea that had occurred to him was the abandoned church. But he himself had never been there, and the only one who knew the way there was Seryozha, keeper of the ancient legends of the pioneer camp.

'You have to go along the Bishop, that way.' Seryozha waved his hand.

'Is it a long way?'

'Well, depends. Yeah, I guess it's a long way. Took us about ten minutes. More. Dunno. Only don't go, Valerych. You could get killed there.'

'What's there?'

'There's something not right there.' Seryozha hesitated. 'Last shift the oldies told us that some kid had gone there and disappeared. Everyone started looking for him, and they found a picture of him hanging on the wall there with the eyes poked out.'

Valerka shuddered.

'There was a priest there ages ago, but they tied him up and drowned him in the Bishop. After that the church totally collapsed and anyone who goes in is done for. And a picture appears on the wall at night and says, "Don't look for me, I'm under the board."'

'What board?' Valerka was now seriously scared.

Seryozha looked around and whispered, 'I don't know.'

'Seryozha, invite your friend to sit down,' called Seryozha's mum.

'No, thanks,' replied Valerka. 'I've got … er… Thanks, I'll be off.'

The church might be sinister, there might be Escaped Convicts in the woods, and Beklya, Rulet, and Siphilyok might be thick hoodlums, but it was still better than being in camp, where vampires hung around pretending to be human.

No relatives had come to see Beklya or his yobs either, as it happened. Everyone was so sick of them at home that they had sent them off to pioneer camp and now it was out of sight, out of mind. Why on earth would they visit? Beklya, bored, had caught Valerka near the canteen and reminded him that Valerka was supposed to show him the place where the Escaped Convicts exchanged food for Finnish knives. Valerka had suggested they high-tail it there straightaway. This was a time when no one was going to tumble to the fact that he had disappeared.

They were walking through the clean grove between the trunks of the pines and the poles of the street lamps. Above, high overhead, everything was moving slowly. The jagged white of the clouds meandered through the conversing emptinesses of the scattered pine tops; the sun was playing; and the chirping of birds seemed like the chirr of counters measuring the parameters of astronomical combinations. Below, a thick coniferous stillness reigned, hot and viscous. It might have been taken for silence, but the attentive listener would discern in it a vast, elusive whisper, perhaps the distant breathing of the mighty river, perhaps the echo of music from the pioneer camp. Or perhaps the rustle made by the shadows of a swaying fern.

'What are you taking the Escaped Convicts?' Valerka asked Beklya.

'Laundry soap, needle and thread, packet of cigarettes.'

Valerka was surprised at how Beklya had thought it all out. At the same time, the particular selection of goods suited Valerka. It was inexpensive, and the cons would not give a Finnish knife in exchange for it. Valerka had already planned how he would pull off his little piece of business so that Beklya would not discover that Valerka had tricked him. In a few days, Valerka would collect Beklya's offering himself, and leave a pistol cartridge in return. Vovka Makerov had been bragging about having one, and Valerka would have to find a way to buy it with the rouble he had brought with him to camp. Getting the cartridge would make Beklya think that the Escaped Convicts had entered into a trading relationship with him, and he would bring a new consignment of goods, in order to obtain the coveted knife. While Beklya was still waiting for the deal to come good, the camp shift would finish.

Valerka had another question. 'How do you know what the cons want?' he asked.

'Basically when it comes to the clink, I know the whole polymer,' boasted Beklya. 'Think about it, Valeryan. When they put you in prison, you, like, get to your cell and they give you a broom and say, "This is a guitar. Crank something out for us." What you going to do?'

Valerka became very agitated at the phrase 'when they put you in prison'.

'They're not going to put me in prison!' he objected.

Beklya grinned patronisingly. He seemed to hold the view that everyone would have to go to prison sooner or later, and only idiots would dispute it.

'You have to give them the broom and say, "After you've tuned it,"' said Beklya, answering himself. 'And if they draw a football goal on the wall, give you a ball, and say, "Score a goal!" OK, so what's your demographic?'

Siphilyok and Rulet were walking to the right and left of Beklya and Valerka, listening intently without saying a word, like hunting dogs beside the hunters.

'You have to say, "Pass it to me!" persisted Beklya. 'And if they get on top of you in the cell and say, "You're a bus, take me to the bus stop"? You, like, get them to the wall and they say, "This ain't mine, keep going!" What do you do?'

'I'm not going to be lugging anyone around,' flared Valerka.

'You have to tell them this is the end of the line,' said Beklya patiently. 'What you doing – twisting a bollocking hypotenuse? I wish you good.'

These words gave Valerka a strange jolt. Of course, Beklya was not lying. It was just that he understood good in his own way. Many other people also understood good differently from the way he, Valerka, did. Therein lay one of life's complexities. You probably could not expect people to believe you, but you could hope they would help you. Yes, people could be stupid, greedy, and cowardly. But they were people. They did not drink one another's blood. And that was why the world remained a wonderful place. At the same time, somewhere in its secret depths, crawling through secret crevices, was cold death. It was clever: it kept itself hidden, but penetrated everywhere, devouring everything in its path. No one noticed it. Except him. Valerka had noticed it.

The pine forest was replaced by a thicket of alder and hazel trees that filled the Bishop clough. In the dense bushes on the bank of the glittering stream stood a small church. Or rather, not so much a church as a roofless red-brick box, with shapeless holes for windows and gouged corners. The walls looked as if sledgehammers had been taken to them. Valerka recalled Serp Ivanych telling of the brutal battle at the Shikhobalovsky dachas. Could these pocks and dents have been left by shelling from the time of the Civil War? The church looked sullen and inhospitable, like an enemy dugout after it had been stormed.

'Bad place,' Valerka warned them in a low voice. 'People go in there and disappear. There's basically some sort of black magic in there.'

Beklya thought for a moment. The shattered entrance to the church was as frightening as a gaping maw.

'Rulet, sloop inside and check it out,' he ordered.

'Vaska, sloop in and check it out,' said Rulet, forwarding the order at once.

'Noo, I'm not going,' said Siphilyok fearfully.

'You what, a scaredy cat, Siphozina?' Rulet was indignant. 'You want my fist in your mug?'

'There are crosses!' explained Siphilyok with superstitious horror.

'What bollocking crosses?'

'Crosses! I'm not going where there are crosses!'

'I'll drag you both in there in a minute!' threatened Beklya.

He tried to grab Rulet by the scruff of the neck and bundle him into the ruins, but Rulet ducked back and scampered out of reach. Siphilyok smartly followed suit.

'Fine, I'll go in myself,' said Valerka, making up his mind.

He stepped carefully onto the crumbling threshold and peered into the temple.

There was nothing terrible there. The same pitted walls, in places covered with the soot from bonfires; green hazel branches sticking out of the empty windows; piles of bricks overgrown with grass; rotten boards; bottles and rusty tin cans; a blue rectangle of sky instead of a ceiling.

The evil force that abducted people was not lurking inside the abandoned church. It forced its way in here from outside.

'The Escaped Convicts left any traces?' asked Beklya, behind him.

He had summoned up the courage to come in after all.

'Yep,' said Valerka. 'There, look. Traces.'

An inscription on the wall, blackened by soot. 'Baldy and Garilla woz ere.'

CHAPTER 9

A DECISION IN THE DARKNESS

Zhanka Shalayeva, the bad, bad girl, was well aware of the impression she and Lyolik were making on the audience while they were dancing 'Chunga-Changa': shapely bodies, tight leotards, short flyaway skirts, upraised wire tails, and snug-fitting hats with Cheburashka[18] ears. Zhanka and Lyolik were portraying monkeys on a tropical island. They shone with impudent smiles, bent this way and that, and squatted, spreading their arms and knees frog-wise; in short, they carried on like little girls. Igor felt in himself the seductiveness of this supposedly childishly innocent but entirely improper dance. Veronika was standing to one side, arms crossed over her breast, her whole appearance seeming to say, 'You prudes, you know nothing of sensuality. So here's a slap in the face for your morals.'

Of course, the music circle's concert and the rest of the artistic presentation also featured choral singing, poetry readings, pantomimes and dramatic sketches, but it was 'Chunga-Changa' that made the deepest impression on the audience. The few dads blushed and the numerous mothers tut-tutted quietly. No one dared give voice to indignation, though, and the dancers finished to applause, albeit nervous. What wrong had they done? None. Youth, its first flowering, knew nothing of shame, and playing

....

[18]   A much-loved character created by the writer Eduard Uspensky, who described Cheburashka as an 'animal unknown to science', with large monkey-like ears.

at cute kiddies merely served as argument that childhood was over and the girls were ripe and ready for the mistakes of youth.

After the concert, Veronika went up to Alevtina Plotkina. 'How did you like our performance?' she asked slyly.

Alevtina Petrovna weighed all the pros and cons.

'Original,' she said arcanely.

Veronika rejoiced vindictively.

Igor pushed his way towards her with difficulty through the crowd of children and parents.

'Let's go for a wander and have a swim, shall we? It's a free day.'

'It's a free day for you, but they've hung the orphan girls on me. Right now I'm going to be baking a raspberry pie with them, and then we've got a tea party at Serp's. We're demonstrating Timur's concern[19] for a generation of heroes.'

Veronika noticed Igor's disappointment and touched his elbow lightly – a rare display of affection from her.

'It's not my fault,' she said gently. 'We'll still have time, won't we?'

Igor went off to wander round the camp on his own.

Out of boredom, he edged his way in among the fans at the stadium, where there was a match in progress between the football teams of the third and the fourth brigades. Here had gathered, for the most part, fathers. They offered encouraging noises and the odd whistle, and generally made out that out on the pitch doing battle were titans such as Spartak and CSKA. The boys, properly worked up, were playing with all their energy, hurtling this way and that, colliding and causing pile-ups and selflessly hurling themselves about. Lyova's team was in the lead and confident. Igor was surprised: Lyova had his players properly trained; they were no longer at a loss, but

....

[19]   The 'Timur movement' was launched in the USSR in the early 1940s to support the families of servicemen during the Great Patriotic War (the name given to the part of World War II in which the Soviet Union fought on the side of the allies, namely June 1941 to May 1945). It was inspired by A.P. Gaidar's short novel *Timur and his Team*, and large numbers of young pioneers and schoolchildren took part in it.

skilfully rounded their opponents, passed to one another, and acted in concert. Lyova himself did not get on the ball and did not rush into attack, but agitatedly sped around various different flash points shouting out orders. He resembled a commissar driving his men into attack, managing to steer the most fervent more precisely and threatening to shoot those who lagged behind.

The PE teacher, Ruslan Maximych, gave a long blast on his whistle to end the match, stepped onto the pitch, and announced the winners. Lyova's team was so knackered they had no energy left for jubilation. Lyova merely patted Tityapkin on the shoulder. Tityapa had torn his trousers at the knee. The losing team, meanwhile, lost their rags.

'Scumbags!' fumed the outsiders. 'It was three on one!'

'I got a brother in the first brigade!' threatened a red-headed lad. 'Him and his mates'll be looking out for you all later!'

Sasha Plotkin took his players to clean themselves up. The losers walked away sullen and offended, and one of them angrily kicked his captain's backside.

Lyova received well-deserved congratulations from the dads, and gravely shook their hands, while Igor studied Lyova's charges, flushed, sweaty, and dirty: Gelbich, Guryanov, Tityapkin, Gorokhov. The boys had certainly pulled themselves together and got organised, and that was why they had been victorious. Yet no time at all ago, these same lads had been conspiring, eager to drive Lyova out of camp. How had they beaten their swords into ploughshares so quickly? Or was everything to be explained by the inconstancy of a child?

Not that Igor spent long chasing his own tail over this mystery.

Igor went to lunch that day with Dimon Malosolov. Dimon was excited; he was noisily slurping his soup and biting off chunks of bread, spraying crumbs everywhere, as if he was in a hurry to go somewhere.

'It's all falling into place, Igoryokha!' he said, lowering his voice. 'Had a bit of a grope, and we been kissing, tongues and all! We find a little hut somewhere and you better believe we'll be planting the parsnip!'

Dimon was bragging about his achievements in the realms of hanky-panky with Irina.

'Plant your parsnip in the open air,' advised Igor.

'Puts her foot down at the open air. Says she doesn't want to do it like a dog.'

'What about before the wedding being a no-no?'

Dimon let out a small chuckle to signify that no virtue could resist a prince like him.

Igor felt sad, even envious. His success with Veronika was much more obvious than Dimon's dubious prospects, but Dimon was about to go rushing off back to Irina, whereas he was left to moon around on his own for God only knew how long.

Igor loafed about until evening, not knowing what to do with himself. He went for a swim, sunbathed, took a nap in his room, read lazily, and even went to visit Dr Nosatov, but the doctor was suffering with a hangover and did not feel up to chasing it away with the hair of the dog – it was, after all, Parents' Day, packed with people; dangerous. Igor took himself off back to his own room.

At last the sun hung over the Zhiguli, and the camp speakers broadcast upbeat songs to the effect that the following day the pioneers would be going camping and fighting. Irina came over to the building; not trusting Igor, she herself received the children back from their parents. Gradually the fourth brigade gathered in full complement. The pioneers were led in formation to assembly. The idea was to part from the parents collectively and solemnly, to avoid snivelling, but some among the brigades, especially the younger ones, were crying anyway. Among the hordes of parents, a few mothers were also wiping their eyes. Igor furtively craned his neck out of the ranks, hunting for Veronika, and was unable to find her. Sasha was taking charge of his brigade on his own.

'Do you know where Nesvetova is?' he asked Irina quietly.

Irina threw Igor a sidelong look; it was plain she saw him as a source of disorder. Igor shrugged his shoulders, puzzled.

'I don't know,' replied Irina. 'Are all the children in their places?'

'The children are all where they should be, at any rate. I ticked them off against the list.'

Then came the beeping of motor boats from the river, supper, washing, and bedtime, and after that began the process of calming the dorms. The pioneers were already hard at the business of sharing and devouring their presents, squabbling, giving one another treats, and striking swaps. Through the doors floated the words, *'Forty-nine, a half is mine!' 'Forty-three, it's all for me!'*[20] The commotion went on until it was almost dark.

Irina established a fragile peace and then scurried off to her quarters. Igor prowled one more time along the corridor, listening out, ready to nag the boys, then went up to his own room. Sasha was drinking his mum's lemonade and eating his mum's biscuits, as if he were a pioneer too.

'Try some,' he offered.

'I don't want any. Has Veronika turned up?'

'Uh-uh,' said Sasha with his mouth full. 'I think she's taking a break with the girls.'

'I might go for a smoke, have a walk,' grunted Igor.

He was becoming vaguely worried about Veronika. She was hardly likely to be drinking wine with someone, and she had no friends among the young leaders. If she was free, Veronika would have preferred Igor's company over a get-together with a group of anyone at all.

On the stoop of Building 3, Igor saw Irina.

'Where has Nesvetova got to?' she asked irritably.

Igor made up his mind. 'I'm going to look for her now,' he answered.

What could have befallen her in the pioneer camp? If there had been an emergency, it would have been known at once: the place was teeming with people. The village drunks were harmless. There were no bears or wolves in the woods, and

....

[20]   In these two phrases, the numbers themselves have no meaning; they are there solely for the rhymes. The phrases are in the nature of spell and counter-spell, the first being a request to share something half and half, the second being a refusal. The premise is that a request framed as a spell must be granted unless it is cancelled by another spell.

what would Veronika be doing in the woods anyway? She would not have skipped off for a swim: she had swum plenty for one summer. Sailed away on a boat? Rubbish. She was here somewhere. Igor remembered Lyova Khlopov disappearing in the same way at the beginning of the shift, but it was nothing; he had turned up, and everyone had then felt sorry for him.

The street lamps were burning over Pioneer Avenue. Near the food block, the dogs had finished ripping into one another and were barking. The sharp flagpole in Company Court was poking the bottom of a moon that was round, with just a morsel nibbled out of its left side by the darkness. The habitual rustling of the bushes was subsiding. The smell of cake and sweets still wafted everywhere, and the dust had not yet settled; it hung over the paths, giving off a ghostly glow.

Veronika was sitting inside a small hip-roofed gazebo in the grounds of the sixth brigade. Igor stopped near the steps, sensing that something was wrong.

'We all lost you,' he said cautiously.

Veronika hesitated, as if listening carefully to herself. At length, she calmly pronounced, 'It's all over between us.'

Igor understood her at once, but did not for a moment believe her lifeless words; he did not even become upset. His heart did not tremble. This simply could not be.

'What's wrong?' he asked gently, climbing up into the gazebo.

'Better not come any closer,' Veronika warned him. There was something strange in her voice.

Igor obediently lowered himself onto the bench opposite.

'Am I to blame? What have I done?'

'This isn't about you.'

She spoke with no trace of any emotion. Her eyes gleamed silver in the shadows.

'So the problem's with Sasha? Or his mother?'

Whistler could easily have snitched to Alevtina Petrovna, and Sasha's mother could easily have given Veronika an ultimatum: either break it off with your lover before it's too late, or say goodbye to your studies. Igor thought it and was immediately ashamed. His surmise would signify that Veronika had made a small-minded choice, and Veronika did not deserve to have Igor suspect her of self-serving a second time. At the same time, such unpleasant but workaday considerations were helping him retain his rationality; the sudden breakup was threatening to dislocate his brain with its egregious senselessness.

'Don't come near me,' repeated Veronika. 'I've thought long and hard and made my decision. It's over now.'

'But why?' Igor became angry.

He was not yet feeling loss; it was more incomprehension that was scrambling his mind.

'Because my relationship with you is wrong. You can see that clearly for yourself. I behaved improperly when I cheated on Sasha. I'm correcting my mistake.'

'Who gives a monkey's about Plotkin?!' shot back Igor.

'In society I will live by society's laws,' replied Veronika, enunciating very clearly. 'Take that as you wish. I am indifferent. Go back to your building.'

Igor rose to his feet. Fury was boiling inside him. Was he a stray cat to be fed in the hallway and thrown back out of the door? And he had no wish to break up with Veronika because of some nonsense of hers.

'I love you and I'm not letting you go. You got that?' He was above Veronika now, looking down at her, and she clutched at the bench with her hands as if to hold herself in place.

'Don't come near me,' she said a third time, but now her voice had lost its tone and been taken over by something hostile, as if danger lay in wait for Igor.

He did not move any closer, nor did he try to hug her or even simply stroke her shoulder to remind her of how easily they had come together previously. He ran down the steps of the gazebo onto the ground and walked away.

Veronika was silent, her blackened eyes staring into the void.

Igor marched toward his own building, pumping himself up so as to warm his soul with anger. But in the darkness, the icy horror of unfolding catastrophe caught up with him.

CHAPTER 10

ON THE BANK OF THE RIVER

'*Neckerchiefs burning warm and bright!*' the girls cried out in tune.

'*On our chests for all to see!*' shouted the boys.

The fourth brigade was stomping in formation to the canteen for lunch.

'*Bugles blast with all their might!*'

'*Hup-two! Forward! Hup-two-three!*'

'Guys, if we don't play Battleships today, I'm going to start eating my sweets,' Gelbich whispered to the boys next to him. 'Or I'll swap them with someone for something.'

Or feed them to Zhanka Shalayeva, Valerka added for Gelbich.

'You can't!' Gorokhov was indignant. 'Everybody waits, you wait too.'

'I got no willpower. Zilch.'

'Let's haul them out during Quiet Hour,' suggested Tityapkin.

So it was agreed.

Life in the camp was following its usual course. When the camp speakers blared out the signal for bedtime, Irina Mikhailovna hustled the pioneers into the dormitories, waited for silence, then handed over to Igor Alexandrovich and headed off to her own room in Building 3. Igor Alexandrovich wandered along the corridor and went upstairs. Gelbich poked his head through the door of Valerka's dorm.

'Fatty's scarpered and Moustachio'll be snagging forty winks,' he informed them. 'Let's move it, boys!'

'Where are you going?' Lyova half rose on his bunk.

'We'll be back in a jiffy,' Gurka reassured him.

There were five of them: Gelbich, Gurka, Valerka, Tityapa, and Gorokh. Stooping, they ran at top speed from the building to the washrooms and from the washrooms to the fence. They climbed the chain link and found themselves near the bush where they had hidden their little boats.

'Wait, boys!' Gurka stopped everyone and took two long pieces of chewing gum from his pocket. 'My mum brought them for me. I'm giving them to you. Brotherhood and that.'

'Cool dude!' The boys were delighted. 'Only how do we split two among five?'

'I'll tear them into pieces,' said Tityapkin. 'I have the eyes of an eagle.'

'Noo, they won't tear evenly and unevenly's not fair.'

'Let's do this,' said Gurka excitedly. 'Tear the chewing gum in half, there'll be four equal parts, you all chew them and then give them to me to chew.'

'That's not fair!' Gorokhov was indignant again. 'We all chew halves and then give you two whole ones? You got a nerve, you big-balled bison!'

Gelbich came up with an alternative. 'Let's count,' he said. 'On whom God sends. First one to get the finger gets nothing. End of story.'

Gelbich started counting, jabbing a long finger at the boys. *'Watermelon, muskmelon, arse bright blue! Watermelon, yellow butter, red arse you! Gorokhov, you!'*

'Bollocks to your blue arse!' Gorokhov practically burst into tears. 'You don't count so the first one's out. You point at who stays in.'

It seemed beyond them to resolve the problem.

Valerka found an answer. 'Look, I've got it,' he said. 'Let's do it like this. I don't chew anything, but I get two sweets from everyone.'

'Winner!' The boys were delighted, and went through their pockets.

This meant that Valerka now had the accumulated capital to play Battleships; without bets in the shape of sweets, the game was shorn of its thrill. The lads meanwhile shared out the gum and chewed it intently, looking into one another's eyes.

'Just don't swallow it,' Valerka advised them charitably. 'If you swallow it, chewing gum can stick to your heart, and then you'll die.'

Tityapkin let out a frightened hiccup. 'Boys, I've swallowed mine,' he whispered, petrified.

From the depths of the green bird cherry tree they hauled out the little ships they had stored there, pieces of pine bark sharpened against bricks, with sticks for masts. They mounted paper sails on the masts. The ships were ready to take to the water.

The bank of the Volga was empty at Quiet Hour. Seagulls wheeled in the sky, shrieking. The water hissed gently, stroking the camp beach all littered by the pioneers, and its strip of shingle along the surf. Good surf was rare here, though: out in the river opposite the camp there was a long sandbank which took the swell out of the incoming waves. A white buoy marked '114' was visible beyond the shoal. In the distance, a towboat with a low barge loaded with a loose pile of something was making its way up the Volga. The blue ridges of the Zhiguli were melting away in the sunlight like blocks of ice.

Gurka selflessly took off his tracksuit trousers, gathered the boats into his arms, stepped into the water, and deployed the flotilla onto a quiet patch of offshore water. The boys, meanwhile, were collecting stones for throwing. The idea was to fire them at the frigates until the boats went belly up. The last survivor would be considered the winner. The vessels were distinguished one from another by inscriptions on the sails, which themselves were made of scraps of newspaper. Valerka's was *Vda*, Tityapkin's was *Zda*, Gurka's was *Siya*, Gorokhov's was *Kva*, Gelbich's was *Bochy*.[21]

....

[21]   The boat names come from the names of newspapers then current in the Soviet Union: *Pravda* ('Truth'), *Krasnaya Zvezda* ('Red Star'), *Sovetskaya Rossiya* ('Soviet Russia'), *Vechernyaya Moskva* ('Moscow Evening News'), and *Gorkovsky Rabochy* ('The Gorky Worker'). The children have folded pages from these newspapers to make their boats, and only part of each paper's name remains visible. *Pravda* – 'vda', *Krasnaya Zvezda* – 'zda', *Sovetskaya Rossiya* – 'siya', *Vechernyaya Moskva* –

'Show me your stones,' Tityapkin demanded of everyone.

The stones were supposed to be the size of a plum, no bigger.

Tityapkin took a tile like a pancake from Gurka and threw it away.

'And you show us yours!' an offended Gurka demanded in return.

He, too, took one stone from Tityapkin and threw it away.

Gelbich stood up in the pose of a javelin thrower and commanded, 'Take your marks … set … go!'

A hail of stones rained down on the flotilla. There was a burst of plopping and splashing, and the small ships started to rock like a flock of ducks. *Siya* all but flipped over and then righted itself. *Zda*'s sail was soaked. Within a minute, the supply of ammunition was used up.

The lads rushed to look for new stones, but as if to spite them, the ones they needed had disappeared among the kopeck-sized shingle. The bombardment lost its intensity.

'Can we use buckshot?' asked Gurka, panting. He was bent over and furiously digging in the sand with his hands, like a dog.

'No!' Gorokhov was also bent double and the word came out in a strangled yell.

Tityapkin was the first to find a pebble, and he immediately launched it at the ships.

'Gorokhov's sunk!' he bawled happily.

Kva was floating sadly upside down.

'Ba-a-alls…!' Upset, Gorokhov flung away his ammunition.

'You'd have done better giving that to me!' said Gurka regretfully. 'I'd have had revenge on Tityapkin.'

Tityapkin immediately redirected his fire to Gurka's *Siya*, while Gurka launched a fusillade at *Zda*. Gelbich joined Tityapa and Gurka, cynically firing at their vessels: he hoped that double-dealing would increase the likelihood of his hitting one of his opponents. Valerka, meanwhile, took shots at Gelbich's *Bochy*. He was a rotten gunner, though, and his stone scored a direct hit on *Siya*. The *Siya* gave a hop, and overturned.

....

'kva', *Gorkovsky Rabochy* – 'bochy'. There is a second layer of humour in the Russian original, in that the name fragments sound funny, like bits of other words, sometimes obscene, sometimes simply amusing.

'Who have you hit, cross-eyes?!' howled Gurka.

Valerka merely smirked. The main thing was that his *Vda* was undefeated.

The wily Gelbich squinted – and his shell accurately sent *Zda* heeling over.

'That's it!' said Tityapkin, drooping. 'As always, the arseholes came out on top.'

Valerka and Gelbich could now take their time. They stood apart, so as not to get in each other's way, and flung their stones in conformity with all the rules, taking aim and swinging. Splashes rocked *Vda* and *Bochy*, but the ships held on.

The other boys sat down on the sand to await the outcome.

'If Vent-face wins, I'll swim to the buoy,' promised Gurka.

An importunate shout came suddenly from beyond the camp fence, 'Hey! Hey! What do you think you're doing there?'

The boys looked round. Behind the chain-link fence they could see Lyova.

'Why did you run away from the dorm?' His voice reached them angrily over the distance. 'It is forbidden to go out during Quiet Hour! Come back in!'

Valerka sensed the boys shrivelling inwardly. Even Gelbich let the hand holding a stone drop. But why should they be afraid of Lyova? Lyova was not a young leader.

'He guessed where we were,' said Gorokhov quietly.

Valerka looked at the boys for a moment, then stared at Lyova with hatred. Lyova was so very, very correct: trousers, white shirt and neckerchief… And he was correct not merely officially, or for show; he was for real. He drank blood only at night; otherwise he was fine.

'Didn't let us finish the game,' sighed Tityapa.

Gelbich shifted uncertainly, then grudgingly hurled his stone, turned, and trudged submissively towards the fence. The others also got to their feet, shook the sand off them, and plodded dejectedly after Gelbich. Lyova waited, looking judgmentally at his comrades through the fence. Valerka he did not seem to notice.

'What about the ships?!' Valerka shouted desperately after the boys.

The day seemed to empty in a rush. True, the lads were not his best friends, but still, they all lived as a group, played together, marched and sang brigade chants together, and they thought along very similar lines. And now they were all walking off, and Valerka was staying behind, not understanding why they could not also have stayed here, on the beach. You never knew what Lyova might want…

Seagulls squawked frantically over the sparkling shallows, swooping above the paper sails of *Vda* and *Bochy*. Valerka looked after the departing boys, and into his soul there crept a deadly fear that he was alone not merely on the bank of the river, but in the whole world.

CHAPTER 11

FETCHING BACK THE BELOVED

Igor tracked down Veronika outside the door to the canteen after lunch.

'Shall we have a smoke?'

'I've given up.'

'So let's talk without cigarettes.'

'Nothing more to talk about.'

'Yes, there is. I want to give Plotkin a political briefing this evening. I'll inform him of the state of affairs on the personal front. I'm sure it will be a fascinating conversation. Come and visit us. You can offer me authoritative support.'

Irony was Igor's way of masking his pain at the rift with Veronika and his fear at the changed state of affairs. The old Veronika would have done no more than wrinkle her nose in derision, showing her superiority over the petty palpitations of petty people. The new version glanced at him expressionlessly and walked away.

Igor spent the day mulling over their night-time encounter. It was his own fault that Veronika had decided to leave him. What had his love prompted him to do? Nothing. Of course, his inactivity did not speak of cowardice or laziness, but even so... He should have told Plotkin everything from the very start. He should have whapped Plotkin round the head with the news and sent him packing. But Igor had not tumbled to that in time. He had fallen into the trap of insouciance, lulled by everything being fine: for him, for Veronika, for Sasha.

What Plotkin was to hear that evening would surely ruin his relationship with Veronika. It was unlikely that the spoilt brat Sashenka was capable of magnanimity and forgiveness. And it was unlikely that the proud girl Veronika was capable of staying with a man before whom she was so guilty. At the same time, did Igor have the right to ruin their life together? Especially if Veronika said she did not want him to. Yes, he did. He believed that what he and Veronika had was true love, and that meant he must fight for it. Let the loser be the one who did not invest the whole of his heart in love.

Of course, Veronika might not return to him even after breaking up with Sasha. She was vain, and did not tolerate the hold of other people's will over her. But if her relationship with Plotkin was not ruined, she most certainly would not return.

These thoughts tormented Igor until evening. And even then, he did not succeed in starting the conversation immediately after lights out. First he had to quieten the boys in their dorms. Then Sasha went off to Company House to iron a shirt and trousers – there was a communal iron in Company. Then Zhenya Tsvetkova's stomach started aching; Igor gave her a tablet and waited for her to drop off. And then it got dark, and his zeal somehow wore off. Igor went outside for a smoke and to gather his courage.

He strolled under the pines, knowing that he was fooling himself and simply stalling for time. He could not face the coming air-clearing with Plotkin. Outlandish fragments of the wooden gingerbread houses, unevenly and uncertainly illuminated by the round moon, jutted from the darkness: an ornamented stoop leading nowhere; a corner of a roof suspended in the void; a soaring sharp-edged facade.

Suddenly, in the distance beyond the tree trunks, Igor spotted Veronika. She was walking from Building 3 towards number 4. Igor stopped, hoping she would not spot him. Veronika must be on her way to see him and Plotkin. In which case, she could meet Sasha on her own and tell him everything herself. It was a faint-hearted, unseemly wish, but Igor, embarrassed, succumbed to it anyway.

He smoked another cigarette, and then another, until he reckoned that up there, in the cubbyhole on the first floor, the most terrible words had already been spoken, and he could stop hiding. Igor threw away his cigarette and set off for the stoop.

Sasha Plotkin was asleep. Simply asleep. He had even forgotten to turn off the lamp on the table. The window, slightly opened, glittered. And there was no Veronika in the room, though Igor thought he caught the subtle scent of her perfume. *What's she done?* wondered Igor. *Flown away?* More likely, he had simply blinked and missed Veronika's escape.

He poked Plotkin in the side.

'What did Veronika say to you?' he asked.

'What Veronika?' stupidly asked a sleepy Sasha.

'Wasn't she here?'

'Here …? No one's been here. Why would Nesvetova come here?'

So she came in, saw Sasha, and left. She had taken pity on him. Or maybe she, too, had lost her nerve. The round moon grinned through the window. Igor flopped feebly onto his bunk. No, he would not say anything to Plotkin today. Tomorrow. Tomorrow.

All the next day, Igor observed Veronika and Sasha. Veronika acted as if everything was just as it had been. She laughed when Plotkin made a joke, and said something cheery herself. Sasha clearly did not suspect a thing. And Igor was no longer tormented by fear of exposure; now he was being eaten up by longing. Veronika was close by – and felt a thousand miles away. Igor watched her giving the salute, tying the girls' neckerchiefs, frowning sternly as she sorted out a quarrel, shielding her eyes from the sun, walking, fixing her hair… He could not lose her. He could not yield. Never. Not for anything.

Irina pulled him up. 'What have you been thinking about all day, Korzukhin?' she asked angrily. 'Your boys are chucking rubbish all over the place! Go and get to work!'

Igor struggled through to the end of the day, and after lights out he gave in and snapped, bellowing at the boys to go to sleep. Sasha, for his part, as if to spite Igor, spent ages fiddling with his stuff, rummaging through his suitcase, re-making his bed, cleaning his parade boots. Igor waited. It was already dark outside the window when Sasha was done.

'Tuck ourselves up?' asked Sasha, stretching a hand towards the light switch.

Igor stopped him. 'We need to talk.'

Sasha stopped, looking questioningly at Igor. Igor had been preparing for this moment for a long time. Now it had come, he had absolutely no idea where to start.

'Cutting to it, Sash,' he said, 'Veronika doesn't love you. It's just she's not turning you down because she's afraid of your family. She loves me. And we've already done everything.'

Igor let out his breath. The stone had been cast; now the avalanche was about to roll.

Sasha looked at him with a kind of tired sadness and disappointment, the way a teacher looks at a pupil who fails to prepare a lesson and then lies that he had to sit for hours at his grandmother's bedside in hospital, even though he has no grandmother.

The stone flew down the slope all on its own; the avalanche did not budge.

'Veronika warned me you'd blindside me with something like this,' Sasha informed him. 'I don't understand why you have to insult and cheapen our feelings for each other. You jealous? It's undignified.'

Igor was left in weightlessness and without air, like a scuba diver from whose mouth someone had suddenly yanked the snorkel.

'Veronika warned him?' So she had tried to indemnify herself against the blow?

At that moment there came a scratch on the window from outside.

The window was on the first floor. No one could have scratched it – unless they had put up a ladder and climbed... Why would they do that? And the sound was hideous, like the shriek of glass being scraped by metal.

Igor was still in a state of bewilderment, as if he was falling endlessly, unable to reach the bottom, the outer limit. He turned his gaze to the window, and beyond the glass, glaring in the light from the lamp, he saw Veronika's face, very pale, inexpressibly beautiful, her black eyes huge wells. Veronika's dark lips moved inaudibly. Igor read the command, 'Open up!'

He did not move; he was paralysed, turned to bone. Plotkin, however, skipped over to the window, rattled the latch, and swung the pane wide open.

Veronika did not climb through the window; her inhuman plastique could not be called 'climbing'. She moulded herself to the opening, bending her arms, legs and body inconceivably, the way young, double-jointed assistants fit themselves into a box which the magician then saws in half.

'Get away!' Veronika ordered Plotkin, her voice toneless.

Sasha leaped back and scurried off to his bunk.

Igor simply sat.

'You invited me, and here I am,' whispered Veronika, smiling at Igor.

Her quiet, gentle voice filled every part of the little room, as if the space itself were speaking. Igor shook his head to rid himself of the delusion, but was unable to take his gaze from Veronika's eyes. There was witchcraft in them, and far, far back, a flicker of crimson. And in her smile, the glint of two sharp fangs.

The truth dawned on Igor. *Veronika's a vampire!*

The thought was completely irrational, but vampires had already made a fleeting appearance somewhere on the periphery, and so reason did not resist admission of the impossible. Igor suddenly remembered Valerka Lagunov, that funny, serious little boy with glasses. The boy had tried to convince him that vampires existed. Igor had not believed him.

'I came yesterday, too,' continued Veronika, moving closer to Igor. 'But I didn't find you ... So I took the other one. Him...'

Veronika looked playfully at Sasha, who shrank, and nodded.

The impossible reality of the vampire was evident to Igor in every detail, but it was so shocking that it seemed alien, imposed on the consciousness by the will of a mocking hypnotist. Inside Igor's head everything started to judder and tumble, like a hail of books cascading from the shelves of an ancient library and bursting open at coloured pictures: *The Hammer of Witches* and the Holy Inquisition, the rampaging women of Salem, decapitated roosters in voodoo rites and revivified dead in Trinidad, a pale Count Dracula in a lace ruffle, coffins, empty graves, the ruins of old castles, cloudy mirrors, decayed robes, copper crucifixes, silver bullets, aspen stakes… Igor had no personal experience; all he had were images and words, like the first time with a woman or first time abroad, and he would never have believed in an infernal vampire, would have decided he had lost his mind, if he had not known Veronika before. She could not be one of *those*.

Horror was starting to make Igor nauseous, but some part of him still saw Veronika as human, and with his horror was mingled a mortal longing. Veronika had become a monster? She was no more? Igor could accept that vampires had appeared, but he could not accept that Veronika had disappeared.

But now he himself was about to disappear, in her fangs. He, Igor.

What was he to do? Spells from fairy tales bubbled up in his mind… 'I rescind my invitation,' Igor barely squeezed out. 'Go away!'

'This is Sashenka's house, too,' replied Veronika slyly. 'Sashenka also invited me to visit.'

Igor looked sideways at Sasha. Sasha had pressed himself into a corner. He was not afraid; he had nothing to fear any more. He had followed the order to get out of the way.

'He's your slave!' Choking, Igor threw his words into Veronika's shining face. 'He has nothing of his own, and no home either! This house is mine alone! Go away!'

It was as if Veronika was suddenly jolted by an electrical impulse. The current contorted her face. She fought with herself, but her body retreated of its own accord, as if someone were controlling it, the way a model aeroplane is controlled by radio. With the agility of a cat, without touching the table or the bed, Veronika retreated, then gave a sudden leap backwards, once again moulding herself to the square of the open window.

'We'll be together, just as you wished, my love,' she promised, and the next instant she was gone, absorbed into the darkness.

CHAPTER 12

FULL MOON

'Valera… Valera…' Someone was tugging at him, to wake him up.

He pried his eyes apart with difficulty. Gor-Sanych had pulled back the canopy of Valerka's little house and was leaning over his bed. His face was covered in shadow, and the pine grove, washed in the pale moonlight, glimmered beyond his shoulder. The boys in the dorm were asleep.

'Valera, get up!' begged the young leader, agitated. 'I need you!'

'Right now?' Valerka was surprised.

'Right now!'

Yawning, Valerka sat up, lowered his feet, and reached for his shirt.

Gor-Sanych was waiting for him by the stoop. He grabbed Valerka's arm and, without saying a word, hustled him away from the building. They hurried past the washhouse, Gor-Sanych looking around as they went, as if they were being hunted, and wriggled their way into the bird cherry near the chain-link fence. Gor-Sanych pushed Valerka down as if he were a rookie in a trench under fire, and stuck his own head out to check their surroundings.

'Who's after us?' asked Valerka grumpily.

Gor-Sanych got down so that he was shielded by the foliage, and looked Valerka in the eyes.

'I've seen a vampire.'

The fog of sleep in Valerka's head dissipated immediately, leaving no trace.

'Who?'

'Veronika Genrikhovna.'

Valerka settled himself properly on the grass. So, Grekhovna too.

'There are lots of them here. Vampires,' said Valerka seriously. 'Lyova Khlopov. Marinka Lebedeva. Alik from the drawing circle. Others, too. Must be.'

'Are you sure about those three?'

'Yes.'

'How?'

'I've seen them bite people.'

Igor Alexandrovich shook his head, distressed. 'How do you keep yourself safe? Like from Lyova?'

'They don't bite during the day. Just at night. And at night I'm in my little house. They can't come in without an invitation. And I'm not stupid enough to invite them.'

Of course. The key was the house. Igor understood. Every night he watched Valerka Lagunov using his sheet to craft himself a crude tent over his bunk. His little house. Valerka was not hiding from mosquitoes. He was hiding from vampires.

'And you're not afraid?' asked Igor.

Valerka looked away and shrugged his shoulders.

'Yes, I'm afraid. But what else can I do? I've got used to it.'

Igor looked at Valerka as if seeing him for the first time. This little boy, nothing to look at, a wimp in glasses, had been living in a nightmare for days, and living in it alone. He had worked the whole thing out, but had no one with whom he could share his discovery, no one to call on for help, and even his young leader – he, Igor Sanych – had paid no attention to him. Only the vampires knew that the boy was right. But the boy had not panicked, not given up; he had come up with a way to defend himself. He was a fighter, a fighter pure and simple. Igor did not sense in himself – alas – the same courage.

'I'm sorry I didn't believe you,' said Igor sincerely.

'Never mind,' replied Valerka awkwardly.

The bushes whispered among themselves in the light breeze from the Volga. Cicadas chirred in the lush grass. Beyond the palisade of trunks, Pioneer Avenue glowed. The moon shone high in the sky; tonight it was full. The pine grove, the bird cherry and the grasses breathed a hot fragrance, as if the smells were liberating the earth from the stifling heat of the overripe summer.

'I love Veronika Genrikhovna,' Igor confessed to Valerka simply. 'And I can't bear it that now she's ... like this.'

The boys were aware that Gor-Sanych loved Grekhovna. Some approved, some disapproved. Valerka felt how much Gor-Sanych was hurting.

'I want to return her to human form,' Igor continued. 'Which means I need to understand everything about vampires.'

'What is there to understand about them?'

Igor picked a small black berry from the bird cherry.

'There is no afterlife,' he said firmly, as if refuting someone. 'And the dead don't come back to life. So vampirism is a disease.'

Valerka did not argue – but nor did he agree.

'In the old days, ignorant people mistook certain sicknesses for dying and being transformed into a demon. You know, someone could become completely unresponsive. They hadn't actually died, and they woke back up. But people said they'd died and been resurrected.'

Gor-Sanych was looking for a rational explanation for the vampires in the pioneer camp.

'They exist according to laws of some kind. We need to work out what they are.'

Valerka had never considered the nature of vampires before.

'Tell me, Valer: Lyova and Veronika. Are they dead?'

'They don't look dead,' offered Valerka cautiously.

Igor rejoiced, as if his diagnosis had been confirmed by a professor of medicine.

'I'll use Veronika as my example. You tell me if I'm wrong. Our vampires eat regular food. They sleep. They're not at all afraid of the sun. They're not characters from Gogol, rising from their graves...'

Valerka had not yet read Gogol.

'If vampirism is a disease, there must be a cure for it. This is the twentieth century. Mankind can already fly into space!'

'You want to hand them over to the medics?' suggested Valerka.

He imagined putting a lead round Lyova's neck and dragging him to the doctor's surgery like a rabid dog, Lyova balking, hissing, and spraying saliva.

'No, not the medics.' Igor shook his head.

Modern science denied what he was interested in: Abominable Snowmen, the Loch Ness monster, Brocken spectres, flying saucers. Modern science would shut a vampire in an asylum and block the doors and windows; there would be your cure.

'In the old days there were rituals to cure people with such illnesses,' said Igor, devising a strategy as he went along. His thoughts were teeming. 'Something'll come back to me. I just need to determine their *modus operandi* ... you know, the way they go about things.'

'Drinking blood is the way they go about things,' grunted Valerka.

'No, that's not enough. How are they different from ordinary people in the daytime?'

Before Valerka's mind's eye appeared Lyova Khlopov in his trousers, white shirt and neckerchief... Then Albert, also in trousers, white shirt and neckerchief... Model pioneers, as if straight from parade inspection and songs.

'They're ... they're correct!' Valerka was dumbfounded by his own conclusion.

'And?' Igor stopped, also beginning to formulate a thought.

'They're correct,' repeated Valerka confidently. 'And being correct is not normal.'

That was right. Of course it was. Everyone was incorrect. Even oh-so correct Anastasiika, top pupil and brigade commander, believed in gnomes and imps.

Igor was struck by the accuracy of Valerka's observation. Veronika, too, had become correct. The phrase she had minted that night: 'In society I will live by society's laws.' Why would she do that? Because vampires needed to hide from people, and the best way to hide was not to attract attention, to become like everyone else, to become a nobody, not to stand out, to submit to the generally accepted order.

'By day they're ideal citizens and at night they drink blood!' Igor amazed himself. 'By day they're like scouts surrounded by enemies. Meaning they're perfectly well aware that they're vampires, and they camouflage themselves.'

'Why don't all the ones they bite become vampires?' asked Valerka. 'Khlopov bit Mukhin, but Mukhin's not a vampire. There are others too.'

'Maybe they're immune to infection?' Igor immediately suggested. 'The consequences of a bite depend on the organism. Some people get infected and turn into vampires, and others don't get infected and don't turn into anything.'

Valerka was not happy with this suggestion. It was not just the vampires who changed; the ones who had been bitten also changed, though they did not become vampires. Like Slavik Mukhin. Or Masha Styazhkina, bitten by Marinka Lebedeva. Valerka recalled an unremarkable incident in the canteen. Slavik had wanted to follow the boys in harassing Old Nyura and throw his spoon into the leftovers tub, but Lyova had forbidden it, and Slavik had not thrown his spoon into the tub. Valerka also recalled Marinka Lebedeva ordering Styazhkina to pick up a piece of rubbish, and Masha had picked up a dry branch from the asphalt. There were many trivial incidents like that. Except they were not trivial. These trivial incidents began to coalesce in Valerka's consciousness into big pictures. The boys had not wanted to play football – and suddenly they had started playing as if they were in the Olympics. The painters from the drawing circle had wanted to cover their papers with cats and butterflies – and suddenly they were drawing upper class toffs with bombs. They were all doing things they did not want to do. And doing them on the orders of a vampire.

'The ones who don't become vampires serve one of the vampires,' whispered Valerka.

Igor stopped again, comprehension dawning.

That first time, when Veronika had not found him at home, she had bitten Sasha. Then she had appeared again. 'Open up!' she had commanded Sasha, and Sasha had opened the window. 'Get away!' she had commanded Sasha, and Sasha had stuffed himself into a corner. She had also said that Igor would lie about their love, and Sasha had not doubted her words… The ones who had been bitten did not merely serve the vampire. They became subordinate. Enslaved. That definition of Sasha that had burst out of him had certainly hit the mark: 'Slave.'

There was a definition of Valerka Lagunov, too: genius.

'Will you help me fight them?' Igor asked Valerka. 'Fighting vampires is a good thing. And you and I are a real collective.'

A feverish chill ripped through Valerka. The summer night suddenly became darker; the full moon shone out as if washed clean, and the honeyed smell of grass was intoxicating.

'I'm with you,' said Valerka firmly.

PART FOUR

241

A VAMPIRE'S FEAR

Thrones running red with the blood of the people
we shall turn red with the blood of our foes.
Gleb Krzhizhanovsky, 'Woman of Warsaw', 1897

CHAPTER 1

BOOBY-TRAPPED

The game was as follows: Yurik Tonkikh had buried his right hand in the sand, his fingers cunningly curled. This was a 'mine'. 'Sapper' Valerka was carefully digging it out, trying not to touch it. If contact were made, the mine would explode: Yurik would quickly yank out his hand, flinging a whole heap of sand in the sapper's face. Not that Valerka was afraid of being blown up. Tonky was a weed; he would not throw sand the way Tityapkin or Gurka would, and what was more, Valerka had protection – his glasses. True, because of them Valerka was considered a sapper of no great interest, and as a result only Yurik had agreed to play with him.

'Idiotic horseplay,' remarked Anastasiika, passing by.

Businesslike, Valerka raked a ditch around the mine and began to clear away the sand from above with his fingertips. The outline of Yurik's hand came into view. Valerka set about blowing on it. Yurik giggled as the sand tickled him lightly. His hand flinched, and his fingers appeared from beneath the sand. Valerka confidently pressed Tonky on the fingernail of his middle finger, and the mine was defused.

'Now you're the sapper,' said Valerka, and immediately slipped his hand into the hot sand with its small stones.

Yurik, sniffling, bent over the mine, and Valerka gazed over Yurik after Anastasiika. She was truly beautiful, in a blue swimming costume, with a wide-brimmed hat, and a towel wrapped around her waist. Against the dazzling sky she seemed woven out of the darkness that swims in your eyes when you look directly at the bright sun for a long time.

Of the six brigades, only four had been brought out on to the beach. The first brigade was on duty, and in the fifth, the nurse, Miss Pasha, had counted too many runny noses. The tots were squealing and splashing, frolicking in the 'paddling pool' by the river bank – an area of shallow water enclosed by wooden walkways. The two peas, Maxim and Kirill, both wearing thick inflatable life jackets and pointed caps with red stars, were patrolling the bridges, and at the same time monitoring the patch of calmer water where the older pioneers were swimming. There the boys were repeatedly attacking the girls amid much splashing and yelling. Only the children had the energy for all this, though. Summer had already overfed the camp, dishing out heat like sweets. Weary of swimming and even sunbathing, the young leaders had covered their heads with panama hats and were simply sitting on the sand in shorts and T-shirts and waiting out the obligatory water-borne procedures.

Gor-Sanych was reading a book, occasionally breaking off to glance at the beach. Every time he met Valerka's eyes, Valerka immediately acted as if they had not had their night-time conversation and that nothing at all connected the two of them. There were vampires everywhere, and secrecy had to be observed. He and Gor-Sanych were like snipers in an ambush: if you moved, you would give yourself away. But Gor-Sanych was a lousy sniper: his face was swollen, his eyes were red, and he looked like a sick man. For Igor, the outcome this morning of the previous night's discoveries was mental and physical ruination.

Some of the 'steamrollers' – sporty lads from the second brigade – and a few of the older girls, who were less self-conscious and more good-looking than the others, were standing in a circle, carelessly tossing a ball around. Every now and then one of the steamrollers would clasp his hands together and knock the ball straight up, high into the air. Zhanka Shalayeva, so sharp and streetwise, turned out to be clumsiness itself in the game. She would miss the ball altogether, or send it sailing sideways, or lose it. Anyone else with such butter fingers would have been thrown out long since, but Zhanka was tolerated because of her gangster connections.

It was Zhanka herself who tired of the game. She left the circle, fixed her black glasses on her nose, and walked over to Gelbich, who was lying on his spread out clothes, absolutely whipped. He resembled an aeroplane that had run out of fuel and crashed.

'What you doing lolling about here?' asked Zhanka. 'They're calling me cack-handed!'

'Yeah, well, if you are cack-handed…' explained Gelbich lazily.

Zhanka dug up some sand with her foot and kicked it onto Gelbich's chest.

'Let's go in the water!' she demanded.

Lyokha Tsybastov was sunbathing next to Gelbich.

'*Little Miss Zhanna went for a dip,*' he wheezed rustily. '*Flipped in on Wednesday, flopped out on Saturday.*'

'What's up, Tsybukhin? You got too many teeth?'

Tsybastysh was silent. This cretinous cow was always picking a fight with him, and he was sick of answering.

'If you don't come, I'll tell Lyolik you're a cocksucker.'

Tangling with Zhanka's armed forces was something no one fancied.

'All right,' agreed Gelbich, resigned.

'Me too, then,' rasped Tsybastysh.

'Me too eats bowls of poo,' retorted Zhanka.

She had appropriated Gelbich and did not want to share him with Tsybastysh.

In the distance, a hydrofoil was buzzing over the scattered sparkles of the Volga. Valerka watched it, squinting. It would be sick to surf the waves rolling towards the shore from the mighty hydrofoil, but the sandbank opposite the beach would take the swell out of them, and, alas, there would be nothing to ride.

Igor was brutally sleep-deprived. Valerka Lagunov might have learned to sleep next to a vampire, but Igor had dozed off only just before first light and his head was now drooping over his book. His backside was numb, his back stiff, and his eyes kept sliding off-centre. He set the book aside and stood up. His brains were running in the heat, like melting chocolate. Igor was wearing sandals on bare feet. He waded out into the water and splashed his face. He loosened up with a few stretches and then strolled along the beach to check on his pioneers: they might have burned up, or be secretly playing cards or throwing sand.

Exhausted by the stifling heat, the pioneers were behaving peacefully.

A little way off, observing his brigade, stood Sasha. His hands were clasped behind his back, and he had stuck a large leaf to his nose and arranged a triangle of newspaper over his head. Igor stood next to Sasha and clasped his hands behind his back in exactly the same way.

'Where's Veronika?'

'She's not feeling well,' Sasha informed him dryly.

The events of the previous day had stopped Igor experiencing any embarrassment in front of Sasha. Sasha had subordinated himself to a vampire and was shorn of his own will, leaving Igor indifferent to his opinion. Even so, Igor wanted to know what was going on in the mind of a man in Sasha's state: what was he thinking, how did he evaluate the situation? Igor understood that his desire was Jesuitical, but so what? He did not feel sorry for Plotkin. And right now he had no strength for sentiment and standing on ceremony.

'Probably worn herself out looking for a victim,' Igor suggested of Veronika. 'Dinner with me didn't work out.'

Igor very much disliked his own words; he did not want to talk about Veronika in that tone, but he needed to make Sasha angry.

'I would advise you to stop acting like a teenager and think seriously about our conversation,' Sasha lectured him.

'Really? We had a conversation yesterday?' Igor was surprised. 'I thought Veronika only turned up to drink my blood.'

'You can say whatever you want. But it has been clearly explained to you that you need to change your behaviour. Stop acting like you're a Don Juan and a Casanova. That's not who you are. Deep down, you're a good person. And Veronika and I are not your enemies. Moderate your vanity and observe the norms of sharing the same space.'

Igor studied Sasha intently. *Was he lying, or did he really not remember that Veronika was a vampire? A vampire: of that there was no doubt.*

'So last night all you did was lecture me about my morals, right?' Igor clarified. 'And Veronika didn't try to bite me?'

'What is she, a dog or something?' snapped Sasha hotly. 'I'm fed up of your verbal antics, Korzukhin! Stop spreading filthy rumours about you having an affair with Veronika. I understand that you don't care about your reputation – I mean, it's not as if you actually have one – but show some respect for the reputation of the young lady.'

Igor finally accepted that for Plotkin, the previous day's visit from the vampire did not appear to have happened. No fangs, no open window, nothing. Just a stern ticking off for the brazen Lovelace. Thus victims often defended their violators and the exploited defended their exploiters.

'Have a haematogen, Plotkin,' said Igor. 'It'll help you when you're giving blood.'

Sasha was about to respond, but at that moment, the torpidity on the beach was suddenly ruptured by a high-pitched shriek. The shrieker was Vika Milovanova from the second brigade. Igor had met her at the Olympics viewing sessions in Serp Ivanych's little house.

Vika had been sitting in the shade of a willow tree all morning, in a swimming costume but wearing a neckerchief and a peaked cap with a visor: she had no wish either to swim or to sunbathe. The neckerchief seemed to announce the firmness of her intentions. But Zhanka Shalayeva did not care about things like that. If there was an opportunity to squash someone, how was she to resist squashing?

Zhanka, Lyolik, and Gelbich were dragging the kicking Vika towards the water, guffawing as they did so. Zhanka and Lyolik held her by the legs, and Gelbich by the arms. Throwing someone into the river was a usual pastime of the stronger ones, and even the young leaders did not punish them for it; they dished out a scolding for the sake of form, and that was it. Of course, no one was going to drown Vika; they would swing her and send her plopping into the water where it was knee-deep, so that she did not have the excuse that she was not swimming because she did not want to get her swimming costume wet. But Vika had barely felt the freshness of the water when she set up a visceral, terrifying howl and flew into a mighty rage. Suddenly possessed of indescribable strength, she snatched up Gelbich with a powerful jerk of both arms, and threw him over herself, wrestler-style. One swing of her leg and Lyolik went flying. Zhanka jumped back just in time to avoid being winded by Vika's heel. Vika flopped backwards onto the sand – and was instantly once more on her feet. With gigantic leaps she raced away from the river bank, flying over the pioneers sunbathing on the sand like a steeplechase champion. The pioneers watched her go, their mouths gaping open in amazement.

'You've totally blown a fuse, Goatzilla!' cackled Zhanka nervously.

Igor was not remotely amused. In the girl's furious, headlong flight he had seen something abnormal, frightening, and inhuman. People only ran like that when they were fleeing a horrifying and deadly danger. But swimming posed not the slightest danger to Vika Milovanova. What was it that had terrified her?

Igor glanced at Valerka. Valerka was sitting in the middle of the beach, his hand buried in the sand. Yurik Tonkikh was diligently digging it out. Valerka could not have failed to notice Vika. He answered Igor with a perplexed look and shrugged silently: *I don't know what's up with that cretin.* Valerka's hand shifted when he shrugged, and Yurik jabbed his finger happily. 'Found the detonator!' he exclaimed.

'You missed,' protested Valerka. 'Ker-bang, Tonky!'

A blast of sand struck Yurik in the face.

CHAPTER 2

MONKEYS AND EAGLETS

After the Parents' Day match, Lyova formed a team from the two middle-school brigades, and many of the boys finally got their freedom from the hated football. Igor reckoned a vampire completely trustworthy when it came to discipline, so he left the team in Lyova's care, rounded up the unclaimed boys, and took them to Company. The boys needed to be fitted into the circles somehow so they would not hang around unsupervised. The number of the unclaimed found itself swelled by the incursion of Gelbich; he was hoping to get into music, where Zhanka Shalayeva was queen bee. Valerka, too, was marching in the general party to Company House. He was indifferent to whether he did drawing with the vampire Albert or singing with the vampire Grekhovna, although at music he would be able to see Anastasiika.

'Last shift the oldies said they had one boy who brought his guitar with him,' Seryozha Domrachev was saying, regaling them along the way. 'He played the guitar like, whoo, could he play. Everyone asked how he'd learned, but he wouldn't say. The oldies took his guitar and looked in the hole and there was a chopped off hand inside. It was a musician's hand. It was the musician playing through the hole, not the boy.'

'How'd they know it was a musician's hand?' asked Slavik Mukhin sceptically.

'The oldies shoved a piece of paper and a pen into the guitar and the hand wrote to them.'

'Yeah and where'd he dig up a hand like that?'

'In the cemetery, where else?' answered Seryozha severely.

'Balls!' Gurka was upset. 'Pity they don't write on graves what a geezer did while he was alive. I need a hand to fix my bike.'

After Parents' Day, Company House was quiet, as if its batteries had run down. Igor let Valerka and Gelbich into the big room where the classes were being held – though Veronika was not in the room. The circle members were not surprised by the newcomers; it was not as if they were actually new. A bored Zhanka immediately made tracks for Gelbich.

'Look what the cat's brought in,' she said. 'What you here for?'

'Not to see you!' replied Gelbich, smiling broadly.

Zhanka looked at Gelbich from head to toe, as if she were trying him on.

'You want me to tell you what your wife's last name'll be? I got the magic to do that.'

'Yeah, go on,' agreed Gelbich eagerly.

The circlers hushed, interested in Zhanka's chicanery.

'Pull out twenty hairs for the fortune-telling,' commanded Zhanka.

Grimacing and hissing with pain, Gelbich began to pull out the hairs.

'Seven… Twelve… Nineteen…' counted Lyolik.

Smirking, Zhanka held out her palm. Gelbich carefully placed his hair on it and scratched his throbbing head. Zhanka squeezed one eye shut, stretched her lips, and mischievously blew the hair onto the floor.

'Your wife's last name will be Gelbich,' she said.

Everyone around her burst out laughing, including Gelbich.

Valerka moved seats, closer to Anastasiika.

'You want a sweet?' he asked in a low voice.

He had specially brought the least crumpled of his cheap sweets for Anastasiika.

Anastasiika examined the present sceptically.

'I like real sweets, not these. Chocolate improves one's tone.'

Valerka was hurt. He squeezed his sweet in his fist. Ah, he had wasted his time coming; he was not appreciated here.

Anastasiika noticed his disappointment.

'All right, come on,' she relented. 'We'll eat half each.'

Igor was talking to Veronika in the corridor. 'I've brought the boys to you,' he said.

'Good. They'll all find something to do.'

Igor was trying to work out if the Veronika standing in front of him was the old one, or was she already someone else?

'Do you remember what happened last night?'

Veronika straightened the neckerchief on her breast and gave a nonchalant shrug.

'Nothing happened. We talked. That was it.'

She was there, but as if behind transparent glass. Igor's attitude to this new Veronika was one of displaced hostility. It was if she were carrying out someone else's criminal orders and she personally was not to be judged. Still, Igor wanted to find out if Veronika was a robot, automatically acting according to a programme, or a soldier: someone who obeyed commands but deep down inside retained something truer to themselves – a love once felt, or at least regret for the loss of that love. Inside Igor himself, beneath his impassive shell, the coals of desolation were smouldering and would not go out. Igor wanted to shatter the glass separating him from Veronika. Then the coals would once again flare into a bright flame.

'We just talked, and nothing else happened?' Igor trapped her gaze. 'I know you've become a vampire.'

Veronika sighed, and looked away, as if this were making her feel awkward.

'Save your stories about the Bermuda Triangle and the Loch Ness monster for the pioneers,' she advised him. 'We're adults. I've taken a decision dictated to me by my conscience, and it's final. Let's not go back over things we've already discussed. It's not easy for me either.'

Is she like Plotkin – unable to see what's right in front of her nose and unaware that she's a vampire? wondered Igor. *By night she drinks blood and turns her victims into slaves, and by day she believes that she simply persuaded them to change their minds? That must be it. I mean, you could go crazy if you knew that at night you grew fangs and a dark force was driving you to find human blood.*

Veronika rounded Igor and headed towards the room where the circlers were waiting.

Inside the room, Zhanka Shalayeva immediately rushed towards her.

'Vnik Grekhovna, me and Lyolik have come up with something totally awesome!' she babbled excitedly. 'We're monkeys in "Chunga-Changa", right, so we don't need wire tails, we need rope! We'll pull each other's tails like we're fighting, and we'll wag our tails. And our arses.'

'Zhanna, what was that you said?' Veronika pulled her up.

The self-confident Zhanka did not bat an eye. Attention had spoiled her; she had no doubt that she had greater licence than everyone else.

'Lyolik, come here!' she yelled.

Lyolik, smiling stupidly, stepped forward, skipping ropes in her hands.

'These are, like, our tails,' said Zhanka, explaining the skipping ropes.

Zhanka and Lyolik stood in line, Zhanka on the left, Lyolik on the right. Zhanka took a folded rope in her left hand, Lyolik one in her right.

'Three, four!' commanded Zhanka. '*Chunga-Changa-a, blue ski-ies above the grou-ound, Chunga-Changa-a, su-ummer all year round!*'

Zhanka and Lyolik, both of them sinuous and slender, started to sing and dance; they twirled their skipping ropes in time and brazenly stuck out their backsides, wiggling them in synch. The effect was provocative and seductive.

'Ew, how indecent!' Anastasiika shuddered squeamishly.

Gelbich was grinning happily, his whole maw stretched wide, while Valerka felt ashamed, as if he had been caught peeping into the girls' toilet.

'Zhanna, Lyolya, stop prancing around!' Veronika irritably cut short the dance and pulled a face. 'No, girls, that is not for the stage!'

Without looking at Zhanka and Lyolik, she went across the room to her place next to the record player. On a chair nearby was a stack of envelopes containing records.

'Boys and girls!' she said to everyone in the room. 'We're changing the repertoire for the Last Bonfire concert. "Chunga-Changa" will not be in it.'

'Why?' Zhanka flew up at once.

'Chunga-Changa' was her star number.

'Because it is not in keeping with the spirit of the pioneer camp,' said Veronika flatly, flipping through the records. 'It's summery and fun, of course, but too childish and frivolous for us.'

'You got a frigging nerve!' snapped Zhanka indignantly.

'Shalayeva, hold your tongue!' answered Veronika angrily.

Zhanka pushed her way roughly to the back of the room, shoving chairs and benches out of the way, and huffily took a seat apart from the collective. Lyolik clumped after her friend in sullen silence. Gelbich hesitated, and then moved over to Zhanka as well. The other circlers maintained a fearful silence.

'The final song will be "Eaglets",' announced Veronika.

Back at the start of the shift, Anastasiika had suggested singing "Eaglets", but Veronika had rejected it in favour of Zhanka Shalayeva and her monkeys. Now Valerka saw Anastasiika proudly straighten and her eyes sparkle with the triumph of restored pre-eminence.

'You've chosen this piece of toffee, huh?' Zhanka shouted angrily from across the room. 'I'll get her back, the little she-goat.'

'Shalayeva!' Veronika barked into the room.

Zhanka bent down, buried her face in her hands, and sobbed at full volume. She despaired with abandon, not ashamed in front of anyone. Everything was on display with her, for public viewing: joy, sorrow, the tricks she played on the people around her.

'I didn't cry when I was turned down!' Anastasiika reminded everyone in her superior way. 'Because I have willpower.'

'Let's pull ourselves together, shall we?' suggested Veronika tiredly.

At that moment the door opened a crack and Lyova Khlopov slid sideways into the room. Trying to be inconspicuous, so as not to hinder the work, he snuck round the wall, swivelling his head, looking for someone. Gelbich was ineptly stroking the sobbing Zhanka on the shoulder. He caught sight of Lyova and tensed up.

'Venka!' whispered Lyova. 'Without you we don't have a team. Come with me!'

Gelbich's face started to twitch, as if struggling to find an expression.

'Venka!' repeated Lyova. It was not a request.

Gelbich stood up, shoulders hunched, and shuffled dejectedly away from Zhanka and towards Lyova Khlopov.

CHAPTER 3

'DARKNESS IS THE FRIEND OF YOUTH'

At dinner Valerka applied the required moral pressure on Vovka Makarov in the form of a glass of compote with dried fruit, the stones of which could be chopped open to get at the kernel, and bought the pistol cartridge for a rouble. A cartridge was useful, not to mention valuable: throw it on the bonfire and it would go off. But, alas, the purchase was intended for Beklya.

After evening meal, the fourth brigade headed for Company to watch a film. Valerka slipped out of the ranks. He was hoping that Irina Mikhailovna would not notice his absence and Igor Sanych would not give him away. Valerka left the camp grounds and made his way through the forest to the abandoned church, where Beklya had left his goods – soap, cigarettes, and a spool of thread – for the Escaped Convicts to exchange.

The orange sun lay on the Zhiguli Mountains beyond the Volga. The pine trunks, at noon incandescent like gold, at sunset had turned purple, as if they had cooled. Alternating light and shadow striped the forest. From deep in the bush came the cry of a lonely bird, as if a wagon had toppled over somewhere and its wheel was still squeaking in its dying turns. Valerka breathed lungfuls of the intoxicating pine fragrance, its tartness diluted with the freshness of fern.

Amid a cluster of hazel, the brick church showed red, resembling a rusty and dilapidated steamship stranded on the bank of the Bishop. Here, fate had an unexpected snag in store for Valerka. Of a sudden Beklya, Rulet, and Siphilyok emerged from the bushes at the edge of the grove. The shitbags had, it appeared, also made their way to the church to collect the offerings left by the Escaped Convicts.

'Freeze, sky sail!' Beklya shouted at Valerka.

Valerka was not scared. He and Beklya were pretty much mates now. Valerka put on a happy smile.

'Shake!' Beklya held out his hand for a handshake.

Valerka put out his hand, but with a hoodlum's dexterity Beklya grabbed him above the elbow and drove a fist under his ribs. Valerka let out a gasp. Beklya twisted Valerka's arm, flipping him round so his back was towards Beklya and he was bent over double.

'What are you doing?' howled Valerka, stupefied.

Rulet and Siphilyok sniggered.

Valerka felt Beklya's hand slip into his pocket.

'Whoa-hoa, a cartridge case!' Beklya informed his toadies with satisfaction.

'Let me go!' demanded Valerka. 'That case is mine!'

Beklya twisted his arm harder, restraining him, and good-naturedly asked, 'You wanted to filch what the cons brought me?'

'Piss off!' said Valerka indignantly. 'I don't take stuff that's not mine.'

'His mouth's running,' said Rulet confidently.

'Four Eyes thinks we got shit for brains,' said Siphilyok, playing along.

'So. It'll cost you three roubles, Rabindranath,' decreed Beklya, grinning. 'You'll get it to me by the end of the shift. Clear?'

Valerka almost froze completely. 'You and me, we're thick as thieves.' He could barely form the words.

'Suck my dick,' replied Beklya.

Valerka suddenly realised what a complete, irredeemable dunderhead he was. How could Beklya be his mate? Bekla was a hoodlum, past, present, and future. He was a hooligan and a thief. He would cheat, go back on his word, betray – and all with a laugh. These were the low rules of the low life: double-cross the simpleton, then fleece him or leave him high and dry. Friendship with Beklya was as valuable as a dollop of glistening gob.

'Hold on to him.' Beklya shoved Valerka at Rulet. 'I'm going to check out the ruin.'

'What the hell do you want him for?' asked Rulet, taking over Valerka's twisted arm. 'Let's do him over and push off, Vasya.'

Squinting, Beklya looked towards the setting sun.

'He'll come in handy when it gets dark. *Darkness is the friend of youth.* Don't let that streptococcus go, you freaks.'

Beklya moved easily towards the church. The shadow of the forest already lay over the clearing in front of the church, but the crowns of the pines were still painfully bright green in the fading sky. The first chill was creeping in.

Beklya's long stride suddenly slowed for some reason, and in front of the breach in the wall he stopped altogether.

'Well.' Beklya hesitated, then called out to his toadies, 'Come here!'

Rulet shoved Valerka forward.

'Best if I take care of Four Eyes and you get yourselves in there,' said Beklya, giving orders.

He gave no explanation for his change of mind, and Rulet and Siphilyok made no attempt to question him. A vague fear hovered somewhere in Valerka's mind.

It was all very strange. On the previous occasion, Rulet and Siphilyok had wimped out of going into the abandoned church, hollering about how there were crosses there. Beklya had not quailed. Now he was clearly afraid. What were the ruins hiding? Or who? Escaped Convicts? The mutilated church rose in the translucent twilight with a kind of immanent threat, as if an armed ambush was hiding behind its walls, as if the church were merely pretending to be dead, while in reality being only badly wounded and still able to inflict a killing blow. But how? What the hell threat could come from those ruins? What could crosses do?

Valerka began to tremble. Beklya wanted to keep hold of him until it was dark. Siphilyok and Rulet were submitting to Beklya just as the footballers submitted to Lyova. And ... Beklya was unable to enter the church. Realisation came, bright as a bolt of lightning: Beklya was a vampire. Beklya had become a vampire, too. Valerka would have seen it at once, but he had been thrown off by the fact that Beklya was not correct, like a pioneer. He did not wear a red neckerchief, did not observe the daily routine, did not participate in the exhibitions and sports competitions. That said, though, he *was* still correct: a correct punk.

Run! Run for it!

Valerka swept his surroundings with a despairing glance. He would have to run into the pine grove. Every other avenue was cut off by a line of impenetrable brush along the bank of the Bishop. In the expanse of the pine forest, he might be able to break away from his pursuers, and his salvation, the camp, would not be far off. First, though, he needed to get rid of Rulet, who had Valerka's arm up his back.

Valerka swung his leg and stabbed his heel into Rulet's shin as hard as he could. Rulet gasped, and curled over as if he had been chopped. Valerka swivelled his shoulder, jerked his arm out of Rulet's grip, and darted forward. The nitwit Siphilyok was also hulking in his way; with a single shove, Valerka knocked him into the grass. Beklya managed to grasp the fact that his prisoner had broken free, and leaped sideways, blocking the way with his big paws outstretched like a goalkeeper. His eyes gleamed eerily black in the twilight; a predator's eyes. Valerka darted aside and rushed towards the only place available – the ruins of the church. Beklya would be unable to follow him in, and Siphilyok and Rulet were a pair of wusses; Valerka hoped he would be able to cope with them. Once he was there, in the church, it would become clear what he was to do next. Valerka flew up onto a pile of brick rubble and ducked into the breach that served as the entrance.

A square box of pitted walls. Holes for windows, from which hazel branches stuck out. Heaps of detritus, mouldering planks, bottles, and other rubbish. Dense shadows in the corners. Pale sky overhead, as if vampires had sucked the blue out of that, too. In the height beyond the edge of the wall, Valerka could see the dark crowns of the pine trees. Their colour had faded; the sun had dropped below the horizon.

'Drag that four-eyed dog out here!' Valerka heard Beklya give the order.

Valerka dashed about the temple. The vampire was thirsty for blood: he had gained power. Valerka remembered Beklya's words: *Darkness is the friend of youth.* That was what the boys said when they were planning to sneak out of the dorm at night. Valerka was flooded with horror. He had nowhere to hide; no one would protect him. He had no home, no friends. Gor-Sanych would not help him. He, Valerka, was alone against the devil. And the church was a trap. What was he to do with Beklya's punklets? Knock them senseless with a brick?

Valerka knew what he had to do. He had to jump out the window, crawl through the thicket, and rush into the woods. Beklya could not guard every window. Perhaps he would get lucky.

Rulet appeared in the gaping hole of the entrance, followed by Siphilyok. Valerka picked up a stray dirty vodka bottle and launched it at Rulet. The bottle shattered loudly against the wall. Valerka flung a heavy lump of brick, then another, and then the piece of soap Beklya had left to swap with the Escaped Convicts. Rulet and Siphilyok crouched down, cowering behind the heaps of rubble. Valerka made a dash for the wall, grabbed hold of the branches poking through the window, pulled himself up, squeezed his eyes shut, and went tumbling into the dense undergrowth outside.

Using his body to batter through the unyielding hazels, Valerka went crashing into an anonymous piece of scrap; it was as if he had landed on bare mattress springs. He floundered frantically, and with one hand clawed his way towards the light, where the thicket ended. Branches scratched him, leaves whipped him, and he kept his glasses pressed to his face with one hand. The sensation was not unlike wintertime in the school cloakroom, where the boys played tag among the ranks of coats and jackets until the attendant shooed them out. Indistinct yelling broke out somewhere behind him as Rulet and Siphilyok also blundered into the jungle.

A sudden explosion – or so it seemed – shook the trembling and tangled mass of bushes on Valerka's right, and Beklya fell out at Valerka. Unwilling to wait for his victim to jump out in front of him, he launched himself into attack – but missed narrowly. Valerka jinked to the left, squeezing past a tree trunk. Beklya snagged his shirt on a branch and lost his chance to catch Valerka. The shirt ripped and tore open, and through the foliage and the twilight and out of the corner of his eye, Valerka saw that the vampire's chest, like the wheelhouse of the river bus, was decorated with a five-pointed star, only not red, but blue, and drawn with a ballpoint pen.

Valerka had no time to think about that. On all fours he crawled out of the bushes and onto the grass. Then he leaped to his feet and rushed into the pine forest.

'Where are you, you dipshits?' Beklya's voice came from the bushes, braying at his patsies. 'You dipsticks! I'll smack you from here to Wednesday! Get your mitts on Four Eyes!'

CHAPTER 4

BLOODSUCKERS

Valerka raced through the neat pine grove in a perfect straight line, like a bullet. He ran towards the camp so fast he might have been accelerating for a jump to the moon that was currently hanging over Storm Petrel. Pines flashed like the boards of a fence; fern sprayed in all directions like green water; cones falling under his feet flattened with a crunch and were squashed into the ground. And behind him in the twilight three shadows charged, soundless and swift – the vampire and his henchmen.

Valerka made it to the bird cherry bushes covering the hole in the fence along the back yard of the food block. It was here that Valerka had fought Beklya's patsies in defence of Anastasiika; here they had taken his tube of 'space food' and matchbox micro-calculator. Valerka dived into the bushes. He was forcing his way through the jagged tear in the chain link when he heard a noise. Beklya had also come crashing into the bird cherry; he had not given up hope of catching his runaway.

In the light of a street lamp, Valerka saw rubbish bins, a pile of empty crates, and the back wall of the food block. From the food block to Building 4 was still a long way, but Valerka knew of no other hiding place beside his own building. Shit. Beklya would still catch up with him, only in the camp rather than the forest. But… the iron door to the kitchen was ajar, meaning that there were grown-ups in the food block. Surely Beklya would not bite Valerka and drink his blood in front of the cooks and scullery maids.

Valerka made up his mind and darted into the food block.

Shelving piled with plates and glasses. A cupboard housing huge aluminium pots with red numbers on the sides. Tin sinks. A butcher's table with a galvanised top. Buckets. Pipes. Enamelled hobs hooked up to huge gas cylinders. Two windows covered with bars. A fan. Doors to the pantry, the canteen, and the toilet. The dark opening of the serving hatch. Up against the ceiling, bath lamps with podgy shades and iron guards. Electricity chirring somewhere. The smell of burnt oil, cabbage, and chlorine. Out of all the staff, the only person in the kitchen was Old Nyura, that bad-tempered, listing, stuttering hag. She was mopping the floor.

'Baba[22] Nyura, hide me!' pleaded Valerka.

'Nuh-uh…' hmmed the scullery maid in astonishment.

Valerka grabbed a large butcher's knife from the table, dodged into the toilet, and clacked the bolt. He would not give up. He would sit in the bog until morning, until the sun took away the vampire's thirst for blood.

Through the door Valerka heard a racket – the wheezing of his pursuers and the scurrying slap of footsteps across the wet floor.

'W-where are you g-going?' mooed Old Nyura angrily. 'I w-washed it.'

'Let me go to him!' Beklya's voice was a strangled hiss. 'He's my carcass.'

'G-get out!'

'Don't touch me!' shrieked Beklya hysterically. 'Push off, rotten blood!'

'G-get out of h-here, you g-ghoul!'

Valerka gathered that the scullery maid was poking Beklya in the belly and chest, and Beklya was being forced to retreat. For some reason he was unable to bite the old woman.

There came the rattling of the iron door and the swoosh of the bolt. Silence hung over the place.

....

[22]   Translated as Old Nyura in narrative passages and left as Baba Nyura in direct speech. The word 'baba' signifies an old woman or a grandmother in children's speech.

'C-come out,' Old Nyura at length ordered Valerka through the door.

Valerka thought for a moment, and then drew back the bolt.

Old Nyura, her head sloping to one side, looked him over. Small, dishevelled, in glasses, a large knife in a whitened fist.

'N-nothing's b-been s-sucking your b-blood?' she asked incredulously, then sighed heavily. 'Everyone g-gets their b-blood s-sucked here.'

Shocked, Valerka uttered not a word. He had not expected anyone else to know about the vampires in the pioneer camp except himself and Gor-Sanych.

'Or are you a b-bloods-sucker yourself, l-little one?' asked Old Nyura. She thought for a moment and then answered her own question. 'Nuh-uh, you w-wouldn't c-come p-poking in here if you w-were a b-bloodsucker.'

'H-h-how do you know?' Valerka seemed to have caught Old Nyura's stammer.

'I b-been w-working here eigh-eight summers. H-how c-could I n-not h-have n-noticed?'

Old Nyura took up the mop she had leaned against the wall and started to wipe off the dirty marks on the floor. She worked with the ordinary peaceableness of someone who had just chased away a mischievous dog rather than a vampire.

Valerka looked out of the window. Darkness was waiting for him outside, like a wild animal.

'Baba Nyura, can I stay here?'

'S-stay, do, I w-won't b-begrudge you. J-just s-sit d-down, don't t-tramp m-my c-clean f-floor.'

Valerka tiptoed across the strip Old Nyura had mopped, put the knife on the table, and sank onto a stool near the stove. Old Nyura was bent over, wringing out a cloth into a bucket. Valerka watched her, but she said nothing more.

Valerka recalled the boys discussing how gnarled Old Nyura had links with the Escaped Convicts. They said she gave them fat pioneers and ate human flesh.

'Who are they, these vampires?' asked Valerka cautiously.

Old Nyura was silent for a moment, then spoke. 'Well, who-who … g-ghouls, who else? They d-drink children's b-blood at night. The ones they d-drink from, they c-call their w-watering t-trough, their c-carcass. Each of them h-has a wh-whole h-herd of c-carcasses. They s-suck a f-few d-drops at a t-time, s-so the c-carcass d-doesn't d-die. And the children, their d-drinking t-troughs, they d-don't even kn-know they're g-giving their s-sweet b-blood t-to these f-filth … f-f-filthy…'

Valerka shuddered with horror and disgust. 'Am I a carcass too?'

Old Nyura hung the wrung out cloth on a pipe and straightened it.

'G-god saved you, for now,' she said. 'Or that g-ghoul w-wouldn't have b-been ch-chasing you. They d-don't b-bite others' c-carcasses. Their own c-come to h-hand, l-like goats. They go to m-milking themselves w-when they're c-called. Afterwards they d-don't remember a th-thing, and they're f-faithful to their b-b-b-bloody shepherd.'

Old Nyura picked up the bucket of dirty water and headed for the door. She fearlessly pushed back the bolt and went outside. Valerka heard her empty the bucket into the bushes with a splash.

Old Nyura returned.

'Why do vampires need carcasses?' Valerka wanted to know. He had to find out as much as possible.

Old Nyura pulled out another stool from under the table and sat down to take the weight off her feet.

'W-what f-for? They c-can't g-go roaming after b-blood e-every n-night. Their own c-cattle. They c-call one and it c-comes to m-milking.'

Valerka went cold. 'And they do that all their lives?' he asked.

'Noo,' Old Nyura waved a reassuring hand. 'The b-bloods-suckers d-don't l-live l-long. Year, n-no m-more. C-carcass feeds him a w-while, then he d-dies and baby is f-free, b-baby w-won't remember a thing, like a b-bad d-dream.'

'Vampires die within a year?' Valerka looked at Old Nyura wide-eyed.

'They g-go to h-h-hell,' asserted Old Nyura.

So they were all doomed? Lyova, Albert, Marinka Lebedeva, Beklya, and even Veronika Genrikhovna. Impossible. The vampires aroused in Valerka unspeakable revulsion, but even so, not long ago these … these creatures had been people, and there was still so much humanity in them that their deaths seemed to Valerka more monstrous than their vampirism.

The wrong done by the vampires was one thing, but death was quite another.

Valerka felt that a yawning chasm had suddenly opened up beside him.

'Impossible!' He would not believe it.

Old Nyura smiled sadly, twisting yet further her already twisted face.

'W-why w-would I lie?'

'How do you know?' persisted Valerka indignantly.

Old Nyura slid off her stool, wheezing and crackling. 'I w-was a b-bloods-sucker m-myself. H-how c-could I n-not kn-know?'

It seemed to Valerka that he was no longer quite normal.

'But you're alive! Why are they going to die?'

'God h-hauled me out of h-h-hell… B-but, ahh, m-messed up, I am.' Old Nyura crumpled her face with her hand. 'L-left leg and arm p-paralysed, t-tongue s-stiff as b-b-bone… This old b-body hardly m-moves… B-but G-god w-was on m-my s-side!'

Old Nyura reached into the collar of her greasy house coat, pulled out a silver cross on a string, and kissed it reverently.

Valerka had no idea what to say.

'Don't g-go b-back to your b-building,' Old Nyura advised him. 'Your b-bloods-sucker will g-get to you again in the night. I was a p-pig-headed b-bloods-sucker l-like that t-too. S-sleep h-here. I'll l-lock you in, iron d-door, c-come m-morning I'll l-let you out.'

Valerka could hardly comprehend what Old Nyura was suggesting. Was Beklya going to shove his way into the dorm? No! But Valerka would still have to get back to the building.

'The young leader will miss me,' Valerka remembered. 'Igor Alexandrovich. I'm in the fourth brigade. You go to the building, tell him about me.'

'I'll g-go,' promised Old Nyura. 'And d-don't you b-be afraid.'

She picked up a purse and hobbled to the door. The door closed, and the padlock clinked in its loops outside. Valerka was alone.

He sat. He was overwhelmed; in his mind something gigantic was shifting. The pioneer camp was a vampires' stockyard? A vampire farm? That explained why the ones who were bitten obeyed the vampires but were not conscious of anything and did not die. But why did the vampires themselves die within a year? Valerka jumped down from his stool and walked across to the window. The lamp over the door to the food block lit up the dustbins, the bird cherry, and the link fence. Behind the fence, pine trunks showed in the darkness. The pioneer camp was asleep. Or rather, the carcasses were sleeping peacefully and the bloodsuckers were moving silently and elusively in the darkness, like hard-working villagers taking care during the bountiful summer to fatten their cattle for winter.

Someone drummed on the iron door, and Valerka jumped.

'Valera! Valera!' came the agitated voice of Gor-Sanych.

A wave of happiness washed over Valerka. He rushed to the door.

'Igor Sanych, I'm here!' he whispered excitedly through the crack.

'Are you all right?'

'Everything's fine! Baba Nyura hid me!'

'What happened, Valerka?'

'Everything's fine!' repeated Valerka. 'Gor-Sanych, you'd better go back to the building. It's dangerous out. There are vampires everywhere!'

'I'm knackered. I've been looking everywhere for you.'

'I'll tell you tomorrow,' promised Valerka. 'I'll tell you a story'll make you shit yourself. Come back in the morning when Baba Nyura's unlocked the door.'

CHAPTER 5

SANDPAPER ON MY EARS

'Up! G-get up!' Old Nyura was poking and prodding Valerka.

Valerka had shifted a few benches in the dining room, and the result had been more or less a bed, albeit without mattress or pillow. Valerka had lain down and instantly fallen asleep. He had slept without dreaming, and had not heard Old Nyura return.

'G-go, little one! The b-boss is c-coming!'

Old Nyura unceremoniously put the befuddled Valerka outside.

A light morning haze had spread over the camp. Illuminated by the low sun, it was filled with the slanting shadows of buildings, trees, and bushes. The world appeared to have found a ghostly double, or perhaps Valerka was simply sleeping on his feet. The black dog Fidel emerged from somewhere and sniffed Valerka in a business-like way, as if making enquiries, and then for some reason rushed eagerly to the rubbish bin rather than the food block door. Then Gor-Sanych appeared. Valerka thought the young leader would sniff him too, but Gor-Sanych started rubbing Valerka's ears.

'I'm awake, I'm awake!' protested Valerka, shaking his head.

'What happened yesterday?' Gor-Sanych searched Valerka with his gaze.

On the way to their building, Valerka recounted everything he had learned from Old Nyura. In the light of the sun, her revelations did not seem as terrifying as they had when it was dark. The world was a wonderful place, and the breaks in it could be repaired. But Gor-Sanych shuddered. Valerka knew he was frightened for his Grekhovna.

'Is that exactly what your Baba Nyura said? That all the vampires would die within one year?'

Gor-Sanych was hoping Valerka had heard wrong or got mixed up.

'Exactly,' said Valerka, not sparing him.

Gor-Sanych hauled out his cigarettes and lit up nervously.

'Yes, but how do they die? And where do the new ones come from?'

'I didn't ask,' answered Valerka guiltily. 'Everything was coming at me all in a great heap...'

'But Baba Nyura managed to survive!' Gor-Sanych, of course, was furiously searching for ways to save Grekhovna. 'How did Baba Nyura manage it?'

'Let's go and have another talk with her,' suggested Valerka sensibly.

If he had been free to do so, Igor would have rushed to the food block then and there and grabbed the scullery maid with her crooked mouth and forced her to tell the whole truth. The world around was too solid and stable, too right in its foundations, even if it did contain all kinds of stupidities and flaws, for life – strong, stubborn life – to be able simply to up and submit to some fallen unclean spirit. Life always fought for itself, life prevailed, and that meant there was a way out. Even if vampires had secretly built their spider's nest in the pioneer camp, it was they who were afraid of life and not the other way around. And that meant they were vulnerable. They had to be overcome.

Silver bugles were sounding reveille through the camp's loudspeakers.

In the dorm, the boys were already dressing. Lyova looked Valerka over, appraising him, but said nothing. Valerka pulled a towel from behind his headboard.

'Where were you last night?' asked Slavik Mukhin.

'Making a bonfire on the shore.'

'Why didn't you invite us?' Gurka waded in, offended. 'I totally make bonfires.'

'I want to come too.' Yurik Tonkikh also sought an invitation.

'The normal way to light a bonfire is with one match,' Gorokhov told him patronisingly. 'Yes, Tonky? You don't know how to do that, you dipstick.'

'I got loads of matches!' protested Yurik.

'A bonfire on the shore is bollocks.' Tityapkin kicked his bedside cabinet in annoyance. 'I was at my gran's in the village, torched her neighbour's barn, motorbike in there.'

'Maybe we could set fire to the hospital here, guys?' said Gurka animatedly.

'Last shift the oldies said that one of them took a tyre from the pier and threw it on a fire,' said Seryozha Domrachev. 'There was so much smoke they brought in a fire helicopter.'

Valerka listened to the boys in silence, thinking about the fact that they were carcasses. They did not know it, but to the vampire Lyova they were not friends, not a football team; they were carcasses whose blood could be drunk, little by little. Lyova noticed Valerka's quick, dark glance, and grinned. Lyova had everything he wanted, and Valerka was an outcast. He was lying about his night-time bonfire because he'd been too scared to sleep in his own bunk.

The camp day was starting as it always did. The brigades lined up in Company Court, the red flag flew up the flagpole, birds chirped in the thickets, the speakers spewed out hearty pioneer songs, and a blast from the klaxon of a moored river bus reached them from the Volga. Standing next to Irina at the head of the brigade, Igor was pretending to look at Whistler, but he was looking at Veronika.

The breeze was ruffling her hair. Her face was as soft and fresh as if she had been sleeping serenely like a child all night. But these days she did not sleep. Igor turned over in his mind how Plotkin would get up and go out, right on the wolf hour, obeying an unknown call. It was Veronika, thirsting for blood and waiting for him somewhere in the darkness. In the sunlight, though, Veronika was as she had been when Igor had fallen in love with her, when he had embraced and kissed her as they lay in the grass on the bank of the Bishop. The Veronika to whom he had told stories of conquistadors going into the rainforest and never coming back, and of the eruption of Santorini that destroyed Atlantis. It was not Plotkin and Svistunova who had separated Igor from that Veronika, but an anonymous ill will; it had captured her and sentenced her to destruction.

Assembly finished, and the young leaders led their brigades back to their buildings.

'Natalya Borisovna has ordered you and Lagunov to go and see her,' Irina told Igor in a low voice.

'What's up?' wondered Igor.

'What's up is that Lagunov did not spend the night in his dorm.'

'How do you know?'

'Khlopov told me.'

'So how does Whistler know?'

'I told her,' answered Irina defiantly.

'Do you never get tired of snitching?' asked Igor angrily.

He looked Irina Kopylova over from head to toe. What was she? he wondered. A bloodsucker? A carcass? Or was she oh-so correct all on her own, without vampirism?

Igor and Valerka met Whistler on Pioneer Avenue.

'Don't try and compost my brains, I won't believe you anyway,' said Whistler with weary contempt. 'For you, camp rules don't have any force, do they? One of you meanders about all night and the other covers for him. Got a nice deal going, you two. How much of this are we supposed to put up with? To hell with it! Here's what's happening, Korzukhin: you get Lagunov's stuff packed up right now, and after lunch I'm sending him on a boat to town. Kapustin'll turn him in to the police, and he'll be in juvenile detention while the police find his father and mother. This little toerag can be their headache, not mine.'

'They're in Baikal!' blurted out Valerka truculently; he had not yet appreciated the threat.

'You'll stay in detention until they come for you. You're a tramp.'

The Senior Pioneer Leader was not joking. It finally got through to Valerka that he was being unceremoniously thrown out of camp. His heart nearly ruptured. Of course he was afraid of the vampires here, but he was even more afraid of letting his father and mother down. Having a son in juvenile detention was an unbearable disgrace.

Dad would be distressed, Mum would cry. What could be more terrible than that? Better to die.

'Let's do this another way!' argued Igor, upset.

'Give all comers head and you'll break the bed,' replied Whistler coarsely.

Igor grimaced. He was struggling. He might still have fought against his boss's decision, but for some reason he did not. Valerka looked at him, bewildered and hopeful, but Gor-Sanych had such a guilty look that Valerka immediately guessed. Gor-Sanych agreed with Whistler.

Icy despair coursed through Valerka. Gor-Sanych believed that Valerka would be safe in the city. The vampires would not get to him there. Valerka's cheeks flushed red with anger. *Oh, Gor-Sanych. And you said we were a collective.*

Valerka took a step back as if he wanted to make a dash for it, but running away was not in his thoughts.

'D'you know why I didn't sleep in the dorm?' he asked Whistler.

'And why is that?' asked the Senior Pioneer Leader, sarcasm twisting her face.

'Because you have vampires in your camp.'

Whistler almost spat at Valerka's feet. 'Your voice is sandpaper on my ears,' she snapped. 'You're sick, Lagunov, and you're not getting any better. Come up with something a bit brighter! I've had it up to here with your fancy stories. That's it, you had it coming. Go home!'

Little Valerka Lagunov looked at the Senior Pioneer Leader through his glasses, as if through the scope of a sniper's rifle.

'You were in charge here last summer, weren't you?' he asked boldly.

'What difference does it make to you?' snarled Whistler, furious now.

'How many of your young leaders and pioneers have died since last summer?'

It was such a wild question that Igor stared at Valerka as if he were a madman. Valerka seemed to Igor to have become glass – brittle, hard, and transparent.

Svistunova was dumbfounded.

'What are you talking about!' she answered, sounding like a schoolgirl bully.

Pioneers passing by turned to give Svistunova frightened looks.

'How many?' Valerka stubbornly repeated.

Igor's brain was working feverishly. If the bloodsuckers died, then of course they would not die in camp; they would die in the city. They died later, after the summer shifts: in autumn, winter, spring. But rumour of the deaths would have to have reached Svistunova. And Svistunova would have to have suspected that something was amiss. She had probably tried to persuade herself that the camp harboured no dark secret. She would have been racked by doubts, though. That was inescapable. She drove them away because she could not find anything unusual in the camp, but the fear had lodged deep and firmly in her soul. It seemed that she had managed to curb it, and then Valerka had landed such a blow that all the locks burst and her fear broke out into the open. The same happens when a person vaguely senses an ailment of some sort, but brushes it off, denies it, and then the doctor comes and says, it's confirmed: you have cancer.

Whistler was frantic. Igor could sense it, deep inside her. She had taken to her heels in headlong flight, running like a cat from a dog.

'Galya Kuznetsova was run over by a car! Novosyolov drowned!' screeched Whistler. 'Vorobyov was basically drunk and froze in a snowdrift! What's that got to do with anything?'

'And how many died of illness?' Valerka pressed his attack.

'Petrova had a heart defect! Congenital! And Rybina had meningitis! And Verka Shestopalova was simply poisoned! Poisoned by tinned food!'

Igor stopped hearing the singing of the birds and the music coming through the speakers. This was how the bloodsuckers died. Illnesses, accidents. And who would ever link them one to another? Students and schoolchildren from different districts of the vast city: there was nothing to unite them. Nothing – except a shift in a pioneer camp. The vampirism remained as elusive as an unidentified flying object.

'But all the ones who've died were here,' said Valerka, quietly summing up. 'With you.'

Svistunova looked at Valerka, then at Igor, her expression hunted.

Igor was convinced that Svistunova did not know about the vampires. She was not in league with the unclean spirit. She was also neither a carcass nor a bloodsucker. She was simply a herdsman on a farm. Why would the vampires want to destroy the Senior Pioneer Leader when it was so convenient for them to raise their own livestock under her management? Perhaps the bloodsuckers were unaware that their lives would be foreshortened. And perhaps not all of them died.

Igor put an arm round Valerka's shoulder, easing him aside. Enough was enough. Whistler was broken. That was enough to stop her harrying them.

Valerka flinched at the touch, as if waking up.

'Enough, Natalya Borisovna,' said Igor, his tone soothing. 'We'll forget this conversation, OK? It's not long now to the end of the shift. We'll get through somehow.'

Svistunova turned without a word and practically ran down Pioneer Avenue.

CHAPTER 6

'NOT UNSETTLING?'

Igor was sitting on a bench in front of the stadium watching the footballers practice. Under Lyova's leadership, a contingent from the fourth brigade was doing battle with a contingent from the third brigade with a view to merging the best forces of both contingents into a common team at the end of the shift. As football, it was all more technical than before, but as a game it was duller. The sacred fire that had driven the boys to do battle with their opponents, their teammates, and the rules had gone out. When Tsybastysh and Makerych had flung themselves into beating Tityapkin, when Gelbich was hoicking Gurka out from between the posts so that Gurka would not stop a goal being scored, when Gorokhov was bellowing that everything was against the law, it had been a more interesting spectacle.

Valerka was not with Igor; he had gone to his singing circle. In Valerka's place, Dimon Malosolov had somehow imperceptibly materialised.

'Anyway, Igor, there's a hundred roubles in it!' he whispered hotly. 'The building's empty, the room's free, but Irishka's supposed to be out with the pioneer girls.'

'So?'

'So go instead of her! And me and her in the room … eh, eh. Whoo.' Dimon rubbed his forefingers together and smiled an ingratiating smile.

He was still eager to seduce Irina. Igor knew Dimon well; he knew how impatient and frivolous he was. It was obvious to

Igor that Dimon was genuinely in love, otherwise he would have lifted his siege long ago and switched to another girl.

'Irina can't stand me. You think she'd she agree to let me help her out?'

Dimon wrinkled his mobile face to signify *I'm begging you! For my sake, of course she will.*

Igor left the players without any concern for their well-being. The vampire Lyova would make sure order was maintained.

Irina was busying herself with girls from the middle brigades who did not want to sign up for any of the circles. The girls were wandering through the unmown grass along the fence, picking flowers and making wreaths. Irina was trying on a wreath and did not look at Igor, but she did flush a little with embarrassment and annoyance.

'I'll keep an eye on them,' he promised.

'Thank you.' Irina barely squeezed out the words.

Now that Irina's fundamental humanity was in the ascendancy over her correctness, Igor found that he could actually like her. She was a good girl, even if she was a stubborn cow. Her correctness was of herself, not prompted by some vampire's designs. It was possible to forgive her. And she was exactly the kind of girlfriend the chaotic Dimon needed.

Dimon enthusiastically dragged Irina away, and it was clear even from Irina's bulky behind that everything was slated to work out for Malosolov this time. Igor felt another keen slap of longing for Veronika.

The girls Irina had been tending went into raptures at the idea of that nice Gor-Sanych spending time with them rather than strict Rin Khalna.

'We are now moving off to Company!' announced Igor.

He wanted to be closer to Veronika, to look at her.

'Why?' asked the girls.

'It will soon be the end of the shift. I suggest you draw cards to give to the boys at the Last Bonfire. You can write your wishes and addresses or basically whatever you want. It will be a memento of the camp.'

Igor knew from experience that for some reason it was important for girls of their age to leave behind a romantic and meaningful memory of themselves. Igor was not mistaken: the girls liked the idea.

They headed, all of them together, to Company House. The girls clung round Igor, hanging on both his arms and chattering nonstop.

'Do you have a wife? Will you be a young leader next summer? What flowers do you like? Have you been to the sea? Is it true that Beklemishev will be put in prison? What would you rather have: a cat, a dog, or a horse?'

On the bench by the entrance to Company, the camp director Kolybalov was talking to the food block supremo. Kolybalov was wearily fanning his sweaty face with a *kapron* hat with holes in, while the lady supremo was looking decidedly disgruntled; she was being distracted from her beloved Captain Kapustin.

Igor left his herd of girls in the corridor and glanced into the room where the dinky young leader Ninochka was busy with the young artists. Easels cluttered the room, and Alik Stakhovsky was walking up and down between them.

'Nina. I need paper – scrapbook size – and scissors, pencils, paints, and a separate cubbyhole,' said Igor.

Within ten minutes he had established the girls in the chess room, which was now empty: the chess players were having a competition somewhere outside.

'What should we draw? What should we write?' asked the girls.

'Draw flowers, butterflies, a bonfire maybe, ships. Write something like "Swan so white, down sublime, don't fall in love with two at one time." Then you need to cut the card out in a nice shape and fold it in half.'

Igor's instructions wholly satisfied the girls.

Igor went out into the corridor. Now that he was not being deafened by the girls' chatter, he could hear music. Veronika's circle was rehearsing a song in the cinema room. Igor made his way furtively to the room and quietly opened the door a crack.

Veronika was sitting near the table with the record player. A record was spinning. Anastasiika Sergushina was standing in front of the circlers and singing loudly:

'*They say life's war and rightly so, and there'll be no retreat, oh no, no, no!*'

Igor looked at Veronika. Her face was strangely detached, as if she were the bird falling from the sky to the rocks.[23]

Valerka suddenly appeared in front of Igor. Igor backed away in surprise, and Valerka slipped out into the corridor after him.

'Has something happened?' he asked anxiously.

'No, I was just, you know, checking…'

Igor did not want to admit that he was pining. Valerka had conceived his hatred of vampires on pure principle, but Igor hated them because of Veronika. That motive might not seem sufficient to Valerka, and his trust might waver.

'I spotted the director here and was thinking maybe I should try and tell him everything?'

Valerka stepped towards the window and looked at Kolybalov. The supremo lady had already left, and the director was sitting on his own, still fanning himself with his hat.

'He won't believe you,' said Valerka decisively. 'Telling him the truth is a no-no.'

'Really?' Igor was surprised.

'Look at Lyova or Albert. They're the ones who are correct. I almost got kicked out. The vampires are better than you and me, Gor-Sanych. They'll take notice of them, not us.'

Valerka tactfully did not mention Veronika in his list of vampires.

A fair-haired little girl looked out of the chess room.

'Igor Sanych, in 'snuff it', do you spell "snuff" with *f* or *ph*?' she yelled.

'Two *f*s,' replied Igor automatically, and then immediately realised what he had said. 'Hold on, what kind of wish is that?'

But the girl had already disappeared.

'I'll risk it,' Igor decided. '*You don't take a risk, you don't drink Validol.*'

After the cool of Company, the warmth of the sun felt like pressure applied by light. Birds chirruped. Children's voices floated in from afar.

Igor perched on the edge of the bench next to Kolybalov.

....

[23]   A reference to a line in the song.

Igor was silent for a moment, then said cautiously: 'Nikolai Petrovich, it seems to me that all is not quite right in our camp.'

Kolybalov sniffed, and offered no reaction, as if there were no one beside him.

'Nikolai Petrovich,' Igor tried again, determined to remind the director that he was there.

'What is not quite right?' asked the director irritably, without looking at him.

Igor thought for a moment. Who was there for him to be afraid of? Kolybalov was not the young leaders' boss. The most he could do was snitch to Whistler. No big deal.

'Some of the children and young leaders in our camp are turning into vampires,' Igor informed him calmly. 'I've seen it for myself.'

Kolybalov went on fanning himself with his hat and staring off into the distance.

'Does that not unsettle you?' inquired Igor politely.

'Sanitary inspectors have audited the camp,' said Kolybalov reluctantly. 'So too the fire brigade. And Public Nutrition. There are no violations of health and safety or work discipline in the camp. There have been no accidents. Everything is in order here. You'd do better to see to your own affairs, my lad. You have pioneers left unsupervised.'

It was as if Kolybalov had not heard Igor mention vampires. As if vampires were as commonplace as head lice, and therefore it was not worth paying them any special attention. Then it hit Igor: the director knew about the bloodsuckers. He had been working at the camp for a long time. He must be aware of the pioneer camp's night-time secrets. But what could he do? Rooting out the vampirism was beyond him. And if you wanted to complain about ghouls, where did you go? The police? The trade union? The Regional Committee?

All this meant that no one had caught the vampires. And everything was in order in the camp. The vampires posed no threat to camp order. Best to let things keep ticking along, unhindered. Retirement was just around the corner.

'Don't you feel sorry for the children?' asked Igor.

'I have children of my own,' objected Kolybalov reasonably.

Irina quite suddenly appeared on the path leading to Company. She was walking so fast and purposefully that her breast was quivering. She was red in the face with rage and shame. She dashed past Igor without slowing her pace.

Behind Irina came a guilty Dimon, also in a hurry. Igor stood up. Dimon grabbed his arm and pulled him aside.

'Bollocks!' he groaned. 'What a bummer, Igoryokh!'

'What, she did a runner?'

'It was all set!' Dimon was almost in tears. 'Bit of this, bit of that. Bit of the other. We were already on the bed. Then that leader of yours came poking in. Svistunova! I rolled under the bed like a scout behind enemy lines. The whole thing's gone to hell in a handcart. Irishka'll never agree now. Talk about bad luck. Bundle me in a bag and boot me halfway to Thursday!'

This was plainly a day of disappointment for one and all.

CHAPTER 7

GUARDIAN ANGEL

Valerka liked the way they all sang enthusiastically together: *'Nothing can scare them from the sky! The eaglets are learning to fly!'*

Then Anastasiika's voice rang out much more beautifully, clear and bright. It freed itself from the chorus and shone alone like the long beam of a lighthouse:

'No simple thing to fight the high, and harder still to be uncompromising!'

Anastasiika was unabashedly enjoying the sound of her own voice. She reached upwards, following the song, as if she was climbing somewhere or being elevated above those around her. Her clear solo triumphed over the disordered chorus.

The pioneer song sincerely stirred Valerka. Company's walls seemed to disappear, and Valerka saw precipitous white cliffs, glistening sea and cannon surf, boiling foam and flying spray, piercing sky and the blinding sun at its zenith. Valerka felt strong, brave, and stubborn – altogether an eaglet, albeit in glasses.

'Well, not bad, not bad,' admitted Veronika Genrikhovna.

'And it would be even better if we removed the lack of talent from the choir,' said Anastasiika nonchalantly.

'And who would you suggest?'

'Semyonova and Lagunov.' Anastasiika named them without hesitation.

Valerka was not offended. Compared with Anastasiika he did not sing; he howled like a hungry dog. Listening would be just as good, as long as he was not thrown out of the circle.

'And Petukhov and Shalayeva,' added Anastasiika.

She could not have forgotten that she had offended Zhanka before. Moreover, it was true that Zhanka squeaked like a rubber doll in choir.

'You said what, you rat?' said Zhanka, angry at once. 'I can't sing, yeah?'

'Singing is not dancing like a monkey.'

'Whose voice from the garbage dump is gently asking for a brick?' Zhanka flew up.

'*Monkey, monkey, nice long tail, monkey, monkey, bricks for sale,*' replied Anastasiika.

'Shalayeva!' Veronika Genrikhovna barked sternly at Zhanka.

Zhanka had already dropped off Veronika's list of favourites. After 'Chunga-Changa' had been cancelled, Zhanka had started losing one position after another. Valerka saw how mad it was making her, but he had no sympathy for her. Shalayeva deserved it. She should not be such a hooligan. Except that in defeat, Zhanka had become more of a hooligan than ever. She was probably hoping to make everyone around her so annoyed that Grekhovna got sick of it and reinstated 'Chunga-Changa'.

I wonder, thought Valerka. *Which is Shalayeva? Bloodsucker or carcass?* Bloodsuckers were correct, and carcasses were obedient, but Zhanka was neither correct nor obedient. Well, perhaps she was obedient, but listening to one of her own, for example Beklya, like Rulet and Siphilyok. Carcasses could be punks if the bloodsucker told them to be so. But a punk bloodsucker like Beklya could not sing in a choir. Punks were not supposed to do that. Punks were supposed to steal, smoke, and take money off weak people. If Zhanka was a punk, that would mean she was not a bloodsucker. And that meant she would not bite Anastasiika.

'I'll get you back, Sergushina!' promised Zhanka furiously. 'You better not walk on your own, you might meet me in a bad mood.'

Anastasiika pretended to be indifferent to Zhanka's threats.

At the end of circle time, Valerka waited for Anastasiika at the door.

'Can I see you back?' he asked glumly.

Anastasiika looked at Valerka thoughtfully and appraisingly. She was holding her coloured bag with both hands and bumping it with her knees.

'It seems to me that you are insufficiently physically developed.'

Of course, Valerka was shorter than her, and he wore glasses.

'Don't judge a person by how they look,' grunted Valerka.

'All right,' said Anastasiika condescendingly. 'Mental development is also important. But we'll go along the fence. There's a place I need to go.'

They left Company and turned towards the building where the camp staff lived. Anastasiika strutted with balletic steps and screwed her eyes up, afraid of meeting Zhanka. Valerka noticed, and said shyly, 'Shalayeva won't attack you when I'm here.'

'Oh, I'm not afraid of her,' objected Anastasiika haughtily. 'My guardian angel always protects me.'

She reached a hand into the neck of her T-shirt and pulled out the gold cross for which Valerka had once fought with Beklya and his jackals.

Anastasiika's gesture immediately reminded Valerka of Old Nyura, who had pulled her cross from the collar of her greasy housecoat in just the same way. The cross protected Old Nyura from the bloodsuckers. Meaning that it was protecting Anastasiika too. Anastasiika was not a carcass. Nobody was drinking her blood. Valerka experienced enormous relief. Being a carcass might not have threatened her physical well-being in any way, but mental health, as Anastasiika had declared, was also important.

'You said every girl has an imp,' Valerka reminded her. 'How does your imp live right next to your angel? They'll fight.'

'Course they won't fight! Are they stupid or what? The imp gives the girl hints what to do, the girl does it, and the guardian angel protects her while she's doing it.'

'What if the imp advises some kind of bollocks?'

In Valerka's personal opinion, an imp would only ever advise bollocks.

'Well, I don't know!' Anastasiika became angry. 'It's none of your business!'

Valerka prudently decided to change the subject.

'You sing beautifully. And the song is beautiful.'

'The melody enables me to demonstrate all the possibilities of my contralto,' said Anastasiika.

'I'm not only talking about the music. It's about waves, about struggle, about birds...' He was inspired by the images in the song: audacity, impulse, flight.

'Poetry doesn't mean anything,' said Anastasiika with an airy wave. 'It's only the sound that matters. A song is a vocal more than anything else.'

Valerka was offended on behalf of the eaglets. The eaglets learned to fly and threw themselves from cliffs, risking death, while little girls were afraid so much as to get on a bicycle, even though if they were to fall off, they would not be smashed to death. Anastasiika herself did not understand where the song's beauty lay. All she wanted was to hear the voice. The meaning whistled on past.

'A song is its words,' said Valerka stubbornly.

'You know nothing about art,' replied Anastasiika carelessly. 'Words are just total piffle.'

'What piffle?' Valerka was surprised.

Anastasiika looked at him as if he were a fool.

'The point is that in camp there's nothing but piffle. Are you completely blind? All these flags, assemblies, pioneer songs, "candles". It's all play.'

Valerka bristled inwardly. Obviously the assemblies and 'candles' were rubbish, because they were invented for the collective and there was no collective. But the red flag was not 'play'. And the star on it was not 'play' either. They were real. No, Anastasiika was mistaken. Though she was not to blame. She was not the only one who did not care about such things. No one did. No one cared about the assemblies and songs and the flag with its star. Red flag, blue flag, or grey-brown-crimson flag. Five-point star or twenty-five. Anastasiika wanted to be admired, and that was why she did not care whether she sang about eaglets or potatoes. But he, Valerka, did care what the song was about. And the courageous eaglets inspired him much more than 'Chunga-Changa'.

'Here it is!' announced Anastasiika suddenly.

They were standing on a bare stretch of ground between the bird cherry and the fence.

Anastasiika looked around, crouched down, and began to rake the ground with her bare hands. Valerka crouched down too.

'This is my "secret",' Anastasiika shared with him in a low voice. 'Don't tell anyone, or you'll be cursed forever and ever and ever and ever.'

She removed the last of the sand with her hands, and a sliver of glass appeared in the earth, covering a little hiding place. Anastasiika leaned forward and reverently admired the contents of her 'secret'. Valerka also leaned forward, putting his palms to his face to stop the sun from blinding him, and looked through the glass. In the 'secret' there were three brightly-coloured buttons, a moth twisted elegantly from a sweet wrapper, a yellow feather, and a large purple bead. Anastasiika pulled a pearlescent nail polish bottle out of her bag.

'I am adding to the composition,' she said importantly. 'Would you like to put something in my "secret" too?'

This was the highest trust a girl could place in a boy. Valerka fumbled feverishly in his pockets. His groping fingers found only a small coin.

There was a sudden commotion in the bird cherry, and Zhanka Shalayeva, sporting a number of scratches, came bowling out into the empty patch like a cat from an ambush. She must have been slyly spying on Anastasiika right from Company, sneaking quietly at a distance until she finally caught the right moment. Zhanka darted towards Anastasiika and with a spiteful laugh viciously stomped her foot right into the 'secret'. There came a crunch from under Zhanka's heel. This was Zhanka's revenge for her setbacks in the circle.

The shameless attack stunned both Valerka and Anastasiika. The brazen Zhanka danced wildly on the 'secret' and squealed:

'Dock, dick, tock tock tick, give the cow's fat arse a lick!'

Without a word, Valerka jumped up and pushed Zhanka as hard as he could with both hands.

Zhanka flew back into the bushes, spreading her long legs. Valerka had a sight of her white knickers with their blue and red polka dots.

'Get out of here!' he howled furiously.

Zhanka was thrashing noisily in the bushes like a mad bear. Valerka shoved his way into the dense thicket and kicked out blindly a few times, trying to connect with the patch of polka-dotted white, while dodging the branches at the same time. Zhanka shrieked.

Valerka rushed back to Anastasiika.

Anastasiika was kneeling over her ruined 'secret' and crying bitterly, trying to straighten out the wings of the crumpled moth with fingers that refused to do as she wanted. There was such despair in the set of her body that Valerka wanted to rush back to Zhanka Shalayeva and this time kill her good and proper, rip her head off.

Valerka stroked Anastasiika's back, his palm finding the knobbles of her spine.

'Don't cry, we'll make a new "secret",' he said. Sympathy was making him tremble. 'I won't let anyone else hurt you.'

CHAPTER 8

APNOEA

Towards evening, not long before the evening meal, Igor went to see Dr Nosatov. In essence, detecting vampires was the direct responsibility of the doctor. He should be the first to notice such a surprising anomaly: who else? But Valentin Sergeich, it appeared, was quietly fermenting himself in the sick bay. Every other day he reeked of something strong and medicinal. With such a lifestyle, the doctor would hardly be able to conduct a value-added study of the functioning of the contingent.

The beautiful, harmonious gingerbread of the sick bay gleamed as the sun picked out the squares of its multi-paned windows. The infirmary had always made Igor burn with jealousy. The doctor as good as had his own house, with running water, no less. Exactly the right place to bring girls. Not to mention that medicine provided a natural route to the creation of a certain intimacy. Valentin Sergeich, however, did not use his official position for personal ends. Or rather he did, but only in relation to alcohol.

A green vegetable garden snuggled round one corner of the sick bay. Miss Pasha, the elderly nurse, was there, weeding the beds. Nosatov did not burden Miss Pasha with work. Igor went up to the stoop and entered without knocking. It was cool in the house, and smelled of medicine. Valentin Sergeich was sitting in the waiting room; he barely had time to clear away a dark, bulbous flask into a wall cupboard.

'Hi.' Igor held out his hand.

The doctor did not look very well. Pale and red eyed. It would have been perfectly possible to take him for a vampire himself, if the real vampires had eschewed work discipline and general decorum.

'You sick or something?' asked Nosatov ungraciously.

Igor lowered himself onto the buckram couch.

'I need a serious talk with you.'

'I won't let you spend the night with anyone,' said the doctor, moving straight to refusal.

'That's not what I had in mind,' said Igor with a grin. 'Tell me, Sergeich, have you ever seen anything, like, strange in our camp? From a doctor's point of view, I mean.'

Nosatov looked at Igor, and there was anguish in his eyes.

'Nope,' he said, not admitting it.

Igor sensed at once that the doctor was being economical with the truth.

'Everyone in good health?'

'Everything's fine,' said the doctor stubbornly. 'Grazes. Cuts. Some overheating, the odd cold, a few dodged bullets. I take ticks out. One had toothache. Gave another a tetanus shot. The usual, Igor.'

Igor was quiet for a moment, pondering whether or not to leave.

'You're lying through your teeth, Sergeich,' he said in a low voice. 'There's something completely off the wall going on here. If you don't see it, they'll run you out when it all comes to light. And if you see it and don't report it, you'll do time.'

Nosatov stood up nervously, almost overturning his chair, and ducked out into the corridor. Igor heard the doctor snap the lock on the front door. Valentin Sergeich came back to the waiting room, made sure the door to the examination room was firmly shut, then resumed his seat and stared at Igor.

'You mean the dead?' he whispered.

Goose bumps on came out on Igor's arms.

'What dead?' he asked, also whispering.

'The dead children?'

'Children die here?' Igor was astonished.

'They're not dead!' breathed the doctor hotly.

Igor wondered if Nosatov had gone mad.

'They come back to life after sunset! No after-effects!'

'Tell me!' said Igor, agitated.

The doctor burrowed in a cupboard, took out a dark flask and a vial, unscrewed the top of the flask, poured into the vial, emptied the vial into his mouth, and sniffed at the sleeve of his doctor's coat.

'Yes, well, anyway, the first time it happened was about two weeks ago.' Valentin Sergeich was now looking somewhere inside himself, where the alcohol was burning away his fear. 'One evening Miss Pasha gave me a jar of strawberries to take to Kapustin. I got to the pier and the bus wasn't there; it had already gone. No one on the shore. I'd kind of turned to come back when I thought: there's a pair of feet sticking out from under the pier! You know yourself there's all kinds of rubbish floating around there, bottles, twigs, rags, shoes… I'd likely imagined it. Then I'm thinking, what if one of the children got sick during the day? Found their way in there and fainted. I should check it out. Long story short: I squeezed under the pier. And there was a little girl lying there. From the first or the second brigade. About thirteen. And the first thing I saw: *facies Hippocratica.*'

'Eh?' asked Igor, uncomprehending.

'Well, the face goes, like, a particular … it sinks. A sign of death. Terrible. I dragged the little girl into the light and checked immediately for everything you can out in the field: apnoea, asystole, corneal opacity, Beloglazov symptom… Biological death! I almost died myself! I sat there in a daze. And suddenly she started moving. She crawled, slowly, like a worm, back under the pier. Lay there. Went quiet. I pulled her out by the legs again and checked a second time. No heartbeat. No breathing. And then she began to wriggle right there under my hands. Got herself free and crawled back under the pier.'

'It's dark under the pier, there's no sun there,' said Igor.

'Long story short: I legged it,' reported the doctor, and once more unscrewed the top of the dark bottle. 'No one saw me there. If the girl was dead, they'd find her anyway. And if she was alive – well, she was alive. She didn't want my help.'

'How do you know that?'

'I'm a doctor. I can feel it. When a person's in a bad way, they cling to a doctor with like invisible hands. But she chased me away. With this horror.'

With a gesture of desperation, Valentin Sergeyevich tipped another vial into his mouth.

'And then you saw her in camp?'

Valentin Sergeyevich again sniffed at his sleeve.

'Yep. Perfectly normal.'

The muslin curtain on the window was fluttering slightly in the warm breeze drifting through the fanlight, and the sunlight admitted through the window was shimmering, playing over the walls. A standing glass medicine cabinet flickered with running fires.

'So … under the pier. Was that the only time?' asked Igor.

Valentin Sergeyevich gave a bitter grin. 'One time doesn't make you hit the bottle.'

Igor remembered the doctor, groggy and in low spirits, solidly refusing the young leader Lenochka's drunken advances the time Dimon Malosolov had organised his get-together on the river bus.

'There were four others after that.' Valentin Sergeich took out his cigarettes but could not bring himself to light up, and idly clicked his lighter. 'All girls. Dragged themselves over here feeling bad: weakness, fever, nausea. I put them in isolation and they … well, in an hour or two they were dead. I took their blood pressure, examined them with a phonendoscope. No pulse. Listened to their chests: silence. Except after sundown they all got up and left. There you have it, Igor.'

The doctor had poured out his soul and was clearly relieved. It struck Igor that Valentin Sergeich had witnessed the transformation of humans into vampires. Dying, sunset, resurrection: it all fitted.

'Yes, but it's not death,' said Igor.

'Not death,' agreed Dr Nosatov.

'So what is it? A deep faint? A coma? A body switch?'

'I don't know.'

'And you don't want to know?'

Valentin Sergeyevich replied with a direct and hostile look. 'I don't need to know, Igor. Why should I?'

　　　　　　　　　

Igor made to object, but refrained. It was true. Why would Valentin Sergeyevich want to get involved? To be fired from his job? To be disappointed in his own competence, acquired with much hard work at the institute and during his internship? Or to acquire a belief in God, in spite of his materialism?

'The shift'll finish and I'll be off to town and everything'll be as it should,' said the doctor. 'And I'll never come here again.'

'Understood,' nodded Igor. 'And these five – the hell with them?'

'Six,' the doctor corrected him.

'Six?'

Valentin Sergeyevich stood up and opened the door to the examination room a crack. On the couch in the little ward, a boy in a blue shirt and shorts was lying. His sandals stood neatly under the couch.

The boy was not moving.

'You want to check the symptoms yourself?' asked the doctor.

Igor realised what kind of nightmare was holding Dr Nosatov's will in its shackles. He had to admit it was understandable. But Igor had seen Veronika the vampire himself. He too had smelled the gunpowder.

'No, I don't,' said Igor. 'And I can't count on you, right?'

'Right. I've seen nothing, heard nothing, know nothing, and I'm not getting involved in anything.'

CHAPTER 9

THE DARK STRATELATES

'Are they dead?' Igor asked straight out. 'In sick bay with the doctor I saw a boy who'd been bitten. His heart wasn't beating.'

Old Nyura started trembling. She could barely squeeze out her answer.

'N-not d-dead. N-not alive either. They s-s-sojourn on the border. They n-need their h-heart to b-beat, it b-beats. N-no n-need, it s-stops.'

'Meaning it's possible to pull them back, right?'

Old Nyura nodded.

It struck Igor that in the technological twentieth century, a vampire should be no different from a human being. It was not enough to deceive the man in the street with outward signs of life. They also had to fool the electrocardiograph and the X-ray machine. A deception such as that required vampires to keep themselves on this side of the line between life and death. The one question, though, was: whose blood would flow from their veins when the doctor inserted a needle into their arms to carry out an analysis? Blood drunk from their victims?

Old Nyura, Igor, and Valerka were sitting in the canteen. Old Nyura had locked both the food block's iron doors and turned off the lights throughout to avoid attracting attention. The high, barred windows of the canteen showed blue in the darkness. The gleam from the Pioneer Avenue street lamps lay on the smooth table tops. The white backgrounds of the posters hanging between the windows deepened, and the painted pioneers peeling potatoes and washing dishes darkened like demons.

'Baba Nyura, there's a lot Valerka and I don't understand,' said Igor by way of understatement. 'We don't have an overall picture of this phenomenon. Please help us.'

Old Nyura sighed heavily.

'Let's start from the beginning,' suggested Igor. 'The carcasses are a herd belonging to the vampire … well, the bloodsucker, yes? The bloodsucker bites them, and then gives them orders and drinks their blood little by little so that no one notices. The carcasses don't know they're carcasses. And the bloodsucker only works at night. But during the day, do they remember they're vampires?'

'Th-they r-remember. I remembered.'

Valerka listened to this interrogation, and felt safe for the first time in many days. Gor-Sanych was an adult. Gor-Sanych had assumed command. He would work out what to ask and how to ask it, and would bring to light all the secrets of the vampires. Gor-Sanych would protect him, Valerka. He and Gor-Sanych were a true collective.

'Yes, but how do you become a bloodsucker?'

Old Nyura shook her head with the effort.

'D-dar … d-dar … d-dark s-stratelates!' she got out, and started to cry.

Her words carried menace and sounded ancient, and they sent chills coursing through Igor. The dining room walls seemed to shift apart and take on a passing purple glow. Igor imagined something colossal and inhuman. Immeasurable heights and abysses, immense forces, infinite spaces, and unearthly hierarchies. Lightning, spears, halos, horns, flaming eyes, and seething lava. At university, Igor had briefly heard the term 'stratelates': it was the name given in the Middle Ages to the leader of an army. But what kind of army? A dark army?

Igor and Valerka waited for Old Nyura to calm herself.

'Who is he – the dark stratelates?' asked Igor cautiously.

'P-prince of d-darkness!' answered Old Nyura.

'The Devil?' Igor quickly suggested.

'N-not the d-devil… H-his s-servant.'

Valerka got up, went to the kitchen, and fetched Old Nyura a laundered waffle towel. Old Nyura wiped her eyes.

'H-he's the one who d-drinks… H-he n-needs them… The b-bloods-suckers … d-don't … for themselves… They're j-just h-his c-cups! They c-collect p-people's b-blood inside themselves, and the s-s-stratelates d-d-drinks them right to the b-b-bottom! W-when he's d-drunk it all, the b-bloodsucker d-dies.'

Igor was silent, trying to comprehend the terrible, shocking picture.

'So the stratelates is the chief vampire?' Igor wanted to clarify everything to the last detail. 'And the bloodsuckers are, like, auxiliaries?'

Old Nyura nodded again.

Igor opened his mouth to ask why such complexity was needed, but the various parts of the system suddenly fell into place by themselves. Yes, the bloodsuckers bit people, but their victims did not fall sick or die. They simply began to submit to the bloodsuckers' orders. And it was not as if you could tell who would be subordinate to whom. Everyone was subordinate to someone. Meaning the bloodsucker left no trace. But the stratelates did. If the stratelates sucked out its victim completely, the victim would die. So the cautious vampire bit a little at a time. And its victims became bloodsuckers, neither alive nor dead, but thirsty for blood. And the stratelates, the prince of darkness, hid behind them. He did not go hunting, where he might be caught; he manufactured himself bloodsuckers, which themselves brought him blood. Hiding behind anonymity, he controlled his providers, and from time to time pitilessly destroyed them, closing the book on them. Logical and inhumane.

'So, how does it work?' Igor looked at Old Nyura, demanding an answer. 'Bloodsuckers who've passed on their blood are no longer needed by the stratelates? Like empty bottles?'

Old Nyura's whole body trembled, but she held back new sobs.

'And how does the stratelates control the bloodsuckers?'

'S-speaks in their h-heads. W-what he t-tells them to d-do, they d-do.'

'Telepathy,' guessed Igor.

The stratelates wordlessly gave the command to appear, and the bloodsucker obediently appeared. The stratelates sucked the carcasses' blood from the bloodsucker, and the spent bloodsucker later died in some manner, all by itself – from illness, in an accident. That was why the bloodsuckers were doomed. They were single use, like ampoules.

'Baba Nyura, how did you survive?' asked Valerka.

Old Nyura sniffed, and crossed herself expansively.

'S-stratelates d-didn't have t-time to d-drink me all up. D-died. F-f-fever s-set in on m-me, b-but m-mum w-went d-down to ch-church. M-made a c-cross over m-me and p-prayed it away. I w-was a l-little g-girl then, so-so l-little, only s-seven...'

'How old are you now?' came in Valerka.

'F-fifty...'

'How did your stratelates die?' Igor retook the initiative.

'We l-lived in the v-village.' Old Nyura gave a feeble wave in the direction of the village of Pervomaiskaya. 'H-he c-came to our f-farm. S-some c-commission. A g-ghoul, he was. H-he w-was one of the b-bosses. N-n-nibbled l-little m-me. I d-drank b-blood f-for h-him – M-mum, uncle, b-brothers. B-by and b-by I h-heard the c-call to g-go to m-my m-master, b-but they p-put him in p-prison. They p-put l-lots in p-prison b-back then. R-rounded them all up one by one. H-he d-died in p-prison.'

'Just like that?' Igor was surprised.

'N-not j-just... S-stratelates n-need a p-proper d-drink every t-time at their m-moon. They d-don't drink, they d-die. M-mine w-was on his own there. The g-guards w-wouldn't l-let any b-bloods-suckers in, and there was n-no man around to b-bite. G-ghoul s-s-starved.'

Igor realised that he had heard something very important.

'What do you mean, "at their moon"?'

'The m-moon on the n-night when h-he t-turns into a s-stratelates, th-that's h-his m-moon. H-he h-has to d-drink b-blood th-that m-moon or d-die.'

Igor became excited.

'So a vampire has to drink blood when the moon's in the same phase as it was when he was turned into a vampire? Otherwise – death?'

'W-well, y-yes,' agreed Old Nyura.

'How else can you kill a stratelates other than starvation?' asked Igor.

Old Nyura looked at her companions – a student from the intelligentsia and a little boy with glasses. For the first time that night Old Nyura grinned.

'B-burn 'em alive,' she said. 'A-a-aspen s-stake through the h-heart. D-drown in h-holy w-water. You'll m-manage?'

Igor and Valerka's spirits sank.

'D-dark s-stratelates is out of y-your l-league,' sighed Old Nyura.

Then Igor asked the most important question.

'Who is he?'

A dog suddenly howled outside the window, a sound so desperate that Igor's hair bristled.

Old Nyura seemed to subside, weighed down; her face became flabby, and her shoulders slumped. She started wriggling clumsily, trying to get out from behind the table.

''Nuff idle ch-chatter,' she grumbled.

'Who?' insisted Igor.

'I d-don't kn-know!' answered Old Nyura peevishly, looking away as she spoke. 'G-get up, th-the b-both of you. It's late! T-time to g-go home. I'll l-lock up.'

They had already agreed with Old Nyura that Valerka would stay overnight in the food block. A little house made out of a sheet was an unreliable shelter. The young leaders' room in Building 4 was also an unreliable shelter, but better than a sheet house: it was, after all, upstairs, and had walls and a door. And physically Igor was stronger.

'I'll have more questions,' Igor warned Old Nyura.

'A-ask m-me t-tom-morrow y-you c-can.'

Igor firmly shook Valerka's hand, and headed for the door. Old Nyura hobbled after him, keys jingling. Valerka looked at her back.

'Baba Nyura, why didn't Beklya bite you? Was he frightened?'

Old Nyura looked round.

'I s-survived m-my m-master,' she said. F-for b-bloods-suckers that's l-like r-r-r- ... t-turning ag-gainst G-god. I'm w-worse than a s-swamp th-thing to them. I b-betrayed the h-holy c-cause. They d-despise m-me. H-have d-done for ages.'

CHAPTER 10

LIFTING THE WEIGHT

The curse of 'work detail' was one which no one ever lifted from the pioneers.

'Why so limp? You're like boiled sausages,' came the chipper voice of Svistunova from the grounds of the third brigade. 'Move it! Move it!'

The fourth brigade was moving glumly and reluctantly. The boys and girls were raking beneath the pines, sweeping the paths, dragging rubbish to the pile. None of them were quarrelling any more. No one tried to instigate a duel (weapons of choice: agricultural implements) in order to brighten up their tedious work. No one was slacking off, either. Almost no one. Igor and Valerka were sitting on the stoop bench. Who was there before whom they should be embarrassed? Brigade discipline was being maintained by the vampires. Irina waved a hand at the useless young leader and his charge. Whistler jogged past, pretending not to notice the shirkers. Perhaps not pretending: from Pioneer Avenue the work detail appeared to be proceeding as it should and everyone seemed full of enthusiasm. Most important was that the rules be observed. And the rules were being observed. An inspection commission suddenly descending from heaven would hand the fourth brigade well-deserved top marks for cleanliness and organisation.

'Lagunov, why the hell are you goofing off?' the girls asked Valerka.

'Hurt my leg,' lied Valerka lazily.

'Luck of the devil!'

The girls had a shrewd idea that Valerka was lying, but it was simpler to believe him. This was the principle, in fact, on which life in the pioneer camp was built. Svistunova and Doctor Nosatov and Director Kolybalov had a shrewd idea what was going on, but it was simpler to believe that there were no vampires, just good boys and girls who played football, drew pictures for peace, sang songs about eaglets, and generally tidied up the grounds. The vampires saw to it that this unspoken agreement was not broken.

'Igor Sanych, what do you think,' asked Valerka in a low voice. 'Who's their head? You know, this … strato … stratelates.'

Igor had been pondering this question half the night.

'I think it's one of the parents.'

'Why?'

'Because Veronika Genrikhovna was bitten on Parents' Day.'

Of course, others had been bitten on other days. Where they had been bitten was unknown. They had dragged themselves over to Dr Nosatov and died on a bunk in his isolation ward. But the doctor had found the first victim out in the open. On the bank of the Volga, to be exact. The dead girl who had been crawling under the pier. The head vampire could have come to the camp in a motorboat and bitten on the bank. And when the opportunity came to enter the camp openly – on Parents' Day – the stratelates had appeared openly. And Veronika had presented herself to him.

'Do we have to kill him?' asked Valerka cautiously.

Igor was silent for a long time. Valerka Lagunov was a child. He thought it was simple: hunt him down, kill him, and everyone would be happy.

'How are we going to find him?' answered Igor, his anguish evident. 'We're not the police. And the bloodsuckers themselves won't tell us anything. And how are we going to kill him? He's a vampire. Burn him alive? Run him through with an aspen stake? How do you see that happening? Speaking for myself, I've never burned anyone alive, and I've never driven a stake through anyone. And outwardly the stratelates is just an ordinary person. They'll nail us for him, we'll do time. We're powerless before these vampires, Valer. The way society is set up, you can't kill a vampire.'

Valerka looked sympathetically at Gor-Sanych. He had come to the same conclusions himself, but had been hoping that Gor-Sanych would come up with an idea – he was older and smarter. But Gor-Sanych had come up with nothing.

'What about Veronika Genrikhovna?'

Igor lowered his head.

Valerka thought that if Anastasiika became a bloodsucker, he would try to kill the stratelates whatever, or at least die himself, so as not to suffer. But Anastasiika was protected by her golden cross. No one was going to save Veronika Genrikhovna. Not the bosses, not the police, nor any cross, nor Gor-Sanych.

There was one other option, however. Probably the last one. Serp Ivanych Iyeronov. Who else was there to pin their hopes on? Everybody respected Serp Ivanych. Listened to him. He was a Civil War veteran, a pensioner of national standing. He could tell someone with influence to help. Serp Ivanych was not someone who could be brushed aside. The question was, would he believe in vampires himself?

'I know who we need to ask,' said Valerka quietly.

'I've already got there myself.' Igor sighed heavily.

Abandoning Veronika was not an option. All chances had to be taken, even the slightest. On one side of the scales was the awkwardness of a strange conversation; on the other was Veronika's life. If Veronika remained a bloodsucker, she would die. She would catch tularaemia, or slip in the street and hit her head on the pavement, or suffer a ruptured appendix and the ambulance be held up on its way to her.

Igor set off to see Serp Ivanych during Quiet Hour. He did not take Valerka with him: why have Valerka at such a conversation? Seriousness was to be the order of the day, and serious was when you were free of children and face to face.

The two sporty peas Maxim and Kirill were sitting on Serp Ivanych's veranda watching the Olympics. With them was the radio technician Sanya, who was not prepared to risk loitering during the day in front of the television in his own room in Company where the director might see him.

'Where's the master of the house?' asked Igor.

'Went upstairs. He'll be right back.'

Igor perched beside them.

The television was showing weightlifting. An athlete in a red single-piece costume was walking unhurriedly along the track. His torso, arms and legs consisted of balloons of muscle. His wrists and knees were wrapped in white bandage. The large hall was noisy: technicians were rolling out television cameras, spectators on the balcony were chattering, the announcer's voice was booming round. On his way to the barbell, the athlete stuck his hands into a bowl of powder and stomped around in what looked like a sandpit. Displaying no strong emotion, he stood over the barbell with its red and blue discs, shook the whole architecture of his mighty body, spread his predatory arms, bent down, and grasped the rod as if the barbell had to be pulled out of the ground like a weed. A jerk and a squat – and the barbell was already on the weightlifter's chest.

The two peas Maxim and Kirill groaned and wriggled their legs in sympathy with the athlete's efforts. The athlete stood up slowly, overcoming the monstrous reverse pull of gravity. The seeming slowness of his movement was reminiscent of the unhurried, drawn-out launch of a rocket from a cosmodrome. Electrical discharges seemed to crackle around the athlete. A howl went up in the hall. Igor looked at the distorted, upturned face of the athlete. The athlete was staring furiously upwards, as if expecting a sign from somewhere up by the ceiling of the sports hall.

It struck Igor that just at the moment, he himself resembled the athlete. The barbell had been lifted from the platform, but it was still lying across the heavyweight's chest: the secret of the vampires had been uncovered, but so far only for Igor. Would the athlete manage to push the barbell over his head: would Igor be able to destroy the stratelates' ruthless cannibalism? Face split wide in a grimace, the Olympic strongman tossed the bar above him and froze, arms outstretched. The barbell hung in the air.

'The Soviet athlete Yurik Vardanyan, in the snatch, has lifted a record weight of two hundred and twenty two and a half kilograms!' reported the announcer.

The two peas drew breath at exactly the same time. Maxim turned to Igor.

'Listen, Igoryokha,' he said. 'We need some men. Firewood's been brought to Concert Clearing. Need to knock up a bit of a bonfire.'

'And?' asked Igor.

'Come after dinner. You'll be useful.'

'I'm not Yurik Vardanyan. I don't set records in the snatch.'

'Yes, we can see that,' said Kirill with a smirk. 'You'll come in handy anyway.'

'All right,' agreed Igor.

Somewhere back in the house, the stairs creaked. Serp Ivanych was coming down from the first floor. He carried on towards the door without giving the veranda a glance. This suited Igor very well. It would not do to talk about vampires in front of the two peas.

Igor caught up with Iyeronov in the yard.

'Serp Ivanych, a moment!' called Igor.

Iyeronov stopped. He was wearing a comical child's panama hat, a sleeveless shirt, and voluminous old man's trousers. On his feet were sandals.

'May I have a word with you? It's important to me.'

'Well, within my area of competence,' Serp Ivanych warned him. 'If this is about how to get a girl to like you, then my advice is out of date.'

'Let's sit on the bench,' suggested Igor.

They settled themselves down, and Serp Ivanych pulled his panama forward to protect his face from the sun.

'Tell me,' said Igor. He hesitated. 'Do you believe in vampires?'

'Only in devils, and striped ones at that. And their grandmother.'

Igor gave a guilty smile. He shared Valerka's liking for the old man. Serp Ivanych gave off an air of calm and kindliness, as if he had already lived through the worst of his life, and the rest was not worth worrying about.

'I'm not having you on, Serp Ivanych. A week ago I'd have thought it all nonsense myself. But everything's changed. Do you know what a stratelates is?'

Serp Ivanych looked very intently at Igor, and his eyes narrowed; his look was ironical and somehow probing.

'I do,' he nodded. 'I come from these parts. It's what we call a ghoul who has other, less important ghouls subject to him. Bloodsuckers, you could say.'

Igor was not quite sure what to say next. He had not been expecting these strange old words to be known to Serp Ivanych. On the other hand, why was he surprised? Iyeronov was eighty years old, though he looked sixty. And in his long life, no doubt, Serp Ivanych had seen all sorts of things. More than he wanted to.

Igor made up his mind. 'They're here!' he declared. 'Here, in camp!'

Serp Ivanych hunched over tiredly, his face darkened, his cheeks sank, and his wrinkles became more pronounced. His short grey stubbly beard suddenly glittered silver, and immense sorrow appeared in his eyes. Looking at him, Igor saw clearly that Serp Ivanovich Iyeronov was, after all, a man of eighty, and not a year younger.

'Eh, my friend,' he said. 'I so hoped I'd never hear those words "they're here" again. Ah, this old fuddlehead's luck wasn't in. We didn't finish them off back then. Well, go on, make your report.'

CHAPTER 11

BATTLE ON THE VOLGA

'The thing is, forty years ago he worked for the NKVD,' Igor was saying.

'What's the NKVD?' interrupted Valerka.

'Today it's the militia.'

'Ah-ha.'

Since his conversation with Serp Ivanovich, Igor had been gripped by an abnormal animation that would not let him go. Serp Ivanych had promised to help, and the dangers Igor had been regarding as mortal had vaporised like smoke. Valerka did not share Igor's enthusiasm. It was all too simple: you went and complained, the army immediately arrived and attacked the enemy, and all the civilian population needed to do was to stand on the side and wait for victory. No, there was something wrong here. It did not work like that.

'He said their section uncovered several vampire networks back then. At first the key aspects of the thing – the set-up – eluded them. Two brigades of operatives were killed. Then they puzzled it out. Arrested four stratelates. All of them died in the cells.'

The night-time streets of old Kuibyshev appeared before Valerka as if he were actually there. Moonlight illuminating rows of brick mansions. The peeling arches of the carriage gates. The pavement blocks. Militiamen in their caps running, tunics belted at the waist and breeches tucked into their high boots. They turn into a back street. From a knocked-out window on the first floor, pale vampires, like giant cockroaches, slink rapidly away this way and that, crawling over the very wall of the building. The militiamen fire their revolvers at the vampires, the shots booming in the silence. The wounded vampires flop to the ground like wet laundry.

'It was all classified, so as not to sow panic in the city. Those were troubling times.'

What had caused the outbreak of vampirism never came to light.

'And the stratelates who bit Baba Nyura…' Valerka reminded him.

'He was one of the four.'

Valerka was silent, pondering.

'Serp Ivanych believed the vampires had been eradicated forever. But they've reappeared. Serp Ivanych wants to pull up the regional office archive, so our case is taken up straight away. And you and I are not to gossip.'

'We don't.'

Still Valerka could not rid himself of an oppressive heaviness of heart.

Igor and Valerka were walking along the lane from the camp to Concert Clearing. The crimson rays of the setting sun were piercing the pine copse. From the nearby Volga came a waft of freshness. Seagulls screeched on the shore.

The Last Bonfire was the most important and biggest event of the camp shift. It was held after the sports championship, the summing-up speeches, and the formal assembly at which the most outstanding pioneers were given awards and the flag was lowered. At the Last Bonfire they sang heart-warming songs, ate sweets, and exchanged addresses. There were a large number of pioneers in the camp – a hundred and eighty – which meant there was no question of romantically sitting around the fire with friends, tossing on twigs. A giant bonfire was built, as high as two people.

The fire was built in the same way each time. Several bundles of long pine logs, each the thickness of the PE teacher's leg, were ferried by launch to the shore of Concert Clearing. In the clearing, a special frame was knocked together out of sawn timber, and the logs were roped to the frame so as to fit the structure out in the form of a marquee. Firewood and brushwood were shoved inside the tent. The whole thing was doused with petrol before the event.

The sun, on the declining arc of its journey, fell behind the Volga onto the ridge of the Zhiguli, like a flaming cannonball onto the parapet of a trench. The piercing light of sunset flooded the deserted Concert Glade. The wooden carcass of the future fire was already half done; it towered, casting a long shadow riddled with holes, like an Indian wigwam. The two peas Maxim and Kirill were hauling logs.

'Bit short on labourers,' remarked Igor.

''S'how many are left,' explained Maxim.

''S'the end of the day,' added Kirill.

The two peas had even showed up to work in their sports gear: tracksuits, T-shirts, and red neckerchiefs.

Or perhaps they had not changed at all since the beginning of the shift.

Igor looked distrustfully round the log tent.

'Won't it collapse when it burns through at the bottom?'

'Yep,' agreed Maxim.

'The pioneers are not to be allowed within five metres of the fire.'

'You're the guy who doesn't fill the pool with water, so no one drowns.'

'Very funny,' replied Kirill.

'So what are we to do?' sighed Igor.

Valerka surreptitiously took his arm.

'Gor-Sanych,' he said quietly and anxiously.

Two figures had appeared in the lane along which Igor and Valerka had walked to the clearing. It seemed likely they were also on their way to help build the bonfire. Igor looked more closely, and recognised boys from the older brigades – the brainy artist Alik Stakhovsky and the hooligan Beklemishev.

'Run!' Valerka suddenly shouted in desperation.

Maxim grabbed Valerka's shoulder with his hand, like a raptor seizing a chick, but Valerka contrived to dodge aside and skip away. Kirill, with a boxer's skill, punched Igor in the stomach, doubling Igor over. Igor's breath flew from his chest, and his heart spun in a void, like a wheel torn from its axle.

'Run!' shouted Valerka again.

Through the tearing pain, Igor realised with horror that the cultured Alik and the hooligan Beklya had no reason to be together. As people, they had nothing in common; they could only be together as bloodsuckers. Valerka had seen that. Meaning the two peas Maxim and Kirill were vampires too. And Concert Clearing was a vampire trap. The bloodsuckers would seize the pesky detectives, the sun would go down, the bloodsuckers would grow fangs, and the prisoners would be bitten and turned into docile carcasses. And stop stirring up the waters.

Little Valerka shot away from big Maxim like a hare from a hound. He sprinted across Concert Clearing towards the forest, in the opposite direction from Beklya and Albert. Maksim dashed after Valerka.

Kirill slammed his fist into Igor's side again, dropping him to the grass. He pinned Igor with his knee, huge and firm like an ancient battering ram. Igor tried with all his might to push the bloodsucker away from him, but Kirill caught Igor's arm, to twist it in a painful hold and immobilise his victim. Igor was no sort of fighter at all, but now he was hammering his fists into Kirill's broad chest and craggy shoulders. The mooing Kirill pressed his weight down on Igor, breaking his resistance.

Emerging from the gloom beneath the flaming pines was another bloodsucker, Lyova Khlopov. He was heading for Valerka. Without even thinking, Valerka turned towards the Volga. The grass, crimson in the setting sun, lashed him. Valerka's run was describing a semi-circle, and Maxim bolted after him in a straight line, shortening the distance.

With an agonising effort, Igor raised himself a few inches to grab Kirill's T-shirt and throw his opponent off him. Kirill recoiled, but Igor managed to catch him by his pioneer neckerchief like a bulldog by the collar. There was a screech of tearing material, and the neckerchief ripped in half. Kirill instantly collapsed and started wheezing, as if his gullet had been sliced rather than his neckerchief torn. Igor slammed his legs down and pushed himself up enough to shove Kirill off his stomach. Kirill fell on his side, frantically trying to put the halves of his torn neckerchief together at his throat. Igor rolled away and jumped to his feet. His legs buckled, but Kirill no longer cared about anything. Convulsively squirming in the grass, he was clutching at the ends of his neckerchief as if he were trying to clamp an opened artery. His face was swollen and his eyes bulged.

Valerka, meanwhile, had not succeeded in slipping away from Maxim along the margin of the beach. Maxim hauled Valerka into a rough embrace. Valerka wriggled in the vampire's paws, howling. Beklya, Alik, and Lyova were running towards Maxim from the direction of the forest. Igor was also dashing towards Maxim. He was closer than the bloodsuckers, and on target to rescue his friend.

'Let him go!' shouted Igor.

Valerka jerked frantically, trying to free himself from captivity. The sun had almost plunged below the horizon. Maxim shook Valerka's legs violently, trying to drive Igor away, whereupon Igor used both his hands to push the vampire and his prisoner Valerka into the river – in the water, Maxim should instinctively unlock his grip. But Maxim did not go tumbling into the Volga. He twisted madly at the edge of the beach, as if on the brink of a precipice, and, keeping his balance, tossed Valerka into the water.

At Concert Clearing, the deep water began right by the shore. Well, not deep, exactly; to the waist or a little higher – but enough to drown. Igor did not think twice. He threw himself in after Valerka.

He went in headfirst, not feeling the cold. His groping hands found something living and he pushed himself upward, his feet dragging along the friable river bed. He straightened, wobbling unsteadily, and lifted Valerka, holding him in front of him under the armpits. Valerka dangled from Igor's hands like a puppy. The first thing he did was check his glasses, and then he started coughing. The water was up to Igor's chest and Valerka's neck.

Four vampires – Maxim, Alik, Beklya, and Lyova – stood in a row on the bank.

'Come out!' smiled Beklya, sharpening his long teeth.

Concert Clearing was now swallowed up in shadow. The sun had gone down.

Igor threw hunted looks this way and that. Behind them on the river, the white buoy was just visible, marking the sandbank.

'Can you swim?' Igor asked Valerka.

'Badly,' answered Valerka, breathing heavily.

The vampires did not move. They waited, looking expressionlessly at Igor and Valerka. Kirill limped up to join them. The vampires' silence seemed as calm and ominous as the darkness in the muzzle of a gun already loaded, aimed at the face, and ready to fire.

'These sh-shits are afraid of water,' said Valerka suddenly, as if there were no vampires around and no one could hear him.

'What?' asked Igor, confused.

'They're afraid of water,' repeated Valerka. 'If they weren't, they would have pulled us out long ago. There are five of them and two of us.'

Valerka stretched out his hand to scoop up some water, and splashed it onto the shore. In unison, as if they were robots, the vampires all took two steps back, then froze again, looking at the humans. It seemed likely they could stand like that until dawn.

Igor did not know what to do. Swimming to the buoy was not the best idea. Perhaps they could wade along the shore to a shallow spot and stay there until the sun came up. They would be in the river, but out of reach of the ghouls.

Something was happening. At the vampires' backs, the twilight seemed to be thickening, and the outline of a human figure was taking shape. Or rather, someone had approached unhurriedly from behind.

'They broke free, master,' said Albert Stakhovsky dully.

The cold water scalded Igor as if it were boiling. Igor felt Valerka's heart begin to thump furiously. The stratelates himself was standing on the shore.

He was examining Igor and Valerka as if they were animals in a zoo. He was not angry, and he made no threats; he knew he would prevail, albeit not just now. Igor could not make out who it was, the stratelates. His figure was gently leaching out in a kind of frail blindness. The dark stratelates was enveloped in mist.

'What can they do to us?' the stratelates asked his bloodsuckers in a low voice, and shrugged. 'They can't do anything.'

At the sound of that voice, everything became clear. Valerka jerked convulsively in Igor's arms. Standing among the bloodsuckers was Serp Ivanych Iyeronov. And speaking the truth, because he had been Igor and Valerka's last hope of destroying the vampires.

'You traitor!' shouted Valerka in a tone of hatred and hurt.

Igor squeezed Valerka more tightly against him, like a Madonna her child.

Serp Ivanych grinned.

'Hey, student,' he called out to Igor. 'Looks like you know how to fight back. Kudos.'

Igor felt himself shivering violently. Ripples coursed over the water around him.

'For that I'll celebrate my moon with your girlfriend,' Serp Ivanych informed him good-naturedly. 'If I'm not mistaken, Veronika Nesvetova. The blood of one who loves and is loved is intoxicating and carries the scent of flowers. I know.'

Igor made no reply. Why would he? It would be no different from talking to a sepulchre.

'Home!' Serp Ivanych gave the command to his bloodsuckers as if they were dogs.

CHAPTER 12

HIS FOOD BLOCK

The vampires had indeed gone, leaving no ambush on the lane. Why waste energy? It was clear that the bloodsuckers already had enough carcasses, and the stratelates had enough bloodsuckers. The stratelates had finished laying up his provisions and could rest until the next crop ripened. What harm could a puny student and a tiny tot of a pioneer do him? None.

Wet and shivering all over, Igor and Valerka broke back into camp through the hole in the fence. They looked around, and immediately headed in the direction of the food block.

Old Nyura was waiting for them in the kitchen.

They undressed to their underwear, wrung out their clothes, and hung them on the hooks where the towels usually dried. Old Nyura lit the cooker burners and gave the boys greasy work coats belonging to the cooks. Igor and Valerka looked very funny in their cooks' coats, but no one was laughing. Old Nyura could sense that something terrible had happened. And the only person to blame for it was her.

'Baba Nyura, why did you hide from us that the stratelates was Iyeronov?' Igor asked at last.

Old Nyura sat down on a stool, put her hands on her knees, and started to cry.

Listening to her inarticulate and stuttering story was pure torture, but listen Igor and Valerka did, holding their breath. The vampires' story had its roots in the distant past – in the Civil War.

Back then, the village of Pervomaiskaya had been called Shikhobalovka, because the local peasants worked at dachas rented out by the merchant Shikhobalov to wealthy residents of Samara. In the summer of 1918, Samara was under the control of the Whites. The Whites were in no doubt that they would quickly prevail over the Bolsheviks. The Whites' forces were advancing up the Volga from Samara to Kazan, and White Cossacks from the Don were moving inexorably to the lower Volga, to Tsaritsyn. The townspeople, reassured by the authorities, went to their dachas as usual in July.

In Shikhobalovka, however, local lads decided to organize a revolution: to attack the Whites and go over to the Reds. More precisely, to rob the rich dacha owners and escape to a place where no one could get to the robbers. The ringleaders of the Shikhobalovka rebellion were the Iyeronov brothers: the elder Matvey and the younger Seryoga.

That night things did not go off remotely as Serp Ivanych had told Valerka. There was no artillery battery at the dachas intended to strafe the Reds' steamships. Nor were there soldiers with rifles. There were ordinary people: officials with their wives and children, telegraph and railway employees, middling merchants. The village revolutionaries fell upon them. Some had their faces punched, others were simply intimidated. Wedding rings were pulled from their fingers, and crosses from their chests. Their purses were gutted, and ladies' jewellery boxes cleaned out. The only man who put up any resistance was an officer being treated with kumis in one of the dachas for a contusion he had suffered at the front. His Browning chattered until he was out of ammunition, whereupon Matvey and Seryoga chased him into the stables. The brothers had no idea that the officer was a dark stratelates.

'Supping on the people's blood?' Seryoga shouted at him, grabbing a pitchfork. 'Now we want your blood!' With that, Seryoga had thrust his pitchfork into the officer's chest.

'A s-stra-stratelates c-can d-drink b-blood any t-time,' said Old Nyura, sobbing. 'D-day and n-night. Th-there's one thing h-he c-can't... If anyone d-demands h-his b-blood from him, he m-must give it. And wh-whoever d-drinks the b-blood of a s-stratelates will b-become a s-stratelates himself.'

Seryoga Iyeronov, village idiot, had shouted about blood out of sheer stupidity – that was what you were supposed to do in a class struggle. For the stratelates, however, it was a sacred order that was not to be disobeyed. The stratelates abruptly grabbed Seryoga and Matvey by the hair and pressed their faces to the wounds in his chest. He pressed them, so that the boys would swallow his pumping blood.

Igor and Valerka felt their hair bristle with revulsion. It was beyond ordinary human nature to accept this ghastly thing that had happened in the stable. But happen it had, and nothing could be done about it. The Iyeronov brothers had unwittingly tasted the blood of a vampire, and were doomed to turn into vampires themselves. To become stratelates.

The revolution at the Shikhobalovsky dachas ended with the robbers seizing a steamboat moored at the dacha dock and making for Tsaritsyn to join up with Budyonny. Old Nyura had not known how things had subsequently turned out for the stratelates brothers. Not badly, as became apparent. Heroes of the Civil War, the brothers only appeared in Samara – more accurately, in Kuibyshev – about fifteen years later. Both had risen high: they sported army tunics with collar tabs and peaked caps, and drove automobiles. And both had long since assimilated the vampire life. They had even changed their names. Seryoga had become Serp and Matvey Molot.[24]

Molot Ivanych had had to look in on Shikhobalovka – something to do with production – and while there had snacked on seven-year-old Nyurka. Soon afterwards, he had ended up in prison. Ended up there by chance, caught up in the purges which in those years rolled on relentlessly, one after another. There was never any rounding up of vampires by the militia – Serp Ivanych

....

[24]   'Serp i molot' (Hammer and Sickle): a symbol representing the unity of agricultural and industrial workers. The hammer and sickle appeared on the state emblem of the Soviet Union, the coats of arms of the Soviet republics, the red star badge on the uniform cap of the Red Army uniform, and elsewhere.

had lied to Igor about that. And Molot Ivanych had simply died in his cell, breaking his teeth trying to chew through the bars on the window. His brother had given him no help.

When blood is food, blood kinship goes by the wayside.

'Are you still afraid of Iyeronov?' Igor asked Old Nyura.

'Y-y-yes.'

The present Serp Ivanych posed no threat whatsoever to Old Nyura, the scullery maid from the village. Her fear was as irrational as the fear of darkness.

Serp Ivanych had lived safely through all the country's woes. More than that: the woes were actually convenient. People were dying or disappearing without trace, and there was always an opportunity for a dark stratelates to find to fresh blood. It became more difficult for him when he retired. But Serp Ivanych knew how to get along. A dacha in a pioneer camp along with his personal pension: could anyone have dreamed up anything better? The summer shifts served the stratelates as blood reaping, when he laid up supplies for the whole year. The pioneer camp became the vampire's personal food block.

'So how does he … bite?' asked Igor, his voice faltering.

It was clear how. The veranda. Evening. Young people in front of the television set, guests of a good-natured old man. The bravura feats of the Olympians on the colour screen. Igor had seen with his own eyes Serp Ivanych sitting in the back row.

The gas from the cylinder hummed in the dark kitchen. A blue wreath of flame illuminated the creased and contorted face of Old Nyura. Glass tumblers glittered faintly in the cupboard. In the upper corner of the window hung a waning moon.

How many times a year does the moon go through its cycle? thought Igor. How many bloodsuckers did the stratelates require in one year? Igor needed to dredge up his astronomy… A lunar cycle was twenty-eight days. The three hundred and sixty-five days of the year divided by the twenty-eight days of the cycle… Thirteen repetitions. A baker's dozen bloodsuckers. Here in camp, the vampire had bitten thirteen people.

Valerka also found something to ask.

'Baba Nyura, are vampires afraid of water?'

'N-not j-just any w-water.' Old Nyura shook her head. 'Ony f-from the Archi-Bishop. The p-priest th-there used to c-consecrate it f-for b-baptisms. Ch-church, there was. T-to this d-day, the w-water reeks of h-holiness. G-ghouls d-don't g-go there.'

The Bishop flowed into the Volga above Concert Clearing. The water of the Bishop, mixing with the water of the Volga, flowed along the bank of the clearing. It was clear why the bloodsuckers, once they had lost the battle, did not pursue Igor and Valerka into the Volga. For the bloodsuckers, the Volga close by the camp was worse than sulphuric acid. Igor recalled the incident on the beach when Vika Milovanova from the second brigade had suddenly gone berserk. Gelbich, Zhanka Shalayeva, and lanky Lyolik had dragged her off for a swim, but Vika had broken away from them ... to avoid falling into the water. Meaning she was a bloodsucker.

'What about the neckerchiefs?' Igor heard again Kirill's ghastly croak as the bloodsucker lost his pioneer neckerchief in the battle. 'How do their neckerchiefs come into this?'

Valerka also remembered the time when Gelbich, that coarse oaf, had ripped off Albert's neckerchief for Zhanka to write a memento for him, and Albert had gone black, like a demon. He had dashed off the avenue, and everyone had thought it was to complain.

Old Nyura pointed to the open door of the canteen. In the doorway, they could see the stretch of wall between the windows, where one of the educational posters of the clean-cut pioneers was hanging. A boy and a girl, carrying a heavy bucket together. The pioneers were depicted in caps and red neckerchiefs, with stars on their chests.

'G-ghouls c-can't g-go out in the sun,' said Old Nyura. 'They'll b-burn to ash. S-so they p-put on everything S-soviet. It's their p-protection d-during the d-day. Red is the c-colour of their b-beloved b-blood. And the s-star is the s-sign of the d-devil.'

'A pentagram,' whispered Igor.

Vague and imprecise feelings took hold of Valerka. There had been a time when certain strange things about the other boys had surprised him, but it had all become familiar; the surprise had worn off, and he had stopped noticing. Pioneer neckerchiefs. A neckerchief was required at assembly and nowhere else – but some of the children wore their neckerchiefs all day. Lyova did, and Albert, Marinka Lebedeva, and others from other brigades. Behaving as if a pioneer was supposed to wear a neckerchief. Lyova had once taken Yurik Tonkikh's pioneer star. And Valerka had seen a five-pointed star drawn with a ballpoint pen on Beklya's chest, when Beklya had attacked him in the bushes near the church and torn his shirt. So this was why the bloodsuckers became correct pioneers, who not only behaved well but also looked as they should. They were using their correctness to hide from both people and the sun.

'What about crosses?' Valerka asked Old Nyura in some agitation.

Anastasiika's cross was keeping her safe. And Beklya, once he had become a bloodsucker, had been unable to enter a church, even an abandoned one.

'G-god exists,' said Old Nyura with conviction. 'He t-took d-death on the c-cross for our s-salvation. The s-sign of his d-death now k-keeps people s-safe. B-but g-ghouls are k-kept s-safe by the s-signs of their d-death. The s-sickle is their m-moon, when they have to d-drink b-blood or d-die. And the h-hammer is for h-hammering an aspen s-stake into them.'

To Valerka, hearing this was even worse than seeing Serp Ivanych as a stratelates. Serp Ivanych was just a traitor, and he was one of a kind, but the vampires' protection from the sun turned inside out what Valerka believed in. He believed in the red flag and the red star, in the hammer and sickle and the Civil War, in eaglets that learned to fly, and an honest collective.

What struck Igor was something else. All the legends about vampires had turned out to be true. Authentic vampires – stratelates – drank blood and were afraid of the sun. Their hearts could stop beating. Those they bit also turned into vampires, into bloodsuckers. And vampires more than likely lived long lives, if Iyeronov's robust health was any indication. And they were unable to refrain from drinking blood.

But it was not only about the vampires. In and of themselves, they did not mean much. It was that the world, so familiar, understood, and dear, was not real. Not a pioneer camp, but a food block. Not morality, but camouflage. Not symbols of state, but magic charms. Not history, but a lie. What was real was something else entirely. His friendship with Valerka. His love for Veronika. The childhood of the dunderheads in the camp who did not know why they were needed here. And also real, perhaps, were the records being set in faraway stadiums.

'When will it be the stratelates' moon?' Igor asked Old Nyura.

It was Valerka who answered. 'The third of August,' he said. 'He told me himself.'

The third of August was the last day of the camp shift. Sunday. The championship. The concert. The bonfire. And the close of the Olympics.

PART 5

A VAMPIRE'S DEATH

We may not rest! Burn, you, burn, but live.
Onward drive! In hot blood onward drive!
R. Rozhdestvensky, 'Onward Drive', 1966

CHAPTER 1

'HALI-HALO!'

'Come on, come on, stop moaning,' Irina Mikhailovna ordered them irritably. 'I'm giving you a pioneer assignment: we'll all take a rake and get to work!'

When young leaders or teachers said they were giving a pioneer assignment, it meant that the work would be boring, hard, and for someone else's benefit.

'We need to pick the rubbish off the shore, so we go home leaving it as clean as it was when we arrived.'

'It was total shit when we got here,' grumped Slavik Mukhin.

'Mukhin, I'll tell your parents what words you know!'

Lyova distracted Irina Mikhailovna. 'Can we take a ball? We'll clean up and play.'

'Only when your work is done,' said Irina Mikhailovna, warning them sternly. 'Khlopov, I'm making you responsible.'

Lyova certainly looked responsible, smartly dressed and in his red neckerchief.

Valerka's squad trailed miserably off to the shore, dragging their rakes.

The Volga sparkled. In the distance, a cargo boat chugged by. Light waves murmured through the pebbles, and away in front of the boys stretched the trampled, littered beach.

'So where's the rubbish?' asked Tityapa mournfully, surveying the expanse.

He did not feel like working, but doing nothing was boring.

Gorokhov waved his hand in front of Gurka's nose. Gurka blinked, inevitably, and Gorokhov immediately smacked him under the chin.

'For frightening the fishy-wishy!'

Gurka snapped his teeth, and Gorokhov immediately chucked him a second time, and a third, and a fourth, admonishing him, 'For ignorance! For ignorance! For ignorance!'

'Th-th-th-thank y-you!' Gurka barely got the words out.

Tityapa also came up with some fun. He scratched Gorokhov on the head and said, 'My arse is itching!'

'You're the arse!' yelled Gorokhov indignantly, and he jumped on Tityapa and threw him to the sand. 'Now say, "Mister, mister, pardon the pisser!"'

'Bundle!' Gurka joyously joined in the yelling and crumpled on top of Gorokhov. 'Boys, flatten us!'

Seryozha Domrachev fell on Gurka, Slavik Mukhin on Seryozha, and Yurik Tonkikh jumped on Slavik, squealing. Tityapkin, crushed by the boys, howled desperately somewhere down in the depths of the bundle.

Valerka and Lyova, separated by the writhing swarm of boys, looked at each other in silence. Lyova could have stopped the rough-housing with a single word, but he did not – probably to make Valerka feel more keenly the bloodsucker's power over the carcasses. In Lyova's eyes could be read the bloodsucker's calm confidence in his own power and invulnerability. Valerka remembered Lyova running up to him to bite him in the battle at Concert Clearing – to break him, overcome him, make him submit. It was the first real attack by a vampire: open and malicious. There, in the clearing, Lyova had not managed to secure victory. But he had not abandoned his intent.

Valerka looked back at Lyova, sullen, implacable.

The boys who had piled into the bundle disentangled themselves and got back to their feet, leaving Tityapa on his own on the sand, wriggling and moaning. But suddenly he rolled over from his side onto all fours and began to fumble with his fingers in the pockmarked sand. A coin – a silver Olympic rouble – glinted in his fingers.

He marvelled at the coin, stunned. 'Wicked!' he gasped. 'Bagsy it's mine!'

He jumped up as good as new, and the boys surrounded him, examining his find.

'Rail grease!' said Slavik Mukhin approvingly.

'Lucky sod!' agreed Seryozha Domrachev.

The lads unashamedly envied Tityapa. A rouble in itself was a very serious sum, and a man with a rouble was a well-to-do and secure person who levied special treatment. And this rouble was no ordinary rouble; it was an Olympic rouble. Needless to say, Tityapa was not worthy of such good fortune.

'I've got four Olympic roubles at home!' boasted Yurik Tonkikh naively, stung by Tityapa's elevation. 'Dad brought them from Moscow. With the rings, the torch, space, and towers! What's yours got?'

'Some bloke on a horse,' answered Tityapa.

'Someone probably lost it on the beach,' came in Valerka.

Gurka was finding it intolerable that another was enjoying good fortune. He rushed away, hunched over, and started digging in the sand with his hands, like a dog.

'I'm gonna find something too!' he shouted.

'We shouldn't dig here,' Seryozha Domrachev warned them. 'Last year the oldies dug on the beach and found human bones.'

'Tityapkin, it's against the law for you to be the only one to have a rouble,' declared Gorokhov. 'It's not yours, it's everybody's! We all squashed you on that spot!'

'Yeah, but I said, "Bags it's mine",' protested Tityapa.

'The first word winds up in a fat cow's belly!'

'The second word's feeble; the first word's got welly!'

'So you're, like, going to hang on to that rouble?' howled Gurka despairingly, giving up digging.

Tityapa hesitated. He himself could feel the unfairness of his success.

'Come on, guys, let's split it,' suggested Slavik Mukhin peaceably. 'A hundred by eight is twelve and a half kopecks.'

'There's no such coin as a half kopeck,' whispered Yurik.

'I don't need anything,' said Lyova, refusing with dignity.

Valerka gave him a sideways glance. Lyova was making out that he was above any distribution. Valerka's reading was that the oh-so correct bloodsucker simply did not know how to participate in an incorrect life, so he was ducking out.

'A hundred by seven is fourteen kopecks,' said Slavik, counting up in his head. 'And two left over. We need to get the young leaders to break the rouble for us.'

'And the two kopecks?' snapped the stickler Gorokhov.

'Two kopecks are bollocks,' noted Slavik.

'Oh yeah, bollocks.' Gorokhov was indignant. 'You're attacked with a knife, you, like, sprint off to call the cops and you don't have two kopecks. And that's it, you're dead.'

'It's free to call the militia,' whispered Yurik again.

'Let's play a game!' said Tityapkin, having a flash of inspiration. 'The winner gets the rouble!'

If they played for it, Tityapkin still had a chance to gain possession of the rouble honestly.

'What'll we play?'

The boys fell to thinking. The game needed to disclose who was most worthy.

'Hali-halo!' Gurka leaped on the spot, as if he had exploded. 'We've got a ball, and Lyovych can call – he doesn't need the rouble.'

'You agree, Lyovych?' The boys looked keenly at Lyova.

Lyova thought for a moment. 'All right,' he said.

Gurka immediately furrowed two lines in the sand with his heel, twenty paces apart. The boys took their places along one trench, and Lyova stood at the other with the ball in his hands. Everyone knew the rules, including the bloodsucker. The game was to get to Lyova; the winner was the one who managed to do so first. Lyova turned away.

'Hali-halo-stop!' he shouted.

While he was shouting, the boys moved decisively forward. All took a big step; Gurka and Tityapkin went so far as to jump.

Lyova turned his head and examined the boys, frozen in a variety of positions. No one moved. Lyova did not attempt to be picky; now was not when it mattered. Rivals had to be sent back once they got a little closer.

Lyova turned back and shouted:

'Hali-halo-stop!'

The boys sprang forward and then again went as stiff as if they had been put under a spell. They stared fixedly at Lyova. Except Gurka. The command 'Stop!' had caught the impetuous Gurka in mid-leap. He turned to stone in mid-air and fell to the sand in a flying pose.

'Zheka Guryanov, you twitched,' said Lyova.

'No way did I twitch!' said Gurka indignantly, lying there as if paralysed. 'I can't exactly hang! Not my fault.'

Lyova suddenly threw the ball hard and hit Slavik Mukhin smack in the chest. Slavik staggered in surprise. The leader had the right to try and dislodge any player with the ball once. If the player did not catch the ball, he lost the position he had gained.

'Zheka and Slavik, go back to the starting line!' ordered Lyova.

This was a bloodsucker's order, and they could not disobey it.

The contest continued.

Playing with the vampire was just like playing with a perfectly programmed robot: he noticed everything and did not miss. Valerka found himself gripped by a grim obduracy. He had to outdo the vampire in some way. Nor was it about the rouble. Why should all the victories go to the vampires? Valerka's eyes were burning into Lyova, and Lyova could see it.

'Hali-halo-stop!' he shouted.

A sudden blow from Lyova's ball winded Seryozha Domrachev.

'Tityapkin, you're moving!'

'I'm breathing! 'S'not me moving.'

'Go back to the starting line!'

Valerka wanted to rush at Lyova and do something to him, but what could he do? Beat Lyova up? Rip off his neckerchief? Push him into the water? Lyova would summon his flunkies to help. And the real mischief was not lurking in Lyova. There were twelve more like him in the camp. The real mischief was in the stratelates. And against Serp Ivanych Iyeronov, Pioneer Valerka Lagunov was powerless.

At the next 'hali-halo', Lyova returned Gorokhov and Yurik to the starting line, and the wedge of boys aimed at him was now headed by Valerka. The boys froze like toy soldiers in a toy war. Except that Valerka felt like a real commander, leading his brigade into a real attack. Lyova was like an enemy tank, and was three steps away.

Valerka gave a predatory smile. He would prevail over the vampire, if only in a game. Anastasiika had been right when she said that a game was the only place where what happened was real. All the rest, where the vampires were currently triumphant, was in the realm of make-believe. And so what if the games turned out to be stupid. Boys play games the way they know.

After all, in a game they were no longer pioneers who could only do things correctly.

Lyova was looking at Valerka with something like regret.

He tossed the ball, caught it, and announced:

'OK, we won't finish the game. We need to give the rouble to the young leaders. They'll find out who lost it. We should do everything honestly.'

CHAPTER 2

PLAN OF CAMPAIGN

The cooks and the food block supremo took for themselves food not doled out to the pioneers: cereals, sugar, pasta, preserves, dried fruit. Bread, vegetables, uneaten portions and leftovers were taken home by the women of Pervomaiskaya village – the scullery maids, cleaners, and laundry women. In the village they kept cattle which they fed in summer with the spoils from the food block. The women tried to get away from work early so that they had time to attend to their own households' needs. Immediately after the evening meal they would quickly carve up the spoils, and then waddle straight for the gates, laden with buckets and bags.

Waiting out the evening's meeting of the assiduous villagers, Igor and Valerka were sitting on the crates at the back door of the food block. Old Nyura had given them a plate of bread, and they were tossing chunks to the puppies from Vaflya's litter. The puppies came scampering out of the cherry and romped around in the grass, while Vaflya lay a short way off, chewing on a bone and observing. The pups did not yet know what bread was, and were tangling themselves up in the rocket cress.

'We'll have to kill him,' said Igor in a low voice.

'Is there really no other way?' Valerka asked cautiously.

'We won't stop him any other way.'

Igor did not add, 'And we won't save Veronika any other way,' but Valerka understood clearly enough. The following day was the end of the shift. The following day the vampire would drink blood. The following day he would summon Veronika

Genrikhovna, and after that she would inevitably die. Valerka shivered. He had no wish for tomorrow to come at all.

'There is a way to overcome the vampire,' said Igor firmly. 'I've thought it out. We don't need aspen stakes and crosses. We just don't let the vampire bite anyone. We starve him to death.'

Valerka quailed. He had never seen Gor-Sanych so serious.

'How do we do that?'

'Remember Baba Nyura saying her stratelates died in prison?'

'Yes,' nodded Valerka.

'We'll do that. We'll put Serp in prison.'

'Yeah but there's no prison here,' said Valerka, taken aback. 'And no militia.'

'But there is the food block. The doors are made of iron. There are bars on the windows. We'll lure Serp into the food block and lock him up for the whole night of his moon. And he'll peg it.'

Valerka looked at the kitchen and the canteen. From the doorway came the indistinct voices of the village women, the clinking of pots, and the clattering of ladles. The food block in no way resembled a crypt suitable for killing a vampire.

'Serp Ivanych would start yelling and bang on the windows. They'd hear him and let him out.'

'Well, yes, my way is not one hundred percent certain,' agreed Igor gloomily. 'But the food block is the strongest building in the camp. Besides, it's out of the way. Of course people might come running and let Serp out, and that would be the end of everything. But we can pin some hope on the fact that tomorrow's a special day.'

'How will that help us?'

'There won't be an evening meal – everyone'll get food at the Last Bonfire. There'll be am dram going on. Loud music. Then they'll all pile into Concert Clearing. The whole daft charade'll drag on practically until dawn.'

'Only the pioneers and young leaders'll go to it. What about the other adults?'

'The other adults'll sit in front of the telly to watch the Olympics closing ceremony.'

Valerka sighed. Doubts tormented him.

'I'm not arguing with your plan, Igor Sanych,' he said guiltily. 'But how will you lure Serp into the food block?'

'I'll think of something,' answered Igor confidently.

Bambook suddenly emerged from somewhere. With the look of a dad who was a little the worse for wear, he sidled up to the pups, sniffed one of them, and then, wagging his tail, made playfully for Vaflya, aiming for the bone under her paw. Vaflya gave a growl, as if to say *You think I'm going to fall for that bollocks.*

'You haven't forgotten about the bloodsuckers, have you?' Valerka reminded Igor. 'At any moment Serp Ivanych could telepath them an order and they'd come flying over and get him out. We need to put them in some kind of prison as well. Except we don't have a second prison.'

'Yes we do,' grinned Igor. 'The boat.'

Valerka looked distrustfully at Igor.

'The river bus? Where is there to lock the vampires in there?'

'The saloon.'

'They'll get out,' Valerka objected at once. 'The door's plywood.'

'I just need to hold them up, if only for a minute. That'll be enough. I'll take the boat out onto the Volga. The bloodsuckers aren't going to leap overboard and start swimming. The river. They won't dive in there.'

Valerka sank into deep thought, picturing the situation. Gor-Sanych really had come up with something altogether unusual.

'Do you know how to steer the ship?'

'It's a river bus. It's not hard. And my father's a captain.'

'In that case maybe it would be better to take Serp Ivanych out on the ship?'

'Yes, that was my first thought, too,' nodded Igor. 'But then I realised: Serp'll attack me. I just wouldn't have time to hop out the wheelhouse and jump into the water. And if Serp got to my blood, the whole thing would be for nothing.'

'Yeah but why won't the bloodsuckers attack you?'

'What do I care about the bloodsuckers if the stratelates has snuffed it?'

Valerka went cold with fear. Gor-Sanych, he realised, had decided to risk himself. Valerka studied him, seeing him with different eyes. Gor-Sanych looked the same as usual: the locks of hair grown long; the dark moustache, the suntan, the faded T-shirt. He was not a muscleman, not handsome, not a braveheart. But there, on Concert Clearing, he had thrown himself into the brawl to save Valerka. And now he was ready to call the enemy's fire onto himself, as soldiers did in war. Valerka felt pride blossom within him that Igor was such a friend. Such a commander. That he, Valerka, had such a collective: small, but courageous enough to go to war with the vampires.

He could express none of this to Gor-Sanych. He did not have the words.

'So how will you get the bloodsuckers onto the bus?'

'Yes, right. I do have an idea...' answered Igor vaguely.

The red evening sun was blazing through the pines. Birds were hopping over the rubbish bins and along the crest of the chain link fence.

Valerka finally asked the most important question.

'What do I do?'

Igor's look was tinged with pity.

'You, Valer, don't have to do anything.'

'Is it because I'm little?' asked Valerka angrily.

'Yes,' answered Igor simply.

'That's not fair! We're a collective!'

'For the sake of a shared victory, Valer, we have to give up our own interests,' pronounced Igor sadly. 'It's difficult. But you have to.'

Valerka wanted to take offence. Adults liked to keep children away from everything interesting. They made out it was for safety, but in reality they were simply taking everything interesting for themselves. Was Gor-Sanych really just another egoist, even if he was also a hero?

Valerka reflected, and reluctantly made his peace. If he and Gor-Sanych were a collective, then he should submit to the commander.

The division of spoils in the kitchen finished, the ladies with their bags and buckets piled out of the food block. Igor and Valerka waited for the exodus to be over.

Since the battle on Concert Clearing, Igor had been spending the nights in the food block; the vampires had no reason to stand on ceremony now. Of course, they were still unable to force their way into Igor's room, but they could send their underlings to drag the young leader outside – to be bitten. Igor had been obliged to come and join Valerka. And Valerka was glad of it.

Old Nyura was mopping the floor.

'Baba Nyura,' said Igor. 'We have an important conversation.'

He climbed impudently onto the butcher's table.

Old Nyura straightened herself, leaning on her mop.

'We have devised a plan for the destruction of the stratelates,' announced Igor.

Old Nyura breathed heavily and crossed herself.

'M-may G-god h-help you, m-my s-sons!' She was almost sobbing.

'Listen up. This is how we're thinking of realising it.' Igor shuffled about the table, experimenting with ways of explaining. 'Tomorrow's the end of the shift. It's the bonfire. Once we've had afternoon snacks, the food block will have nothing to do. None of the workers will stay on here, will they?'

'Y-yes, th-that's what h-happens each t-time,' confirmed Old Nyura.

'We need someone to open the kitchen door tomorrow night. Iyeronov will turn up at the food block at sunset. As soon as he's inside, the door has to be shut and locked. And that'll be that. No one'll come and help Iyeronov. He'll spend his most important night without a victim and at dawn he'll snuff it.'

Igor looked Old Nyura in the eye.

'I'll be somewhere else. The only person who can lock up Iyeronov is you.'

Old Nyura's face went white and sagged, like dough.

It was easy enough to say it: they caught him in their trap and that was the end of the vampire. But how would it be in practice? In the morning, the cooks would come back to the food block and find that nice man and pensioner of national standing, Serp Ivanych, dead. Nightmare! Disgrace! Who went off leaving the old man in the canteen?

Scandal! And then some.

'No-o-o-o-o-o!' Old Nyura backed away, bleating.

Igor slid off the table, stepped over to her, and took her by the shoulders.

'It would look like an accident,' he said, setting about trying to persuade her. 'You know. Serp felt like a drop of compote in the evening. Went over to the canteen. One of the ladies opened up for him. And a bit later locked up. An oversight.'

'An oversight? How?' came in Valerka.

'I don't know. Got a bit tipsy and distracted. Thought Serp had already gone. Padlocked up. Anything can happen! Of course the militia will come along later and interrogate everyone, but no one'll confess, and that includes you, Baba Nyura. There'll be no way to get at the truth.'

'N-n-n-no.' Old Nyura was shaking her head this way and that, like a horse. 'I af-f-fraid. I af-f-fraid!'

'Of the militia?' asked Igor, defeated.

'S-s-stratelates!' Old Nyura breathed out fervently, her whole body shaking. 'I af-f-fraid t-to t-talk to him! I c-can't l-look h-him in the eye.'

Igor was at a loss. He had not expected such faintheartedness from Old Nyura.

Some kind of searing strength seemed to lift Valerka up.

'Give me the key!' he suddenly demanded hotly. 'I'll open the door and close it myself. Give it to me! It'll be better if I do it. I won't let you down!'

CHAPTER 3

CLINICAL PICTURE

Valerka's a child, Igor was thinking. *He doesn't yet know how to be too anxious to drop off.* Igor envied him. Valerka was snoozing serenely on the hard benches, while Igor was sitting by the window and looking out over the camp. The bright moon gave the air a radioactive glow, but the gloom remained gloom. The columns of pine trees, the piles of bushes, and the geometry of the gingerbreads fused together to give the appearance of an internal construction of the darkness, a secret device of midnight.

Nothing had yet changed in the world, but its static balance had already been overwhelmed by the invisible kinetics of violation. Everything would happen tomorrow. The vampire would die in the trap – or manage to break out, at which point Veronika would be doomed. Not long before, Igor had been regretting not having access to miracles. He would never see an Indian yogi plunge into a trance for centuries, or hear the incantations of an exorcist casting out demons. Fata Morgana would never show him a bustling desert city long since submerged in the sand. No sinister ancient kraken, overgrown with seaweed and barnacles, would ever rise from the depths of the sea to surface beside his ship. Alas, in his country, science and society saw all this as nonsense, and had rejected it as a relic of the past and a deformity of bourgeois culture. But now he, Igor, was sitting by a window in a pioneer camp canteen, thinking about a vampire. And the vampire was living in a dacha, receiving a pension, wearing a red neckerchief, and protecting himself with the hammer and sickle. Miracles in this country masqueraded as the everyday, but science denied them, because otherwise one would have to cast doubt on the everyday, and the everyday was not to be subjected to doubt. This denial had been helping the vampire drink blood and kill people.

Igor did not fall asleep until just before dawn. Shortly thereafter, Old Nyura came and chased him and Valerka away. They shuffled off to their own building and grabbed a little more sleep in their rightful places. Then came breakfast and heads like lead. But there was no question of giving in to weakness. The day that had just started was the day of the fight.

Igor had not told Valerka everything about his plan to destroy the vampire. There was no need to disconcert the lad. Not to mention that lurking within the plan were a number of shortcomings. For example, Igor did not know who all the bloodsuckers were. True, he had calculated that there were thirteen of them, but he knew only eight. Igor was counting on finding out the identities of the others from Dr Nosatov. He had to compel Valentin Sergeich to name them. After which he had to compel Nosatov to make sure all the bloodsuckers assembled on the river bus at the right time. If he failed to appeal to the conscience of the cowardly doctor, he would have to resort to cynical blackmail.

Igor strode over to the sick bay, thoughts whirring.

Doctor Nosatov was in the waiting room, sober and not even hung over.

'I don't want to send you scurrying back to the bottle, Sergeich,' said Igor, 'but I've come about those children again. The ones … well, you know. I need their names.'

'Why?' The doctor immediately looked distrustful.

'I'm going to try and stop what's happening to them.'

'You're not a doctor.'

'Medicine, in the shape of you, has proved itself powerless,' Igor reminded him.

Valentin Sergeich looked at Igor from under his brows. Igor waited. The doctor dithered for a moment, assailed by grave doubts, then opened up a cabinet, took out a shabby exercise book – his register – and put it on the table.

'Start from the 19th,' he told Igor morosely. 'Five cases. The sixth – the first – I didn't enter. The entries in pencil, not pen.'

Igor realised that at the end of the shift the doctor intended simply to take a rubber to all mention of his awful patients, and forget about the whole episode forever.

'Give me a piece of paper,' said Igor. 'I'll make a list.'

Igor turned the pages of the register, taking his time, and soon his sheet of paper showed a column of five names: *Maltseva, Galya, 1st brigade; Rybkina, Oksana, 3rd brigade; Vechter, Sveta, 2nd brigade; Glushenko, Misha, 3rd brigade; Yurevich, Nina, young leader.* Meaning the girl Dr Nosatov had found under the pier was Marinka Lebedeva or Vika Milovanova. Igor completed the list: *Lebedeva, Marina, 4th brigade; Milovanova, Vika, 2nd brigade; Khlopov, Lyova, 4th brigade; Stakhovsky, Alik, 1st brigade; Beklemishev, Sasha, 2nd brigade; Buravtsev, Maxim, young leader; Tkachuk, Kirill, young leader; Nesvetova, Veronika, young leader.* The Young Pioneer Camp Storm Petrel's baker's dozen. The stratelates' Olympic catch.

It struck Igor that a camp was the best place for a vampire to go about laying in supplies. There were young people there, crowded together. The young were restless; something was always happening to them. They got themselves killed more often than adults, whose lives had settled firmly into a rut. And who were they, these young things? No one. The young held no positions of responsibility and had no common sense. Their deaths did not have the same consequences as the death of a man burdened with children, work, commitments, and a penchant for compromise. Very convenient for the vampire. The only people more convenient for him than young people would be a bunch of old sots, but drunkards had a narrow social circle. They would find it harder to raise a herd of carcasses for themselves, and were unreliable breadwinners.

Igor pushed his paper towards Dr Nosatov.

'These young people will be dead within a year,' he said. 'For real.'

The doctor's face creased with suffering as he read through the list. Then he pushed the sheet aside.

'What can I do?' he asked. 'I don't know the diagnosis. No tests have been carried out. I don't have a clinical picture.'

'Yeah, well I do. Help me.'

Valentin Sergeich's reluctance to participate had him wriggling on his chair.

'Shit, you're a doctor,' Igor pressed him. 'You're supposed to save people!'

'They need to go to hospital. Full examination. Check-up.'

'Give over pissing yourself.'

Dr Nosatov slumped as if his spine had been broken.

'Listen. This is what you need to do,' said Igor coldly. 'You're going to take this list and go and see Whistler right now. Tell her that after football, when the whole camp is together in the stadium, she is to announce that at ten p.m. those specified on this list are to come and see you here, in sick bay. Got it?'

Igor had it all very well thought out: the time and the plan of action.

'How am I going to convince Svistunova?' persisted the doctor.

'Well, tell her it's all down to tick bites. You need to give these kids injections before they leave camp.'

'So why didn't I give them emergency prophylaxis straight away?'

'Shit!' Igor flew up. 'What do you get from ticks?'

'Encephalitis. Lyme disease. Ehrlichiosis. Anaplasmosis. A load of other things. And pretty often those infections provoke other diseases.'

'There!' Igor gave the doctor an encouraging pat on the shoulder. 'Lie. Tell her you gave them the shot for encephalitis the day they were bitten and now you've decided to inject them for anaplo … plasmosis. You know, like you can't have both shots at once. Whistler doesn't know.'

'What if she asks them if they were bitten by a tick?'

'Why would she check up on you? Still. All right, we'll cover ourselves. Tell her that this anaplasmosis aggravates other diseases, causes fainting, loss of coordination, impairment of cognitive function. Hell, pile it on. Tell her it could be contagious, like flu. She won't even ask questions.'

It was a good move. Igor praised himself. Whistler, of course, would immediately link the mythical infection to the deaths of the young leaders and pioneers. And she would not delve into the details of the vaccination, because in that case she would be shown to be guilty: she had known about the danger but not raised the alarm.

'Even so, Igor, I'm afraid of bringing myself to Svistunova's attention. Can't we get by without her? I'll send Miss Pasha round the camp. She'll find everyone on the list herself and warn them.'

'That won't work!' Igor firmly objected. 'The people on the list are healthy. And they haven't been bitten by ticks. Why would they come over here to see you? One of them'll take it into their head not to come, but I need them all. So it has to be Whistler ordering them. They'll listen to the Senior Pioneer Leader, but they won't give a monkey's about what you say, or me, or Miss Pasha.'

The doctor was suffering agonies, pacing nervously round his office. His medicine cabinet set up a frightened rattle of its delicate glass.

'What am I supposed to do when these thirteen come pouring in here?' The doctor looked Igor in the eye. 'Seeing those dead souls again will be too much for me.'

'You don't need to see them,' Igor reassured him. 'Lock the door and put up a notice up outside telling them to go straight to the river bus.'

'Where?' asked the doctor, uncomprehending.

'The river bus.'

'Why?'

Igor was already worn down by Valentin Sergeich's embarrassing faintheartedness. 'Do you really want to know?' he asked angrily.

The doctor quickly looked away.

'No, I do not.'

He sighed, and let out a whimper, as if he were about to burst into tears.

'I only want to know one thing: when will this all be over?'

'Do as we've agreed, and then it will be over,' Igor promised.

CHAPTER 4

KISSING ON THE PIER

A jumping game was in full swing by the entrance to the canteen. Two girls were standing on the path with a length of tatty and much-knotted elastic pulled tight round their legs, while a third girl was jumping up and down as if she were on springs. She twisted nimbly sideways and backwards, crossed and spread her legs and waved her arms to keep her balance. Her long ponytail bounced, and her skirt billowed.

'*Moony hawkers, lunar walkers,*' the jumper was chanting in time to her springing. '*Landed* plunk! *Got roaring drunk.*' The jumper skilfully changed her aerobatic manoeuvres. '*Ribbon this side – queen at noontide, ribbon that side – ginger cat. Pretty wrap and cheery clap – and hear the great big trigger snap! Berry berry bonbon, ker-boom the ciggy long gone, inside the sweet a skunk and our Yelena's boy's a punk!*'

Igor was waiting for his brigade to assemble after lunch, and stood watching. The skipping game was something very simple and real, because as far as it was concerned, pioneers and vampires did not exist. Igor thought of Veronika. Only recently she, too, had been just such a little girl. Of course, that little girl was still there inside Veronika even now, just as inside Igor himself was still the little boy who had played war games and chopped nettles with a stick. One could be angry at anything in life but this little girl.

Veronika came out of the canteen with Sasha Plotkin.

'I need to talk to you alone,' Igor told her.

'We have nothing to talk about,' replied Veronika coldly.

'It's important,' insisted Igor.

'I believe I warned you to get off Veronika's back?' inquired Sasha, a quaver in his voice. 'Do you really not get it?'

Sasha was acting like a knight, a noble defender of the weak. He knew that Igor would not get into a fist fight, and so was carrying himself defiantly. Igor paid him no attention to him. Veronika likewise.

'I'll pester you until you do talk to me.'

'Looks like you're asking for my fist in your face!' blared Sasha.

'Don't attract interest to yourself by shunning me,' Igor went on, threatening Veronika with the thing that vampires feared no less than holy water.

'OK, fine,' agreed Veronika reluctantly. 'A little walk. Sasha, chill. Assemble the brigade and head into the building.'

'Only not for long, Korzukhin,' said Sasha. 'Call me if you need to, Nika.'

Igor watched with grim curiosity as Sasha Plotkin made his businesslike way towards the pioneers. This is what the submission of the carcass to the bloodsucker looked like in everyday life.

'Let's take a stroll to the pier,' suggested Igor.

They were walking along the avenue as if nothing had happened: no breakup, no turning into a vampire, no stratelates' terrible promise. And the red neckerchief around Veronika's neck seemed of no particular significance, either. It was just a neckerchief.

'I've guessed what happened,' said Igor. 'Iyeronov bit you on Parents' Day, when you and the orphan girls went to his tea party. And then you bit Sasha, didn't you? Probably not just him, but that's not important now.'

'You're talking complete rubbish.' Veronika frowned with irritation.

'There's no one around. Who is there you need to pretend you're a normal person in front of?' Igor shrugged his shoulders. 'I saw you with my own eyes coming into my room through the window. On the first floor. And you had fangs.'

'Crap!' said Veronika, decisively denying it.

'I'm not a carcass like your Sasha who's going to believe whatever you tell me to believe.'

Veronika stayed silent.

'I know why you need a pioneer neckerchief. I know why you betrayed our love and went back to Plotkin. I know what you do at night. I know your heart doesn't beat. And I know who Iyeronov is.'

Beyond the iron gates, the plaster bugler stood tall on her pedestal, the same as ever. On his way by, Igor stroked the bugler's chapped and peeling silver knee. Horrors more horrifying than a walking sculpture had been uncovered in the pioneer camp. And the plaster girl had never been alive.

'No, Igor, you have no notion of who Serp Ivanovich is.' Veronika's face twisted in a grin that carried none of her usual haughtiness.

At the mention of Iyeronov, her eyes had darkened. Igor remembered that dark fire. It lit up only in moments of triumph and bliss.

'There's such power in him, like he's a god. He has no barriers. He knows everything about people. He makes the world comprehensible. And when I'm with him I feel all-powerful.'

Against his own volition, Igor felt jealous of the vampire. 'How is it you find Serp so inspiring?' he asked grimly.

It was not, of course, about intimacy. Intimacy was too simple.

'It's a mystery to me, too.' Veronika spoke slowly, as if listening attentively to her own pleasure. 'Nothing like this has ever happened to me before. I don't think I've ever met anyone else with such a remarkable story and such a clear way of explaining life. If you are one with him, you receive everything you need: love, freedom, truth. Everything acquires its own meaning. Everything done for him is part of a great cause. I've never felt so needed. It's as if I've been entrusted with a flag to carry.'

'He drinks your blood, and the rest is narcosis,' said Igor harshly.

'Yes, he needs my blood,' agreed Veronika easily. 'So what? Some need insulin, he needs blood. I don't begrudge him my blood. He's an old man. He was badly wounded in the Civil War. He's sick. But age and suffering don't detract from the greatness of his spirit.'

Igor had brought Veronika out onto the pier, stretching away as it did into the river from the shore. The motor ship would soon dock here, but for now the pier remained empty, like an unfinished bridge. The planks creaked beneath their feet. The waves slapped lightly against the piles and the hanging tyres. Reflections from the water ran across Veronika's face.

'You weren't like this with me,' remarked Igor, not sparing Veronika's vanity. 'With me, you couldn't tolerate anyone giving you orders. You didn't want to be told how to live or what to think about life.'

'Don't be offended, Igor,' said Veronika, gently stroking his elbow. 'It's just that everything with you was … kind of shallow. Make-believe. We went for walks, laughed, kissed, slept together … but the big wide world was as scary as ever. That's why I was so … unbearable. Spiky. But when you have a master, the world is not scary. Of course it still has lots of danger and inconvenience. But now I know why, and I know I'll cope.'

Igor was very nearly shaking with hatred for the vampire.

'It's all lies and deceit!' He was looking into Veronika's dark eyes, but those eyes were like ice holes. 'Tonight Serp will drink your blood, and in a few days you'll be dead! There won't be anything for you at all!'

'And I agree, if that's what he needs,' answered Veronika boldly, even happily. 'You think that'll frighten me? Stop me? You've never felt what I feel now! You've never been alive the way I'm alive!'

To hear this was unbearably painful for Igor.

In the distance, a hydrofoil was flying along the Volga. It sparkled in the sun like gunshot.

Igor grabbed Veronika by the shoulders.

'Say what you want,' he breathed in her face, 'but I don't believe you. I don't believe you've fallen out of love with me. Yes, you gave me up for the sake of safety. Yes, you've agreed to die for a vampire. But you haven't fallen out of love with me.'

Veronika looked at him as she would a killer. He laid his palm on her breast – and there was dead silence. Her heart was not beating.

'Don't touch me,' she sighed almost voicelessly.

'Wriggle and I'll push you in the water,' Igor warned her. 'I know you can't go in the water. And I know you won't bite me in the daytime.'

He leaned forward and greedily pressed his lips to hers, cold and soft. Veronika froze at the edge of the pier, not daring to move. Igor wrapped one arm around her, squeezing her desperately against him, kissing her as he had never kissed her before. This was his beloved Veronika – stolen, deceived, turned into a monster, but still his Veronika. And beneath his palm he felt a sudden, shy pulse; and a second beat; and a third. Veronika's heart had woken up. It had jolted itself into life, without command.

Igor pulled away from her lips, just an inch.

'I won't throw you in the water,' he whispered. 'But I need you to do one thing. For me.'

Veronika's face was wild; blue spots swam across it.

'When your master calls for you today, tell him you'll wait for him in the food block. Let him go there. It doesn't matter where you'll be at that time.'

Veronika was silent, troubled.

'Tell him!' repeated Igor. 'I'm trusting you because I love you. You love me too. You've forgotten, but I know it for you. And I won't give you up.'

CHAPTER 5

THE VAMPIRES ARE HAPPY

'*The sea is fretting* ones!'[25] commanded Anastasiika. '*The sea is fretting* twos! *The sea is fretting* threes! *Shapes from the sea now freeze!*'

The boys and girls froze in outlandish poses.

The brigade needed something to occupy them before the football championship began, and Anastasiika had suggested a game of 'The sea is fretting'. Irina had approved, and so, naturally enough, had Igor. Those who were minded to play lined up under the pines in front of Anastasiika. Those not so minded sat on the bare earth and acted as judges.

Anastasiika hypercritically examined the nautical figures.

'Clockwork or stone?' she asked Slavik Mukhin.

Slavik had hunched over into an incomprehensible contortion and was holding his palms spread out beside his nose.

'Clockwork,' replied Slavik.

Anastasiika touched him to 'wind him up'. Slavik wiggled his hands.

Anastasiika thought for a moment. 'I don't know who you are,' she said, dissatisfied. 'A freak, not a nautical figure. A crocozebra. A cross between a bulldog and a rhinoceros.'

The judges could not guess the figure either.

'Probably a geranium,' suggested Lenochka Romanova.

'How did a geranium get in the sea?' asked Anastasiika, surprised.

....

[25]   A popular children's game.

'The captain's wife gave it to him and he chucked it in the sea. Geraniums smell disgusting.'

'It's a whale!' shouted Slavik angrily. ''S'his mouth and teeth!'

'Whales don't have teeth,' objected Anastasiika. 'Only a shark has teeth.'

'Whale! Whale!' hollered the boy judges. 'Dead ringer!'

'A bad figure,' declared Anastasiika. 'You're out, Mukhin.'

'Unfair!' exploded Gorokhov. 'Everyone can see it's a whale, 's'just you looking at it crooked!'

'I don't recall giving you permission to speak,' snapped Anastasiika by way of rebuke.

Valerka was sitting among the judges, admiring Anastasiika, the flowing movements of her hands as she depicted the waves. Lyova Khlopov and Marinka Lebedeva were also among the judges. If they had been required to sweep the grounds, collect scrap metal, or take part in a sports competition, the bloodsuckers would most likely have been in the vanguard, but they were unable to play games. There were no rules on how to show a whale, or even a geranium thrown overboard by the captain.

Igor strolled on a little further. The river bus was already tying up, and the blare of its klaxon could be heard from the river beyond the pines. Igor had been wanting to intercept Dimon Malosolov, but he missed him. Dimon had scooted straight off looking for Irina in her building, and Igor had to wait for the two of them to have out whatever it was they wanted to say. It would not be worth irritating Dimon by distracting him from his meeting with his beloved. He needed Dimon to be feeling kind and pliable.

Igor glanced discreetly at Lyova and Marinka. The little bloodsuckers no longer awoke hatred in him. On the contrary, they had become rather pitiful. Veronika's grim candour had made a dispiriting impression on Igor. It was one thing for bloodsuckers to submit to their stratelates the way the carcasses submitted to the bloodsuckers: order received – order carried out. It was quite another for the bloodsuckers to give themselves heart and soul to their enslaver and serve him devoutly and be ready to do anything for his sake. The bloodsuckers were making a religion of their stratelates. To them, the vampire's wishes were sacred commandments and the will of heaven. They would heedlessly lay down their lives for their master. Like dogs, they were happy to be at their master's boots.

'*The sea is fretting* ones!' commanded Anastasiika. '*The sea is fretting* twos! *The sea is fretting* threes! *Shapes from the sea now freeze!*'

The judges studied the figures with interest.

Zhenka Tsvetkova was simply standing there, hands above her head in the shape of a little house.

'Clockwork or stone?' Anastasiika asked Zhenka.

'Stone.'

Once again, Anastasiika was at a complete loss to identify the figure.

'I'm a sea princess,' said Zhenka, giving her a clue. 'This is my crown.'

'Crown my bollocks!' wailed Gorokhov. 'That's more like a peaked cap!'

'There's no such thing as sea princesses in real life!' The silly invention made Anastasiika angry. 'The figure of a sea princess is not allowed. You're out, Tsvetkova!'

'Sea princesses exist!' Zhenka became indignant.

'No, they don't. Look, everyone agrees!' Anastasiika stretched her hand expressively in the direction of the community of judges, the male contingent of which had burst into exclamations of approval, and the female part – exclamations of indignation.

Igor did not see the continuation of the argument. Dimon came out of the building.

Igor hurried up to him.

'Dimon, hang on, I need you for something.'

Dimon's face was trembling like a child's.

'She told me to go to blazes!' babbled Dimon, taking no notice of Igor.

'Who?' Igor was astonished.

'Irishka! She told me never to go near her again!' Dimon fished out his cigarettes and agitatedly lit up right by the building. 'She can't forget your bigwig almost walking in on us.'

Igor realised that Dimon was referring to the incident when he had found a quiet place in the building for himself and Irina only to have Whistler come barging in. Dimon had spent the entire shift nudging Irina towards his bed, and it had been a titanic job, because Irina's moral principles were up to withstanding a direct hit from an atom bomb. Even so, Dimon had managed it. Only for Whistler unwittingly to bring all his achievements crashing down. Daring a second attempt was beyond Irina, and in frustration she had ruthlessly kicked Dimon out of her life so that he would not tempt her.

'Lend me some of the green stuff,' Dimon asked earnestly. 'I'm going to go to the doctor, buy some booze from him, and get out of my tiny.'

Dimon was planning to roll head over heels down the slope of his bitter destiny.

'The doctor's downed all the booze himself,' Igor said. 'I sympathise, Dimon. But I need you for something. Get me the keys to the ship again.'

'What for?'

'I need them.'

Dimon gave Igor a look of misery and condemnation.

'My life's fallen apart, and you want to get a girl onto the boat?'

'It's not exactly straightforward for me either,' replied Igor, rattled.

'Piss off, Igoryokha!' said Dimon, offended. 'You've spent the whole shift on a high.'

'Dimon, this is really important.'

'I've had it up to here with Palych! He doesn't think I'm an actual person. He won't give me anything.'

'No, come on, you'll be able to talk him into it again.'

'Nope. I'm off to get pissed as a newt,' said Dimon angrily.

He shoved Igor out of the way and walked off. Igor's plan to capture the bloodsuckers was on its way to hell in a handcart. In desperation, Igor grabbed Dimon by the sleeve.

'Wait!' he said hotly. 'Quid pro quo. You give me the key to the steamer and I'll give Irina a prod in your direction.'

'A prod? How?' Dimon slowed down at once.

'Doesn't matter!' Igor flapped his hand; right now he was ready to promise anything under the sun. 'When the concert starts, she'll be waiting for you in the building.'

'Word of honour?' Dimon was stupid, and very trusting.

'Bring me the key!'

'Roger that!' cried Dimon, already brighter and more lively. 'I'm out of here. Hello, Palych!'

Meanwhile, beneath the pine trees, the nautical figure contest was continuing. Gurka was spawled on his back, an arm and a leg sticking up.

'Clockwork or stone?' Anastasiika asked him haughtily.

'Hurry up and guess!' howled Gurka. "Smurder holding this!'

'Clockwork or stone?'

Gurka's strength failed and he dropped his leg.

'I was a shipwrecked boat!' he shouted. 'That was my masts sticking up!'

'You're out,' said Anastasiika coldly. 'You broke your figure.'

'I did not break it! I was clockwork! I was showing how the ship went down to the bottom and its masts all fell off! The ship's lying on the bottom like this.'

Gurka stretched out his arms and legs as if on the command 'Attention!', and closed his eyes.

All my masts have fallen off, too, thought Igor.

He tracked Irina down in the young leaders' room. Irina was sitting on Sasha Plotkin's bed, for some reason without her glasses. There was something intimate about that; Igor stopped in his tracks. Irina wiped her face with her palm, put on her glasses, and made to get up.

'No need,' Igor stopped her, sitting himself down opposite her.

Irina, it turned out, was crying. The indomitable Irina Kopylova was crying. Chubby, plain, ever ordinary, she had suddenly become human and very endearing. Yes, there was something there for Dimon Malosolov to fall in love with.

'We're leaving tomorrow,' said Igor, 'and we won't see each other again.'

'I won't be sorry,' sniffed Irina.

'And Dimon won't show up again, either. And he's really got it bad for you.'

'Did he put you up to this?' asked Irina without looking at Igor.

'No. But we're old mates. I know him well. And I'm not happy either that everything's fallen apart between him and you. He thinks super-short term, like Pinocchio: you told him to get lost, and like an idiot he got lost.'

It occurred to Igor that Veronika had also told him to get lost.

'Don't go poking your nose in, Korzukhin!' snapped Irina fiercely. But she did not get up from the bunk to take herself off and terminate all discussion.

'You're grown-ups. You like each other. You're not hurting anyone. Why did you have to end it?'

'I don't need any more of that kind of disgrace!' answered Irina furiously.

'What disgrace?' Igor was astonished. 'You absolutely haven't done a thing! If you mean Whistler, she's up to her ears in her own problems. She's long ago forgotten about that. And so what, she lives with the PE teacher, not registered, and anyway she didn't say a dicky bird about it. The obstacles you've got are all right here.' Igor leaned forward, stretched out his hand, and unceremoniously jabbed Irina in the forehead with his finger.

Unexpectedly, Irina did not bat away his hand.

'Maybe that's right,' she said stubbornly. 'But you have to live by the rules.'

The rules presupposed going first to the registry office and then to the bedroom. All reasonable and fair. Except that it would not work with Dimon. He would not last until the registry office. And if he did not get it now, he would zip off for it somewhere else.

'You're right,' agreed Igor sincerely. 'We're a society, not a herd, so we must live by rules. But the question is: what rules? I don't know who dreamed up the rules for us, but somehow even a good person feels too cramped in them. And the man is unhappy, even though he's not guilty of anything.'

Igor was no longer talking about Dimon, but about himself. And he was no longer thinking that he would never visit Stonehenge or the Egyptian pyramids – bollocks to them, the pyramids. Igor was thinking that vampires were evil, and no one disagreed with that, but the rules, alas, would not let anyone defeat the vampires. In his tussle with the vampires, he, Igor, had to duck and dive and be as cunning as if he were a crook. Why? Why were the rules more convenient for vampires than for humans? Well. The vampires, at least, were happy. And Irina was not a vampire, although she, like any bloodsucker, was devoted heart and soul to the rules – the solemn order of things.

Irina was silent, pressing her lips together. Her eyes were full of tears.

'Anyway, Kopylova,' Igor finished tiredly, 'if you follow the rules, you'll lose Dimon. He's not the brightest bulb in the chandelier. He won't understand you.'

Irina was not a cretin. Everything Igor was saying, she already knew. Of course she did.

'Don't go to the concert,' asked Igor candidly. 'I promised Dimon I'd try and change your mind and that you'd meet again.'

Irina did not answer – but she did not object. Igor took it as agreement.

CHAPTER 6

EVERYTHING TAKEN AWAY

Manly songs about sports records and peaceful fighting were booming from the camp loudspeakers. The camp was preparing for the football championship. The young leaders were assembling their pioneers at the stadium. Valerka and Yurik were walking along the narrow, bush-lined path behind Building 2.

'Mum wanted to sign me up for football so that I developed physically, but Dad said chess would be more useful in life,' Yurik was saying.

Behind them sounded the hurried tramp of feet, and someone's hard hand suddenly pinched Valerka's neck, squeezing it fiercely and doubling him over.

'Gotcha, grayling!' gloated Beklya, breathing on the nape of Valerka's neck.

'W-wha-at?' shouted a terrified Yurik in a reedy voice.

'Beat it!' Rulet barked at him.

'Go to hell!' took up Siphilyok.

'I'll tell the leaders!' promised Yurik, weeping as he retreated.

Beklya rammed Valerka's head into the thicket and drove him forward, apparently so he could settle with Valerka without witnesses.

In a secluded clearing behind the acacia, Beklya kneed Valerka in the backside several times, then let him go.

'Let's break his glasses!' Rulet balled his fists and danced animatedly in front of Valerka, as if trying to work out where to hit him.

Valerka was not the least bit afraid of Beklya and his curs now, although it looked like he was about to receive a royal thrashing from them. Valerka looked on Beklya as a bloodsucker, not a hoodlum, and a bloodsucker did not bite while the sun was up, so there was nothing to fear.

'You owe me three roubles,' said Beklya with a smirk.

'You sure you don't mean five?' asked Valerka boldly.

'Getting fresh, are we, Mazepa?' Beklya's fist piled into Valerka's solar plexus.

Valerka crouched over in pain, coughing.

'You're going to have every injury that's ever dragged itself into A & E, you get that?'

'I don't owe you anything!' croaked Valerka, choking.

'Get us the three roubles!' Rulet was twitching hysterically.

'Bring us the money!' Siphilyok sang along.

'Yep, yep, in a sec,' wheezed Valerka. 'I'll just iron your shoelaces...'

The punks would likely have set to beating Valerka up, but the bushes quivered, and out of the thicket and into the clearing came Lyova Khlopov in tracksuit trousers, T-shirt, and red neckerchief. Behind Lyova appeared Tityapa, Slavik Mukhin, Gorokhov, and Gelbich. And hovering shyly and in some agitation behind their shoulders was Yurik.

'Oh!' scoffed Beklya loudly. 'The full Guadeloupe has arrived!'

Valerka was taken aback. He had not expected any help – it was not as if he had any friends – and suddenly a sworn enemy had come to his rescue. A vampire. And not alone, but with his own company. Inside Valerka, unwanted gratitude mixed with deep-seated hatred, and his convictions tottered as if on stilts.

'Let go of him, Beklemishev!' ordered Lyova sternly.

'Or what?' clowned Beklya.

Lyova looked Beklya in the eyes without a word. Valerka switched his gaze back and forth between them, trying to understand: did Beklya and Lyova know they were both bloodsuckers? Were the bloodsuckers really going to fight over him like two cats over a herring head? Beklya, the punk, was taller and more rambunctious than Lyova, but Lyova, the pioneer, was supported by a noble uprightness that lent him strength, and a steadfast, athletic character. The carcasses, meanwhile, simply drilled one another with fierce looks, ready to do the bidding of their masters. Of a sudden, Valerka felt that he, too, wanted to be in Lyova's team, because Lyova was a valiant and fair commander.

'There are more of us, Beklemishev,' warned Lyova.

Beklya, making out that he really did not give a monkey's, nonchalantly pushed Valerka away.

'Take your Four Eyes,' he guffawed. 'I'm not going to miss this piece of shit.'

Lyova put an arm around Valerka's shoulders.

'Let's go,' he said calmly.

'I'll find you in town!' Beklya threw one last threat at Valerka.

As they walked to the stadium, Lyova said nothing more. Yurik was quiet, too. He stayed close to Valerka and sniffed in embarrassment. He felt somehow awkward, as if Valerka had suffered through something he had done.

'Beklya won't find you,' Gelbich reassured Valerka. 'It's a big city.'

Valerka did not think Beklya would even look for him.

'I'd have knocked Rulet out with one swing of my left,' bragged Tityapa belatedly.

'Support us, Lagunov,' Lyova asked humbly when they reached the stadium.

By evening, the blue of the sky had started to thicken and the clouds had yellowed in the heat. There were no free places on the benches, and half the spectators were on their feet, hopping about. A complete racket was the order of the day. Pushing and shoving broke out from time to time in different sections of the crowd, and the young leaders rushed in to calm the ruckus.

'Teams to the pitch!' ordered Ruslan Maximych, the PE teacher, shouting into a megaphone.

The teams made a disorganised entrance into general view. The noise from the spectators grew as they welcomed their own players. The 'steamrollers' – boys from the senior brigades – inspected their rivals and sniggered derisively. They were sure of victory, because the oldies had always been victorious in all competitions. It was not as if the steamrollers created an impression of immense might, though. They were a little taller than Lyova's footballers – except Gelbich, of course – and their voices were coarse and unpleasant. That was all. In a word, more posing than pre-eminence.

The young leaders Kirill and Maxim, the steamrollers' coaches, gave them a pep talk.

'Act aggressively. You are stronger!'

'Lean on them psychologically. You are older!'

Whistler came out onto the pitch. The PE teacher Ruslan handed her the megaphone.

'Boys and girls!' Natalya Borisovna's electronic voice carried easily over the hubbub of the spectators. 'Welcome to the main event of our Olympic shift: the football championship!' New howls arose from the crowd.

'Why so quiet?' thundered the Senior Pioneer Leader, trying to raise the degree of rapture. 'Hurrah for our future champions!!!'

'Hurrah!!!' the audience hollered wildly.

The PE teacher took the megaphone.

'The team of the first and second brigades against the team of the third and fourth!' he announced. 'The captains: Gorelkin Vovchik and Khlopov Leonid!'

Lyova pursed his lips, but did not correct him.

'On my whistle, the match will start. Let the first half begin!'

Valerka and Yurik were sitting directly on the ground and watching both teams prepare for the skirmish. The PE teacher put the ball in the centre of the pitch, retired to a safe distance, looked at his watch, and blew his whistle. The players rushed furiously towards the ball and piled into a scrum. The spectators again raised their voices in concert, yelling wildly.

Valerka's thoughts were far from the stadium. Valerka was trying to understand why Lyova had saved him from Beklya. No matter how many explanations whizzed around in his head, they all came down to one thing: Lyova was good. Lyova was not pretending to be a pioneer, any more than Beklya was pretending to be a punk. Granted, there was that time in Concert Clearing when Lyova had wanted to bite him. What of it? After sundown, the bloodsucker part of the vampires awakened. But Lyova was

a good person. The bad person was the one who had made him
a vampire.

The steamrollers' style was blunt and straightforward. They
piled into Lyova's team, all of them in a herd; they broke easily
through the enemy defence, raced for the goal, and scored.
Gurka, who was defending the goal, legged it somewhere or
other, nowhere near the ball. The crowd whooped and hollered.
They were happy. Nobody was expecting an actual contest from
the match; all were counting on a chance to admire the little
ones being beaten up. The oldies were expected to provide
general pleasure by pulverising the rookies. Therein resided the
sacrificial essence of the championship.

The girls from the older brigades joined together in an
organised chant: '*If! our boys! come out on top! We will kiss! them
all non-stop!*

From Lyova's original team, Gurka, Tityapa, and Gorokh had
survived, and from the second squad (not Valerka's) Gelbich,
Tsybastysh, and Makerov. Lyova gathered his players in the
centre of the pitch and tried to impress something on them,
like a ringleader talking to his conspirators. The steamrollers
ran around, relaxed and shouting back to the yelling spectators.

The PE teacher gave a blast on his whistle, and Lyova's team
raced at once into the attack. The ball gave every appearance of
having been switched. It flew in long zigzags from one of Lyova's
players to another, as if someone had pre-drawn its trajectory,
while the steamrollers charged about in completely the wrong
places. Gelbich soared over the field like a gaunt bird of prey and
swept the ball into the opponents' net.

The spectators could not have cared less who was being
thrashed – the tots or the non-tots. The spectators rejoiced, and
the steamrollers were clearly surprised at the lack of sympathy.

Kirill and Maxim bustled anxiously here and there, but the
oldies' star had already tumbled from the sky. Emboldened by
success, Lyova's team was no longer willing to relinquish the
initiative. Valerka watched in silence as the onslaught against
the steamrollers unfolded on the pitch. Football had bored the
hell out of Valerka the whole shift, but now he was following it
with a kind of grim avidity. The boys appeared to have cracked

the mystery of the intricate mechanism of victory. The secret was that there was no need to try and outrun everyone or hold the ball for as long as possible. The job was a team job, and the task of each individual was to help the team where they could and not try to do everything all on their own. Valerka, too, understood this.

Lyova stayed out of the thick of things; he ran around giving orders.

'Pass to Makarov! Lay it off to Koshkin! Make a run into the third zone! Pass to Gelbich! Send it out to the right wing!'

One of the steamrollers scythed Lyova down, but he did not let up.

The boys seemed to Valerka to be under a spell. The deft manner in which they made overlapping runs and kept the ball from the steamrollers brought it home to Valerka that he was jealous. The boys had merged into a team, while he had turned his back on football. He had been over-hasty. Then again, how could he have imagined what a vampire might be capable of? He remembered being sorry that there was no special machine where you could press a button and everyone would straight away pay heed and hey presto a team would materialise. It turned out that there was such a machine.

The lads were hammering in goal after goal. The steamrollers were going spare. The spectators were braying with laughter at them, and each goal was accompanied by a mocking roar. Zhanka, her eyes screwed up, was screeching frantically, flushed red with pride for Gelbich, who was leading the line. Even the sullen Lyolik was wearing a clumsy smile, despite the fact that the team with boys from her brigade was the one losing.

The PE teacher was becoming grimmer by the second. He had originally been rooting for the stronger boys, but they had cheated him of his expectations. The PE teacher resorted to excuses and abuse.

'Morons. I'm telling you. Morons.'

The two peas Kirill and Maxim were charging about after the PE teacher, as if their own shame as coaches would be less noticeable if they were near him.

There was nothing for it. The PE teacher blew his whistle. The match was over.

The sweat-soaked and dishevelled steamrollers were standing on the pitch, unable to believe their defeat.

Lyova's lads were breathing heavily, still uncomprehending.

'With a score of 6-1 the team from the middle brigades are the winners,' announced Ruslan nonchalantly, as if the victory was worth nothing.

The spectators hollered with delight. It's always nice when idols crumble.

The Senior Pioneer Leader stepped smartly out onto the pitch and took the megaphone. Her experienced organiser's instincts were prompting her not to close the shift with discord. Triumph for some and a debacle for others would be a bad look.

'I think you've all done well!' she shouted cheerfully. 'Right, boys and girls?'

The spectators offered Whistler their generous support.

'In the Olympics, the main thing is taking part! Everybody wins! Hurrah for our boys!'

'Hurrah!!!' took up the crowd.

Whistler whispered something in Ruslan's ear. Valerka understood what.

'You should have made it a draw! You're the moron around here.'

The footballers were leaving the pitch. The boys headed in the direction of Valerka and Yurik. Lyova dropped to the ground next to Valerka, as if by chance.

'Sick, what we did to them?' he asked quietly.

Valerka offered his sullen agreement. 'Sick,' he said.

'You made a mistake, Lagunov.' Lyova was chafing his knees and not looking at Valerka. 'I called you to join us and you didn't come. And you needed to.'

Valerka felt as if he had been doused with something cold. Yes, Lyova was good: selfless and honest. Yes, he had saved Valerka from Beklya. Yes, he had created the genuine collective of which Valerka dreamed. But that changed nothing, because Lyova was a vampire. Meaning the vampires had even taken away his – Valerka's – dream.

'Wait, wait, girls and boys, listen up!' shouted Whistler into the megaphone. 'There will now be a half hour break for everyone to get dressed for solemn assembly. And I have an announcement!' A piece of paper appeared in Whistler's hand. 'If I call out your name, you are to go and see the doctor in sick bay at ten o'clock this evening...'

Valerka smirked to himself. Gor-Sanych's plan was in motion.

CHAPTER 7

UNDER THE RED FLAG

The building was in upheaval. The young leaders had finally allowed the brigade to get ready to leave the camp. Igor was on duty in the storeroom, making sure there were no outrages akin to the disappearance of Tsybastov's jeans. The pioneers, shoving and cursing, were sorting out their bags, backpacks, and suitcases. At night, after the bonfire, there would be no time for fussing about with their belongings, and in the morning even less. Boarding the motor ship was planned for straight after breakfast.

Irina was keeping order in the corridor. Pioneers were rushing back and forth, exchanging things that had become mixed up over the course of the shift.

'Styazhkina, where are you? Give me my blouse!' shouted Lenochka Romanova.

An indignant Anastasiika drew herself up in front of Irina. In her hand she held a beautiful foreign travel bag.

'This is utter stupidity, Irina Mikhailovna!' she declared angrily. 'You said to leave everyday clothes for when we went away, and now we need our parade uniform for assembly! So it's turned out the other way round!'

'Don't make me angry, Sergushina,' answered Irina. 'Go to your dorm. Stop getting in my way.'

Valerka spent no time breaking his head over such trifles. His clothes would be parade clothes to begin with, and then be rebadged as everyday clothes. Job done. Idiots could get changed if they wanted to.

The boys scattered their junk on their bunks, not so much for the purpose of getting anything done as to convince themselves that they had gone to uncommon lengths to observe decorum and do their stocktake.

'Guys, come and visit me. Dad'll take us fishing,' said Seryozha Domrachev, issuing a general invitation.

'I'll come!' Gurka promised immediately. 'I'll bring both my older brother's nets. He's like a totally top poacher, he's even been shot at.'

'Come to Metallurg in the autumn,' said Lyova firmly. 'We have a junior football team there at the stadium. Zheka Guryanov, Kolka Gorokhov, and Tityapych, I'm inviting you pres … personally. We need good players.'

'I'll be there on the first of September for sure!' promised Gurka.

Slavik Mukhin twirled a cap with a visor in his hands, made up his mind, and slapped it on Tityapa's head.

'I'm giving it you as a keepsake,' he said. 'You liked it.'

'Not fair!' barged in Gorokhov at once. "Fyour giving anything, you got to give it to everyone.'

'How can I give one hat to everyone?'

'Then don't give him anything!'

'Let's all give each other hats!' said Tityapa, quickly coming up with an idea so as not to lose his present. He pulled out his wrinkled panama and tossed it to Gorokhov. 'Here!'

Gorokhov spun the hat in his hands and started grumbling. 'I haven't got a hat of my own! I didn't bring one with me.'

He clearly did not want to part with his newly-acquired panama.

'Give your socks,' suggested Slavik Mukhin.

Gorokhov immediately whipped off his socks and flung them over to Yurik Tonkikh.

'Thank you,' said Yurik politely. 'Here, Valerka!'

Yurik held out his nursery school cap to Valerka.

Valerka went out wearing Yurik's cap.

Gelbich, the brigade flag-bearer, was kicking his heels near the stoop. He was already dressed for assembly: ironed trousers, white shirt, shoulder sash, neckerchief, and cap. He was bored, and amusing himself with the rolled-up flag, twisting it this way and that, and landing blows on an imaginary opponent.

'Oh, Valeryan!' rejoiced Gelbich. 'Come here. I'm going to kill you! Stay still! Aaaahh! Aaahhh!'

Gelbich whacked Valerka with the flag, in the ribs and then around the head.

'Brains out!' he said with satisfaction.

Valerka did not like how freely Gelbich was handling the flag. Of course, a brigade flag was a piece of nonsense, but even so, it should not be treated like that.

'A flag isn't a toy,' said Valerka, displeased.

'What, then?' Gelbich instantly latched on, sensing fun.

He unfurled the red cloth and waved it in front of Valerka's face.

'Kiss it!' he ordered. 'Kiss it!'

The way people poke a chained dog with a stick and keep repeating: 'Bite it! Gnaw it!'

Valerka tried to grab the flag. Gelbich nimbly hopped away.

'Let's have a fight!' he suggested eagerly. 'A bayonet attack! I stab you and you, like, peg it.'

Gelbich made a lunge with the unfurled flag, striking Valerka in the chest. Valerka rushed forward to grab the flag and inadvertently stepped on the cloth. At the same moment, Gelbich hopped backwards and yanked the flagpole. The silk tore treacherously. Gelbich lifted the flag in fright, and gasped: the cloth was hanging from the pole, attached to it by a single corner, like the head of a mop.

'What have you done, you four-eyed goat?' howled Gelbich.

Valerka himself stopped dead, and let the name-calling pass. He tilted the flag and examined the damage.

'We can stitch that,' he said confidently. 'I'll zoom off and get some thread from the girls.'

'If Fatty sees this she'll beat me to a pulp.'

'Hide,' Valerka advised him. 'It's your own fault.'

He ran to the building and bumped into Anastasiika right at the entrance.

'Sergushina, help!' he begged earnestly. 'Give me some red thread.'

'I don't bring mouliné with me to camp,' replied Anastasiika haughtily. 'Needlework requires tranquillity, and there isn't any of that here.'

Valerka had no idea what mouliné was.

'We've ripped the flag,' he admitted. 'We need to stick it back on.'

Anastasiika measured Valerka from head to foot with an icy glance. She was brigade commander, and she had to walk under cover of the flag.

'Morons,' she said. 'Wait a minute. I'll bring you some.'

Valerka waited on the stoop for her to come back, dancing with impatience.

She returned with a needle threaded with a long black thread. She raised the needle, point upwards, and handed it to Valerka.

'Here's your needle! But if the flag is horrible, I'll draw conclusions. You understand?'

'Understood!' said Valerka gruffly.

Hiding behind an acacia, he and Gelbich repaired the flag, more or less. It looked almost as it had done, only slightly wrinkled.

'It's shit, but we can live with it,' said Gelbich, letting out a relieved breath.

Fortunately, Irina Mikhailovna, lining up the brigade in front of the building, did not notice. Irina Mikhailovna had her own worries now.

'How can you forget your own brigade's motto?' she scolded. 'The motto's written on the stand, you see it a hundred times every day! Are you sure you haven't forgotten your own names? The brigade is "Danko"! Our motto is … *Burn as bright…* Well, go on!'

'*As a fireman's light,*' suggested the airhead Zhenka Tsvetkova.

'I'm going to kill you all with my own hands!' promised Irina Mikhailovna.

The whole camp assembled in Company Court. Grown-ups stood by the flagpole: Whistler, the PE teacher Ruslan Maximych, Marina Fyodorovna, the senior tutor, whom nobody remembered, Doctor Nosatov, Director Kolybalov and, of course, Serp Ivanych Iyeronov. Sanya, the radio technician, was fussing about. As usual, some of his wires were refusing to play nicely together, and his amplifiers were dead.

At last came the thunder of the drums. The tramp of many feet sounded in unison. Each brigade did a lap of honour of the square and assumed its place. The flag-bearing group, marching in formation, carried out the large company flag. The pioneers' actions had been practised over the course of the shift, and everything came out accurately and expressively. There were no outsiders at the assembly, and the beauty of the parade was reserved exclusively for those in camp, as if an inspection were being made of a secret society.

It struck Valerka that the camp was indeed a secret society. Nor was it about the vampires. The point was in a mystery of an altogether different kind. Its presence distinguished their life from the life of nature. It distinguished the even pioneer formation from the disorder of the acacia; it distinguished the bugler's song of summons from the merry song of the birds; it distinguished marching in regular rectangles from the free movement of the clouds. Valerka now knew this secret. And his disappointment in it was bitter.

They, people, were themselves to blame. They cared nothing for the mystery hidden in the scarlet flags and the five-pointed stars and the hammer and sickle. People, it turned out, had no need of that mystery. But the vampires did. The vampires did more than sow deception and drink blood; they perverted the whole essence of the sickle and hammer, the whole essence of the flag and the star. But to Valerka that essence was very dear. What else was there to hold dear? Olympic roubles? Soon enough, the vampires would pay for their sacrilege. Not all the vampires, of course. But one of them, at least.

'Boys and girls!' shouted Whistler fervently into the microphone. 'Today we are finishing our glorious Olympic shift! We did well! Hurrah for all of us!'

'Hurrah!!!' swept through the brigades.

Then Whistler read out the names of the winners of the various competitions, and the camp heroes came forward to receive their certificates. Whistler saluted them, and the others clapped, hands raised above their heads. There were heroes by the barrow-load, and Valerka could not wait until they were done. Mind you, what was the hurry? The stratelates was not going to run away now, and would not perpetrate anything awful: there he was, standing by the flagpole.

'And now: attention!' commanded Whistler. 'Lowering the flag on our shift is entrusted to the one who raised it. Serp Ivanych Iyeronov!'

The tall Serp Ivanych leaned slightly towards the microphone.

'Ah, but I did not raise the flag alone,' he reminded the assembly slyly. 'I would like help from the one who helped me before. Otherwise, what if I can't manage it?'

The pioneers broke into ready laughter. Valerka went cold.

'Valery Lagunov from the fourth brigade, step forward!' Whistler joined in with joy, as if she had not been the one to kick Valerka out of the camp.

Someone behind him pushed Valerka out of the ranks.

Under the gaze of the whole company, Valerka made his way forward, his legs cotton wool. Fear had swept over him, as if he had been invited straight into the maw of the stratelates.

'Don't be shy!' shouted Whistler cheerily.

Stumbling, Valerka reached the flagpole. Serp Ivanych had already caught hold of the halyard to which the flag was attached. He gave Valerka a friendly smile, but in his smile Valerka saw only the pitiless hunger of a vampire consumed by longing in the light of his beloved, accursed moon. Yes, the stratelates had chosen his prey, although he could change his mind. Valerka looked directly into Iyeronov's black eyes.

'Let's do this together, eh?' the old vampire suggested in a low, mocking voice. 'We do all right, don't we?'

CHAPTER 8

'THE EAGLETS ARE LEARNING TO KNOCK'

The final concert was held in the stadium instead of Concert Clearing. For one thing, there were benches around the stadium. For another, the log wigwam readied for the Last Bonfire had been precipitately doused with petrol by one of the camp staff, meaning a match struck by any prankster could send the whole thing up while the concert was still going on. If unpleasantness were to be avoided, it was best for the time being not to let the pioneers into the clearing.

After the ceremonial assembly, Igor stopped Valerka.

'You all right?'

Igor studied Valerka, surprised at himself. How had he presumed to lay such a responsibility on this puny, bespectacled boy?

'I'm ready,' said Valerka seriously. 'Are you?'

Igor was also ready. Before the assembly, he had popped in to see Old Nyura, and Dimon Malosolov had just handed him the bunch of keys to the boat.

'Here.' Igor handed Valerka a simple single key to the padlock which hung on the back door of the food block.

'Has Baba Nyura already done a bunk?'

'Yes. She signed me with a cross and promised to pray all night.'

'We'll manage. We don't need her,' said Valerka confidently.

Igor sighed. The sun was tumbling down towards the Zhiguli and blazing through the pines. There was something ominous in its red evening flame, like a trail of blood.

'Well, good luck!' Igor held out his hand to Valerka.

'And you.'

Valerka's narrow hand was as firm as an adult's.

A hot spark seemed to shoot through the handshake. Valerka was sure that Gor-Sanych was a reliable friend, and would not let him down, and therefore in his turn Valerka would not let Gor-Sanych down. Valerka had never had such friends before.

Valerka watched Igor go, until he disappeared behind the bushes.

It would not be a good idea for Valerka to appear in his own building, and he was not going to the concert. The best thing for him to do was to go to the food block, let himself in as agreed, and wait there in ambush for the stratelates. Valerka made his way along the avenue.

Anastasiika suddenly emerged from a side path and fell in step beside him.

'I think we need to say our goodbyes before the end of the shift,' she said. 'So I could walk you halfway, for instance. Are you sleeping in the canteen again?'

'How do you know?' asked Valerka in surprise.

'Everyone knows you quarrelled with Khlopov and went to live in the canteen. Just like a dog. All the stray dogs live around the canteen.'

'You want to say goodbye but call me names,' Valerka reproached her.

'Fine. If you need an apology, I'm sorry. But it's true.'

Valerka knew that the following day he would part with Anastasiika, and they might never meet again. Although everything depended on him. He knew where Anastasiika went to school, and he would be sure to find her in the autumn, only there was no need to talk about that now. If she was minded to be sad and kind, let her; she was usually overly mean and arrogant. And it was easier to be friends with a girl in town, because there were always too many prying eyes around camp.

'I've been studying you, but I haven't found everything out yet,' said Anastasiika. 'Tell me, what do you collect at home?'

Valerka did not collect anything, but he lied. 'Model aeroplanes, calendars, stamps.'

'I collect calendars with flowers on them. If you've got some, I'll swap you.'

'I'll get some,' said Valerka solemnly.

'Have you been to the sea?'

'To Anapa twice.'

'That's good. I've been to Jūrmala. I'll give you an amber, and you'll give me a seashell, one you can hear the sound of the surf in.'

Valerka started working out where he might get hold of a seashell.

'What constellations do you know?'

'Er...' Valerka hesitated. 'The Great Bear. Orion.'

'You can show me them later. But first we'll enter into correspondence. We must write each other one letter a week.'

'I can do two,' offered Valerka generously.

Anastasiika reined him in. 'We are not yet in such a close relationship,' she said.

It struck Valerka that this was all kiddies' stuff. Anastasiika with her letters and calendars seemed altogether like a little girl to him. He was off to kill the stratelates and she was talking about seashells. Well, one day he would tell Anastasiika how he and Gor-Sanych had battled with vampires in the pioneer camp. Anastasiika would be blown away, and appreciate him, Valerka, properly.

Despite what she had said about half way, Anastasiika walked with Valerka all the way to the food block. There was no one in the back yard, not even the dogs. Valerka used his key to unlock the padlock, pulled it from its loops, and swung open the iron door as if he owned the place. Anastasiika peeked warily into the kitchen.

'Is this where you actually live?' she asked from inside. 'Where do you sleep? On the floor?'

'I push benches together.'

Valerka stood outside with the lock in his hand, and held the door open, waiting for Anastasiika to finish looking and come back out.

Out of the blue, a whirlwind struck Valerka, knocking him off his feet and onto the ground. He had no idea what it was.

The stratelates! he panicked. But it was not the stratelates. It was the beanpole Lyolik, Zhanka Shalayeva's friend, hurtling at Valerka and sending him flying. Zhanka herself was there too. Like a flash she slammed the iron kitchen door with both hands, sending a loud boom through the whole camp. Valerka pushed himself up a few inches and saw that Gelbich was also taking part in the attack. Venka grabbed the lock that had fallen out of Valerka's hand, rushed to the door, and pushed the shank into the loops.

'What are you doing?' yelled Valerka furiously.

Without hesitating, Lyolik planted her foot straight in his ribs. Gelbich turned the key to fasten the lock, then yanked it out of the keyhole. Anastasiika was left on the other side of the door, in the kitchen.

'Hey, rat!' shouted Zhanka cheerfully, smacking the iron door with her hands. 'You're going to sit there, you got that? You can kiss your precious concert goodbye!'

Valerka realised that all this was the next stage in Zhanka's revenge against Anastasiika. Zhanka could not bear the humiliation of Valerka kicking her after she had ruined the 'secret'. Zhanka was a scheming punk. She and her flunkies had once more tracked down Anastasiika and Valerka, and improvised this new, cruel revenge.

'Sing yourself a solo!' shouted Zhanka, mocking Anastasiika through the door. 'Dog's arse! Liver sausage! Prostitute!'

Valerka heard Anastasiika pounding angrily on the door.

'Sing me "The Eaglets Are Learning to Knock"!' jeered Zhanka. She was beside herself.

It was a disaster. A total, total disaster. A dog's arse. Anastasiika would not make it to the final concert, and she had so wanted to dazzle the audience with her singing. Mind you … concert? Singing? The sun's disk was on the horizon and the whole operation was hanging by a thread. From somewhere far away, the pitiless stratelates was already striding towards the food block, but the food block was closed. Meaning Gor-Sanych had stolen the ship and exposed himself to the bloodsuckers' bites for nothing. He would turn into a carcass. Into a slave. Meaning the stratelates would drink someone's blood today, and the whole thing would never end. And it was all Valerka's fault; he had failed in his task. This could not get any worse.

Anastasiika pounded on the door, calling, 'Lagunov, let me out! Lagunov!'

With a roar, Valerka jumped up and leaped at Gelbich like a madman. The dumbfounded Venka had no time to dodge, and Valerka violently seized Gelbich's right hand, trying to prise open his fist and take the coveted key. Gelbich thrashed stupidly, randomly jabbing his other fist, connecting now with Valerka's side, now with his shoulder. Lyolik threw herself at Valerka from behind, dragging him by the collar, and viciously slammed her weighty fist into Valerka's back, shaking his whole fragile frame like a pillow being beaten from both sides. Kicking up a cloud of dust, they scrapped like dishevelled fighting cocks and a big mad hen. The red light of sunset lit them up.

'You were my friend!' Valerka wheezed at Gelbich.

'Huh?!' howled Gelbich helplessly.

He was protecting Zhanka, his girl, just as Valerka was protecting Anastasiika.

Lyolik punched Valerka boxer-style on the side of his face, knocking him off Gelbich. The glasses flew from Valerka's face, and Lyolik kicked out at them.

'Duff him up, the blind bat!' shrieked Zhanka excitedly from the side.

Gelbich was torn by conflicting feelings, and he was in a much worse state than Valerka. How could this be happening? They had played together, enjoyed their free time together, and now here they were fighting like sworn enemies. Gelbich was almost in tears, not knowing what to do.

'Here's the key, Valerych!' He showed the key in his palm, then swung his arm and hurled it behind the rubbish dump and over the fence into the bird cherry.

No key, no discord.

'Look out!' barked Lyolik just then. 'Shalayeva, let's get out of here!'

Zhanka and Lyolik were gone in a twinkling, dashing headlong away from the food block. When they were in fighting mood, their thinking was quick and unerring. Gelbich whirled on his heels as if he had been scalded, and also bolted, chasing after the girls.

Valerka hurtled towards the door.

'I'm here! I'm here!' he shouted to Anastasiika, imprisoned in the food block.

'Let me out!' sobbed Anastasiika behind the iron door.

'A sec! Just a sec!'

Valerka circled like a kite over the ground, myopically hunting for his glasses. There they were!

One arm had sustained a fracture, the lenses were cracked... No matter.

Valerka planted the glasses on his nose. The world became sharp again.

Find the key! He must find the key! Fast. More than fast! He, Valerka, still had a chance to prevail! He and Gor-Sanych still had a chance to prevail!

Valerka swiftly climbed the rickety chain link fence.

CHAPTER 9

WILD ANIMALS AND A CAGE

Two sheets of paper were pinned to the door of the sick bay. One was a list of the thirteen bloodsuckers, and the other had an announcement: 'Sick bay closed. Assemble on the dock.' Igor found a pencil, crossed out 'on the dock' and wrote: 'in the river bus saloon.'

Igor made his way through camp using the back yards, so that no one would slow him down. A bunch of keys distended his pocket. The iron leaves of the gate were wide open. The plaster pioneer girl soundlessly blasted her bugle, escorting the sun behind the ridge of the Zhiguli. The moored motor ship stood at the pier.

The world was new-painted with the crimson of sunset. The white buoy with its number 114 appeared to have blushed red. The white superstructure of the boat was an intense pink, and the blue stripe on the hull violet. The light feathery clouds in the sky resembled a flock of flamingos. The Volga glittered amber, dazzling in the glow, but near the piles the little waves were suddenly lit from within by a sullen ruby flame. Only the moon remained blurred and pale: the earth's sunset had not touched its distant cosmic orbit.

It struck Igor that the waning of the moon was the same now as it had been many, many years before, when the country boy Seryoga had turned into the awful stratelates. Everything around was the same too: the Volga, the seagulls and the Zhiguli mountains, the quaint houses on the shore and the tall pines. And now, just as then, a little ship lay quietly moored at the pier, only not a steamship with a chimney and paddle wheels, but a decorative river bus. And in the pioneer camp, just as in the Shikhobalovsky dachas, there still lived defenceless people. It was as if Igor had been transported to the past, as if a time machine had started up, as if the Civil War was still going on.

Igor bent over a rusty bracket welded to the pier's support – there was a bracket instead of a bollard – and with an effort unwound the intractable rope – the mooring line. Then he made his way to the superstructure and opened the passage to the bulwark. Beneath the roof of the superstructure it was already proper twilight. Igor unfastened the door to the forward passenger saloon, went down the steps, and looked around. The ceiling practically brushing his head, the sealed windows, the benches. Igor went back up to the deck and unlocked the door to the wheelhouse. He went in, closed the door behind him, turned the lock, and climbed the stairs. That was it: he had seized the ship. Now he had to wait for the vampires. He would see them from the windows of the wheelhouse, but the vampires would not be able to make him out against the sun. Igor hopped up into the high captain's armchair.

The foredeck with its benches, the flagpole with its pennant, the strip of boardwalk, the shore, the plaster bugler girl, the iron gates of the camp… No one yet.

The first to appear were two girls, and that was a great stroke of luck. Children would not ask 'Where's the doctor?' 'Why's the meeting on the ship?' Children would take it as a given. The rest of the bloodsuckers would then simply follow suit, without delving too deeply into it. The girls hovered for a moment on the pier, looking around, then stepped aboard. Igor could hear them talking as they made their way down to the saloon.

Next through the camp gates came Ninochka Sergeyevna, the little young leader from the art circle, and with her, Alik Stakhovsky. Alik gallantly gave Ninochka his hand, helping her to step from the asphalt onto the pier. After Nina and Alik came two more girls, followed by a younger boy. Then Igor noticed Beklya. Beklya loitered on the pier for a while, then crossed onto the boat and dived down into the saloon, although he quickly reappeared on the upper deck in front of the wheelhouse. He took out a cigarette and unashamedly lit up.

Voices and laughter floated up from the saloon. To all appearances, the youngsters gathered there were just regular pioneers. Igor even felt a creeping suspicion that he had misidentified the bloodsuckers, but he pushed the thought aside. At last he saw Lyova Khlopov. Lyova was bringing Marinka Lebedeva. Meaning the headcount was already ten. Three were still missing – but they were the most dangerous and important. Igor started to get nervous.

The two peas Maxim and Kirill skipped through the gate and hurried to the pier. Soon their heavy footsteps sounded on the stairs down to the saloon. The only one missing now was Veronika. Igor felt jolts of panic starting to beat inside him. He took a look out of the back window of the wheelhouse. Beyond the Volga over the Zhiguli a sliver of sun was blazing. Soon the children and adults in the cabin would begin to turn into vampires, and there was no telling what they would do once they realised they were trapped. Igor turned back towards the camp gates again, and with relief caught sight of Veronika. She walked the length of the tarmac and along the pier, and disappeared under the wing of the superstructure.

Igor darted out of the wheelhouse onto the deck.

'Beklemishev,' he ordered in the tone of a young leader, 'get into the saloon.'

'Bollocks with bells on,' said Beklya in a surly tone, but he complied.

In his sweaty fist, Igor was clutching the key.

He closed the plywood door to the passenger compartment behind Beklya, quickly slid the key into the keyhole, and turned it a complete revolution. The door could be unlocked from either side only with the key. The bloodsuckers had walked smack into the trap, every one of them.

Without waiting for his prisoners to react, Igor rushed to the captain's post.

The lock on the wheelhouse door. The steps up. The ignition key. So many keys, locks, doors, and stairs today... The ship's generators fed current to the engine, and the dials on the instrument panel trembled. Igor decisively pressed the starter button on its spring. The engine in the hold came to life and started to rumble quietly. The wheelhouse floor vibrated slightly. Igor caught hold of the lever and shifted it from neutral to reverse, gently increasing the number of revs. Under the stern of the boat – Igor knew this – the agitated water foamed and seethed. Igor shifted the helm, setting the rudder to the angle required to turn the vessel.

The river bus moved quietly away from the pier, pulling the loose end of its mooring rope, as if backing away from the pier into the expanse of the river.

The Zhiguli were already obscuring the sun. Scarlet rays were striking the sky in a fan.

How many seconds would the bloodsuckers need to work it all out?

The wheelhouse now resembled an aquarium, suffused with the departing light. Standing at the helm, Igor felt like a pilot guiding a falling plane away from a city. Would he have time to eject? That was already unimportant.

From the bowels of the little boat came a furious thumping: the bloodsuckers were pounding on the locked saloon door. The river bus was edging away from the pier, but the pier was still too close. The saloon door cracked. It was plywood; what else could be expected of it? Igor saw the bloodsuckers rush out on to the fore deck. Maxim and Kirill led the charge, followed by Beklya, then Lyova Khlopov and Alik Stakhovsky, then Nina and Veronika, and then the little girls. The bloodsuckers hurled themselves at the railing. Maxim swung over the gunwale … and hung above the water, not daring to jump. The side of the boat and the pier were separated by about five metres of water. Water which still held onto scraps of sacredness, and so was impassable to the vampires.

The river bus, its diesel rumbling, was moving further and further away from the pier, turning in an arc with its bow towards the fairway. Igor looked at the bloodsuckers from the wheelhouse, and the bloodsuckers, turning around, looked at him from the deck. There was no talk between the bloodsuckers; it was as if they were acting in accordance with an order given to all. It was awful for Igor to see Veronika in the crowd, the same as all the others, as if their personalities had disappeared and all that remained was a single will, and that not their own.

The shore continued to recede, and around the bus the darkening river spread out. Now Igor was alone with a baker's dozen bloodsuckers. The sun could no longer help him. And the bloodsuckers could force him to steer the vessel back to the pier. Igor shuddered; he saw how this might go, and it was not good.

The bloodsuckers moved silently to the superstructure and climbed up its walls towards the wheelhouse. Igor stiffened in horror. The bloodsuckers clung to the walls with the tenacity of insects. In a twinkling they were swarming all over the wheelhouse on every side, the way wasps swarm on a lump of sugar. Their bodies blocked all the windows, and inside the wheelhouse it went dark. Igor stared, stupefied, at the pale faces and the spread hands pressed against the glass. Bottomless, black vampire eyes stared from all directions.

Igor had not told Valerka what he intended to do with the river bus. Well, he was not planning to leave the vessel to float downstream by itself. With no one at the helm, the river bus might well collide with another steamship on the river, or it might be driven ashore, whereupon the vampires would disembark and run to the camp. They would manage to get back before dawn, free the stratelates, feed him – and all would be lost. Igor planned to plough the bus into the sandbank, far enough that it would not slip back into the water. The sandbar, marked by its buoy, stretched out just ahead.

Igor put the engine into neutral, then engaged forward gear, shifted the rudder, and increased the propeller speed to maximum. The vampires were blocking the view, but with his inner compass, like a migratory bird, Igor could sense the position of the buoy. Now the vessel was heading straight for the sandbank.

The bloodsucker Kirill hammered on the glass with his fist. He was unable to crack the plexiglass, but the pane gave a jump, and one side popped out of its retaining rubber weather strip. Kirill pressed with both hands, pushing the glass inward through the window opening. Igor realised that the bloodsuckers were about to burst into the wheelhouse.

Just at that moment, the boat ploughed gently into the sandbank. Losing thrust, the ship was carried by inertia into the sandbar, driving its bow up into the air. The jolt sent the bloodsuckers skittering off the front side of the wheelhouse, and for a moment Igor saw again the vastness of the Volga, the dark blue sky, the dying glow over the hump of the Zhiguli, and the buoy, bobbing on the waves from the river bus. Plastered over one another like worms, the bloodsuckers once again stuck themselves to the window, and Kirill shoved his head and shoulder into the crack. He squeezed his way into the wheelhouse in a signally inhuman fashion, like toothpaste wriggling out of a tube. Igor threw the lever to stop the engine, yanked the key out of the ignition, and hurtled away from the vampire at full tilt.

He skittered down the ladder, twisted the barrel of the lock, flung open the door, dashed out of the wheelhouse, and ran smack into two little girls blocking the way to the side. The girls latched onto Igor. He hurled them aside in horror, only for Alik Stakhovsky to come at him from his blind side. Igor planted both hands on Alik's chest and shoved him. Alik gave a sudden twist of his head, describing an inhuman movement, as if his head were on a hinge, and tried to sink his long fangs into Igor's wrist. Igor pushed Alik at one of the others; it was so dark now that it was impossible to make out who. Igor had very nearly made it to the little gate in the railing when Veronika grabbed him. Pale, dishevelled, monstrous Veronika.

Had she done as he asked? Had she told the stratelates to go to the food block?

Igor thrust out his elbow, the way an animal trainer playing the part of a criminal thrusts out his elbow for a dog to grab … but an animal trainer wears a special bite sleeve. Veronika sank her sharp teeth into Igor's arm. The other bloodsuckers froze, devouring with their eyes the blood spurting from beneath Veronika's fangs.

With difficulty, Igor raised his hand so that he could see Veronika's face and her eyes. He felt no pain at all. An unspeakable bliss flowed from the place of the bite, across his shoulder and through his body, and he felt a longing, strong enough to madden him, for the bite to last forever.

'You told the stratelates…?' Igor could barely raise a whisper.

Pain was burning in Veronika's blackened eyes. She had not wanted to bite him, but she could not stop herself. Bloodlust had smothered her will. Veronika did no more than bow her head slightly, to signify *Yes, I told him.*

In a last effort, Igor desperately wrenched himself out of his monstrous pleasure. He knocked open the guardrail door with his heel and fell backwards from the side. Veronika had not unclenched her jaws, and she went flying with him.

The blow from the water sobered Igor up like a slap in the face. He went down over his head, and Veronika, thrashing, unhooked herself from him. There was a flicker as her shadow dissolved into the fragile, changing twilight.

The cold water pressed against Igor on all sides, and sharp pain suddenly flared in his bitten arm as if a switch had been thrown. Igor's feet grazed the bottom of the sandbank, and he braced himself and stood up, emerging up to his chest.

Above him hulked the white hull of the steamship, high and even, like a wall. Or rather, not the hull, but the wing of the superstructure. Crawling rapidly upwards on its vertical surface was the soaking wet Veronika: crawling, writhing and howling, scorched by the water. Beyond the wide open gate in the railings loomed the dark figures of the bloodsuckers, and in the light dancing off the waves, Alik Stakhovsky could be seen, fallen to his knees, his long tongue greedily licking dark drops of blood from the gate.

Igor flopped noisily back into the water, and backstroked away.

The vampires watched him from the side of the boat, like wild animals looking out of a cage.

CHAPTER 10

HIS MOON

Valerka was searching for the key in the bush of bird cherry, where the zonked-out Gelbich had junked it. Valerka dug desperately through unyielding branches and foliage, shook trunks, and ferreted about in the woody debris near the roots. The greenery whipped him all over like bathhouse besoms, twigs tore at his hands and face, sharp knobs ripped his shirt, mulch slithered inside his collar. Valerka did not give up. Everything depended on the key.

The sun had already set beyond the far bank of the Volga, and the pine trunks were black against the departing azure. The pale, waning moon rolled out into the sky like a broken wheel. Faintly, from far away, came the sound of music and many voices raised together: the final concert had started in the stadium. The paths alongside the buildings were empty, and the mercury lamps burned over the deserted Pioneer Avenue, illuminating nothing. In Company House, three windows on the ground floor glimmered an iridescent blue: the camp staff, their presence not required at the event, were watching the closing ceremony of the Olympics on the TV.

A dull gleam in the gloom of the bird cherry: the key. Valerka grasped it greedily, like a diver in the depths of the sea grasping a sinking coin. Except that to Valerka the key was dearer than any coin, dearer than any treasure.

The stratelates was not yet on his way to the food block; of that Valerka had no doubt – he would not have missed the vampire. Valerka swung over the fence, overturning a rubbish bin, and rushed to the kitchen door. Flinging the lock down against the wall, where he would be easily able to find it again, he swung the door open and burst into the darkness of the interior.

Where was Anastasiika? She had long since stopped knocking. The kitchen with its cookers and sinks, its butcher's table and crockery cupboards… The pantry with its shelves and fridges… Empty. Valerka darted into the dining hall. The big windows with their grilles, the pattern of their bars resembling the rising sun, like on the emblem of the USSR. On the walls between the windows, the posters of pioneers. Long rows of tables and benches. Anastasiika was sitting on the floor in the far corner. Her face pressed against her knees, she was crying quietly.

Valerka had no time to stand on ceremony.

'Come on!' He tried to take Anastasiika's hand.

'I'm not going!' she sobbed hopelessly. 'I'm not going anywhere. I'm staying here!'

Valerka had no choice but to sit down beside her.

'Look, it's not the worst thing that you didn't get to the concert. No harm done,' he said, trying to console Anastasiika. 'Everyone knows you have the most beautiful voice of all.'

'You don't understand anything, you idiot! This is all your fault.'

Valerka knew that Anastasiika was wrong. It was Zhanka Shalayeva's fault, not his. He had been fighting one against three. But Anastasiika needed to dump all her hurt on someone. All right, he was fine to be the victim – only not here.

'We have to get out!' Valerka touched Anastasiika's shoulder. 'It's important!'

'Nothing's important now.'

Valerka was already out of time. The iron door clanged softly, and the figure of a man blocked the doorway. Tall, lean, stooping. Valerka could see him through the open serving hatch. It was Serp Ivanych Iyeronov. The stratelates had come to the food block for the victim of his moon.

Valerka clamped his palm over Anastasiika's mouth.

'Quiet!' he whispered. 'Quiet! Don't move a muscle!'

His face told Anastasiika that this was very serious.

'All is not as it appears in the camp,' said Valerka almost soundlessly. 'Don't ask anything. It's not Serp Ivanych. It's not a human being at all.'

Anastasiika's eyes goggled.

'I'm not lying and I'm not crazy. And he's come here to kill!'

Valerka warily removed his palm. Anastasiika remained silent.

'You don't have to believe me,' added Valerka, looking through the serving hatch. 'But we have to scarper before he catches us!'

Serp Ivanych did not hurry. He looked round the kitchen and pantry, searching. Then he opened the door to the dining room. From where he was, at the door, he could not yet see that in the far dark corner behind the rank of tables someone was hiding.

Valerka waited, biding his time.

Fear was thumping inside him, but Valerka did not give in to it. He felt himself on the very edge of a precipice: one tiny move and he would fall. That changed nothing, though: he had to break out of his narcosis and move. His heart may well be beating so hard that his chest was hurting, but the fight was not over. He still had a chance to slip past the stratelates and dash from the dining room to the kitchen and outside into the yard. Then he could slam the outer door, shove the padlock into its loops, and lock the vampire in.

'What's going on?' asked Anastasiika.

Valerka felt a surge of joy: she was whispering, meaning she believed him.

'I'll explain later. Right now we're going to crawl along the floor on our knees so we're hidden by the tables. Serp'll come into the canteen and we'll run out the door. You got that?'

Anastasiika's face, wet with tears, gleamed faintly in the darkness.

'Come on, get going,' said Valerka, hurrying her.

Anastasiika hesitated, and Valerka gave her a shove. She got awkwardly onto all fours and crawled along the wall, as if they were playing a silly game. Valerka crawled quickly after her. Her knees pattered quietly.

The stratelates took a step into the canteen. Then another. Suddenly, noisily, he gave the nearest table a shove and blocked Anastasiika's way with it.

Iyeronov seemed to Valerka to be towering over them almost to the ceiling.

He looked down, his expression mocking.

'He-he-hello,' stammered Anastasiika. She was in shock.

'Stand up, stand up,' Serp Ivanych advised them good-naturedly.

Valerka and Anastasiika rose to their feet, still separated from the vampire by a line of tables and benches.

'You modern pioneers find dubious ways to entertain yourselves.' Serp Ivanych smiled wryly. 'I'm afraid your young leaders would not approve of your slipping away together.'

Serp Ivanych was pretending that he was just a pensioner, not a vampire.

Valerka joined in at once. 'We won't do it again,' he said. 'We were just talking here. Can we go now?'

But Serp Ivanych had recognised him. How many pioneers were there in the camp who wore glasses?

'No, you may not,' Iyeronov answered softly, and fell silent.

He seemed to spend a moment listening carefully to himself and receiving an answer to a question.

'You're a gutsy lad,' he suddenly said to Valerka. 'You and your friend actually managed to rob me of my beloved's blood today.'

'Blood?' Anastasiika opened her mouth stupidly.

'But it didn't all work out, did it? One of the trappers has himself fallen into the trap.'

The vampire smiled, and bared his long fangs.

'Still, it was a good idea. It's a long time since I last met such daredevil hunters.'

Anastasiika looked at Valerka in astonishment.

'There's no such thing as this,' she said. She spoke perfectly reasonably, but behind the sobriety of her thinking Valerka caught an impulse towards madness.

'There is, my dear,' Serp Ivanych assured her.

I have do something! thought Valerka.

'I'm not afraid of you!' he shouted at the stratelates, although he was terribly afraid.

Serp Ivanych was wearing a light summer jacket thrown over an ordinary T-shirt. The sort of clothes worn by drunks and dacha dwellers. With a movement of his shoulders he shrugged off his jacket, caught it, and tossed it carelessly aside. Then he threw his head back, holding his face up to the moonlight as if it were rain, and breathed in deeply.

'I like breathing,' he admitted. 'I like it when the heart is working.'

'Who is he?' Anastasiika asked Valerka in a trembling voice, as if Iyeronov were a foreigner and unable to answer for himself.

'He's a vampire.' He said the word bleakly.

'Imagine, children.' Serp Ivanych spread his arms, bathing in the cold, dead glow. 'In this place many, many years ago I tasted blood for the first time, and to this day I have never experienced anything more beautiful. My moon has brought me here again.'

Where the food block now stood must have been, back in the Civil War years, the stable into which the Iyeronov brothers had chased the White Guard officer during their raid on the Shikhobalovsky dachas. It was here that Sergey Iyeronov had stabbed him with a pitchfork and yelled *Now we want your blood!*

Serp Ivanych was changing, imperceptibly. He grew taller. His slouch disappeared. His T-shirt pulled tight around his swollen muscles, as if Serp Ivanych had turned into a gymnast from a parade in his younger years. Except that an athlete like him would not have been accepted into the parade, because his chest and shoulders were smothered with tattoos, like a convict's: blue five-pointed stars, stars, stars.

Serp Ivanych suddenly winked merrily at Valerka.

'You and me, though, eh. We're old pals, aren't we? I'm letting you go. Go on, go. I won't touch you. It's her blood calling to me now, not yours.'

Serp Ivanych pointed his finger at Anastasiika.

'You and your friend stole my beloved from me, but you've brought your own girlfriend instead. Well. I'll accept her in payment of your debt.' The stratelates was showboating now, like a regular hoodlum. 'This is exalted pleasure you are giving me, young man. Her blood will go nicely with your despair. Like wine and music.'

'Don't give me to him!' Anastasiika made the words with her lips alone.

Not for one moment was Valerka tempted to save himself at the cost of Anastasiika. What was he – a good-for-nothing? A coward? He would never submit to the vampire.

Valerka set his hands against the table and gave it a mighty shove forward, expecting to knock the stratelates to the floor with the impact. The iron legs of the table rasped. The table thudded into Iyeronov as if it had cannoned into a cliff wall. Valerka very nearly went sprawling on his stomach on the table top, but the stratelates did not so much as flinch.

If the vampire was not to be taken down with a battering ram, then defence was needed: he would have to build a barricade. Straining, Valerka hefted a second table and with a clatter lumped it on top of the one leaning against Serp Ivanych. On top of that he piled a bench, then overturned a third table with a crash, and hauled up a fourth. Anastasiika squealed, covering her face with spread fingers.

Serp Ivanych made an inconceivable leap, soaring to the ceiling, and froze there, on the ceiling, clinging to it by his arms and legs like a monstrous spider. He twisted his head and looked down, his face empty of all expression, his lips moving like black worms. This was no longer a human being; it was some kind of hideous creature. It crawled swiftly to another spot and halted, measuring, and then suddenly fell away from its support and came hurtling down directly on top of Anastasiika.

A single merciless kick knocked Valerka out of the way.

Anastasiika was lying on the floor and the stratelates was hunched over her on all fours. He now resembled a huge wolf crushing with its body a captured lamb. He shook his head, readying himself to tear at her with his teeth. Anastasiika was too scared to move. Her eyes widened halfway across her face.

From the vampire's fanged mouth popped a long, sharp tongue. It dabbed at Anastasiika's throat and lifted the golden cross on its ragged chain. The vampire quickly retracted its tongue into his mouth, greedily gulping down its pickings. How could it help, this little cross, against such a monster? Valerka lunged at the vampire only once more to meet a flying foot and be flung aside.

'Go away!' The dark stratelates directed a visceral grunt at Valerka, as if his mouth was stuffed with earth from a grave.

Valerka would not stop. He rose to his feet. His glasses were askew, and only one lens was left in the frame. His nose was bleeding, his shirt was torn, and there was a gaping gash in his knee. The little, lacerated Valerka in no way resembled those neat and correct pioneers adorning the posters on the walls. The moon, a chunk of itself gnawed away, shone brilliantly through the mesh over the windows, the bars of which represented the rising sun. And for Valerka, there was no longer any other sun.

'Let her go!' raged Valerka, and his voice carried such frightening authority that the vampire looked round balefully, as if against his own will. 'Let her go! Come to me, on your knees, you piece of shit! I want your blood!'

CHAPTER 11

LORD OF THE DOOMED

His groping feet found the bottom. Helping himself with his hands, Igor stood up and, able to walk now, waded towards the shore. The warmed water still retained the heat of the day, and it was only in the air that it felt colder. Igor climbed out onto the lip of the shore and looked around. On the dark, uncertain flatness of the Volga, the distant river bus showed a mysterious blue, grounded on the sandbank. Not a sound came from it. The Milky Way stretched across the whole sky, as thin as smoke and barely visible. At Igor's back, the pine grove reached up and breathed. Above the grove glittered the icy moon with its melted edge. The celestial light of the stratelates.

Igor pulled off his wet clothes, wrung them out, and tugged them back on. The hand that Veronika had bitten ached, reminding him that what had happened out there on board the river bus had been real. Igor felt for the bunch of keys in his pocket, and no, he had not lost them. His pack of cigarettes was soggy, though, and lighting up was out of the question. A shame; a smoke would be good, to mark the deed just done. It had worked.

Fine. Cigarettes were not the most important thing. The most important thing was Valerka. How was he faring in camp? Had he succeeded in locking the vampire in the food block? Igor needed to get on and find out. Victory would be secured only at dawn. Igor strode hurriedly toward the pines – the copse that separated the camp from Concert Clearing.

The copse was empty, and brightly lit by the glow of the moon. The thin, straight trunks showed silver. Very soon, people would be rushing here – pioneers flocking from the camp to the Last Bonfire – but for now, the light and dark were frozen in unbroken stillness. And suddenly Igor saw someone.

That someone was coming towards Igor, staggering as if drunk or mortally wounded. He stumbled, clutching at the trees. He kept stopping, as if he was losing his strength and was ready to fall onto the grass, but each time he suddenly twitched, straightened up, and ran a few more steps. He was shuddering, inwardly battered by unaccountable blows. It was as if he did not want to walk, and indeed could not, but something beyond comprehension was pushing him forward.

It was Serp Ivanych Iyeronov.

Igor could not believe his eyes. Had the vampire really broken out of the trap? Had Valerka Lagunov failed? Was the whole thing shot to pieces? Had the plan he and Valerka concocted fallen apart and left the dark stratelates free? But what was he doing in this wood? And why did he look so strange?

Igor hid behind a trunk. Iyeronov hobbled past, noticing nothing. He put Igor in mind of a broken robot with its engine cutting out intermittently, levers skewed this way and that, and gears out of alignment, but still driven by its implacable program to carry out its appointed task. Igor hurried stealthily after Iyeronov. He had to understand what had befallen the vampire – and their operation.

Iyeronov dragged himself as far as Concert Clearing. In the middle of the clearing towered the planned bonfire, a hip-roofed structure built of thin logs and filled with firewood and brushwood. A few days ago near this wigwam, Igor and Valerka had almost fallen victim to the claws of the bloodsuckers. Serp Ivanych crumpled onto all fours, flattened himself to the ground, and wriggled awkwardly into the wigwam.

Igor watched, his amazement knowing no bounds. What on earth did Serp want in there? Why had he crawled into a structure destined to be burned? What was going on, full stop? And what was he, Igor, to do? The wood had already been doused with gasoline; all it needed was a spark and the whole thing would go up. Igor swung into action, ready to rush into the wigwam and drag Serp Ivanych out – by his legs, if he had to; and then stopped. Serp Ivanych? No! Not Serp Ivanych. A vampire who had wanted to drink Veronika's blood that very night. It was not the old man Iyeronov who would burn, but the Dark Stratelates, the Lord of the Doomed. Let him burn! Good riddance. Igor breathed heavily, shaken by his own hatred.

The road between the clearing and the camp was filled with voices and noise: the young leaders were bringing the pioneers to celebrate the Last Bonfire. Igor peered across to the entrance to the clearing, where light from hand-held lanterns was flickering. Then he took another look at the wooden wigwam. In there, too, he could see faint flashes of light. Kneeling in a pile of firewood and brushwood, Serp Ivanych was trying to strike a match. He wanted to set the bonfire alight – and himself at its core. In the darkness beyond the logs, Igor glimpsed the stratelates' face, twisted by suffering: huge eyes and grey stubble.

And suddenly Igor understood everything. The vampire, of course, was not suicidal. After all, he had been fighting for his hideous life for so many years, destroying others, insinuating himself into positions of power, lying, covering himself with stars... Now he was acting against his own will. That was why his movements were so ugly. The vampire was carrying out an order. A pitiless order. The kind that he himself had repeatedly given to others.

The horror of it made the hairs on the back of Igor's neck bristle.

A conflagration erupted in the depths of the wigwam. For a moment it illuminated the old man on his knees, then it broke out in all directions, running along the logs and engulfing the whole structure in seconds. Upwards it swept, a mighty, crackling torrent of fire. A shadow jittered in the flame and melted away, swallowed up in the fierce glow of the inferno; and inside the bonfire something was turning, rising up, and flipping over... The fire was bubbling with its own short-lived creation.

Concert Clearing resounded with shrieks of delight. Just as the pioneers came bounding out of the forest, the enormous fire shot up spontaneously in the dark, empty space, as if to welcome their arrival. Bright, hot light swept round in a wide circle. The boys and girls raced towards the fire, yelling, and the young leaders spread their arms and tried to slow down the charge.

'No pushing! No pushing!' shouted Whistler into her megaphone. 'Do not go closer than five metres! Observe order and caution!'

No one knew that a vampire's bones were crackling and popping along with the firewood on the pioneer bonfire. Smoke billowed, blotting out the Milky Way and the moon. The children's joy was absolutely pure. A fire of such humungous proportions could not be set anywhere else nor with anyone else. Not at the dacha with parents, not on a camping trip with teachers, not in town on rough ground with friends. Only in pioneer camp.

The stratelates' monstrous death shook Igor. Yes, it was right for the vampire to die and in so doing free his slaves… It was right, but not like that. Not in front of his conqueror, and not in so bestial a fashion – in the hellfire of an inquisitorial pyre. Igor was not prepared for such a gruesome spectacle. And dark tentacles of doubt were beginning to worm their way into his soul. Was his conscience still alive, if he had contributed to this barbaric execution? Did his character simply lack backbone? Was he afraid to accept himself as he was? Or had he never been fully convinced that Iyeronov was a vampire, a real vampire, who simply could not be dealt with in any normal human way? One frame haunted Igor, and he could not get rid of it. The stratelates kneeling inside the log marquee, striking matches.

'In a circle! Round dance! Come on, everybody in a circle!' Whistler shouted merrily into her megaphone.

Her ardent pioneering was at last in harmony with the pioneers' own wishes. For the sake of participating in a fire like this one, the pioneers had agreed to forget everything: who was older or younger, which of them had been praised and which reprimanded, who had talent and who was unteachable. The pioneers grabbed one another's hands and formed a ring around the fire. The young leaders led the round dance, not really believing in the unaccustomed unity, and as the children went round and round in the dance, their faces floated, irradiated by the flames. In these faces there was no anger or guile, simply intoxication with the shared fun.

To the bone-weary Igor, the fun was unbearable. Igor knew what they did not: that the pioneer bonfire was in reality a bonfire lit for a funeral.

From the crowd of pioneers he fished out Yurik Tonkikh.

'Yura, where's Valerka Lagunov?'

'I've lost him myself,' said Yurik. 'Maybe he wanted to sleep?'

'Yes, OK. I'll have a look.'

Igor strode quickly from the clearing in the direction of the camp. A nagging suspicion was troubling him. There was a connection here: Valerka's absence and the vampire's bonfire.

The pine trees. The chain link fence. The plaster bugler girl. The iron gates. The avenue with its street lamps. Not a single soul around. The acacia. The stands. The path to the food block.

The iron door to the kitchen was ajar, and the lock and key lay on the ground. Igor stepped into the darkened food block. In the kitchen, everything looked pretty much as it always did. So too in the pantry. But in the dining room, Igor's heart gave a jump. The tables and benches were skewed and overturned, as if elephants had chosen this room for a brawl. Such bedlam was hardly likely to be the work of the stratelates. Clearly Valerka had fought here.

Where had he gone, Valerka Lagunov?

Igor ran from the food block to Building 4. The pioneer camp was uncommonly empty, as if a neutron bomb had fallen and all the people had instantly evaporated, while the buildings and things remained intact.

The door to the building was also open. No light was burning anywhere. No voices, no rustling; the only sound was the floorboards creaking underfoot. The whole brigade was at the bonfire, Sasha Plotkin with them. Igor glanced into Valerka's dormitory. Valerka was lying on his bunk, face to the wall. Igor rushed over to him – and at the last moment recoiled. It was Anastasiika Sergushina. She was sleeping in her clothes, and had not even taken off her shoes. Why was she here? Igor could not bring himself to wake her.

He went outside. The stratelates' moon was shining behind the crowns of the pines. Where else should look for Valerka? Igor made his way out onto Pioneer Avenue. The street lamps burned lifelessly with a quiet whirr. The old mutt Mukhtar sloped out from under a bench, went up to Igor, gave him a half-hearted sniff, and trotted away without interest. The decorative gingerbread houses stood beneath the pines, like gift boxes without gifts.

In the dappled darkness Igor suddenly noticed glowing blue lights playing on the bushes behind Iyeronov's little house. They were reflections from the television. Who had turned on the television in the dead vampire's house? His ghost? Igor quickened his pace.

Valerka was sitting on a chair in the middle of the veranda, as if it were his house, and silently staring at the screen. Valerka's appearance astonished Igor. His clothes were crumpled, torn, and covered with dirt. His face and hands were badly scratched. His cheek was bruised. His hair was a dirty mop. One lens was missing from his glasses. Igor cautiously lowered himself onto a nearby chair.

'Are you all right?' he asked timidly.

'Yes.'

Igor hesitated.

'Was it you sent the stratelates into the bonfire?'

'Yes.'

The television was showing the closing ceremony of the Olympics.

A giant torch with the Olympic flame soared into the rose-pink evening sky. Thousands of artists performed choreographed dances on the green arena while waves of colourful banners rolled from side to side. Music rang out, simultaneously exultant and sorrowful. The people in the stands were shouting and clapping their hands, snapping their cameras, laughing and throwing their arms round one another's shoulders. There, in the stadium, a miracle was taking place: rivalry, envy, and evil intent had disappeared, and everyone was gripped by a sense of kinship on the planet; hearts were softened by sadness at the transience of the age, and it suddenly became piercingly clear that the world was beautiful and that life should be lived without discord. A huge Misha with a cloud of balloons floated onto the field. He raised his paw in farewell and slowly soared over the arena, while people waved and wiped away their tears. On the screen a dark-skinned lady was crying, pressing her delicate fingers to her soft lips and blowing Misha a kiss.

'There was no other way,' said Valerka in a low voice.

'I know,' whispered Igor.

And above the distant stadium, golden salutes exploded, one, then another, then another. Cries of 'Goodbye, till we meet again!' scattered over the whole country.

CHAPTER 12

ONCE UPON A TIME IN THE USSR

The boys had made their beds and were sprawling on top of them. There was nothing for them to do.

'Near our house there's another house,' Slavik Mukhin was saying. 'Old. Totally abandoned. It's got a brick wall going straight into the ground. There's definitely treasure there. Gold, most like, or some kind of machine gun.'

'Machine gun's all right,' said Tityapkin. 'Bollocks to gold, completely useless. I'd rather have a machine gun.'

'We all wanted to find the treasure, but no one can break the wall.'

Gurka was fired up at once. 'Shit, I can break walls!' he exclaimed. 'I can cook up a bomb! I'm going to so blow up that wall, all the bricks'll fly to the moon!'

'Treasure's dangerous,' warned Seryozha Domrachev. 'There's always corpses guarding it. You're, like, digging up the treasure and out crawls a corpse and, like, *whooooaaa!*'

'When you get to the treasure you mustn't tell anyone about it,' added Gorokhov. 'Otherwise the cops'll be straight round swiping it all for themselves, that's the law. They'll give you a certificate of honour. Good for wiping your arse.'

The boys were waiting to be called to board the boat. Waiting, as was the whole brigade and the whole camp. The day before, the young leaders had promised that they would start loading up after breakfast, but that morning Rin Halna and Gor-Sanych had announced that the river bus had broken down and they had to stay in the building until the breakdown was fixed. So there the boys were.

Lyova was not with them. He had fallen ill and been taken to sick bay. Valerka was not participating in discussing the problems of treasure-hunting either. He was lying on his bunk without his glasses, staring at the ceiling. The lads knew that Valerka had had a fight with Lyolik and Gelbich, and that was why his face was battered and he was upset. The boys met his troubles with understanding; they did not laugh at him or tease him.

Yurik Tonkikh sat down next to Valerka.

'Come and see me at my place,' he said. 'We'll make a model plane together. I've written my address for you...'

Yurik slipped a piece of paper with the address into Valerka's hand.

At last, Irina Mikhailovna's cheery voice sounded from the corridor. 'Boys, girls, we're leaving! Don't forget your things! Boarding time!'

All morning Irina and Igor had been taking turns running from the building to the pier, because out on the Volga, Dimon Malosolov had been engaged in trying to save the river bus, in other words, had been performing an act of heroism. Irina had been worried about Dimon, and Igor about the bus.

Igor had returned the keys to the steamship to Dimon that night, and Dimon had not even suspected that the boat-jacking had been the work of Igor's hands. The river bus had been discovered grounded on the sandbank by pioneers returning from the Last Campfire along the shore rather than the road. The pioneers had reported to Whistler. While Whistler was still trying to work out what was going on, dawn had broken. Whistler had woken up Captain Kapustin.

The enraged Kapustin was unable to blame Dimon for anything. There he was, Dimon: sober and holding the keys. The craft had been hijacked by hooligans. Dimon easily assured the captain that there was no need to call for a tugboat from town. He himself would this very instant restore to the Captain the well-being proper to his post.

Dimon was bursting with happiness. Everything had worked out with Irina, and he was ready to move mountains. Irina was accompanying him to his act of heroism, having lost any need whatever for independence. On the pier, Dimon heroically stripped down to his blue boxers, took the keys in his teeth, and swam vigorously out to the river bus. Irina became terribly anxious while her beloved was subduing the raging waters, climbing aboard, starting the engine, skilfully hauling the vessel off the sandbank in reverse with a series of jolts, and driving it triumphantly back to the pier.

Dimon was not shocked by what he saw on the steamship. The former bloodsuckers – well, they were the hooligan element, and they had not disappeared from the river bus. They had merely spread themselves all over the craft and were lying feebly on the benches, many of them feverish, shaking and nauseous. The usual signs of a hangover. No mystery there. The gang had forced their way onto the boat, broken down the saloon door, and overdosed on some kind of poison. Someone had foolishly loosed the boat's moorings, and it had set off into the river of its own accord. The pisspots had tried to save the situation by pressing out the wheelhouse windscreen and getting themselves to the helm, but without the keys they were unable to start the engine and get back to the pier. The river bus had been carried on to the sandbank, and woe had driven the pisspots to get hammered out of their tinies.

This version of events wholly suited Captain Kapustin. Igor too.

The only one not to believe it was Svistunova. Fine: Beklemishev was a punk and Nesvetova was a stroppy young thing, but how could Maxim and Kirill – athletes – be party to a knees-up? Or role model Khlopov or cultured Stakhovsky? And, for goodness' sake, the little girls from the middle brigades. No, the picture did not add up. These alkies were the ones on Dr Nosatov's list: well then, let the doctor bother his head with them. The shift was ending and she needed to put the whole thing out of her mind. Whistler dispatched the hangovers to the doctor and preferred not to notice anything strange.

On his way to the pier, Igor dropped in on Old Nyura in the food block. Old Nyura had managed to tidy up the canteen before the cooks arrived. Igor could not bring himself to tell her the truth of the stratelates' death. He lied. He said that the vampire, locked in the food block, had crumbled into dust at dawn, and that was the end of him. Old Nyura believed it. She put her arms around Igor and burst into sobbing. Igor stroked her back and thought that Old Nyura's terror was past. Old Nyura was free. And he and Valerka were not.

When the camp speakers announced that it was boarding time, Irina gave Igor the task of lining up the brigade on the path by the building while she went to the isolation ward to fetch the former bloodsuckers Marinka Lebedeva and Lyova Khlopov. The pioneers poured out with their suitcases and bags. Valerka paired up with Vovka Makerov; they had not become friends during the shift, so Valerka could stay silent. He was the only one of the whole brigade who had put on his pioneer neckerchief. He had also discreetly torn to pieces the note with Yurik's address. He did not need to know where Yurik lived. And Yurik did not need to invite him into his house.

Gelbich, unruly as ever, broke the line and pushed his way through to Valerka.

'Valerych, what the hell?' he said, sounding offended, as if Valerka was the one who owed him an apology. 'This is all bollocks!'

He held out his hand to Valerka. It was clear that he wanted to make peace. Valerka answered Venka with a calm shake of the hand.

'Done.'

A whisper rustled through the brigade. 'Gelbich beat Lagunov up and now he's asking for forgiveness! Gelbich is a wuss, he's blubbing, he's scared of jail!'

Anastasiika did not even look round at Valerka. That morning at breakfast she had not so much as glanced at him once. Nor had Valerka looked at her. The previous night he had brought Anastasiika from the food block to his building, settled her in his place, and left her. He would never be going back to her. He had to rip Anastasiika from his heart.

Valerka sensed it: Anastasiika was afraid of him now. What she had seen that night in the food block had stunned her, shattered her conception of the world. Anastasiika now reminded Valerka of a spoiled kitten who had suddenly been thrashed by her master. Brutally thrashed, and for no reason. The kitten understood nothing and was hiding from the one who used to caress it but had suddenly turned into an abuser. Well. Hiding was good. The kitten would find another owner, a good one. But the abuser was burning inside with pain and longing.

The third brigade walked along the avenue, chattering excitedly.

'Let's move!' commanded Igor Alexandrovich.

The fourth brigade followed in line behind the third.

On the pier, overseeing the boarding, were Whistler, Ruslan the PE teacher, the senior tutor, and Doctor Nosatov. The radio technician Sanya had the young leader Lenochka to one side and was whispering something to her, looking embarrassed. The director Kolybalov was not present. Serp Ivanych was also absent, of course. Not that anyone had been expecting him to attend. He was an old man; these days, fond farewells were not good for his health.

Igor's thinking was that Iyeronov would probably not be missed until the evening, when he failed to turn up for the meal. He would not be found anywhere in camp. Most likely that would be the signal for investigators to descend on the place with dogs, searching every inch of the beach and the woods. They, too, would find nothing. The vampire had burned to ashes in the pioneer bonfire, the smoke of which had dissipated in the sky. The strange case of the missing pensioner of national standing would eventually be sent to the archives with its mysteries forever unsolved. The old man had no relatives; there was no one to mourn his passing.

'Attention, Igoryokha,' said Dimon, cordially distributing orders. 'Your pioneers are to make their way to the upper bow. Irishka's already taken the sick ones up there. No pushing!'

Igor ceded the initiative to Dimon and did not interfere.

Doctor Nosatov unobtrusively approached Igor.

'Is it over?' he asked, as if a propos of nothing much at all.

'It's over,' confirmed Igor.

Igor went down to the aft saloon assigned to the third brigade. The children were making a racket. Veronika was squeezed into a corner, huddled up in her jacket, pressing her wrap to her lips. Her face was colourless and damp with sweat. Like all the wretched bloodsuckers, Veronika was swinging between fever and cold, shaking with chills and turning inside out. Other people's blood left a hangover more brutal than vodka. Igor perched beside her on the edge of the bench.

'How are you?' he asked.

'Be easier to snuff it,' she answered.

She placed her cold, damp hand over his and twined her cold, damp fingers in his.

Sasha Plotkin popped up from somewhere right at that moment.

'Korzukhin, can't you see she's ill?' he hissed jealously. 'Get out of here and go to your own place.'

'Sasha,' Veronika suddenly said quietly, 'you do that. You go to your own place.'

'What do you mean?' asked Sasha, uncomprehending. 'My place is here.'

'Anywhere but here.'

'What? How not here?' exclaimed Sasha, righteously indignant.

'Plotkin, leave her alone,' explained Igor tiredly. 'Are you completely stupid or what? She doesn't need you. Not now, not ever. Just piss off, OK?'

The engine set up a powerful rumble on the other side of the wall, and vibrations trembled along the hull. Igor felt the propeller shaft spinning beneath the saloon floor. The steamship shuddered as its whole bulk detached itself from the pier. The boys all scrambled to the windows to admire the foam-flecked whirlpools of waves.

The ship worked its way away from the shore. Whistler, the PE teacher, the doctor, the tutor, and the radio technician Sanya waved to the bus, and the pioneers shouted back from the upper decks. The captain gave a blast on the klaxon. Goodbye, pioneer camp.

The day was cloudy and windy. The flat surface of the ruffled Volga had gone an impenetrable grey. It was as if the sullen expanse was preoccupied with something of its own and indifferent to people. The bow split the waves in two, sending up spray. Seagulls scurried and shrieked but were swept aside.

'If you've got a sweater, put it on,' ordered Irina Mikhailovna.

Valerka stood up and walked to the deck rail. Irina gave him a sidelong look but did not tell him to stay back. There was a kind of fierce aloofness about Lagunov today, and Irina decided not to mess with him.

Igor appeared beneath the wing of the superstructure. He went up on deck and stopped beside Valerka. In the distance beyond the strip of water stretched the jagged line of the forest. The decorative little houses of the pioneer camp had already slunk away somewhere out of sight.

'Do you feel anything?' asked Igor.

'No,' shrugged Valerka. 'Everything's just like it always is.'

But everything was not as it always was. Both of them knew it.

Igor put his hand on Valerka's thin, firm shoulder.

'What's on your mind, Valerka?'

Valerka said nothing for a moment. The wind ruffled the ends of his red neckerchief.

'I don't want to drink blood,' he said. 'I don't want to the way Serp Ivanych did.'

'Serp Ivanych' came out as if Iyeronov was his grandad.

'I'm your friend.' Igor squeezed Valerka's shoulder to make him feel the solidity of his promise. 'I won't leave you. We'll fight together.'

Valerka dropped his head, as if all his strength were gone.

'Serp Ivanych stopped being a stratelates,' he said quietly. 'Serp Ivanych turned into my bloodsucker and obeyed my order. So you can stop being a stratelates. You just have to find out how.'

'I told you, I'm with you,' repeated Igor.

He took a deep breath of wide Volga freshness, and thought that he and Valerka would manage it. This ancient evil could not overcome a human being unless that human being surrendered their will to it. He and Valerka had sufficient stubbornness for another battle. They would prevail. They would prevail, and live great and beautiful lives. After 1980 would come 1990, and after 1990–2000. They would see the millennium change, and everything around them would become new, entirely new. How much time still lay ahead of them! There would be 2001, 2002, 2010, and 2020… And there, in the unimaginable year 2020, everything that was happening now would already seem like a dear old fairy tale. And they would laugh untroubled laughter, remembering, as if through the prism of a rainbow, how one hot Olympic summer they bravely did battle with a vampire.

ABOUT THE AUTHOR

Alexei Ivanov has written fifteen novels, published between 1992 (*Dormitory on the Blood*) and 2023 (*The Armoured Steamships*, a novel that reflects Ivanov's long-time interest in the Russian Civil War). Ivanov's novels have been nominated three times for the National Bestseller prize, and for several other awards within Russia, including the Big Book Award. His works have been adapted for the big and small screen, most notably his 2003 novel *The Geographer Drank Away his Globe*, which was made into a multi-award-winning film starring Konstantin Khabensky. *The Food Block* ('Pishcheblok') has been made into a television serial which first aired on Russian television in 2021 and has since been followed up by a 2023 sequel, *The Food Block 2*.

Richard Coombes has been a classicist, a musician, an international tax specialist, and now translates Russian-language literature (verse, prose, and song lyrics) into English. Richard's recently published translations include Elena Dolgopyat's short story collection *Someone Else's Life* ('Chuzhaya zhizn'), published in 2023 by Glagoslav; other short stories by Elena Dolgopyat and poetry by Lyudmila Knyazeva, Dmitry Vodennikov and Tatyana Voltskaya in a variety of literary journals; poetry in the bilingual World War II poetry collection *Poems from the Front* ('Frontovaya lira'), published in Russia in 2021; and poetry in the bilingual anti-war anthology *Disbelief*, published in January 2023. A follow-up anthology by the 'Disbelief' team, called *Dislocation*, will be published in 2024. Richard's translation of *Liza's Waterfall* (Pavel Basinsky's documentary-thriller 'Posmotrite na menya') is complete and awaiting publication.

- *A History of Belarus by Lubov Bazan*
- *Children's Fashion of the Russian Empire by Alexander Vasiliev*
- *Empire of Corruption: The Russian National Pastime by Vladimir Soloviev*
- *Heroes of the 90s: People and Money. The Modern History of Russian Capitalism* by Alexander Solovev, Vladislav Dorofeev and Valeria Bashkirova
- *Fifty Highlights from the Russian Literature* (Dutch Edition) *by Maarten Tengbergen*
- *Bajesvolk* (Dutch Edition) *by Michail Chodorkovsky*
- *Dagboek van Keizerin Alexandra* (Dutch Edition)
- *Myths about Russia* by Vladimir Medinskiy
- *Boris Yeltsin: The Decade that Shook the World* by Boris Minaev
- *A Man Of Change: A study of the political life of Boris Yeltsin*
- *Sberbank: The Rebirth of Russia's Financial Giant* by Evgeny Karasyuk
- *To Get Ukraine* by Oleksandr Shyshko
- *Asystole by Oleg Pavlov*
- *Gnedich by Maria Rybakova*
- *Marina Tsvetaeva: The Essential Poetry*
- *Multiple Personalities by Tatyana Shcherbina*
- *The Investigator by Margarita Khemlin*
- *The Exile by Zinaida Tulub*
- *Leo Tolstoy: Flight from Paradise by Pavel Basinsky*
- *Moscow in the 1930 by Natalia Gromova*
- *Laurus* (Dutch edition) *by Evgenij Vodolazkin*
- *Prisoner by Anna Nemzer*
- *The Crime of Chernobyl: The Nuclear Goulag by Wladimir Tchertkoff*
- *Alpine Ballad by Vasil Bykau*
- *The Complete Correspondence of Hryhory Skovoroda*
- *The Tale of Aypi by Ak Welsapar*
- *Selected Poems by Lydia Grigorieva*
- *The Fantastic Worlds of Yuri Vynnychuk*
- *The Garden of Divine Songs and Collected Poetry of Hryhory Skovoroda*
- *Adventures in the Slavic Kitchen: A Book of Essays with Recipes* by Igor Klekh
- *Seven Signs of the Lion by Michael M. Naydan*

- *Forefathers' Eve* by Adam Mickiewicz
- *One-Two* by Igor Eliseev
- *Girls, be Good* by Bojan Babić
- *Time of the Octopus* by Anatoly Kucherena
- *The Grand Harmony* by Bohdan Ihor Antonych
- *The Selected Lyric Poetry Of Maksym Rylsky*
- *The Shining Light* by Galymkair Mutanov
- *The Frontier: 28 Contemporary Ukrainian Poets - An Anthology*
- *Acropolis: The Wawel Plays* by Stanisław Wyspiański
- *Contours of the City* by Attyla Mohylny
- *Conversations Before Silence: The Selected Poetry of Oles Ilchenko*
- *The Secret History of my Sojourn in Russia* by Jaroslav Hašek
- *Mirror Sand: An Anthology of Russian Short Poems*
- *Maybe We're Leaving* by Jan Balaban
- *Death of the Snake Catcher* by Ak Welsapar
- *A Brown Man in Russia* by Vijay Menon
- *Hard Times* by Ostap Vyshnia
- *The Flying Dutchman* by Anatoly Kudryavitsky
- *Nikolai Gumilev's Africa* by Nikolai Gumilev
- *Combustions* by Srđan Srdić
- *The Sonnets* by Adam Mickiewicz
- *Dramatic Works* by Zygmunt Krasiński
- *Four Plays* by Juliusz Słowacki
- *Little Zinnobers* by Elena Chizhova
- *We Are Building Capitalism! Moscow in Transition 1992-1997* by Robert Stephenson
- *The Nuremberg Trials* by Alexander Zvyagintsev
- *The Hemingway Game* by Evgeni Grishkovets
- *A Flame Out at Sea* by Dmitry Novikov
- *Jesus' Cat* by Grig
- *Want a Baby and Other Plays* by Sergei Tretyakov
- *Mikhail Bulgakov: The Life and Times* by Marietta Chudakova
- *Leonardo's Handwriting* by Dina Rubina
- *A Burglar of the Better Sort* by Tytus Czyżewski
- *The Mouseiad and other Mock Epics* by Ignacy Krasicki

- *Ravens before Noah* by Susanna Harutyunyan
- *An English Queen and Stalingrad* by Natalia Kulishenko
- *Point Zero* by Narek Malian
- *Absolute Zero* by Artem Chekh
- *Olanda* by Rafał Wojasiński
- *Robinsons* by Aram Pachyan
- *The Monastery* by Zakhar Prilepin
- *The Selected Poetry of Bohdan Rubchak: Songs of Love, Songs of Death, Songs of the Moon*
- *Mebet* by Alexander Grigorenko
- *The Orchestra* by Vladimir Gonik
- *Everyday Stories* by Mima Mihajlović
- *Slavdom* by Ľudovít Štúr
- *The Code of Civilization* by Vyacheslav Nikonov
- *Where Was the Angel Going?* by Jan Balaban
- *De Zwarte Kip (Dutch Edition)* by Antoni Pogorelski
- *Głosy / Voices* by Jan Polkowski
- *Sergei Tretyakov: A Revolutionary Writer in Stalin's Russia* by Robert Leach
- *Opstand (Dutch Edition)* by Władysław Reymont
- *Dramatic Works* by Cyprian Kamil Norwid
- *Children's First Book of Chess* by Natalie Shevando and Matthew McMillion
- *Precursor* by Vasyl Shevchuk
- *The Vow: A Requiem for the Fifties* by Jiří Kratochvil
- *De Bibliothecaris (Dutch edition)* by Mikhail Jelizarov
- *Subterranean Fire* by Natalka Bilotserkivets
- *Vladimir Vysotsky: Selected Works*
- *Behind the Silk Curtain* by Gulistan Khamzayeva
- *The Village Teacher and Other Stories* by Theodore Odrach
- *Duel* by Borys Antonenko-Davydovych
- *War Poems* by Alexander Korotko
- *Ballads and Romances* by Adam Mickiewicz
- *The Revolt of the Animals* by Wladyslaw Reymont
- *Poems about my Psychiatrist* by Andrzej Kotański
- *Someone Else's Life* by Elena Dolgopyat
- *Selected Works: Poetry, Drama, Prose* by Jan Kochanowski

- *The Riven Heart of Moscow (Sivtsev Vrazhek) by Mikhail Osorgin*
- *Bera and Cucumber by Alexander Korotko*
- *The Big Fellow by Anastasiia Marsiz*
- *Boryslav in Flames by Ivan Franko*
- *The Witch of Konotop by Hryhoriy Kvitka-Osnovyanenko*
- *De afdeling (Dutch edition) by Aleksej Salnikov*
- *Ilget by Alexander Grigorenko*
- *Tefil by Rafał Wojasiński*
- *The Food Block by Alexei Ivanov*
- *A Dream of Annapurna by Igor Zavilinsky*
- *Letter Z by Oleksandr Sambrus*
- *Liza's Waterfall: The Hidden Story of a Russian Feminist by Pavel Basinsky*
- *Biography of Sergei Prokofiev by Igor Vishnevetsky*
- *A City Drawn from Memory by Elena Chizhova*
- *Guide to M. Bulgakov's The Master and Margarita by Ksenia Atarova and Georgy Lesskis*

And more forthcoming ...

GLAGOSLAV PUBLICATIONS

www.glagoslav.com

www.ingramcontent.com/pod-product-compliance
Lightning Source LLC
Chambersburg PA
CBHW021754190726
48290CB00005B/1265